On

Celeste Daniels is a poet and content editor. Born in Decatur, Georgia, Daniels has lived abroad in Europe and Asia, having experience as one voice of many in the Black, southern culture and being the only Black person in a room. When not writing about romance and time travel, she is pursuing her master's in library and information science and chasing after her Lab-Rottie mix, Kobe.

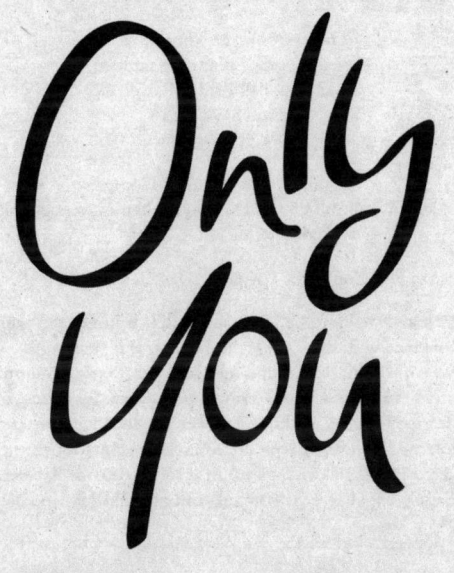

Only You

CELESTE DANIELS

hera

Penguin
Random
House

First published in the United Kingdom in 2025 by

Hera Books, an imprint of
Canelo Digital Publishing Limited,
20 Vauxhall Bridge Road,
London SW1V 2SA
United Kingdom

A Penguin Random House Company
The authorised representative in the EEA is Dorling Kindersley Verlag GmbH. Arnulfstr. 124,
80636 Munich, Germany

Copyright © Celeste Daniels 2025

The moral right of Celeste Daniels to be identified as the creator of this work has been asserted
in accordance with the Copyright, Designs and Patents Act, 1988.
All rights reserved. No part of this publication may be reproduced or transmitted in any form or
by any means, electronic or mechanical, including photocopy, recording, or any information
storage and retrieval system, without permission in writing from the publisher.
No part of this book may be used or reproduced in any manner for the purpose of training
artificial intelligence technologies or systems. In accordance with Article 4(3) of the DSM
Directive 2019/790, Canelo expressly reserves this work from the text and data mining exception.

A CIP catalogue record for this book is available from the British Library.

Print ISBN 978 1 83598 242 6
Ebook ISBN 978 1 83598 240 2

This book is a work of fiction. Names, characters, businesses, organizations, places and events are
either the product of the author's imagination or are used fictitiously. Any resemblance to actual
persons, living or dead, events or locales is entirely coincidental.

Printed and bound in Great Britain by Clays Ltd, Elcograf S.p.A.

Look for more great books at
www.herabooks.com | www.dk.com

I

To my granddad, Andrew.

Your love story is one of my favorites.

'One day you'll learn: It's not about what makes sense. It's about what happened.'

J.M.D.

Chapter One

July 2013

The only accurate way to describe Danielle Richardson would be to call her a dreamer.

For as long as she could remember that's how she visualised people, places and the impossible things to know at her age. Her eyes were often glued to the TV, wondering what would happen next to the characters because there was never an end, even though her parents tried to convince her otherwise. Dani was sure there was always a 'next'.

Everyone thought she had learned to think like that from music, the endless possibilities of it. It was the go-to explanation when people asked her about her cello skills or her interest in composition. It was the easiest one, the most reassuring.

The real lesson came from her dreams, the ones she had grown up with for years, always starring her as the same set of characters. It didn't matter that she didn't look the same or live in the same place. It also didn't matter that sometimes – more often than not as she got older – the dreams felt real. She couldn't relate to people that said they could only remember a few things about their dreams or that the details were often illogical. For her, dreams were other lives and truths and heartaches she was glad to never have experienced herself.

But she always remembered them, even when she wished for nothing more than to forget.

Dani laid on the chaise in a typical university office – the brown furniture, shelves lining the walls, the dull carpets, a certain staleness in the air that mixed with the smell of books – tossing her favourite stress ball and catching it deftly as her counsellor, courtesy of Howard University, took notes. The woman had sand-coloured skin and curly brown hair that Dani would have been envious of before she found out how well box braids suited her. She wore rings on every finger and gold jewellery that contrasted against her perpetual dark clothing. Dani's favourite feature about her was her poker face, a mildly unamused expression that rarely changed except for the occasional glance over her square frame glasses giving Dani a clue that she was being annoying.

She waited for Dr Castillo to diagnose her latest dream. It was a repeat of one of the earliest she could remember. She was sailing from the Ivory Coast, practising sword fighting on the deck of a ship to pass the time until she arrived in Paris. It was a tamer dream than usual, so Dani appreciated it.

'And why do you think this particular dream is recurring?'

Dani shrugged. 'Because that's what it does,' she said. 'It's a dream.' She tossed the ball again, catching it effortlessly.

'Dani,' Dr Castillo warned. She hummed in reply. 'I can't help but feel as though you're not taking this seriously.'

'It seems stupid to get worked up over something that only happens in my sleep.'

'So, you don't find it strange that you've dreamed of yourself in different bodies for years? Like you are disconnected from your own?'

'There are stranger things in the world.'

'Even the endings?' Dani's hand faltered, a sudden ache forming in her chest, and she barely caught the ball as it fell. Dr Castillo leaned forward, persistent. 'How does that make you feel?'

Dani drummed her fingers on the green ball.

'Well, as you know, sleep and death are cousins. My family is very close.' She almost snickered at the exasperated sigh her therapist released.

'Dani, you're stalling. You've been in sessions off and on for years for this very reason,' Dr Castillo pointed out, hints of her Bronx accent slipping in. A telltale sign that she was getting frustrated. 'I think it's time for you to be more proactive in your therapy journey. Whatever you've been avoiding – whether trauma or an actual mental condition – won't stop here. It will follow you. The only way to resolve it is to face it. Do you realise that?'

Dani threw the ball again, noticing the time on her watch, and snatched it out of the air. 'I'll get back to you on that next month,' she said, rolling to her feet and rushing out.

'Dani—'

She rushed out of the room and didn't look back, only taking a deep breath when she was outside the building. It was always so stuffy in there. She heard her phone chime, and she looked down to see a text from her dad.

Just checking in.

The usual, she texted back before tucking her phone away.

Her phone buzzed again seconds later. Her dad had sent a heart emoji. She sent one back, looking at the time. Her class started in fifteen minutes. Gripping the strap of her bag, she headed over to a building nearby, ready to put all thoughts of therapy aside.

Ten minutes later, she was in one of the classrooms in Lulu Vere Childers Hall with a notebook and pen resting on her desk. More students filed in, but she paid no attention to them as she went over her latest composition, jotting down some questions she wanted to ask her professor after class. She looked up briefly

3

when a guy with brown skin and a low-cut fade with the barest hint of waves carrying a guitar case took a seat at the front of the class. His chocolate brown eyes were thoughtful and focused as he tuned his acoustic guitar.

He's cute, she thought before turning her attention back to her notebook. She didn't wonder why he was here; her professor often had guests visit their class.

Just as she thought of him, Dr Allen came in with his usual easy-going gait contrasting the distinguished, salt-and-pepper goatee hinting at his age where his unwrinkled and unblemished brown skin didn't, and sharp hazel eyes that made him seem more intimidating than he was.

'Good morning, musicians,' he greeted in his naturally bellowing voice. 'Hope you had a great Halloween and didn't terrorise anyone.'

Dani chuckled politely with the rest of the class, although hers held a certain fondness. She had Dr Allen last semester and while he could be a little corny, she appreciated that he always seemed happy to be in class.

'Now, as we start to prepare our compositions, I want to circle back to a topic that I covered in the previous course, Music 314,' he said, rolling up his sleeves, ready to get started. 'If you didn't take that course with me, that's all right. The question is quite simple: Is any music truly original?'

A few hands raised around the class, but Dani lowered hers when two in particular shot up.

'No,' answered Dre, a percussionist majoring in Jazz Studies, his dreads swaying around his face as he spoke. 'Everything is borrowed from something else. With technology and exposure, it's almost impossible for anything to be original.'

'That's not true,' another student interjected, Lauren, a flutist from her performance class. She always had long nails and loved wearing dark academia themed outfits with afro puffs. 'Everything has a start. Even if the original idea is thought of by multiple people, the execution is completely different.'

Dani smirked as she watched the two debate; they always had opposing ideas.

She felt a pair of eyes linger on her and turned to look at the guest at the front of the room. He looked at her with a slight tilt towards the heated conversation, silently asking *What's going on?* She tilted her head towards the two before shrugging, letting him know this was normal. He smirked and they shared a quiet laugh. Dani found herself smiling as she turned back to the great debaters.

'But that's interpretation, not originality,' Dre argued. 'Only if you're second,' Lauren said with a steely look.

'Okay, good,' Dr Allen interrupted, before the argument could spiral out of control. 'Both are good points. So, let's try to apply them. I have one of my favourite musicians, Mr Jones, here.'

The guy holding the guitar waved awkwardly. Dani gave a small wave back, which made the corner of his mouth quirk upward.

'He's going to play a song. I want you to decide whether it's original or not. Jones, take it away.'

He nodded before turning his focus to his guitar, his fingers running through a basic chord before taking off. Dani's jaw dropped slightly as she listened. Mr Jones was clearly talented given the way his fingers flew over the strings with incredible ease. However, that wasn't the part that caught her attention. It was the *song*.

She had never heard it before, didn't even know if it was freestyled or not, but it felt like a memory, a melody whose name was on the tip of her tongue. It pulled her into a trance, filling in all the blank spaces to all the songs she had created over the years. It felt like something was righting itself within her as she watched him play, a feeling of coming home after being gone for too long. For a moment, she was drifting, falling into the headspace where it was just her and the music dancing around each other. Nothing to hide and nowhere to run.

Nothing but pure joy.

Mr Jones finished with a lingering high note and there was a beat of silence before the class started to clap. Dani blinked, coming back to herself. She immediately flipped to a new page and jotted down notes as ideas flooded her brain.

'Thank you, Jones. That was fantastic,' Dr Allen said as the class quietened down. 'So, I'll ask again. Is it original?'

'Definitely,' Dani jumped in, eager to talk about it even as her fingers itched to keep writing her composition. 'While he started off with melodies we're familiar with, he made sure to bring contrast melodies, giving the song a new energy. It started to sound like John Coltrane's "Giant Steps" in the style but that's kind of the point. No one can be separated from their influences. How we put them together is where the originality comes from.'

The class was silent. She rubbed her neck awkwardly. Had she started rambling again?

She looked between her professor and his guest. They both had looks of awe on their faces, with Dr Allen even going as far as to applaud. 'Ladies and gents, Danielle, the know-it-all,' Dr Allen teased, tipping an invisible hat in her direction. 'We appreciate you always.'

'It's Dani,' she said, rolling her eyes playfully as the class laughed.

'Of course,' Dr Allen chuckled. 'But let's make sure. Now, Jones was that a freestyle or a cover?'

'Freestyle,' he answered. 'But Dani is right. I wanted to see if I could do a version of "Giant Steps" like I had my senior year here. Being in this room brought back that memory. Other than that, I just played with different melodies, to see what could create a feeling of tension and excitement.' Jones looked and caught her eye, smirking playfully. 'I find that's usually the best part of a song.'

Was that a challenge? Dani smirked back at him and leaned forward. 'Says who?'

Their eyes met and, for some reason, in the back of her mind there was an audible *click*. Her smirk dropped as a headache hit her full force. It felt her brain was being pulled apart while a rush of images filled it. She froze, unable to move as they crashed over her. She clinched the edge of her desk, groaning as she pressed her fingers to her temples, the pressure doing very little against the agonising pain.

Just as quickly as it started, it was over. The class and her professor's voice slowly came back.

'Dani, are you all right?' She blinked until Dr Allen's face came into focus. She looked around, suddenly leaning back when she realised the guitarist was hovering over her. She couldn't understand why but sudden proximity felt over-whelming. She didn't know what was happening, but she knew she had to get out *now*.

'S—sorry.' Haphazardly, she packed her bag and rushed out of the room, the voices around her echoing as she stumbled over her desk.

She started to run through the campus to her car. Her mind felt like it was tunnelling, focusing on one thing at a time: Get to her car. Get to her apartment. Go up the steps. Find her keys – where are her keys? Open the door. Get to her room. Everything revolved around the pressing thought *getoutgetout-getout*. She slammed the door to her room closed, locking it. She collapsed onto the floor, trying to catch her breath as she stared at the ceiling.

After a few minutes, the world finally stilled.

She rubbed her clammy hands against her jeans as the tight-ness in her chest faded. Dani's heart beat wildly in her chest. She laid down as she tried to come back to her body, emotions rolling through her rapidly. One moment, she was excited like she was lingering on a cliff edge, and then the next she felt terror like she just jumped off.

'What is happening to me?'

The silence of her apartment had no comforting words for her.

Chapter Two

I'm fine. It was a random migraine. Nothing to worry about, Dani tried to reason with herself the next morning. After a long night of staring at the ceiling and researching all her symptoms until she was sure it wasn't a sign of an upcoming aneurysm, all she was left with was the embarrassment of running out of class. She blamed that stranger and his hypnotising music. He and his stupid, cute smile were the cause of something wrong—

'Nope,' she declared as she tossed her bag over her shoulder, turned to her full-length mirror, and pointed at herself. 'You are fine. You are going to go to orchestra practice and work on your composition and everything will be fine. Then, you will pick up your favourite tacos for dinner and go home because everything is *fine*. Got it?'

Mirror Dani nodded enthusiastically, enough for her to leave the room confidently. She grabbed her cello and lugged it out to her car before driving to the auditorium, greeting people in a blur; her pep talk had made her late. She chatted to a viola player and the second chair cello, quickly tuning her instrument. Finishing just in time, the director came in mere seconds after she checked her last string.

'All right, people,' the conductor, Dr Carver, said as he went to the podium. 'As I said last practice, today is our first run-through of the entire concert. We only have a few weeks to make it perfect, so let's not waste time. On my count.'

Dani took her position and let the worries of her question-able feelings melt away, focusing on the music.

–

'Good work today,' Dr Carver told her after practice. 'And before you ask, yes, I finally picked the pieces for our next concert and will be giving you the sheet music for it next practice.'

'Yes,' Dani said, pumping her fist in victory, understanding this was no small feat. As one of the few Black conductors to have led a major symphony orchestra, he took teaching the next generation of musicians *very* seriously. Dr Carver very rarely gave out advanced copies of sheet music, wanting the orchestra to bond over learning together. However, his desire to train her to be a conductor often meant he gave her more leeway. She wasn't set on the goal, but she did appreciate the advantages.

'Don't get too excited yet,' he said. 'First, I wanted to intro-duce you to someone.'

He walked towards the auditorium seats, where small clusters of people talked. Dani almost stopped short at the sight of a familiar face among them. Her mind only vaguely registered that she was still following Dr Carver and *not* walking up to the guitarist – Mr Jones – from yesterday.

'Danielle, this is Ross, a former student of mine,' he intro-duced.

Dani snatched her eyes from Mr Jones and looked at the person next to him.

'Hi,' she said, holding her hand out. 'Nice to meet you.'

'Likewise. You play beautifully,' Ross complimented as he shook her hand. Dani forced a smile, despite how on edge she felt with Jones's eye on her. God, she hoped he didn't bring up the migraine here. She didn't need Dr Carver thinking she was sick and giving away a potential solo.

'Ross plays violin with the New York Philharmonic,' Dr Carver explained. 'They're holding auditions soon. I wanted him to come see you.'

'Oh, really,' she said, stunned by her teacher's generosity.

'Really and honestly, as long as you play like that, your spot is all but guaranteed,' Ross praised. 'How long have you wanted to go to New York?'

'Oh, um, not long,' she said, tucking a loose braid behind her ear. 'I'm still prepping my audition piece.'

'Well, in that case, the only tip I would give is to make your sight-reading as good as your practised materials,' he suggested. 'But even if you don't make it, you'll leave an impression.'

Dani waved off the compliment. 'They probably see thousands of musicians. I doubt they would remember me.'

'You'd be surprised,' Mr Jones interjected, his deep voice slipping effortlessly into the conversation.

'Oh, Dani, this is Jones,' Ross introduced. 'He studied music, too. Not orchestra like us, but if you ever need someone to play bass, this is your guy.' Ross clasped Mr Jones – just Jones, she guessed – on the shoulder, and he smiled modestly.

'Okay, okay,' Jones said, shrugging off Ross's hand. 'Don't overdo it. Nice to meet you, Dani.'

She raised a brow at him but smiled politely.

'You, too.' She looked towards Dr Carver. 'I actually have to go, so…'

'Of course. Carry on. Just think about the auditions, okay?' he urged.

'Sure, and thanks for the tip, Ross. Bye, guys.' She did her best to make sure it didn't look like she was running away, settling for a speed walk instead of a sprint. The sound of footsteps echoed behind her but there were too many people to tell if anyone was following her. Her hands were jittery as she gripped the railing, descending the front steps. Maybe she just needed to go to the hospital after all…

'Hey.'

Dani stopped short. She cursed under her breath before turning slowly.

Jones's gaze punched her right in the gut. His eyes burned with intense concern as they met hers. After a moment, he broke eye contact. She swallowed nervously, wondering if she looked as embarrassed as she felt. When he looked back at her, his concern was gone, replaced by a friendly, distracting smile, as if it were never there. Dani narrowed her eyes at the change. There was something inherently familiar about the sudden change and him. It made her nerves stand on their end in anticipation because—

'I know you.'

'What?'

'I–I mean I remember you from class. Sorry about storming out. I had a bad headache but I'm fine now,' she explained.

'Okay,' he said. 'Um… get better soon.'

She nodded in a hurry before scurrying towards her car, cringing as she repeated the conversation in her head. Of course, she knew him; she just met him yesterday. *But that's not what I meant.* The thought was a bit chilling as she paused, her hand on the door handle of her car.

For a moment, she had felt like she had seen Jones hide away his emotions a thousand times. Just like the headache, the sense of déjà vu was overwhelming, but it disappeared too quickly to understand. She shook her head and chalked it up to exhaustion. There were too many things in life happening for her to be stuck on a random headache and a random guy.

After all, she was fine.

–

Stephen Jones watched Danielle walk towards the parking lot, dazed by her words as everything clicked. *I think I know you*, he thought as he walked back to the auditorium.

Before that moment, he wanted to believe his memories were real but there was always a seed of doubt. Minds were fickle and what could be 'memories' could be vivid delusions. After all, his life was pretty normal, and he doubted that he would actually experience the epic love that haunted him for years. But here she was, right in front of him once more – and he doubted he would ever see her again.

Truthfully, as he pulled out a small notebook from his back pocket, he hoped he wouldn't. He flipped open to the page he had written on that morning, documenting the piano scales he had practised. He had only completed eight out of twelve. Jones chuckled humourlessly at the timing of everything.

He hadn't planned on being on campus today. He rarely visited Howard since graduating a few years ago. Allen had invited him out of the blue to be a guest and he didn't have anything previously planned. It was coincidence that led him here. But, as he had known for years, this was inevitable. It always was, no matter how much it shouldn't be.

Like all his lives before, he'd found her again.

'Shit,' he mumbled, closing the notebook, tucking it away just as he approached Ross back in the auditorium.

'All good?' Ross asked.

'Yep.'

Ross handed over a to-go coffee cup. 'Don't forget this. You know how you are, and this is a theatre.'

Jones smiled as he grabbed it. 'I was coming back for it,' he lied.

'Yeah, yeah. Let's go.'

He fell in step just behind his friend, taking a sip of his coffee and winced. It was ice cold. He threw it away in the nearest trash can.

He didn't have time to waste on bad coffee.

Chapter Three

Paris

March 1895

Captain Damien's favourite part of the day was sparring with recruits. They only received a few for the Republican Guard every spring and even fewer lasted long enough to put on an official uniform, much less grow in rank. Part of his job was to vet aspiring corporals, usually from the countryside looking for prestige, and test their resilience.

He couldn't resist the smirk that came to his face every time one stepped forward to take up his challenge: land a single blow. This time it was four against one, which was impressive. Even after discovering that Damien was the best, most recruits tried to defeat him on their own, steal their moment of glory, instead of using strategy. Maybe there was hope for this group yet.

It took no more than two minutes for Damien to get them on the ground. The soldiers around him were rowdy, shouting from the sidelines and probably making bets while enjoying the show. Damien did nothing to discourage his audience even when he spotted his superior scowling at the edge of the crowd.

Uniform crisp, beard neat, and stars decorating his chest, the man's experience was etched in the hard lines of his face, speaking to his status. General Roulet made his way through the raucous group. Some were smart enough to quiet as he passed. Damien, however, laughed and threw his hands up.

'General,' he called. 'You're finally here to join the fun.'

'And what fun might that be?'

'It would be teaching the lesson of resilience to these fine recruits, of course.' Damien grinned as one of the recruits groaned.

The general smiled but there was nothing approving about it.

'I don't know who is more foolish, them for thinking they can take on a high-ranking officer, or you for slacking on your duties for this petty contest.' His gaze turned sharp, and everyone grew quiet. 'Recruits, go back to your *caserns*. Captain Cadieux, take over for Captain Damien. Captain, come with me.' The lingering smile left Damien's face and his eyes hardened. 'The rest of you, get back to your posts.'

The crowd slowly dispersed as Damien made his way over to General Roulet, falling in step with him. The general said nothing as he led him towards his office. Most soldiers would stay several paces behind their general, but Damien stayed by Roulet's side. He always pushed for more, to be equal despite the hierarchy. Granted, General Roulet was no better; he let Damien get away with it.

'How concerned should I be about this?' Damien asked quietly, nodding to the guards as they passed.

'Not at all,' General Roulet told him as they walked the halls of *Caserne des Célestins*. Damien could vaguely hear the stomp of the horses as they passed the cavalry training grounds. Damien waited for Roulet to explain further but the general motioned for the captain to be quiet as they continued to pass other officers in the echoing stone hallways. They climbed three sets of stairs until they reached the fourth floor, heading to an office that overlooked the casern's main training ground.

'You remember the favour I asked of you last month?' Roulet asked, sitting behind the desk.

'The protection job for your landlord friend,' Damien recalled.

'Correct. His ship finally docked, and he has requested our presence this afternoon. I figured you wouldn't have much to do today.'

Damien chuckled. With the turbulence surrounding the city and people constantly accusing each other of being spies or zealots of one cause or another, there was always something to do. Still, constantly fighting zealous protestors was wearisome. They weren't real soldiers. There was spirit but no skill, like handling gangly children.

'Do you know what this friend of yours needs protection from?'

'Not particularly. Only that there was some kind of investment that needed to be handled in person.'

'How delightfully vague.' Damien checked his pocket for his money, his belt for his sabre and revolver before heading to the door. 'Where is he staying?'

'Just outside of Paris, in Saint Germain,' Roulet said as he gathered his own revolver and hat. 'When we get in there, control yourself. I want none of your usual antics. Do you understand me?'

'I'm no fool,' Damien replied.

'True, but I know your temper,' he said, his gaze narrowing. 'I have given him my word that you are a brave, *level-headed* soldier. Do not make me a liar.'

Damien narrowed his eyes, mirroring his general, but relented, nodding once in agreement. He heard Roulet let out a sigh of relief and knew why. It was a good day when Damien decided to co-operate.

–

Several hours later, Roulet knocked on the door of a summer villa with an expansive yard. While it was not as grand as other homes of former nobility, it spoke to the family's wealth. Whatever land General Roulet's friend held, it profited well. Before he could contemplate much longer, the door opened, revealing a tall man with smooth, sand-coloured skin, only a few shades lighter than Damien's own and an intimidating glare. By the man's protective stance, a revolver resting comfortably in his hand, the man had to be a soldier.

His guard went up; he had a feeling that there wasn't much need for 'protection' in this household.

He stayed silent as the man led them through the house without a word. More men were scattered around, talking or eating, quietening as they spotted the guests. They were a direct contrast to their opulent surroundings of marble and gold finery, dressed in bright, patterned tunics and trousers with weapons within arm's reach, alert eyes betraying their laid-back demeanours.

After the long walk down the hall, they approached a study, the south-facing windows letting in plenty of light. There, in the centre of the room, a man stood over a map of Africa. He was an imposing figure, tall like his guards, his skin the colour of coffee. Unlike his men, he wore a French-style suit, though quite colourful with the flowers embroidered on the coat. While Black people weren't rare in Paris, Damien usually saw people of his background in an inferior state, often working the lowest stations available. Yet, this man seemed to bow to no one. It made him even more daunting despite the pleasant smile he presented when he spotted General Roulet.

'Good to see you, old friend.' The man's accent rounded out many of French's hard consonants, holding his hand out to shake. It was musical yet odd to Damien's ears.

Roulet clasped the man's hand without hesitation. 'You as well,' he said. 'I see you came with a small army.'

'One can never be too careful in foreign lands,' the man replied, watching Damien slyly from the corner of his eye. 'But no need to rush off and tell your newest king.'

'President,' General Roulet corrected. 'We're long past the days of Versailles.'

'Is that what you call them now?' The man's smile turned mischievous but followed with a hearty laugh, his friendly demeanour returning. 'Either way, me and my men will be returning as soon as my daughter is settled here.'

'How is Mademoiselle Sabine?' Roulet asked.

'Spirited as ever,' his friend replied, grinning proudly. 'If her mother were here, she'd probably have a fit about how much she takes after me. Were she a boy, she'd have been a terrific soldier, but we will have to settle for finding her a strong husband.' The men shared a laugh before turning to Damien.

'Damien, this is Kwame Kouassi, one of our liaisons from the Ivory Coast.'

'Pleased to make your acquaintance,' Damien said gruffly nodding once.

Kwame looked at him curiously before chuckling.

'The pleasure is mine,' he replied. He gestured to some seats nearby. Damien and the general sat down on the sofa and Kwame sat down on an armchair in front of it. 'Your general speaks highly of you and your skill. I have been a first-hand witness to them through your training sessions over the years and must admit, I am impressed.'

'Thank you.' Damien remained stoic, unsurprised by the common praise. The words had lost their lustre years ago. What did raise an alarm was the mention of 'years', because while Damien prided himself on being a top-notch soldier, he'd never seen Kwame before. Why wouldn't he make himself known?

'General Roulet has also told me that money isn't as common as it once was. We are indeed much removed from the days of Versailles.' Kwame chuckled as Damien tensed at the words. 'Be still, young man. I mean no mockery. I am simply here to present a quite lucrative offer.'

'Of that, I have no doubt,' Damien said, his eyes lingering on the art that littered the walls. 'Though it begs the question of what could be so important to protect?'

Kwame raised a brow before chuckling. 'Perhaps your general has not kept you well informed.' Damien clenched his jaw as Kwame clarified, 'My home country is Côte d'Ivoire.'

Ah, Damien thought, *the new colony*. He had seen headlines about the country in the news years ago, a few of his comrades being stationed there. He had inquired about doing the same to General Roulet, but the general was adamant about keeping him in France.

'France has been working to… mend its international relations with us for the past few decades with little success until I came along,' Kwame continued. 'You see, young man, there would be no Côte d'Ivoire without me, my land, and my influence with the Grand-Bassam kings. Cousins of cousins and whatnot. Bloodlines are a tricky thing, don't you agree, Captain? Anyway, not all my countrymen agree with my position and that's caused some… strain, to put it lightly.'

He didn't want to be seen, Damien decided right then. His statement alone showed that he was clever, too clever to be seen as a shiny object of the French upper crust. They may have been a hundred years past the days of the guillotine, but some were still fond of the thought.

He was also sure Kwame knew of his orphan roots and put him firmly in his place with that one statement. Kwame was someone to know while Damien would never be. It was a fact and a warning.

'So, you need protection,' Damien said, ignoring the slight.

'Not quite.' He hesitated, before intertwining his fingers. 'As I mentioned earlier, I have a daughter who is quite rambunctious, but like all women, must get married. Now, while there are plenty who want her hand back home, I am well aware that my countrymen don't see the exchange as an opportunity as I have and may see her as an opportunity to seek revenge on me. Luckily, there have also been some requests here that have piqued my interest, but I have my concerns.

'Let's not feign ignorance, gentlemen. There will be plenty of people who will embrace her for her wealth while shunning her for her African roots. Now, while she can be trained to be a proper French lady, I have a feeling it would help tremendously if she were to be surrounded by the right company and I need both of you for that to happen.'

'I agree,' Roulet said, eyes darkening. 'You need not worry. I will keep her under my care, and Damien will help ensure she is not taken advantage of.'

Damien clenched his jaw to hold back his immediate refusal. He had assumed he would help with assembling a team, helping the man's soldiers adjust to the French system, perhaps even provide some training. Instead, he was being demoted to a *guard*. No, a glorified chaperone! For a landowner's daughter, no less. Yet, he couldn't say no right after Roulet's agreement.

At least, not yet.

'Thank you, my friend. And I hope you understand, Captain Damien, this is a different battle than you are used to,' Kwame continued. 'You must always practise discretion and vigilance. While not technically royalty, she will be the target of many, some more surprising than others. Should you make a mistake, she will pay the price. Do you understand?'

'Yes,' Damien reluctantly answered. 'I… promise to protect her.'

Kwame smirked. 'Good. Now, we just have to tell her.'

–

Damien let himself fall a few steps behind the two. He didn't want Kwame to see even a hint of his anger. All his preparation, the years of literal sweat and blood, all thrown down the drain. He could already feel his skills withering away as Kwame led them into the expansive garden behind the house.

She's probably sewing or picking flowers.

However, he heard the familiar sound of metal clashing, instead. The whistle of the air being cut, and feet shifting among the dirt. It sounded as if someone were… fighting?

Sure enough, as they rounded the corner, he saw a young woman holding a foil, sparring with one of her father's soldiers. Only she wore proper protective clothing while the man looked as if he rolled out of bed, his tunic rumpled and smudged with dirt. The two moved around the garden, the girl was surprisingly agile, her fencing skirt allowing her to move fluidly.

He watched her parry with calculating eyes. She had good speed and instincts, but her balance needed improvement. She tended to lean forward, and hunched her shoulders in defence, causing her to sway between moves. She had a good foundation but for the more complicated manoeuvres, she seemed unsure, hesitant. Nothing a couple of adjustments and more practice couldn't change. Perhaps she should…

'Keep your back straight,' he called out.

The girl narrowly dodged the soldier's lunge before stepping back and pulling off her mask. Her curly hair spilling over her shoulder and her cheeks two red spots from exertion, she looked at Damien.

A shot of electricity ran through him as their eyes met. She was beautiful, something he expected. She was not as statuesque as her father, although her hazel eyes were just as demanding, hints of muscle showing along her arms, her brown skin unblemished, and lips enviably full. *Pretty girl*, he thought.

He crossed his arms as the girl let her foil rest at her side, an eyebrow quirked. 'Pardon?'

'Your centre is too low. Great for defence but leaves you too slow to respond.'

Sabine's lips pursed as she looked Damien up and down. He raised a brow, and she stood taller under his gaze, undaunted. Something about the expression made it hard for him to hold back a smile. He could imagine her as a soldier, charging towards him on the first day of training. She already had the sword.

'He's right,' the soldier behind her said. She didn't spare him a glance, simply nodding as she kept her eyes on Damien. 'Is this a new teacher, Father?'

'Of sorts.'

'Well, that's not foreboding at all.' She dropped her sword and smiled before joining them, hugging Kwame around his waist. 'Good afternoon,' she greeted.

Kwame softened and gathered her in a warm embrace. 'Afternoon, Sabine,' he said, placing an arm around her shoulders.

Damien frowned at the display, not recalling a time he'd seen such an affectionate father. He couldn't even remember the last time he saw one *look* at their daughter unless it was to scold them. Kwame turned her towards them, and he followed Roulet's lead, nodding politely in greeting. He bit back a grin when her curious gaze lingered on him.

'Sabine, you've met General Roulet.'

Sabine curtsied. 'Nice to see you again, General.'

'You as well, Sabine. Your skills are coming along nicely.'

'Well, I won't be ready for a battlefield anytime soon, but I can at least land a hit or two,' she quipped.

Kwame and the general laughed, and the focus shifted to him. 'This is Captain Damien,' Kwame told her.

He bowed to her. 'It's a pleasure to meet you, Mademoiselle,' he said.

'You as well, Captain. Thank you for the advice. I'll make sure to consider it in future lessons.'

'I am honoured.'

'Captain Damien will be joining you when you move to General Roulet's home,' Kwame informed her. Sabine's eyes widened, and she opened her mouth, but her father lifted his hand before she could speak. 'Just for added protection. I'll have to take the men with me once I leave in two weeks' time.'

While he came off as callous to many, Damien prided himself on being aware to a fault. As a Black man in the French military, his life depended on it. So, he didn't miss the many emotions that rushed over her face nor the fear that flashed on it when she looked at Roulet. The moment of vulnerability followed by the quickness of how she steeled herself back to being a gracious host caused a pang in his chest.

How many times had he done the same?

'That's… good,' she replied. 'Perhaps, he could become my new teacher.'

'If the lady wishes,' Damien encouraged, but kept his voice even. When she looked at him again, the wariness faded a little and for a moment, it felt like the dynamics were reversed: them against well-meaning but unmoveable leaders. They both looked away.

'Very well,' Kwame said. 'It's settled. Resume your studies.'

'I thank you for your generosity, Father,' she said sarcastically, though her eyes softened as he kissed her forehead. 'I'll see you at dinner.'

' 'Til then,' he promised. 'Gentlemen, let's talk details.'

The trio headed back inside with the general and Kwame talking through the details of Damien's post while he did his best not to think too much about the young woman practising in the garden.

'What do you think?' General Roulet asked Damien an hour later as they stood on the railway platform that would take them back to Paris. Damien leaned on one of the columns as he watched civilians chat amongst themselves animatedly. In comparison to the colourful, bustling household they had just left, everyone else looked dull.

'She's different than I expected,' Damien commented. 'Older. I'm surprised she has not married yet.'

'Yes, with the transition of French rule being so recent, Kwame hasn't had much time to think of it until now,' the general reasoned.

'If she's supposedly training to be a lady, why is she learning to fence?' Damien asked.

'It's a hobby she picked up from her father,' Roulet told him. 'After Kwame's wife passed, it gave them something to bond over. He also didn't want his daughter to feel vulnerable in the world.'

'Curious.' Something stirred inside him as he remembered the way their eyes had met and recalled the defiance in her gaze. He looked up to see Roulet looking at him suspiciously.

'You seemed to be reluctant about the job in the study. Though Kwame can be persistent, I can smooth things over with him if you're not comfortable.'

'You would champion for a fool like me?' Damien teased.

'Answer honestly,' he commanded, facing him. 'What do you truly think of Sabine?'

Damien sighed. Not for the first time, he wished that Roulet was like him. It would be much easier to explain how he saw more similarities between him and a stranger than the comrades he'd made over the years. Not just her insistence on annoying the most powerful person in the room, but different like him.

African with no tribe. French with no name. Caught in a world that didn't know what to do with them.

Looking at Sabine, he could feel a sense of kinship, a chance for once, not to be the only one in a crowd. It was a foolish reason to take a job, but he couldn't deny his curiosity.

'I think it'll be interesting to see her father convince her to marry. She's a fighter,' he said. 'The job pays enough, and my assignments are a bore. Maybe a change of pace will be useful.'

The general hummed before checking his timepiece, as if he were trying to seem relaxed. Damien knew the general well enough that there was more on his mind. He counted forty-seven seconds before the general spoke. 'She'll have a lady's maid attending her,' General Roulet mentioned. Damien almost chuckled.

So, that's what worried his superior offer, not that he blamed him. Her beauty combined with her father's confidence made Sabine undeniably intriguing. But there were many women in Paris and more who would not cause a potential headache for him down the road.

'She's pretty, but nothing special in any other regard.' The words tasted like ash on his tongue.

'If you're sure…'

'I am,' he said confidently. 'I won't disappoint you. You have my word.'

Chapter Four

Paris

March 1895

'I don't want you to leave,' Sabine told her father as he packed the last of his things, which made little sense to her. The villa was theirs and they were wealthy enough to fill it with whatever they wanted. Beyond travel clothes, money and a blade – he would never forget that – her father didn't need to take anything else to their home in the Ivory Coast. He only had a few keepsakes he never parted with, no matter where he went.

She had been one of them but too many things had changed over the last decade.

He clasped his travel bag close. 'I'll be back soon enough.'

'For my wedding,' she stated, hoping she hid her exasperation well.

Her father chuckled. 'Of course not,' he said. 'I have to pick your husband first.'

Sabine stood up and turned her back on her father to roll her eyes. 'I have been too obedient to be shipped off like this,' she mumbled in French.

They usually spoke in Fante behind closed doors and among family. French was for political gatherings and impressing foreigners. Yet, she slipped into her mother's language as naturally as she would've when her mother was alive.

Amelie… Sabine contemplated the name for a moment.

It was not lost on Sabine that France practically owned her home country and used it as a means of production. However, she also knew that unlike what most Frenchmen believed, it wasn't a lone effort. Rather, it was a collaboration, for better or worse. Even knowing that, she was also aware her parents shouldn't have met, they shouldn't have married, and she shouldn't exist.

It was supposed to be a family trip for her mother to see a new world with Sabine's maternal grandfather, as he set up a trading post. Her father, full of charisma and an instinct for forming connections, was supposed to help. Unfortunately, he had fallen in love with Amelie instead. As a result, Sabine's grandfather abandoned Amelie in the country, disowning her when he discovered the relationship.

Her parents had lived a quiet life, but her mother didn't make it past Sabine's eighth birthday. From then on, her father went back to doing what he did best: charming and connecting with people. He became key in making Ivory Coast an official French trading post.

Of course, no one from her tribe saw the full result of her father's actions until much later. She barely understood the magnitude of his decision to strengthen their relationship with France. All she knew was there was no going back.

'*Mon trésor*,' her father said gently, turning her to face him. He smiled kindly before tapping her forehead. 'Your accent sounds just like your mother's,' he told her in French before switching back to Fante. 'And you are right. You rarely disappointed me, which is why I must give you the best life possible. That will always be my intention for you. Do you understand?'

'Yes,' she said just as she heard a carriage pull up. She looked out the window and spotted General Roulet stepping out before holding his hand out to steady his wife. 'Be back soon, please,' she pleaded.

He looked at her curiously, as he always did the few times she had allowed desperation to show.

'*Ama*.' Sabine's throat went dry at her day-born name, something he rarely called her since her mother died. His gaze softened before giving her forehead another kiss. 'I always return. Always.'

—

The first night at General Roulet's home was decent.

His estate was as grand as one would expect given his status, even standing shoulder to shoulder with the homes of other bureaucrats. Sabine was awed by the pastel orange townhouse with its curved archways and intricate stonework, making each window look like a piece of art. But despite it and the welcoming Parisian weather, something about it felt cold.

The staff were polite as they took her belongings. Her personal maid, Sandra, was straight-laced and quiet, unlike most she had previously encountered who were intrigued by her background. With them, she would usually pretend not to speak fluent French to avoid conversation. With Sandra, however, it was unnecessary.

In fact, Sabine's background was never a topic at all as Madame Roulet asked questions about what she wanted to do while in town and invited her to one party or another. The woman was sturdy and bubbly despite her greying hair, a splash of red colouring her pale face as she spoke rapidly.

She couldn't help but think how far out of their way the Roulets must have gone to make her comfortable, from welcoming her, to the various open invitations. It almost felt like staying with family with how at ease she felt. And yet, the night still felt too cool, and the bed was too soft. It felt like she was being coddled by feathers and stone. Sighing, she looked out the window, watching the stars crawl across the sky.

She wished her father were here.

—

'Good morning,' she greeted the Roulets at breakfast the next morning. She wore a burgundy day dress that Sandra helped her pick out from her minimal wardrobe. Most of the clothes she owned didn't fit the French style so she didn't bother bringing them from the villa. Besides, going shopping with Madame Roulet would probably be a good way to build their relationship.

'Good morning, Sabine.' Madame Roulet welcomed her with a bright smile. 'How did you sleep?'

'Well, thank you,' she lied. A servant placed a plate in front of her, a modest breakfast of bread, cheese and a small cluster of fruit with a cup of coffee. It was lighter than she was used to, but she made no comment, figuring today would be full of adjustments.

'So, I was talking to my husband last night about taking you into town tomorrow,' Madame Roulet mentioned. 'He was a bit wary but promised me it would be safe enough for us to go. We can do some shopping and have lunch with a dear friend of mine, Madame Dupont. How does that sound?'

'It sounds nice.'

'Splendid! I'll send a letter right after breakfast,' Mrs. Roulet said excitedly. Sabine smiled back. She had a feeling the woman liked a full day on her schedule.

Surely enough, the general's wife inquired, 'Perhaps we should invite them over tonight for dinner? That way you can become acquainted with her and her husband.'

'Isn't that awfully soon?' she asked, making her voice sound smaller and shy. 'I don't feel prepared. I still feel a bit tired. I apologise for my reluctance, but my nerves…'

'Oh, no, no.' Madame Roulet waved her hand. 'You're our guest. Of course, you need some time to adjust. I tend to get enthusiastic with newcomers, but by all means, please rest.' Sabine wondered if she would have to apologise again but Madame Roulet had already waltzed on to the next topic of conversation.

Breakfast was the shortest meal of the day, so Sabine was left with plenty of time to explore. The townhouse was smaller than her father's villa but filled with imported vases, portraits that lined the halls and hardwood floors covered in exotic rugs. It spoke the language of every house she had lived in for the past few years: unapologetically wealthy. Quite impressive, but equally bland.

She walked from the sunroom that overlooked the garden. Again, it was smaller than she was used to, but the hedges were high, allowing for privacy. There, she spotted someone circling the tree with a foil, carefully avoiding the flowers as they lunged and parried an invisible opponent. She approached the window slowly, recognising the familiar face of Captain Damien.

Though it didn't happen often, there had been men that had caught Sabine's eye, whether for their looks or charm. She didn't mind conversation, but rarely met someone who could keep her attention. With Damien, something felt strange. Alien, even. Every time she had looked at him yesterday, she wanted to step closer. She was so *curious*.

His eyes were light brown, framed by black hair and russet skin. He easily towered over her when they were side by side. His gaze was cold, calculating, as he moved but she remembered the hints of a smirk from their previous conversation. He clearly had the power of a soldier; the sharp angles of his face matching the small scars that appeared above his cheekbones. Everything about him warned her that he was a threat; but his smirk, a look that she found sly and charming, made her think twice.

Her face flushed when she remembered the playfulness and heat in his eyes. She saw it again when he looked up from his imaginary sparring partner.

They stared at one another for a long moment before he motioned for her to join him. She took a deep breath, steeling herself as she stepped outside.

'I wondered when you would wake,' he said in lieu of a greeting.

'I'm guessing you rise with the dawn.'

He shrugged. 'A habit, princess.'

'I think the technical term would be "mademoiselle",' she corrected him. He raised his brows at her before smirking.

'Very well, *Mademoiselle* Kouassi.' He did a shallow bow and she grimaced at his sarcasm. He chuckled when he saw her face, making her school it into a cool expression. She refused to be his amusement.

'Why did you invite me over?'

He went around the tree and picked up an extra foil. 'I was hoping we could start your fencing lessons today,' he said, holding out the weapon to her. 'Unless you prefer to rest.'

The challenge in his voice was clear, and it sparked her competitiveness. It would be smarter for her to excuse herself, as she told Madame Roulet she was tired. She grabbed the sword anyway. 'I'm well rested.'

Damien smirked once more before stepping back and lifting his foil. 'Let's hope so.' And then he lunged.

The lesson lasted for hours. Damien made it a mix of sparring to see her technique and practice to improve it. Sabine thought herself to be a good sport, but as the sun crawled across the sky, she found herself doubting this fact. She should have known better than to fight in a dress or challenge a soldier. She held back a groan, wishing she had quit much earlier.

Sabine grunted as she lunged at Damien with what was left of her strength. To her embarrassment, he merely sidestepped her attack, letting her land on the ground. She growled before throwing the foil aside.

'The least you can do is catch me,' she spat.

Damien shrugged before kneeling in front of her. 'The more you get acquainted with the ground, the less you'll be defeated by it.'

Sabine huffed before standing. 'I'm starting to regret replacing Seydou,' she said, rubbing her back.

'There will be no one to coddle you in the real world, princess,' Damien chided.

She placed her hands on her hips defiantly. 'May I remind you, *again*, that my technical title is mademoiselle and I doubt

I'll be flinging a sword around in real life.' Sabine rolled her eyes at the notion. 'I'd be better off with a handy pistol.'

Damien seemed unperturbed by her frustration. She would dare say he almost seemed smug.

Feeling bold and determined to gain some footing, she grabbed her foil and sauntered over to him. She walked in a slow and steady circle around him, letting her blade drag behind her. 'I'm well aware there is no mercy in French high society,' she explained, her voice softening. 'In that setting, I'm sure I'd run circles around you, Captain.'

Sabine stopped in front of him, a hair's breadth away. A charge crawled over her skin when their eyes met that almost made her breathless. She looked away as she took two steps back, pointing to the ground. 'Don't move from that circle,' she ordered. 'If I can take you down, then practice is done for today and tomorrow.'

Damien raised his eyebrows at the circle before smirking at her. 'Very well, princess.'

He took a defensive stance and beckoned her to charge. She took a deep breath, looking for a weak spot and lunged. She lasted longer than before, even landing a few lucky hits until Damien drew her in too close with a false opening and struck. Sabine hissed, clutched her arm, and lost her footing. She prepared herself for the fall, not expecting the arms that grabbed her, pulling her upright.

She panted as she tried to reorient herself, breathing in the smell of him. Under the sweat and grime was something smoky and inviting, his light brown eyes calming her. However, just as quickly as the moment came, so did the piercing gazes of the house's staff. She could only imagine the gossip that would spread. Before she could make the situation more scandalous, she stepped back, realising belatedly that she had been clutching his tunic for balance.

'Well done,' Damien commented after a moment. 'You're improving. Slowly, but you're doing well.' He took her foil from her hand. 'We'll continue tomorrow. You can go to another lesson. Perhaps, sewing.'

'I despise sewing,' she muttered, not missing his soft laugh as he sauntered off. She didn't look as he left. Instead, she planted her feet and practised the manoeuvres she had been complaining about mere moments ago.

She found it was an effective way to keep the hum of desire under her skin at bay.

Chapter Five

July 2013

'What are you doing?'

Dani jumped at the voice behind her, turning to see her friend and other roommate, Talia, standing behind her with a bowl of popcorn. She pressed her hand to her chest over her racing heart.

'You know, I really need you to make more noise when you move,' Dani said.

Talia rolled her eyes as she stepped around her to the couch. 'I'm sure I make plenty of noise.'

Dani pursed her lips, saying nothing else about the bold-faced lie. Talia may have been 5´10 with broad shoulders but the most intimidating thing about her was that you never heard her coming, like she had been a ninja in a past life. A sour taste filled Dani's mouth at the thought.

Her mind was still shuffling through her dreams. Lately, they had been stronger than usual, easier to remember, too. She had experienced them enough to know the high points, but the details were starting to filter in. She was living Sabine's life day by day now. Well, Sabine and Damien's.

She would say it was like reading a book or experiencing a 3D film, but she felt every aspect of their emotions and it kept jumping back between the two without warning until she was turned around about who *she* was. Why were her dreams changing now? Almost like…

33

'Dani!'

Her attention moved from the spot on the wall she was staring at back to Talia, who was looking at her in concern. 'You sure you're okay? You've been staring off in the distance for five minutes.'

'Y—Yeah.' Dani her waved off. 'Just… running through my solo for orchestra.'

'Well, you could at least sit down. You're creeping me out just lurking like that.'

Dani's feet shuffled reluctantly to the couch, plopping down on the opposite side. 'What are you watching?'

'BBC's *Pride and Prejudice*.' Dani groaned, pushing herself to get up just as Talia grabbed her arm. 'Wait, wait, you promised we could watch it one day! It's good I swear!'

'No, I'm not getting in the middle of yours and Riley's debate,' Dani declared as she tried to pry Talia's hand off her. She knew the story since she read it in her high school literature class. But she was wholly unprepared for the film versus mini-series debate that was apparently popular among Jane Austen fans. Riley, Dani's best friend from freshman year, was vehemently *for* the 2005 film, while Talia was a diehard fan of the mini-series. This difference led to multiple arguments about which was better, often pulling in whoever was around to join their side.

Personally, Dani didn't care for either, finding the story both boring and overdramatic; Riley and Talia agreed that was the worst opinion of all three.

'I promise I won't even tell her you watched it,' Talia whined while Dani tried to wiggle out of her friend's vice grip.

'Fine, fine! Just get off of me.'

'Yay!'

Talia let her go and Dani took a deep breath. She dug her hand into Talia's popcorn defiantly and sat back, humming in acknowledgement whenever Talia told her a titbit about the show.

Halfway through the second episode, Dani found that she didn't mind the show, the acting making it much more engaging than the book.

The antics reminded her of a modern romcom, with just enough going on to keep her intrigued even with the classic setting. She didn't dare voice this opinion, already knowing the irony of someone who studied 200-year-old composers saying she wasn't a fan of historical storytelling. Dani was munching on popcorn when something about how Elizabeth spoke to Mr Wickham conjured up an uncomfortable feeling.

'You're watching this in French?' Dani asked. Talia raised a brow at her.

'Yes…' her friend drawled. 'This is my way of studying for my French class. That's why the English subtitles are on for you. You didn't notice this whole time?' she quizzed.

'No,' Dani said, dazed as she focused on the language. She suddenly understood the words just as well as she knew English. *How was that possible?* She swallowed nervously, racking her brain for an excuse. She was sure she hadn't been reading the subtitles. But perhaps she was just tired. Her dreams were, after all, keeping her up as it is. 'I obviously wasn't paying close enough attention,' Dani stood, shaking her head. 'But I need to do some work for my composition class.'

'Okay…' She felt Talia's eyes follow her as she stood.

'I'm fine, Tal,' Dani said, answering her friend's unspoken question. The look in Talia's eyes told her she didn't believe her but, luckily, something happened on screen that captured her attention. Dani took that as her cue to leave, quickly making her way back to her room. She leaned against her door in a daze.

'*Quand il me prend dans ses bras, qu'il me… pout? Moi?* Fuck.'

So, she wasn't fluent if she was already butchering '*La Vie En Rose*'. The words were awkward, stumbling as they fell off her tongue. They didn't come with knowledge of what each word actually meant but rather a memory of hearing the song.

She forced her jaw to unclench as she went to her side table and pulled out her dream journal. All the details she remembered from the past few nights were there, filling up multiple pages. What was once a sparse collection of details was now a plethora of stories. She almost dared to call them diary entries.

She flipped to a fresh page and wrote down:

> *Don't know French but understand it now??*

What was happening to her mind? Was something wrong? Did she have a condition she didn't know about? She had heard of people with multiple personality disorders having full backstories for each personality – or waking up from a coma, suddenly fluent in a foreign tongue. Was this a mental break-down? Had she suffered some trauma she couldn't recall? She groaned, dropping the pen to cover her eyes with her hands.

She didn't have time to have a breakdown. It was her senior year. She was one step closer to playing with the New York Philharmonic and she could *not* go crazy now. Her parents and therapists couldn't finally be right after all these years. A lump rose in Dani's throat as she wondered what could be wrong with her, lying across her bed to stare at the ceiling.

If her mind snapped, she couldn't play like she wanted to. Her dream of being a professional cellist, travelling the world to play concerts and maybe even being part of a film soundtrack, would be gone. Her mind swirled with daunting questions that made her lightheaded, having to remind herself that she needed to breathe.

Maybe the stress would take me out first, she thought. She placed her hands over her stomach and started to slow down her breathing. She played elevator music in her head, something mindless. Before she knew it, it had transformed into a familiar freestyle piece, one that had been stuck in her head for over a week. She sat up suddenly.

Jones. The dreams started when she met him. Maybe he was some kind of trigger. If she could figure out what it was, maybe it would stop. It wasn't much but it was better than sitting in her room waiting for a panic attack. She scrambled for her laptop and opened her school email.

Hi Dr Allen, she wrote, *I have a question…*

Chapter Six

June 1895

'The weather is quite nice, don't you think?'

'Must you always start our strolls with the same observation?' Sabine scoffed as she looked over her shoulder towards him. 'You've yet to complain. Why start now?'

'I believe two months is long enough to endure.'

'Says the one never willing to contribute,' Sabine said quickly. 'If you have a more interesting observation, please delight us both.'

Damien smirked at the frustration in her voice, already amused by her impatience. Truly, it was the best part of his days. When General Roulet said protecting her would be one of his hardest jobs, he thought it would be due to Sabine being stubborn or helping her adjust to French society – but no.

There was a lack of anything to do other than watch her. Most faux pas were avoided thanks to Madame Roulet, and Sabine was prim and proper at every turn. She stayed home reading most days until she had to meet an acquaintance Madame Roulet invited to the house, which was practically every other day. Those meant dinners and after-dinner conversations before finally retiring for the night to wake up and do it all over again without showing a hint of disdain.

The boredom he could endure, but the restlessness was new. His only outlet for any energy was their daily strolls through the

Jardin du Luxembourg and their occasional fencing sessions. Seeing her façade slip for a moment was a relief; he didn't understand how she hadn't gone mad by now.

'Mademoiselle Kouassi, you and I both know that is not my role.'

'Perhaps, we should switch. You make conversation and I brood.' She looked over her shoulder and frowned, scrunching her brows together in what he guessed was supposed to be an imitation of him.

'Brooding is my specialty,' he simply said.

'How do you not go mad not speaking all the time?' she asked, glancing over her shoulder once more. He always stayed a few steps behind her, far enough to represent her status, near enough to interfere when pickpockets lingered too close.

'The same way you don't go mad having to make so many conversations about nothing.'

'Ah,' she said. 'Endurance.'

Damien almost laughed as they walked past a group of people listening to a street musician. They were too comfortable for the public setting. Quips during fencing practice was one thing but outside the house, there were many prying ears. He had to remember to be more careful.

When she looked back again, he made sure to observe the crowd. No angry commoners today, but the tide could always turn. Protests had occurred over less than a beautiful, wealthy foreigner strolling through the street.

Beautiful. Damien scoffed at himself.

'And what do you find so funny?' Sabine asked. 'Life,' Damien answered easily. 'It's ironic.'

'How so?'

'How not? People kill themselves to stay alive, which they can barely enjoy for one reason or another. Always family or position or something else equally petty. I assume Côte d'Ivoire is not so different.'

'From what I've seen, you Frenchmen seem determined to enjoy yourselves to the fullest,' she snapped.

39

Damien looked at her in mild shock, and she blushed at her sudden outburst.

'I mean, there are bigger concerns at the moment. Right now, the main hope for my country is a peaceful... transition.'

Damien grimaced but understood. He had heard more than enough tales of Africa. Everyday there were merchants seizing the chance to bring home exotic goods and jewels, and the lengths they were willing to go for them. Gold, cocoa, ivory and diamonds all within arm's reach, supposedly. *All at a cost*, he thought, as he looked back at Sabine.

He was well aware of the price of France's expansion – the amount of African blood spilled for it – but he felt separated from it. He didn't agree with his home country's land race with the English and Germans, but he couldn't help but wonder what price those in Mali and Benin had to pay for 'French advancement'? What did *she* have to pay for another country's greed?

When they passed the crowd, he stepped closer until they were side-by-side.

'That's the wish of sensible people, but these are not sensible times. Not yet, anyway,' he replied in a low voice. 'Some people like to dance in the ashes of their own fires.'

'I hope it keeps them warm at night.'

Damien chuckled and she looked at him curiously before asking, 'What is your name? I mean, your last name. Everyone calls you by your first name.'

'You already know it,' he told her. She looked at him inquiringly as he joined her side. 'I don't have a last name, nor did I adopt one. I have no family. I grew up on the streets until the general found me. Damien is a name I chose for myself and the only one I care about.'

He waited for the look of pity or for her to insist on picking a name for him as so many had done over the years.

Instead, she said, 'That's... commendable.'

He tilted his head. 'How so?'

'Some men are so defeated in life they won't even claim their name.' 'Have you encountered men like that?'

'Almost…' She paused at the window of a dress shop. It was adorned with dresses of all the latest styles in vibrant colours, beckoning them inside. Sabine seemed particularly mesmerised by the deep blue one off to the side.

'My father seemed to be that way after my mother died,' she said suddenly. 'Many didn't know they were in love or even married, though I found it obvious. I once hoped for a love as deep as theirs but now… seeing how destroyed my father was after she passed, I don't know if I could bear it.'

Damien was silent, having trouble picturing Kwame in such a state. The man's only leeway seemed to be with Sabine and even she had only so much sway.

'I wish I understood,' Sabine admitted. 'It seems as though he would cast away the world for her. Even now, I feel as though his involvement in giving our country to the French seems to be in dedication to her. How can you be so captivated by someone? How can they rule your thoughts so effortlessly, even when they're gone?'

How indeed, he pondered as he stared into her forlorn eyes. He couldn't imagine loving someone more than a few nights, much less a lifetime and beyond.

'I'm sure that's a mystery that has been pondered for centuries,' Damien said finally. 'Lucky for you, people don't expect it of you. Many would prefer that you don't give in to such folly.'

Sabine smiled but didn't seem reassured by the words. 'Yes. That's the right thing to do.'

The wistfulness in Sabine's voice made Damien curious. An interesting story laid there, waiting to be asked about. Words scratched at the back of his throat, itching to deepen the conversation, but he bit them back. It was neither the time nor the place and he had already risked enough.

Still, he didn't step back as he asked her, 'Have you received any word from your father?'

'Yes. He has met with the Bassam kings once more. There's some unrest in the city—'

'Tell me the best part,' he interjected. It wasn't her first time receiving a letter from her father. It was always a summary of business, which Sabine would read aloud so he could update General Roulet. However, the last paragraph was just for Sabine, to update her on what was happening at home. That was his favourite part, the snippets giving him a glimpse of a different world. They seemed to be hers as well as he watched a smile slowly spread across her face, her eyes lighting up as she reminisced.

'He saw my grandmother,' she told him. 'He had arrived just in time for my cousin's first child be born and they had a huge feast to celebrate. I'm jealous. I've craved my grandmother's kedjenou since I read his letter.'

Damien watched her shoulders relax for the first time since they left the house and felt relieved before letting himself fall under the spell of her story of a world far, far away.

Today, for one moment, the grim reality could wait.

–

'Kwame will be back from the Ivory Coast in a few days.'

General Roulet and Damien were in the general's home study, standing on opposite sides of the general's desk. The room was the exact opposite of the rest of the house, which was bright and welcoming. The walls were sapphire blue, books and charts filled the space, hiding away secrets. Some were keys to victories while others were notes on defeats. Roulet had allowed Damien to peruse the books at his leisure, but Damien had little patience for battle strategy, much to the general's disappointment. But Damien treated that the same way he treated the lingering concern in Roulet's eyes over the years; he ignored it.

'He and Sabine will be attending several parties over the next week,' Roulet continued. 'They have a few allies here but are looking for more, so there will definitely be plenty of mingling.'

Roulet pored over papers while Damien waited for instructions, his eyes glancing at proclamations and tactics he wouldn't be a part of due to his post. Damien felt his restlessness surge up. His hands itched for a sword, ready for battle. Taking a deep breath, he let it out slowly; he had to prepare for another battle, one harder for him to comprehend.

'The party is fully staffed, but Kwame wants someone to keep a close eye on Sabine,' he continued. 'He wants to ensure she's only connecting with the correct guests.'

'I'll make sure of that,' Damien reassured him.

Roulet hummed, looking at him critically; he waited. 'You seem better. Much calmer.'

'Sabine insists on being active. Keeps away the boredom,' he replied, which was true.

'As long as no boundaries are being crossed...' Roulet looked at him sharply, and Damien stopped himself from exhaling in exasperation.

'I've kept my word. She is safe and well. And *untouched.*'

'Good.' Roulet seemed to hesitate before speaking again. 'I hope you understand that while this is a favour for a good friend, I do worry about you.'

There was a softness in Roulet's gaze that always made Damien uncomfortable. He had been unable to place it when he was younger, often flitting between the barracks and the general's home. Now, he was well acquainted with the worry-prideful mix that lingered in Roulet's eyes.

'I am well,' he reassured the man stiffly.

Roulet nodded before becoming his superior again. 'You should go inform Sabine of the party arrangements. Perhaps she will be excited to make new friends.'

–

Sabine stopped herself from rubbing her face as her cheeks burned from all the smiling. She was currently caught in a circle of lawmakers' wives telling her about the latest opera they'd attended. Sabine wondered if the retelling would be as long as the show Madame Roulet had taken her to last month. While dreadful then, this was worse. Why must polite conversation go on for so long?

Despite it being her third party, her tolerance for them wasn't getting any better. She would usually feel a little better with her father around, but he was always commanding an audience of men in General Roulet's study while she was forced to the drawing rooms for more appropriate conversations. Although, no matter how the conversations went they always turned back to—

'I must say, you have the loveliest necklace.' Sabine gritted her teeth before smiling graciously at one of the ladies; she didn't remember her name. She touched the three strand, beaded necklace as if she had just remembered she was wearing it.

'Thank you. It was a gift from my father,' she said, repeating the words she had said every time she wore it. 'He had an artisan from home make it for me.'

'And what material is it?'

'Ivory.'

'My, it's beautiful,' the woman said, a shine of greed in her eyes.

She reached out and touched the strand, running her fingers across the beads. Sabine forced herself not to pull away, even though she clearly remembered the way the woman recoiled at the sight of her and her father when she first entered the house. Sabine didn't know this woman's connections nor her husband's position and the possibility of ruining business for her father was enough to keep her still.

'Hopefully, there will be more where that came from.'

Sabine felt her shoulders relax once the woman removed her hand.

'I'm sure there will be. My father knows value when he sees it,' Sabine reassured her. 'If you'll excuse me for a moment.'

She needed fresh air *now*. She walked out of the room and down the hall, wandering aimlessly. Or perhaps not, since she soon found herself at the door that led to the garden. She only meant to crack the door open, but the cool breeze beckoned her outside. Her eyes immediately went to the sky as she stepped foot on the grass.

The lights from the house made the stars hard to see, not that there were many to see in Paris, even on good days. She sighed as she closed her eyes. She had to give up the stars as well?

'Careful, princess.'

Sabine jumped and spun around, finding Damien holding the door open.

'You go missing too long, you worry guests.'

'Oh,' she said. 'Right. I just needed a moment.'

'I'm afraid that I can only give you a minute or two more,' he teased.

Gratitude flooded Sabine and she stopped herself from flinging her arms around him in relief. She clasped her hands together, looking at the stars, trying to see if there were any constellations she recognised. There weren't, of course, but she wondered what she was missing. Perhaps Damien would tell her tomorrow. She asked him questions all the time now and he always answered, no matter how reluctantly.

She wanted to call him a friend, something she desperately needed. It may have been easier to ignore the desire for one if Damien wasn't always around, if their backgrounds were different, and if he didn't look so lonely. Was he lonely everywhere or just here?

Sabine winced at the idea of even uttering the words. She couldn't ask him that. That question was inappropriate, and people knew who she was now. She had to start building her future, didn't she? Running away was only a fantasy.

Stars were a much safer option.

'All right, I'm… ready,' she said, facing Damien once more. He nodded and held the door open for her. She stepped back inside the hallway, the sound of the party filtering back in, bringing back the tension in her shoulders. She took a few steps back towards the drawing room when she remembered something.

'Take this for me.' She reached behind her head to take off the necklace. She huffed as she futilely tried to separate the clasp and chain.

'Let me.' Sabine froze as she felt Damien's words caress the back of her neck. His hands were warm but callous as they replaced hers, their fingers brushing. She swallowed as a thrill ran down her spine. He had never dared to get so close to her before. His fingers continued to brush against her skin until the necklace loosened. The cool beads slipped from around her neck before disappearing.

She cleared her throat and pressed her palms to her cheeks, hoping they weren't red. 'I'll come back for it at the end of the night.'

She didn't dare look at Damien, pushing the moment to the back of her mind as she re-entered the room. She did her best to focus on the conversation, jumping in with a titbit here and there to blend in. Still, the wife from before immediately noticed.

'Oh, your necklace is gone.'

'Yes, my father wanted to borrow it quickly,' she lied. 'It seemed one of the husbands was quite interested in the craftsmanship.'

The woman's eyes lit up and she could already see the future unfolding. The woman was sure to prattle about her love for the piece to her husband who would go to her father about acquiring ivory who would then go home to obtain more through whatever means necessary. And another piece of her home would be gone to traders while she stayed here enabling it all and powerless to stop it.

46

It's business, she thought. It didn't stop the knot that formed in her stomach as she continued to chat all night, smiling through it.

–

Sabine watched her maid, Sandra, carefully take her hair out of its updo. The feeling of pressure releasing was marvellous and she allowed herself to bask in it after such a long night. The only miracle was that there would be no more parties this week and that the next event Madame Roulet would drag her to was another opera in three days' time. She would finally get to rest.

She tensed when she heard a knock on the door.

'Princess,' Damien called through the door. 'Are you decent?'

'It's *mademoiselle* and yes,' she answered sternly. 'You may retire, Sandra.'

Sandra gave a curious look over her shoulder, but said nothing as she stepped outside, Damien entering.

'I believe you forgot this.' He held out his hand, revealing her ivory necklace.

She gasped, hurrying to grab it. 'Thank you.' Placing it carefully in her jewellery box, her shoulders slumped in exhaustion. 'I survived another day.'

'Surely the party wasn't that bad?' Damien smirked. 'I make great company.'

She looked at him from over her shoulder, serious despite the surge of gratitude that filled her chest. 'Thank you for tonight. I realised I never thank you for anything.'

'You never have to,' he promised. 'I'm here to protect you. I will not go back on my word.'

'I guess you're growing quite fond of me.' She sat on her bed, one leg tucked under her, the other dangling off the edge. 'And before you worry, I shall not run off and ruin the fun by telling General Roulet. Although it would be amusing to watch him scold you like a child.' A shadow seemed to pass over Damien's face, and she faltered. 'Perhaps… I am mistaken,' she revised. 'I shouldn't joke about such things. My humour could use some work. I'll just—'

'You're not wrong,' Damien cut in. 'Truthfully, Roulet may have me scrub the latrines, if not demote me, for how close we have become.'

'Surely, it can't be that serious?'

He opened his mouth, but nothing came out. The silence built between them until it was uncomfortable. Eventually, he looked away. 'I should let you rest,' he said finally. 'Goodnight, Mademoiselle.'

He quickly turned on his heel, slamming the door behind him. Sabine bit her lip and looked out the window.

What could he have possibly wanted to say, and why did her stomach burn with the need to know?

–

The manicured lawns of the Luxembourg Gardens stretched far and wide before them the next day. Colourful flowers blooming alongside the paths. Trees in neat lines supplied occasional shade as they visited the various statues and fountains. Usually there were plenty of people walking or lounging in the grass. Today there were only a few, due to the storm clouds above them. When Damien suggested staying inside for the same reason, Sabine merely scoffed.

'Why would I be scared of a little rain?' she had asked, before throwing on her coat.

They walked along the paths quietly, Damien's eyes on their surroundings while Sabine looked around curiously. Her eyes lit up at every new flower she spotted, before gently touching their petals. She would flit from one to the next while Damien watched her, fascinated by her excitement.

Sabine belonged outside. He had never thought that of a lady – or any woman before – but seeing her among the flowers, she looked like an extension of nature and her appreciation for fresh air and plants didn't feel superficial. He wondered how often she had gone outside when she was young.

'All the time,' she told him a little later. They sat on a bench near a fountain, eating a light lunch. The chef had packed brie, bread, apples and thinly sliced ham for them to share. She ate like a lady, but he could tell through her precision, it was practised. 'My mother loved tending to the small farm we had. I liked racing with my father for what felt like hours. When I would visit my grandmother, all the village kids would play outside every day. It's not like here, where everyone is always hiding.' Her eyes filled with longing, and she started to pick at her sandwich.

'I'm surprised you're not spending more time with your father.'

Sabine smiled, but there was no joy. 'He's a soldier on a mission. He has things to do. I will see him when it's done.'

'Being a liaison is a full-time job.'

Sabine snorted. 'Among other things.'

'Ah, so he's not a stand-up citizen.'

She shrugged and gave him a knowing look. 'You French should know more than anyone else that landowning can be a tricky business.'

Damien hummed in agreement but said nothing more.

'He works hard and is not one to be trifled with,' she continued. 'He can make General Roulet look soft-hearted in the right context.'

'Ha! I doubt that,' he denied with a shake of his head, stopping when he saw the troubled expression on her face. 'Mademoiselle…'

'You shouldn't do that. Too many people have gotten hurt by underestimating him. Including me.'

'Are you afraid of your father?'

'No,' she answered quickly. 'My father protects me. It's only when we disagree that I… worry about the consequences.' She looked at him, her gaze so piercing he almost shivered.

This is dangerous, his mind warned. He wanted to ask, but she started smiling again.

'Either way, you shouldn't doubt the kindness of your general. After all, he is letting me stay in his home.'

'Very true,' Damien agreed, letting the conversation drift to a new topic.

'It's interesting to me how he never had children,' Sabine mentioned. 'I guess he views his soldiers as his sons.'

The comment was offhanded, but it still made Damien tense. There was again the implication he kept trying to ignore. Had it really become so obvious?

Sabine huffed. 'Oh, what is it now? It's the second time you've stiffened up when I've mentioned the man,' she fussed. 'What's wrong?'

'It's nothing.'

'Talk to me.' She slid closer to him, placing her hand on his shoulder. 'You bear my burdens. How shall we be friends if I do not bear yours?'

Damien clutched her wrist and put it back at her side. She struggled to pull away, but he pinned it there.

'You have luxuries you do not understand,' he said, his eyes boring into hers. 'Ones I cannot indulge in. Truths that contradict my vow of protection. I do not have free rein with you. I am not allowed to be comfortable with you. You warned me of such implication mere moments ago, remember?'

'This has nothing to do with my father, and I refuse to have him dictate every aspect of my life,' she said defiantly, pushing forward. 'Since when have you cared for such restrictions anyway?'

He said nothing, only letting go of her and turning away before she saw the answer in his eyes.

He never cared to be restricted. That didn't change the fact that he knew he should be, instead of holding necklaces, sharing stories and giving her leeway at every turn. The price would be high if he made a mistake with her. He would lose Roulet's trust, a thought that left a bitter taste in his mouth.

Before he could stop himself, he spoke. 'Roulet's changed.'

'How?' Sabine asked carefully.

'Your father cares for you,' Damien said suddenly. 'Yes... I am well aware of that fact,' she said, puzzled. 'How do you know?'

'Because I'm his first priority,' she told him. 'I may not always agree with his methods, but I'm not a pawn to him. I can trust him because I know he will not sell me, not like other power-hungry men. He raised me at his side. He's always chosen what is best for me.'

Damien stared at her intently, the confession heavy on his tongue until it finally escaped. 'I see Roulet as a brother-in-arms,' he explained. 'He was the one who took me off the streets, made me a soldier. I became the best and people always gave him credit for finding and training me, as though I did it for him. I didn't care; he's a good leader. I would fight for him the way I would fight for any one of my soldiers. But now...'

Sabine waited patiently for him to find the right words. 'I think he sees me the way your father sees you,' he admitted. 'I don't know what to do with that, how to feel about it.'

Sabine nodded slowly, contemplating his words. After a moment of silence, she placed a hand over his. 'You do nothing.'

'What?' Damien asked incredulously.

She giggled before facing him, unintentionally bringing herself closer to him than before. 'Roulet may see you as his son, but he's not insisting upon a title or credit or more respect. He's letting you be yourself. You can't stop people from caring for you or change how they do so. Just as you can't stop how you care for someone else,' she told him. 'So, don't worry about it.'

Damien raised his eyebrows. 'If you say so.'

'I do.' She stood. 'As the smarter one of us, you have to listen to me.'

'Your fencing strategy says otherwise.' She scowled and he laughed, light re-entering the conversation for a moment. He quickly sobered as he looked up at her. Strong, brave and daring as always. He felt a low hum under his skin, something that always lingered under his fondness for her.

'Will you take your advice on letting someone care for you in their own way without question?'

'Yes,' she said smugly, crossing her arms with a playful grin.

Heat built under his collar as he stared up at her. He looked around, seeing the area was clear of any visitors, anticipation making his heartbeat speed up. He was going to get into so much trouble. Still, he shrugged nonchalantly as he stood. 'Very well,' he agreed.

Without further hesitation, Damien cupped the back of Sabine's neck and pulled her into a kiss.

Sabine froze at the sudden touch. His lips were demanding on hers, but he noted the way she held onto his arm, tugging him closer. He let himself get lost in the touch of the lady that was finally in his arms, instead of across the room. How many times had he thought about this when remembering the way her face flushed after helping her with her necklace? How easy it was to always step closer over stepping back? Every brush of her lips fuelled his desire, wanting more. The way she parted her lips to sigh tempted him to go further – to cross another line – but she was already trembling.

Slowly, he pulled away. Sabine panted as she tried to catch her breath, subconsciously leaning forward for more. Damien's lips brushed over her heated cheeks, his words a whisper in her ear.

'I won't apologise,' he told her. 'I was taking your advice.'

He pulled away too soon and Sabine blinked at him, her eyes still wide in surprise. 'Ready to return?' he asked.

'Yes, I believe so,' she said, still a bit breathless. He motioned for her to lead the way.

With one last look over her shoulder, she started walking along the path to the exit. He didn't linger by her side, instead staying two steps behind. His face remained impassive, but his heart jumped every time she touched her lips or looked over her shoulder to make sure he was still there.

Chapter Seven

Paris

June 1895

Damien did his best not to seem more energised than usual when they returned to the house, forcing himself to relax as they were informed of a last-minute dinner party. He made sure to seem almost bored when Sabine came down hours later, dressed beautifully in a green gown and ivory jewellery. He made sure not to spare more than a cursory glance when men tried to whisper in her ear during dances and dinner. And he most definitely did not appear smug when she would inevitably dismiss them. He ignored how every inch between them felt like torture and how every look out the corner of her eye was a small victory.

He knew the penalty would be high should someone discover what had transpired in the gardens, but he felt a surge of pride at how dazed Sabine appeared after their kiss. Yet. He couldn't help but wonder if perhaps he had read her reaction wrong when, after they arrived at the house, she kept distance between them. She didn't dare to converse with him even when there was a perfect opening to do so. Perhaps the moment was supposed to be fleeting, buried over time.

Damien grimaced as he walked through the halls of Roulet's home, taking a small break from the party. He didn't want to cause her discomfort – and he should know better. Sabine was beautiful, but there were plenty of stories where a beautiful woman was the downfall of a man. He had a good life. Did he need to risk his position or comfort for one person?

'Damien.'

He stopped short of the doorway to the sunroom and peered inside, barely making out Sabine's silhouette as he stepped towards her cautiously. What was usually a prism of light over an intimate living room surrounded by tall, leafy plants was now mere shadows. Sabine herself was almost invisible to him even from a few feet away.

'Personally, I didn't take you for one that enjoyed the dark,' he commented as he approached the chaise she sat on.

'It's the best way to see the moon.' She pointed out the window.

He walked over to the glass, peering out. Sure enough, a crescent moon peeked just above the towering hedges that surrounded the backyard.

'I see,' he said, lingering on the twinkling night sky before he turned his attention back to her. 'What...' He lost his train of thought as the moonlight caught her eyes.

Her face looked soft and inviting, her mouth forming a natural pout, eyes clear and bright. Yet, there was a furrow in her brow. He reached out to smooth it without thinking. Sabine gasped sharply, the sound loud in the silent room. He pulled back instantly and cleared his throat. 'We should head back.'

'Right, um...' She swallowed nervously, looking at him. 'You...' Sabine's eyes flickered over his face and to his mouth before looking away.

Damien waited before stepping back, figuring he should leave first. 'Why did you do it?' she asked suddenly.

He paused, standing in the doorway. The light beckoned him to go. Leave the mystery behind and join the party. Find a girl that he could forget about. The old comfort was tempting. And yet...

He stepped back into the shadows until he was only a few feet from her. 'Come here, and I'll tell you,' he dared.

Sabine slid from the chaise, the swaying of her hips accentuated by her silk dress as she walked towards him. Her hair was twisted into an elaborate pleat instead of her brunette waves she had this afternoon, leaving her neck and shoulders bare. Closing the distance, she stopped mere inches away, lifting her chin defiantly. Damien wrapped his arm around her waist and pulled her closer. Her hands shook but she balled them into fists, never looking away from him.

Always the fighter, he thought before leaning down. Her eyes darted over his face quickly, her body tensed as he closed the meagre distance between them.

'Sabine,' he called gently.

Her eyes met his, bold. He almost chuckled but doubted she would take it well. Instead, he cupped her face, running his thumb over her cheekbone. She sighed, her body relaxing under his touch until her eyes closed. Only then did he lean forward.

Their lips met softly, and Damien stayed still until he felt Sabine stretch up to press her lips firmly against his. He kissed her slowly, coaxing her lips to part. She did so, sighing into his mouth as he took her bottom lip between his. She slid her hands up, wrapping her arms around his neck. Sabine moaned quietly, the sound still filling the room and Damien smiled against her lips. He gave in to one more lingering kiss before pulling away.

Sabine rested her cheek against his, her eyelashes tickling him as they fluttered open.

Damien memorised the look on her face, how she swayed towards him for more, before reluctantly letting her go. 'We should go back, princess.'

He turned before she could ask him for anything, like stay in the darkness with her, but he had already crossed enough lines for the night.

—

'Are you all right?'

Sabine looked up from where she was picking at her breakfast and to her father. General Roulet and his wife were visiting a friend, so it was just them in the dining room for once.

'I'm fine. Just a little tired from the party,' she told him, but he didn't look convinced. He leaned forward and took her hand.

'If any of the guests made you uncomfortable…'

She shook her head before he could finish the suggestion. 'No, not at all.'

She ate a couple of berries before her thoughts started to wander back to last night. Her lips still tingled whenever she thought of Damien, reliving the kiss all over again. It felt like torture waiting to train with him, much less looking at him. She popped a strawberry in her mouth before peering at her father from the corner of her eye.

This was an awful situation. Her father was looking for her husband and she was sneaking off to kiss soldiers! Well, not yet – *not at all*, she reprimanded herself. She couldn't do this. To think if someone caught her… a shiver went down her spine and she had to close her eyes for a moment as a face from long ago popped into her mind. She remembered running her fingers over the wide bridge of his nose, his broad smile as he told her to quit messing with him, not meaning a word he said.

She couldn't do this. '*Mon trésor.*'

Eyes snapping open, she looked at her concerned father. 'Do you feel ill?'

'No. I… I'm just contemplating the future. Everything seems to be changing so fast. I don't think I'm ready for what's coming.'

'My dear, no one is ever truly ready for change. As long as we find the strength not to cower before it, we will come out stronger.' He took her hand. 'And who knows. Maybe you will welcome these changes.'

'But what if it's not something I want?' She felt childish asking the moment the words left her lips.

'Wants pass. Needs do not. Do you know what you need?'

Sabine bit the inside of her cheek. Of course she did. She needed choices. She needed sunlight against her skin. She needed a chance to be herself. Every time she thought of the upcoming months, they were grey and filled with shadows, like Paris. Yet, when she thought of what made her happiest, her thoughts always wandered back to the garden…

Her lips tingled.

'Yes,' she answered.

'Good,' her father said. He kissed the back of her hand. 'Focus on that. Then, all the strength you need will come to you.'

'Yes, Father.' She smiled at him before continuing her breakfast.

Hours later, Sabine walked with Damien through the Luxembourg Gardens. She waited until they were by the fountain again, alone once more, before she took his hand. She pulled him behind a tree, away from the prying eyes of other visitors. Damien followed her willingly.

'Kiss me again,' she demanded.

Damien looked at her, his shock at her confidence melting into a knowing smile. 'Your wish is my command.'

Chapter Eight

Her father always said time was a valuable resource no one could afford to waste.

'There will always be people who rely on us to use it wisely. How they spend their time will always be a result of how we use ours,' he had once said, adulthood and responsibilities too far away for her to understand why her father was gone so much of the day.

When Sabine thought about it, time was the only thing she truly claimed for herself. As such, she decided to spend it the way she loved: reading, sword practice, kissing Damien in dark corners, shopping and learning the ins and outs of French high society from stations to rumours. She made the correct acquaintances, staying by Madame Roulet's side whenever she walked out the house. At every event she made sure to leave an impression of being amiable, if not a bit ignorant of the culture, despite it being drilled into her for the past few years. She was a lady, just smart enough to be appropriate, oblivious enough to be approachable. The days were a blur while the nights stretched out longer, especially when Damien would dare to sneak into her room.

Seasons passed, and it became harder for Sabine to look past these moments, dismissing any worries about future husbands that came to mind. Perhaps her father hadn't had as much luck as he anticipated. Maybe it wouldn't be a big deal to wait another year for a husband. Or perhaps he would lower his standards to something more... accessible.

She didn't linger on the last thought as she gasped into Damien's ear.

She had snuck the soldier into her room after feigning a headache to skip afternoon tea. Madame Roulet didn't seem to be put off by this, insisting Sabine go straight to her room. She reminded herself that she had to stay quiet as Damien bit her collarbone, and she slipped into a haze of lust under the afternoon light.

Sabine had come to realise that, when it came to satisfying curiosity, touch worked much differently than other longings. She had craved a lot of things in her life: the taste of alcohol, the shine of jewellery and even the thrill of a good fight. They were all satisfied so quickly.

Yet, the desire for touch lingered much longer, flaring up when she least expected it. Every time Damien's fingers trailed over her skin, she wanted more. She wanted his kisses to last longer, for each caress to be more intimate than the last, to have the same control over his body that he had over hers. She sought out the thrill of him towering over her while knowing he would never push past her boundaries. It was a heady and addictive feeling that she could never quite sate.

'Careful, princess,' Damien said when Sabine reached for his belt, grabbing her wrists. 'Your crown might fall off if you let a simple knight take your virtue.'

She scoffed as she sat up and cupped his face. 'It's my virtue to give,' she told him. 'And as far as I can see, I won't have a husband for some time. Why not fully enjoy my time with you?'

His eyes dimmed, and he moved her hands to her side. 'You may be surprised how quick the process will be.'

Sabine narrowed her eyes at him. 'Why do you say that?'

'I don't know how closely you've been listening to the rumours but there's a particularly interesting one.' Damien trailed his finger up her thigh, goosebumps rising where he touched her. 'Something about former aristocrats looking for a foothold in Africa.'

Any warmth left in Sabine disappeared as she processed what the words meant. 'What? My father would never marry me to someone like that. Surely, he would set his sights on someone of higher status. A count or duke, a son of a Bassam king— not a foreigner with no status.'

'We may no longer have statuses but we don't need them when land pays more.'

'I... No. No,' Sabine protested. 'He wouldn't do this without telling me! We've been to plenty of parties, but no one of consequence approached me.'

'Maybe he didn't want you to get worked up.' Damien smirked but there was no mirth in it. 'He, like everyone else who knows you well enough, knows you have a temper.'

'This isn't the time for your jokes,' Sabine snapped, getting out of bed.

'Where are you going?' Damien asked as Sabine, only wearing her undergarments, looked for her dress.

'I'm going to speak to my father,' she said, making her hair presentable.

Damien shook his head but got up to help tie her corset and slide on a short-sleeved afternoon dress. He had fixed his uniform just as someone knocked on the door; he moved quietly behind it.

'Come in,' Sabine said, an edge present in her voice. The door swung open, hiding Damien as Madame Roulet entered with a wide grin, practically vibrating in excitement.

'I do hope you're feeling better,' she said politely. 'Your father is here and would like to speak with you in the parlour. I told him you may still be under the weather, but he said it was urgent.'

Sabine forced a smile on her face. 'Oh, I am feeling much better. Tell him, I will be there shortly.'

Madame Roulet clapped her hands together excitedly before exiting, and Sabine's mouth dropped into a frown as she stomped to her vanity.

'You can't enter angry,' Damien said, not moving from his spot. 'You're not supposed to know.'

'My father always said to pay attention to the world around me,' Sabine grumbled as she added a jewelled bird hairpin to her brunette tresses, an heirloom from her mother. The reminder always softened her father, and she wanted every advantage she could get.

The walk from her room to the parlour seemed longer than usual and gave her nothing but time to digest what was going to happen. She tried to remain calm, but her body shook with rage. Her father had never decided anything without her. To think he may have made the biggest choice of her life without a word was infuriating. By the time she approached the door, she was ready to fight tooth and nail because she would be damned if she were expected to take this without question.

She stomped inside the room, making her father look up. He appeared calm as he stood from the table. There was coffee and puff pastries that the cook only made when Madame Roulet was in the mood to celebrate. As if he were about to deliver the news she had been waiting for all her life. She almost scoffed before remembering he would not accept the disrespect.

'*Mon trésor,*' he greeted, kissing her cheek.

'You're marrying me off,' she hissed in Fante as he pulled away. He sighed before gesturing for her to sit. She plopped in the seat across from him stiffly.

'I should have known the news would travel to you before I could tell you myself.' 'You decided without me.'

He shrugged. 'I didn't have an offer until this morning. There was nothing to decide.'

'Yes, there was,' she snapped. 'I have never met this man, much less looked him in the eyes to see his intentions. Yet, you have agreed to make me his wife!'

He looked at her as if she had lost her mind.

'Quiet as it is kept, he is nobility, Sabine,' he said. 'With the type of power they have, there is nothing to decide. Who would dismiss such an offer?'

The words stung more than she expected, mostly because she thought she would never hear them. Did her thoughts not matter at all?

'I am not doing it,' Sabine told him, shaking her head slowly. 'You will have to drag me down that aisle. You have no right to cast me away like this.' Foolishly, she thought she would spark his temper, but he just looked tired.

'Sabine, I have all the power in the world to make the marriage happen. Don't you understand? You are not a sacrifice. I'm guaranteeing power for our family that will never be questioned.'

'How?' she shouted, her voice thick with tears she didn't want to shed. 'I'm already in this strange country with even stranger people to secure a future for us. But for you to decide without any kind of warning is cruel! How could you…' She took a shuddering breath as she tried to ignore the pure devastation coursing through her, but her father's sunken eyes did nothing to stop it from drowning out her anger.

'You told me that I was the most precious thing in this world to you. I should have known better,' she said, standing quickly. She turned to leave, but her father grabbed her and pulled her into his chest. 'Let go of me!'

'Don't ask me to do that yet,' he said, his voice, too, thick with tears. 'Do you not see how this breaks my heart?'

Sabine stopped struggling and hid her tears in his chest, fingers twisting into his shirt. He let her cry for a few moments, before lifting her face and wiping the tears trailing down her cheeks.

'You were the only reason I had left to live after I lost your mother. Everything I do is to protect this family, to protect you. I cannot ignore your need to marry and when you spoke of changes at breakfast a few months ago, I saw it as a sign that you were ready.'

Sabine's heart broke further, and she turned away from him. If only he knew…

'I met with his father and he is exactly what you need. They are happy and have the power that guarantees you will be cared for, *mon trésor*. I didn't do this to punish you.'

'I thought… I'm not ready to lose myself to marriage or a child. I'm not ready to lose my home forever,' she whispered, the truth slipping out of her mouth unexpectedly. She knew that staying in France was the goal, but when faced with the reality, she couldn't picture a future in Paris. If she married someone of importance, every day she would be stifled and trapped in a gilded house for the sake of her father's business. Would she ever see her home again?

'You won't lose anything,' he reassured her, placing a calming hand on her shoulder. He turned around and kissed her forehead. 'You will never lose me. Just like you won't lose yourself. Marriage can enhance your life in ways you do not yet understand. You must remember that. Do you promise me you will do so?'

'I have no choice,' she answered, resigned.

Her father's eyes steeled, his shoulders straightening up. It was as if he was looking straight through her, reminding her to remember who *she* was.

'You always have a choice. It's up to you to choose the right one. The one best for you *and* our legacy. That is your role. I have never guided you wrong and, more than ever, I need you to trust me. Will you, Sabine?'

She bowed her head, unable to look at her father. So much of this moment felt wrong, but she couldn't dispute the logic nor push away the offer without a better explanation. For all she knew, this might be the best choice for her when it came to marriage.

But Damien… Sabine closed her eyes. No matter how she looked at the situation, she couldn't find it within herself to be the daughter he wanted. Not now, when he was unknowingly breaking her heart again.

'You ask me this when we both know there's only one correct answer,' she whispered, the anger in her voice reigniting. 'We both know what would happen if I were to make a different choice.'

Her father tensed. She glared at him, opening her mouth to yell, words that had been buried in her for years ready to fly. Suddenly, he clamped her mouth shut. She gasped under his hand, but he put a finger to his lips, nodding to the exit. Shuffling near the door could be heard, a shadow just visible beneath. He towered over her, his eyes warning her as he moved his hand back to his side.

'What is your choice, my daughter?' her father pressed, switching back to French.

Sabine looked, swallowing her resentment. 'I... accept,' she said reluctantly. He smiled and she could hear excited chatter behind the door.

'I knew you wouldn't let me down,' he whispered in Fante, wrapping his arms around her so tightly it was as if he never wanted to let go.

-

Damien watched from the garden as Sabine moved around her room in a daze while preparing for bed, constantly rubbing her eyes. He could guess the outcome of Sabine's conversation with her father, and a hollow feeling sat heavy in his chest. He was no fool; he had known that his relationship with Sabine would be a passing affair, but it didn't make it that much easier for him to accept. He wanted more time, more conversation. So much more than he could or *should* ask for.

Still, he tossed pebbles at her window to get her attention. There was one person more devastated than him right now and he had to be there for her.

Sabine froze when she saw him and wiped her face before opening the window. He climbed up quietly as she returned to her vanity, her eyes vacant. She brushed her hair, staring at her reflection as if she were searching for something, eyes red-rimmed. Whatever it was, she didn't seem to find it, the grip on her brush as tight as the one she usually had on her foil. He kissed the top of her head, his hand on her shoulder. She put her hand over his and intertwined their fingers.

'You're stronger than this. Whatever it is, you will overcome it with grace,' he murmured.

'I'm getting married.' Damien knew to expect the words but they were still a stab to the heart, like she was making a callous joke. The way she wiped her tears told him she was not. 'What's so graceful about being forced to be a stranger's property?'

'Sabine…' Damien was lost for words. What could one say when something so special was all over before it could start? He met her gaze in the mirror. There was still defeat but there was also a desperation he was familiar with, the feeling of needing to cling to the truth, however small. The same look was reflected in his eyes.

'If I asked you to stay with me tonight, what would you say?' she asked quietly. 'I would tell you no one would be able to take me from your side.'

She tightened her grip on his hand as she stood and brought his face to hers, kissing him as if it were the last time. 'Stay… please,' she murmured against his lips.

He answered by pulling her into an embrace.

Damien was taken by surprise by how eagerly Sabine kissed him. She didn't seem nervous, her fingers sure as she loosened his uniform, silently urging him to take it off. Yet, when he stepped back so he could properly remove his tunic, she turned away. Wearing only pants, he stepped behind her, rubbing her arms. She leaned back into the embrace, her pulse fluttering against her neck.

'There's no need to be afraid,' Damien whispered into her hair, kissing her ear before leaning down to kiss her neck. She shivered, grabbing his wrist, and pulling it across her waist.

'Says the soldier,' she replied, her voice slightly wavering. 'I'm sure you've had plenty in your bed.'

'You say that as if I were only ever supposed to bed you.'

Sabine turned, staring at him defiantly, a true force in the making. 'Of course, you were.'

He smirked. 'Quite the request from someone engaged.' She flinched, but he pushed through, not seeing a reason to deny it. 'Isn't that a bit selfish?'

She pulled him closer. 'Maybe I want to be selfish,' she whispered. She hesitated before placing her hand on his bare chest. He wondered if she could feel his heartbeat quickening from the way her eyes roamed over him with hunger. 'You make me want all the things I shouldn't.'

Not knowing what to say, he kissed her, substituting words for action.

Sabine followed his lead, their kisses fast and desperate. He reminded himself to slow down, not wanting to overwhelm her. He pulled back and her cinnamon eyes fluttered open in confusion. Smiling to reassure her, he reached for the fabric of her nightgown. He watched her swallow nervously as he tugged it higher inch by painful inch until he could gently pull it over her head. He took a moment to admire her laid bare before him. He had dreamed too many times of this moment, and his imagination didn't do her any justice. She was beautiful and glorious, even though her nerves were palpable.

Her eyes started to dart around the room, but he touched her chin, tilting it until she could only focus on him. She took a staggering breath when their eyes met. He took her hands and placed them around his neck, drawing her closer. He felt sparks skittering across his skin when they were chest to chest and he coaxed her closer to kiss him. She moaned quietly when his tongue touched her lips, persuading her mouth to open.

Her gasp tasted sweet as he moved them towards the bed. Sabine let him, seeming calmer as he laid her down, her curls spread across her pillows like a halo. Her lidded gaze urged him to continue, and he didn't dare turn away as he rid himself of his clothes. Usually, Sabine's widened eyes would stroke his ego, but he didn't feel the same sense of pride. Instead, something delicate replaced it. He traced her face, memorising the softness of her skin. The world shrank down to them and the candlelit room.

'I want to take you so badly,' he whispered. He leaned down to briefly press their lips together. 'Tell me I can.'

'You can,' she said even quieter. 'I need you to.'

He crashed their lips together, his desire raging as he kissed down to her breast, taking her nipple in his mouth. Sabine arched into the touch with a gasp. A quiet moan escaped her mouth a moment later as he lapped at the bud while running his fingers up her thigh, parting her legs.

He watched her closely as he stroked her core, noticing how tightly her eyes closed as her face pressed against her pillow. Her breaths were shallow as she ran her fingers through his hair. She grabbed the short strands tightly as he continued to tease her, his lips unrelenting on her skin and fingers eager inside her.

'D–Damien,' she said, the name caressing his skin as her hands gripped his shoulders and her legs shook at the sensation. She trembled, a blush high on her cheeks. He bit at her bottom lip, the only moment of roughness he allowed himself. 'I want— I—'

'Shhh…' he told her, not wanting to possibly be overheard. This moment was between them, and he wanted it to stay like that. He pulled his fingers out and spread her thighs farther apart. He heard her breaths turn shaky once again and looked up. She was staring at the ceiling, her fear returning. He couldn't have that. He brought her chin down until she was staring at him.

'Da–mhmm…' she trailed off as he caressed the sides of her body, making her relax. He kissed her neck as he nudged his

68

cock inside her. Sabine whimpered and he stroked her hair as he pushed further inside, sinking in inch by inch. He returned to her lips, letting her bite and scratch him all she needed. Soon the kisses turned soft, and her body relaxed. He didn't hesitate to pull back and thrust into her. Her eyes shot open, and she yelped against his lips before pulling away.

'Damien,' she moaned as he continued to plunge into her, moving her legs around his waist so he could go deeper. She practically shook out of her skin, her grip on the sheets so tight he wondered for a moment if they would rip. Surely, she was close to the wave of pleasure like him, he reached between their bodies to coax her to her peak.

Her head fell back, and he covered her mouth right as she let out a long moan mixed with his name. He snapped his hips faster and faster, moving his fingers desperately. He cussed under his breath as she became impossibly tight around him, coming with an arch and muffled scream. Her nails dug into his skin in a way that made his eyes roll back as he slowed down but didn't stop. He continued until he seized up, groaning into her neck as he spilled into her.

Stars twinkled innocently outside the window as silence fell over them like a comforting blanket. Damien kissed her neck and fell into bed beside her. They both took a moment to catch their breath, Sabine eventually shifting closer to him as her eyes started to close. He laughed softly before kissing the back of her hand, biting one of her fingers playfully.

'I'm doomed.'

He looked to see her eye was cracked open. 'How so?'

Sabine sat up and pushed him down onto his back. She straddled him, her sudden energy throwing him off balance. 'How am I supposed to give myself to another man now after knowing you this way?' she asked before kissing him.

Damien gave into the feeling, wanting to be as close to her as possible. He rolled them over, so they were resting on their sides, and Sabine tangled their legs together as she continued to kiss him. Damien chuckled against her lips as she trailed kisses over his chest, stirring his arousal again. He pulled her close and pinned her to his chest. She wriggled in his arms, but he kissed her again to calm her. She eventually settled down before biting his lip.

'I'm trying to be nice,' he warned her in between kisses.

'Who says I want you to be?' she teased.

He rolled her on her back and pinned her wrists. 'Those are very dangerous words, princess.'

The playful light immediately vanished from her eyes.

'Don't call me that,' she told him. 'When we're alone, I want you to call me by my name. I don't want to hear you call me by a title or nickname.'

Damien softened at the request. 'All right,' he agreed. 'From now on, I shall only ever call you Sabine. With reverence to rival a priest and his god.'

Sabine grinned as she shook her head. 'Ah, are you a devoted follower now?'

'My prayers shall adorn you like silk from China.' He leaned down to kiss her wrist.

Sabine giggled as he continued to kiss every inch of skin he could reach. His lips dragged across her cheekbones as he asked, 'Will you accept my devotion, Sabine?' Her breath hitched, and he pulled back, watching her pupils dilate.

'With every breath I take.' She sat up to run her fingers through his hair. 'I'll talk to my father.'

'I'm sure he won't object to you having a long engagement.'

'No,' she said.

A certainty entered her expression, and he was taken back to their first practice, showing the determination that drove him mad in the best way. It was a moment that had changed everything and now, here was the look again, ready to take more.

'I mean… I'll change his mind.'

'You… do you think that's possible?'

Sabine nodded. 'You're the beloved soldier of his closest ally with a steady income. That's not without its merit. Not to mention, you can protect me. There's no reason why I couldn't have you. And even if there were reasons...' She tightened her grip on his hair for a moment, her eyes darkening. 'He already made me leave my home. He cannot make me leave you.'

'Even if he tried, I would find you,' Damien told her. 'No one's going to take me away from you. Not even if you wish me to be gone. I vow to be yours.'

Her eyes lit up at the words, and their lips met once then twice before Sabine hugged him, his head resting on her chest. He let her soft breathing lull him to sleep. Before he drifted to sleep, he heard her whisper, 'And I yours.'

Chapter Nine

They say the best way to improve memory isn't to try remembering every detail. Instead, they say to recognise a unique detail creating a mental picture of the best moment and then store it in a familiar place — a memory palace.

Jones's friends thought it was a dumb term, but he had a soft spot for the whimsy of it. He appreciated the idea that a memory was a grand thing, something to be protected at all costs. After all, who was someone without their memories but a shadow of who they were supposed to be?

At this point in his life, Jones had many palaces. Some were humble, like his childhood home in Atlanta, filled with mental pictures of his friends and family. Others were as grand as a French chateau, pieced together through longing gazes and the scent of lilies and hyacinth. But what they all had in common was a soundtrack, a set of songs that held those moments together. When he couldn't find a fitting song, he wrote one. He didn't care if it was used for a project or tucked into a closet somewhere. The only thing that mattered was that he had it. That he had found a way to remember.

'Whatcha doing over there?' Jair asked. 'Writing a symphony?'

The melody that was playing, the second movement of a flute concerto, disappeared as Jones's eyes shot open, coming back to the present. He was in a burger joint with his friend, in the middle of jotting down a song idea when the waitress had passed by, her lilac perfume lingering behind her.

He swallowed, noticing his throat was dry as the memories of Sabine and Damien's first night faded. He grabbed the water in front of him and took a long drink.

'Haven't tried that in years,' Jones said, finishing the series of chords he was writing down before he got lost in his memories. 'And no. I'm trying to figure out a song but it's all over the place.'

'Lemme see.' Jair held his hand out and Jones passed over his notebook. A former drummer, Jair had great insight, which was probably why he was such a successful producer in New York. A few number one hit songs had made him big enough to have his own studio; Jones had become his go-to bassist over the years.

'It's a wreck but there's some good stuff in there.' Jair handed back the notebook. 'Bring it to the studio and we'll figure something out.'

'I'm down,' Jones said before biting into a burger. He closed his eyes, savouring the greasy taste. Good food was the easiest thing to remember.

'Who knows? Maybe this will finally make you give in to my offer.' Jones groaned but it wasn't over the food anymore.

'Man, you are like a dog with a bone. Let that shit go already.'

'Hell no. You are holding me back from making serious bank,' Jair exclaimed. 'My biggest hit is *still* "Tied All Up".'

'All I did was the bassline.'

'And that made it a hit and you know it. Honestly, if anyone's the asshole, it's you.' Jones chuckled at his friend's persistence as he reflected on the track he wrote two years ago.

They were practically shut in the studio for two days over that song, but it was worth it. Months later he would hear it on the radio non-stop. A couple weeks after that, Jair would call him to tell him the song went to number one. It would be months later before a residual cheque would arrive in the mail, making Jones go online to check the song's credits.

He was listed twice, as a bassist and as a producer.

'I told you I owe you one for that,' Jones said. 'And I paid you back.' 'But you won't join my team as a producer.'

'Nope.'

'Jones, for real, you were meant to do this! You got the ear for it,' Jair insisted.

He shrugged. 'I'm good on it.'

'Why? What's wrong with doing exactly what you're doing now but better?'

I've done it already. But he couldn't tell his friend about production skills from a past life, nor was it the main reason. Jones was sure he wouldn't mind being a producer. He would be good at it, but there was more to the job than just the fun stuff.

There was moving to New York and being in the studio for hours. Having to concentrate for days on end on multiple projects, something he already struggled with now as just a bassist. Thinking about handling someone else's music, their message to the world, with his crowded mind? There was no way he could make that commitment, not without ruining something along the way.

As the silence stretched between them, Jair's face fell, sensing the direction of his friend's thoughts. Jones grabbed some fries off his plate to buy time, ignoring the fact that they were cold.

'Because New York sucks,' he said with a smirk.

'You shut the fuck up. It's the best city in the world,' Jair declared, truly a Brooklyn native.

The tense atmosphere eased, and Jones was thankful that he would never have to have this conversation with the girl that was starting to creep into his brain.

His phone chirped in his pocket, and he looked. He raised a brow at the string of numbers, wondering if it was a scam message. He froze when he opened it.

Hi! This is Dani from Dr Allen's class. I got your number from him. I have a couple of composition questions and was hoping you can help me. Are you free anytime soon?

His first thought was, *I should say no.* It would be better for everyone if he made an excuse, said he was travelling over the weekend or moving. Instead, before the possibility could even settle in, he was typing back.

Hey Dani! Yeah, I have some time tomorrow afternoon. Where do you want to meet?

He pocketed his phone and tried to concentrate on Jair and not the massive decision he'd made.

Chapter Ten

Paris

March 1896

'I must express my gratitude to Madame Roulet. Her words have done your beauty an injustice.' Lamont Laurent kissed the back of her hand and smiled. 'Though, I will say your aura enhances it splendidly.'

These were the first words her betrothed had spoken to her. It made her ill.

Still, she smiled politely. The proper thing to do would be to blush or appear smitten but she didn't need to go that far out of her way to please him; she was already promised to him.

'Your words are kind.' Her face felt it was on the verge of breaking, her smile too wide to be natural. 'You reflect the beauty of your homeland as well. France is exquisite.'

Lamont lit up, and he looked around at the few people who had surely overheard the exchange, including his mother, Madame Genevieve Laurent. She had been watching Sabine carefully since she had arrived. Sabine tried not to seem bothered by the scrutiny, but it was starting to wear on her. It was becoming too much, but it was a party, and she was finally meeting her future husband. She had to stay.

'I'm glad you find it appealing,' Lamont said. 'Truthfully, I was concerned that the chill would be troublesome for you.'

'Then, you should know that my people are known for their resilience,' she told him, careful to keep any bitterness or insinuation from her words. Still, she noticed his mother narrow her eyes.

That's not good.

'Though, I could use some fresh air,' she added.

'Then, I shall provide it.' Lamont held out his arm. Sabine took it and let him lead her to a quiet path outside. She pretended to straighten her dress to cover how her eyes darted to Damien, who nodded once. She held back a breath of relief. The trio were quiet as they walked.

'I hope you've enjoyed your time in Paris so far.'

'How could I not?' she said, forcing her voice to stay neutral. 'The journey was more taxing than expected but Paris has a lot to offer.'

'How so?'

'I'm not used to such long journeys. I hadn't taken many until recently.' 'Travelling suits you.'

Sabine shrugged. 'I guess we'll find out over time.' 'Perhaps we should go to Nice for our honeymoon.' Genuinely curious, Sabine asked, 'And what's there?'

'Oh, you would enjoy it. They have beautiful beaches, a chance for you to relax all day. I wouldn't dare subject you to sports like tennis. I can be a bit competitive.' He laughed. 'Otherwise, doesn't that sound like the perfect holiday?'

It was practically bait, the way he put it. She wondered what type of woman he saw her as. Sabine could argue or tell him she liked being outdoors rather than being tended to all day, which wouldn't help her. She needed to get married. It would be better to concede now, keep the illusion until the fateful day.

So, she smiled politely. 'Of course.'

Lamont seemed satisfied with her response, and Sabine fought not to scowl at him. It wasn't ladylike.

'I have a feeling we will have a great marriage,' he said as they continued to walk.

Sabine chuckled at the irony but kept her response light-hearted. 'It will be quite the treat. However, I do not believe your mother is too fond of me.'

'Don't worry about that.' Lamont placed his hands on her arms, rubbing them. 'Only I have to be fond of you.' He leaned closer, and Sabine tensed before stepping back. She cleared her throat and turned away.

'We should return before people think we're being indecent,' she excused quickly. He sighed in frustration behind her, and she frowned. The nerve of him.

'I suppose you are right,' he agreed reluctantly.

She turned to him, and he was holding out his arm again. She didn't want to touch him, but took her place by his side, swallowing her discomfort.

Later that night, Sabine's new maids chattered around her as they prepared her for bed, but she tuned them out.

Had she been too harsh in her judgement of Lamont? He didn't know she studied history or knew how to fight, how gardens were her favourite place in the world because it reminded her of home. He had been eager to meet her, so she could understand his frustration at her lack of reception. Yet, she couldn't shake her dislike of him.

'Mademoiselle Kouassi.'

Sabine closed her eyes to clear her mind before turning to Damien. His face was the usual aloof mask of a guard, but she could spot the protective glint in his eyes.

'I have a message for you from your father, remember?'

'Yes, I do,' Sabine said quickly. 'Sandra, you are dismissed.'

'But the Laurents might find it inappropriate if they find out I left you two alone,' Sandra warned, suspicious eyes landing on the soldier, but one pointed look from Sabine made her avert her gaze. She ushered the other maids out even as she continued to glare at Damien on her way out.

Sabine shook her head when the door closed. 'I should send her back.'

'She only wants to look out for you,' Damien told her.

Sabine looked at him in surprise. 'And here I thought you were sworn enemies,' she commented. It was no secret to her that Sandra wasn't fond of how often they broke conventions of their stations, whether asking for moments of privacy like this or Damien sneaking Sabine treats during parties.

'Oh no, she despises me,' he said, and Sabine cracked the first genuine smile that night. 'But I know she would never betray you. She never says negative things about you.'

'That's… fascinating,' Sabine stated, voice flat. Damien rubbed her arms, and she looked up at him, yearning for his touch. She had craved it all night. He indulged her with a sweet, lingering kiss, savouring the tender moment. Too soon, he was already stopping.

'I can't stay much longer,' he whispered.

Sabine fisted her hand in the collar of his uniform but nodded. Laying her head on his chest, she indulged in the few moments they had left. 'I thank God that you're here.'

Damien kissed the top of her head. 'As do I.'

–

A week later, she was sitting in the drawing room with Lamont, his mother and the Roulets. The conversation was polite as they discussed upcoming events and light business. Sabine only chimed in with the occasional word or two, spending more energy trying to *look* interested. With her father gone, it was an easier act than she thought it would be. Without him, she could get away with being less than spectacular. From the pointed way Genevieve ignored Sabine, that seemed to be the preference no matter how much Madame Roulet tried to include her in the conversation.

Sabine took a delicate sip of her tea as Damien entered the room. She made sure her eyes didn't linger as he delivered a note to the general, murmuring a message in his ear. Luckily, she had another chance to look at him when the general stood up. Damien's lip quirked up the smallest bit when he met her gaze. She took another sip to hide her smile.

'I'm afraid I have other matters to attend to,' General Roulet announced. 'Madame Laurent, please send my regards to your husband. We must catch up one of these days.'

'Wait, dear, we have to discuss the wedding date,' Madame Roulet exclaimed before the general could leave. Sabine's eyes widened and her eyes immediately landed on Damien. His brows furrowed for a moment before he smoothed his expression.

'Ah yes,' General Roulet said. 'Well, Sabine has been in France for a year but such an affair would take time to prepare, especially with her father overseas.'

'So, perhaps, next summer would be a good time?' Madame Roulet suggested, looking at Sabine. 'I understand Côte d'Ivoire is much warmer than France, there's not much we can do about the temperature but surely, we can be more accommodating to you and your family then.'

Sabine opened her mouth to agree, more than comfortable with the year-long delay, when Genevieve spoke.

'Absolutely not. We'll have it in autumn.'

Sabine's jaw dropped and she was glad she wasn't the only one. Madame Roulet seemed just as taken aback.

'Madame Laurent, surely you can't be serious,' Madame Roulet said, her previously jovial tone sounding strained. 'We wouldn't want the wedding to seem rushed. We all know how easily a reputation can be ruined over an indecent rumour.'

'What would be so indecent?' Genevieve said. 'Kwame has been a friend of our family's for years. We may know the agreement is fairly recent but surely that doesn't need to be public information. Seven months is more than enough time for the arrangement to be deemed decent, is it not?'

'Still, it may not be wise to take the chance.'

'Well, unfortunately, we and Kwame have business that cannot be delayed. So, improper or not, this marriage must be taken care of sooner than later.'

'I'm inclined to agree with my mother,' Lamont said. 'Besides, the timing will be perfect. We'll be visiting Marseille this winter. It would be a great way to spend our first Christmas together.'

Genevieve peered at Sabine and set down her teacup. 'Don't be sad, my dear. October is a splendid time to get married.'

'I'm… merely shocked,' Sabien said. 'I didn't expect our union so soon, but it sounds wonderful. I shall lean on Madame Roulet for arrangements, yes?'

'Oh, yes! We shall have it here. It will delightful,' Madame Roulet exclaimed, her excitement leaving no room for argument. Genevieve pursed her lips but said nothing. Lamont looked relieved before smiling at Sabine. She smiled back, her face hurting from the strain.

'Fantastic. I'll let Kwame know.' The general tipped his head towards the room before he and Damien walked out, the soldier not looking back. Sabine blinked a couple of times, reminding herself to breathe as Genevieve and Madame Roulet discussed wedding details. She saw movement out the corner of her eye of Lamont, gesturing that they go outside. She forced herself to stand.

'We are going to get some fresh air,' Lamont announced to the madams, who barely looked up, not pausing their conversation. He held out his hand and Sabine took it delicately, following him outside.

She slipped her hand out of his once they were outside. They walked slowly around the perimeter, workers skipping away when the couple approached.

'It's a beautiful day,' Lamont said.

'Yes,' she replied, wondering if he felt as awkward as she did. It was hard to start a conversation with someone when she didn't have anything in common with them. For a man that was allegedly so good for her, it would have been nice to be notified exactly what traits her father admired about him.

'I know this may seem a bit overwhelming,' he said. 'I, myself, did not think that my mother would suggest such a date, but let's take the blessings as they come.'

'That's an optimistic outlook,' she said dully. Lamont looked at her with furrowed brows and she forced a smile on her face. 'You seem like quite a hopeful person while I feel so overwhelmed,' she amended. He smiled again; his ego successfully stroked.

'Well, perhaps this will replace your worries.' Lamont reached into his pocket and pulled out a small, leather box. He stopped walking and waited until she was facing him before opening it. Her jaw dropped at the sight. Inside was a large emerald ring surrounded by small pearls. It was one of the largest gemstones she had ever seen.

'I see you're speechless,' Lamont said smugly. 'Here.' He took it out of the box and slipped it on her left ring finger with ease. 'Ah! A perfect fit.'

'Indeed,' she said, unable to take her eyes off it.

'And now you have something to look forward to.' He gently took her hand and kissed the ring.

-

That night, Sabine held the ring, looking at it from different angles. Even hours later, it was still as overwhelming as it was when Lamont first slipped it on her finger. Madame Roulet's eyes had widened at the sight of it.

'What does this mean?' Sabine asked when the Laurents were finally gone.

'That we need to start building up your trousseau,' she said. 'Immediately.'

A ping on her window interrupted her musings and she looked out. Sure enough, Damien was outside in a simple black tunic and pants rather than his uniform. She extinguished the candle burning on her bedside table and opened the window. Damien climbed in quietly, joining her on her bed.

'I didn't think you would come tonight,' she said.

'I wouldn't miss the time,' he said. 'Especially…'

She sighed, fiddling with the ring. She held it out for Damien to see. 'Lamont gave me this after you left. It's my engagement ring.'

Damien held it in his palm, and she could see his eyebrows raise in the faint moonlight. 'It's…'

'Ostentatious,' she filled in, leaning back against the headboard.

'Not a fan of gems?'

'Oh, on the contrary,' she said. 'I love jewellery. Just not this. I'm more of a fan of rubies over emeralds.' She took the ring from his hand and placed it on the table with the candle. She beckoned him closer, and he moved so that his back was to her chest, her legs on either side of him. She ran her fingers over the spikey buzz of his shorn hair. 'I don't know how I'm going to do this.'

'I don't know either,' he said.

'With a summer date, I had a year,' she murmured. 'Maybe I could have tried to get my father to withdraw his consent, convince him to postpone until the Laurents got sick of waiting or convince him that me and Lamont are incompatible.'

'Do you really believe your father would relent?'

'…With time, I had a chance. But seven months isn't enough, especially if the reason is directly tied to my father's land agreements.'

'Then that's the reality,' Damien said grimly.

Sabine felt tears of guilt fill her eyes. He tried to smile but there was a lingering pain there. She buried her face in his shoulder, wrapping her arms tighter around him. She could feel his heartbeat under her palm. It was soothing and cruel under the light of their reality. Every moment they shared was theft. How could they continue after she was married?

Sabine tried to quiet the tears, but sobs escaped her lips. Damien just stroked her hand, whispering that it was okay.

She shook her head vehemently. 'I hate it,' she told him. 'I don't want to be anyone else's.'

83

He stiffened before pulling back. She opened her mouth to ask what was wrong, but he crashed his lips against hers. Her tears continued, but she was pliant as he laid her down. He kept his lips on her as his fingers travelled under her night gown. She shivered as heat flooded throughout her body, legs separating easily as pleasure bloomed under her skin from his attention. Her fingers slid over the fabric of Damien's clothes, her hand not catching onto any buttons like they would with his uniform.

'Take off your clothes,' she said, something she wouldn't have been brave enough to demand months before. He obliged and she did the same, their clothes rustling softly as they hit the ground. Her hands were all over him by the time he came back. She didn't need him to guide her as she settled in his lap, knees brushing his hips. She kissed him hungrily, not wasting any time as she guided him into her.

Damien groaned quietly at the tight heat while Sabine stilled to adjust to the size of him. Damien stroked her back as he leaned forward to lap at one of her collarbones. Sabine bit her lip to muffle her moan, legs trembling as they bracketed his hips, gripping his forearms as he rocked into her. She pulled at his hair, making him moan the way she liked before capturing his lips for herself, welcoming the familiar taste of him.

He tasted like home.

She gasped when he bucked his hips faster. She scratched down his shoulders, moaning his name.

'Faster,' she moaned in his ear. 'Please. For me.'

Damien quickly flipped them around, laying her down on the bed. She threw her head back at the sudden change and pulled him down. Their kisses were a flurry of tongues and panting, as if they had to devour the other right at that moment.

'I… I'm almost…' she tried to articulate but between his powerful thrusts and how he continued to touch her most vulnerable spots, her brain stopped short. Damien didn't reply but took her hand instead, intertwining their fingers as she came; he quickly followed her.

She sighed as she tried to catch her breath, loving the way Damien's body covered her own. She felt him kissing her shoulder and neck softly before finally moving to her lips. She felt boneless, giddy as her orgasm ran through her. She looked out the window and saw the moon was farther across the sky than before. The reality weighed her down as she sat up slowly.

'I want you to stay the night,' she murmured. 'But you have to leave soon.'

He followed her gaze before kissing her shoulder. 'But not right now,' he murmured against her skin.

She sighed tiredly, trying find the strength to be somewhat responsible. 'Damien...'

He leaned up and stole a kiss, melting away her worries as she cupped his face and enjoyed the heat between them. She had felt cold for so long...

'I'll leave before Sandra comes,' he reassured her. 'Don't worry, Sabine. Tonight, I'll stay by your side.'

Chapter Eleven

Paris

April 1896

There was a moment when Sabine first woke up; the sun had just started to rise on the horizon, making the sky blush. She would watch the sky change in a trance, savouring the quiet and the smell of Damien on the pillow that she would switch with her own the moment he left. In those moments, she could pretend she had woken up early and that Damien had only left their bed to make breakfast for them in their home.

Then, the sunlight would fill her room, and Sandra would knock on her door. It was her only warning before the madness would start.

A month had already passed, and, most days, Sabine could hardly believe she was engaged. The announcement had been sent to the paper and Madame Roulet made sure they visited every linen shop in the city after Sabine had shown her her 'meagre' trousseau. She had some dresses from when she arrived, a few jewels, including her ivory necklace and emerald ring, and some swathes of kita fabric, but not much else. According to her guardian, she needed much, much more.

'We need it to at least match your ring,' Madame Roulet told her. 'You need sheets, napkins, a new nightgown, and the lack of linens! Not to mention we still have to get the dressmaker to design your gown... I shall tell the general to ask your father for more ivory.'

When she and Madame Roulet weren't running around town, Lamont would visit her. Since the wedding date loomed so close, both Genevieve and Madame Roulet were keen on them spending as much time as possible to learn more about each other. He always showed up with an eager smile and bland conversation that did nothing for the restlessness under her skin since she no longer had time to fence or go for a walk through the gardens.

To try and combat that, perhaps inject some kind of novelty into their interactions, she suggested they spend the afternoon horseback riding outside the city. It didn't take long for her to realise that it was a mistake.

'Easy, slow down, Sabine,' he admonished. 'You'll scare the horse.'

It was his third reprimand and the second time he had reached over to grab her reins, as if she were moments from going out of control. She bit the inside of her cheek to stop herself from snatching away the reins.

'You don't need to worry. As I've said before, I've ridden horses for a while,' she said, straining to keep her voice calm.

'But these are Anglo-Arabians,' Lamont emphasised. 'I highly doubt you've ridden these before. Why, my father only has these due to a bet he made with a diplomat. Can you believe it?'

She didn't answer nor did she bother to tell him that she learned to horseback ride on Andalusians when her father made an under-the-table trade deal with a Spanish diplomat. She could only imagine how he would react to that.

'Now, if you look out west,' Lamont said next to her, 'you will see—'

'I don't care,' Sabine cut in and Lamont froze. She had never spoken harshly with him before. Truthfully, she had done her best to spare his feelings, but it was becoming more impossible with each passing day.

'Why would you not care?' he asked. 'You said you wanted to explore.'

Sabine rolled her eyes before dismounting her horse, stomping down the path that led back towards their carriage.

'Sabine, *mon coeur*,' Lamont called but she didn't stop.

A few moments later, his footsteps followed, and she wished she weren't wearing a dress, if only so she could outrun him.

'My darling, slow down.' He grabbed her arm, but she snatched it out of his grip before turning to him.

'Are you sure you feel all right? I should have known the heat is too much for you,' he chided.

'The weather is cooling, and I grew up in a place much warmer than this,' she said through gritted teeth. 'The thing that is upsetting me is *you*.'

'Excuse me?'

'You are irritating! You have been following me around like a hen. Not even my father was so overbearing!'

'I apologise.' Lamont's face reddened, already trying to reach out to her. She narrowed her eyes at him, silently warning him.

'I figured we could use the day for ourselves to get to know each other better,' he reasoned, still looking baffled at her reaction. 'I'm glad we've made each other's acquaintance. You're a charming girl but I want to try to get to know you better.'

Sabine looked at him with genuine confusion, stepping back when he attempted to embrace her.

'Who is this "charming girl" you speak of?' she asked. 'You have no inkling of who I am. How can you when you've never asked me a true question?'

'What do you mean? Of course, I know you,' Lamont refuted, his feet shifting with discomfort.

Sabine held back a scoff as she crossed her arms. 'What do you know about me?' she asked him.

'You are graceful and gentle.' She hummed at the vague description. 'You're quite the social butterfly.'

She couldn't help but throw her head back and laugh. 'Monsieur Laurent, my favourite activity is swordsmanship,' she corrected. 'Those acquaintances I've made are strictly to strengthen my father's relationships for his business endeavours, and there is nothing graceful about my feelings towards you.'

Lamont's jaw dropped and Sabine sighed tiredly.

'I'm surprised you are unaware of the nature of this arrangement,' she continued. 'You are a little boy looking for praise from a woman whom you were taught from birth would be in your shadow, clapping for you. No matter the expectations of me as your wife, I refuse to be her. Though I understand that life and duty will have its way, let it be known that I do not care to bond with you in the present nor in the future.'

A neigh interrupted them, and she saw the horses starting to trot away.

'We should head back,' she said. She lifted her dress so she could catch up with her horse, mounting it in one easy lift. She watched Lamont do the same before heading back, neither of them saying another word.

-

'He's so immature,' Sabine yelled, every word accompanied by a swing of her foil. Damien parried the wild swings easily, letting her get her anger out. It had been a coincidence that he happened to be at Roulet's house during the day, having to deliver a message to the general. He hadn't expected to see her, knowing she was going to be with Lamont the entire afternoon. However, the moment she stomped inside the house, she demanded a fencing lesson from him.

Practice would be a generous label on the session, with her mostly ranting between strikes. She didn't even take time to change from her riding outfit. He knew he should remind her that the staff could be listening but figured she would only erupt later at a more inopportune moment.

Still, he couldn't resist the correction, 'Watch your backfoot.' She made the adjustment before groaning.

'And to think my form is getting worse because of him,' she said. She turned away from Damien, her shoulders moving with deep breaths, but the tension never left them. He wanted to massage them until she relaxed but knew they were only metres away from the house. Her exclamations were already enough of a risk. Instead, he stood by her, staring at the garden wall with her.

'Worried or defeated?' he asked.

'What?'

'From my experience, most anger boils down to the two,' he said, looking out the corner of his eye. 'So... worried or defeated?'

Sabine's grip on her sword tightened.

'Both,' she confessed. 'Defeated that *he's* the one I'll have to be legally tied to. Everything I have will be owned by someone so condescending and oblivious. Worried because... how will I survive this marriage? Just the thought of him—' She shivered.

Damien didn't know what to say. It was hard enough over-hearing their discussions of the wedding date and knowing that every other afternoon was spent with another man. Yet, the jealousy took a back seat at her misery. He doubted that anything he did would be enough to help her endure a life that she hated.

Still, it didn't mean he couldn't try.

He stepped back and drew a circle around him. Sabine watched him with furrowed brows. 'What are you doing?'

'Land a hit,' he said. 'If you do, you'll get a prize.'

'I highly doubt that I can do that now. I haven't practised in weeks.'

'It doesn't matter. I know you. If you want it to happen, then it will,' he said. 'So, do it.'

Sabine stared at him for a moment, a shine coming to her eyes before she stepped closer to the circle. She took her stance, and, at his nod, she raised her foil.

Sabine wasn't wrong about being out of practice. Her balance was lacking, and her footwork was clumsy, and she slower than before. Still, she continued to try, circling him relentlessly. Sweat broke out across her forehead as she tried to land a hit, her frown deepening at every failed attempt. He was tempted to go easy, but he knew that wasn't what she needed. She needed a challenge. She needed to endure. So, she kept going, kept fighting.

He watched her form grow sloppy and opened his mouth to call time when she stumbled. He reached out to catch her, only for her to sidestep him and land a hit on his back. He turned in shock to see her smirking, her now inside the circle.

'A lovely trick,' he said.

She shrugged. 'I figured I would try something new.'

He shook his head but couldn't hide his smile. 'Very well. I'll have your prize tonight.'

She pouted for a moment before looking over her shoulder. She quickly looked away and cleared her throat.

'Evening, General,' she greeted. Damien peered over her shoulder before stepping aside, making sure he was a respectful distance from Sabine.

'Good evening, Sabine,' he greeted. 'I'm surprised you're still here, Captain. I was on my way to the caserns to speak with you.'

'I apologise, General. I ran into the captain when I returned from my excursion with Lamont. I remembered that we haven't had a lesson in so long. I insisted on him staying,' she said.

'That's quite all right,' General Roulet said. 'However, I must steal him away.'

'Of course.' Sabine took the practice sword from Damien. 'Thank you for your indulgence, Captain.'

'I hope I don't make terrible company,' he teased.

Sabine looked at him with a smirk, but her eyes were soft. 'You're the best company I could ask for,' she reassured him. 'Second to the general, of course.'

General Roulet chuckled before motioning for Damien to follow. Damien let his eyes linger on her for a few more seconds before tearing them away.

He made sure to give as much attention as possible to the general as he reported about disturbances around town and reports from overseas, but his mind couldn't help but linger on Sabine. Were it not for her teasing the general, her words would've been cause for concern. Yet, she said them anyway. She wanted to make sure he knew.

And for that, he knew he would endure anything with just one word from her. He would grant any request, even if it took him away from his bed in the middle of the night and risked his future. He would do anything for the look of glee on her face, like the one he saw under the moonlight when he presented her with a golden bangle engraved with flowers, small rubies dotting their centres.

The way she panted in his ear, writhing underneath him moments later, the world could burn for all he cared.

Chapter Twelve

Washington, D.C.

July 2013

As Dani got off at the Smithsonian train stop, she became very aware that what she was about to do could be a terrible idea. Having only talked to Jones twice, both times very briefly, she knew next to nothing about him. And yet, the moment he offered to go somewhere with her, she couldn't say yes quickly enough. She would never have guessed he would ask to meet her at the National Mall but tried to keep an open mind.

She spotted him in front of the lawn of the Smithsonian Institute, typing on his phone. She took a moment to look him over, trying to find anything familiar but there was nothing that reminded her of Damien or triggered thoughts of anyone else. Maybe it really was déjà vu.

Jones looked up from his phone and spotted her on the walkway. He waved his hand, and she returned the gesture as she walked over to him.

'Nice to see you again,' he said. 'You look better.'

'Turns out naps are miracles,' she bluffed. 'How are you?'

'Good,' he said, shifting awkwardly. 'Surprised, honestly. I didn't expect you to reach out, well, ever.'

'Me too, but… I've just been stuck on this piece for so long and Dr Allen told me a little more about you, so I figured you could help. Although, I don't see how a museum can do that.' Dani looked around warily. While she'd lived in D.C. for a few years, she had only been to the area twice and both times were when she first arrived.

'Well, I would usually suggest travelling for writer's block, but since you have classes, I figured this was the next best thing.'

'Do they have a music museum?'

'No, but it sounds like you don't need to go to a music museum,' he said. 'When's the last time you enjoyed art for the sake of it just being art?'

Dani thought through the last few months of her life. There was practice, film night with her friends, a couple of parties for birthdays, concerts for class, trips home for the holiday, more classes, more compositions… She winced as she realised that grad school had taken over her life much more than she originally thought. When was the last time she listened to music for fun and not just for noise in the background?

'Okay, you have a point,' she relented. 'So, where are we going?'

He held out his arms wide. 'Pick a direction.'

'Like some kind of choose your own adventure?'

'You do realise that's literally life, right? Choosing your own adventure and hoping it's a good one,' he said.

'Well, excuse me, Yoda,' she teased.

'I'm Obi-Wan at best.' They both laughed, and she looked around at the nearby buildings. She pointed to the one in front of them, feeling oddly nervous. 'Ah, throwing out the big guns. Okay, let's go.'

Jones led the way to the National Museum of Natural History, which thankfully wasn't filled to the brim with school kids like she imagined. Not that she had time to really linger on the thought of them as she immediately went wide-eyed. While she had seen *Night at the Museum*, it could hardly prepare her for the scale of the building. The towering, marble entrance and life-sized elephant made her stop and stare. There were also so many signs for displays, she didn't know where to go first.

'Right or left?'

'Huh?' She turned to Jones, forgetting he was next to her for a moment. He cracked a smile before pointing in either direction. She looked at the signs for fossils and mammals.

'Seems like we're supposed to go right first,' she said.

'Cool.' He started walking towards the stairs in the back. Dani stared at him in confusion before following.

'Umm, where are you going?'

'To the top,' he said as he started up the stairs.

'Why?'

'To keep you on your toes. Come on!' She took one look round the first floor before following him. He was far enough ahead that she barely caught him turn the corner into the geology exhibit. She walked a little faster to follow. She stopped short when she entered, trying to spot Jones among the crowd futilely. She moved carefully, barely glancing at the stones on display. She wanted to stop and look at the moon rocks but continued, her desire to catch up to Jones stronger.

It wasn't until she reached the gems and minerals gallery that she slowed down. She looked around the hall before giving up and reaching into her purse to get her phone. *If he ditched me, I swear...* The thought stopped short as she spotted a ring in one of the displays.

Among the diamond necklaces and rings her eyes landed on a very familiar piece of jewellery. Her throat tightened as the emerald ring Lamont had gifted her in her dreams glittered under the museum glass display. It was just as she had remembered and, for a moment, she could almost feel its weight on her finger. She looked at the plaque under it.

> *Originally a possession of an influential French family, this emerald ring was a wedding gift from Lamont Laurent to his Akan wife, a key connection in the colonisation of the Côte d'Ivoire and the expansion of France's territory in the late 1800s.*

Dani dropped her phone at the sight and pressed her hand to the glass. This was impossible. The ring shouldn't be real. It was a dream. Yes, they'd been getting more vivid lately, but they were illusions. They had to be. But Dani had never been to the museum before, had never seen the ring or one like it in person. Which meant...

'I didn't take you as a jewellery fan.'

Dani flinched and spun around to see Jones waiting for her. The smirk on his face dropped when he saw her expression. 'What's wrong?'

'I... the ring.' She pointed to the glass. Jones stepped closer to the display, and she swore that she saw his eyes widen too but he stepped back and said, 'Wow. That's... really something. I don't think I've seen a ring that big in person.'

His laugh afterwards sounded forced, but she was sure she was just projecting. She had to be. She closed her eyes as she felt her heartbeat quicken.

'Danielle, are you okay?' She felt his hand on her shoulder and it centred her enough to slow her mind down. *This is for fun*, she reminded herself. *You're fine. You're fine.* She opened her eyes again, picking up her phone, trying to keep her nerves at bay as she turned away from the display. 'Are you getting another headache?'

'No, no,' she said. 'I was just... lightheaded for a sec. I probably didn't drink enough water today.'

'Then let's get you some water.'

'I'm fine,' she said quickly. 'We're supposed to be on an adventure so let's go.'

'Dani, if you're sick—'

'I'm okay,' she insisted, looking him in the eye. His gaze was wary and she grabbed his hand, putting it to her forehead. 'See? No fever or anything.' Jones stared at her, scrutinising her before seeming to let whatever worries he had go.

'Okay,' he relented.

'But no more hide and seek,' she said.

'We'll take it easy,' he said. He looked down at where she was still holding his hand. She blushed, not realising she was holding onto him. She was about to pull away when he squeezed her hand.

'Let's go.' He tugged her along and she fell in step beside him. Next to him, she caught a whiff of his cologne. It smelled like night and orchids. She couldn't help but lean closer to him, putting her arm through his, her thoughts beginning to drift to Paris. *No*, she thought as he led her to the Ocean Hall. *Stay right here.*

After walking around the Natural History Museum, Dani had calmed down long enough to actually start paying attention to the displays. Jones had let her 'ooh' and 'ah' to her heart's content before they went to the National Museum of African Art and the Hirshhorn Museum. Jones asked her if she heard any music from the pieces she lingered on. Remembering that she was supposed to be experiencing an art block for her composition, she went along with his attempt to get her to make music on the spot. Sometimes, she would have an answer, explaining what the art piece sounded like to her, sometimes she didn't and shot the question back at him.

As far as a creative challenge, she didn't mind it. After hours though, she was tired and ready to head home.

'I don't think you could work as a guru,' Dani declared as they exited their third museum. 'I feel no closer to my composition being completed than when we first started.'

Jones chuckled as he led her to a bench. 'You gotta admit it was a good attempt.'

'Debatable.' She plopped down, grateful to be off her feet.

'Stubborn,' he shot back. She stuck out her tongue in lieu of an answer, getting another laugh out of him. She liked the sound of it.

'Thanks for today,' she said. 'It may not have worked but I had a good time.' She almost added *with you* but figured that was too much. It was their first time hanging out and despite holding hands for a bit, she didn't want to get too familiar too quickly. He was still a stranger, no matter how comfortable she felt at the moment.

'I hope I don't make terrible company,' he teased.

Dani smirked, but her eyes were soft. 'You're the best company I could ask for,' she reassured him. He held out his hand. She didn't hesitate to place her hand in his and let him pull her to her feet.

'Don't be afraid to reach out,' he told her.

'For guidance?'

He shrugged. 'Or company.' She smiled, looking down at her feet as she felt a flutter in her stomach. Sweet and cute? She was doomed.

'See you around.' She turned her heel and started to walk towards the train station, feeling like she was practically skipping as she recalled the feel of his hand in hers. Suddenly, she stopped, the giddiness seeping out of her as she remembered his words.

I hope I don't make terrible company.

Her eyes widened and she retraced her steps. Jones looked at her curiously.

'Did you forget somet—'

'You know,' she said. It was a painfully vague accusation – she barely knew what exactly she was accusing him of – but the way his face dropped was enough of an answer. It rocked something in her, and she felt unsteady on her feet, but she bore her eyes into him, not daring to look away. 'You *know.*'

'…Yeah,' he admitted. 'I know.'

–

'How is this happening?'

Jones almost chuckled at Danielle's question. He had been searching for that answer almost his entire life.

'I wish I could tell you,' he said. 'I was just like you, thinking it was dreams or some movie that I forgot about. One day, the memories got triggered and after a while, I could remember everything perfectly. I don't know why.'

They sat in a nearby cafe she had suggested. The coffee shop bustled around them, filling the awkward silence. Jones saw the way Danielle clutched her paper coffee cup like a lifeline and sympathised with her. He understood her confusion, the overwhelming questions of if this was real and, if it was, why.

'Okay, but… are you sure they're the same people? We could both just be crazy.'

'That's one explanation,' he said. 'I'm sure dreaming of a love affair between a Black French soldier and a rich mixed Ivorian girl is a new sign of anxiety.'

Danielle scowled at him and took a sip of her coffee. 'Okay. So, clearly we share that memory. But I have others like—'

'Sarah, David, Selene, Demir, Shayla, Donovan, Sienna and Devlin,' he rattled off. 'I remember them, too.' Danielle's jaw dropped before quickly closing, and she turned her attention to the mug of coffee warming her hands.

'Okay. I— okay…' Danielle tapped her hands on the table before leaning forward. 'Let's say that it's real. All the memories are real. That ring—' He felt a chill run down his spine as he remembered the emerald ring in the display. Had he known it was there, he would never have led her into that building. 'I mean, I remember them but it's like now things are coming into focus.'

'That's how it started for me, too,' he revealed, leaning towards her. 'It'll take some time but eventually everything will come back.'

'Everything?' She looked at him in panic and he couldn't help but place his hands over hers, trying his best to comfort her. She let the touch linger but slipped her hands away as she worried her bottom lip. He sighed, sitting back.

'Danielle—'

'Dani,' she corrected quickly.

'Dani,' he repeated. 'I know you want me to tell you the ins and outs, but this is new to me too. I wasn't even sure if everything was real until that day I saw you.'

'And what about me was so familiar?'

Jones's mind went back to the lecture a couple weeks ago. He had been instantly attracted to her, wanted to talk to her about music before she bolted out the door. He was surprised to see her the next day. He was happy to see she was better and even wondered if he should try visiting Dr Allen's class again. It was all attraction until…

'You said you knew me. Something about how you said it… it just made sense.' Her expression fell, and she looked at the table.

Jones frowned, feeling helpless. He wished he knew the right thing to say to her. There was a feeling of familiarity but also hesitation. It was like meeting a friend after years apart – which, in a way, was true. There was uncertainty, wondering which parts of them were the same, which had changed.

'Jones,' she said. 'Or…'

'Stephen,' he filled in. 'But Jones is fine.'

'Jones, we can't do this,' she said. 'You know why we can't do this.'

'Dani—'

'It doesn't end well,' she interrupted. 'I may not remember everything, but I do remember that. And I may not remember all the details, but I know, whatever it is, I don't want a repeat. I'm sorry.'

She stood up quickly and practically ran out the cafe. Jones put his elbows on the table and leaned into his hands. Her reaction was reasonable, and she was right; they couldn't be together. Several lifetimes had proven that.

It didn't hurt any less to watch her walk away. And he knew there was no way to tell her he was dying already.

Chapter Thirteen

Paris

May 1896

Damien watched the recruit shift nervously, his eyes constantly roaming, giving away where he planned to strike, but the captain didn't move. He stayed still, large and intimidating, while the recruit decided on his next move. He shifted to the left.

Easy, Damien thought right as the man lunged. He sidestepped the move, knocking him off balance and sending him tumbling. Damien chuckled as he stepped over him.

'Again,' he commanded. The recruit, Leo, got up with a huff. This time he didn't take as long to decide his next move, but the result was the same. Meanwhile, Damien assessed his skills. Leo had only been training with the Republican Guard for a few days since transferring from the cavalry. He was a good soldier but had room for improvement with his hand-to-hand combat. His stance was too open and he still looked terrified. Yet, there was a doggedness in him every now and then that reassured Damien. Even though the moves were sloppy, they were decisive. *I can work with that.*

So, he told the recruit to try again and again for hours. Every time Leo got up, his legs got shakier. Damien waited patiently, letting the recruit attack first but still outmanoeuvring him easily. Leo groaned and Damien crouched down to pat his shoulder.

'Not the worst,' he commented before stepping over him while the crowd of soldiers around them whooped excitedly. They pulled Leo up from the cobblestone streets in front of their favourite tavern.

Usually, they would go a few times a week but with him splitting his time between the estate and the caserns, it had been much longer since he had spent time like this with the other soldiers. Even with the underlying desire to see Sabine as soon as possible, he loved being back home.

One soldier handed Damien a cup of cider and he sat at a table where Roulet watched the rowdy group with the tiniest of smiles.

'That was quite tame for you,' he commented. 'Usually, you rush in there like a Spanish bull.'

'What can I say?' Damien shrugged. 'I've adjusted.'

Roulet hummed as Damien downed his drink. 'Not sure if I should be happy that my prized captain is losing his fire.'

'Ha!' Damien shook his head at the general. 'Never that. I've merely found better outlets.'

'Ah, yes.' Roulet's gaze focused on him. 'You have been coming back less and less.'

'I've found a room close to you,' Damien reasoned. 'Sabine prefers I be close with the whispers of unrest, especially given the country's past.'

'The nobility has long been done away with.'

Damien held back a scoff. He may be a loyal soldier, but he was no fool. The titles may be gone, but the land and money stayed exactly where they were, in the tight grip of the aristocracy. The up-and-coming bourgeoisie only disguised that to a certain degree.

'Yet, there's still turmoil,' he pointed out politely. 'Madame Sabine is still fairly new to the country. The lack of her father's presence still makes her uneasy.'

'And you find kinship with her?' Roulet's gaze was sharp, but Damien looked straight ahead.

'There's a way of life we understand. She was raised by a fighter, as was I. Both deemed outsiders. We're warier than most.'

Roulet sighed. 'Yes, unfortunately. While I respect my friend, I truly wish he hadn't involved her so heavily in his business. She's still struggling to accept the engagement. My guess is that she will have trouble settling in as a wife.' Roulet leaned towards him. 'I hope you are doing nothing to interfere with that transition.'

Damien's throat went dry at the knowing look. Sometimes, he truly hated that Roulet was so insightful.

'I've told you I would not.'

'She's a beautiful girl.'

Damien bristled at the comment, his hands tightening into fists. 'Many are,' he said, an edge entering his voice. Inches apart, Damien wondered who would reach for a weapon first.

'Do *not* touch her,' Roulet warned. 'And stay at the casern tonight. That's an order.'

'Yes, sir,' Damien forced out, knowing better than to delay his answer.

The two glare at each other, neither backing down. Roulet dismissed him with a wave. Damien didn't say anything else as he stood up, soldiers scrambling out of his way. Stepping outside the tavern, he punched the wall, the pain in his chest overshadowing the one in his hand.

He was growing tired of the rules that only allowed him to have part of what he wanted.

It had been that way his whole life, from Roulet forging him to be a soldier as a child to being Sabine's secret lover. Roulet had to hide how he viewed Damien as a son. Sabine had to lie to her family to be able to show him love. It seemed the only way people could show they cared for him was by giving him only half of what he needed.

He slumped against the wall, closing his eyes.

He hated picturing only impossible things but couldn't resist the fantasy. It used to be living with Roulet as his son or being a war hero. Now, it was living on a farm far away with Sabine. They would be safe and alone. She would ride horses all day while he worked the land. Their children would run free. In the evenings, they would sit together and look at the stars, wanting nothing else in the world.

He opened his eyes, and they landed on grey stone, his heart sinking.

Perhaps Roulet was right. He needed to quit now, save both him and Sabine while he could. That was the smartest strategy, the only real one left. He looked down at his side, where his sword rested against this hip. It was a standard issued weapon; one he had quickly replaced when he became captain with a blade he had personally commissioned. That sword was his most prized possession; he had traded it for Sabine's bracelet without a second thought.

I love her.

And that bested logic every time. They may have never exchanged the words aloud, but he knew it was the truth. It was the only reason either of them would risk so much. Without a doubt, being in love with Sabine was the most reckless thing he had ever done but it was also the only thing that kept him going. And Damien was not one to give up.

Hours later, he entered Sabine's room again, burying his nose in her hair as she pulled him into her. He could deal with Roulet's disappointment later. For now, he focused on the one thing that made surviving each day easier.

–

'It's quite amazing when you think about it,' Pauline, the blonde, blue-eyed daughter of one lawmaker or another, said to Sabine.

She wished she could keep up with all the names, but despite how much time she spent going over them with Madame Roulet, she was still unfamiliar with the Laurent family's friends. She hated to admit how overwhelmed swirling crowds of people made her. She wanted to stop hosting and just sit down. Unfortunately, Pauline was insistent on conversing with her.

'I mean, you got the crown jewel of suitors, don't you think?' she asked, a jealous glint in her eye.

Sabine smiled. 'We suit each other well,' she answered civilly. Sabine started to step around her, but Pauline followed suit, blocking her.

'Yes, but you were unaware of him before your arrival in Paris, were you not?' she continued. Sabine hid her hands behind her back, resisting the urge to force the woman out of her way. She had to maintain relations because… she couldn't remember anymore. Why was she here?

'How did you know out of all the suitors in the world that he was so "suitable"? Or was it all that land that pulled you two together?'

'My, my, Pauline, you're quite concerned about my upcoming marriage,' Sabine warned with a smile.

Her eyes widened in faux innocence. 'Forgive me, I only meant to dispel a few rumours. People say you have long been acquainted, but none have ever seen you two together.'

'There's no need for theatrics,' someone said behind her. Sabine looked over her shoulder to see Lamont with a goblet of water, handing it to her, standing close but not enough to touch her. 'Sabine is modest, and I respect such grace in a woman.' Turning to Sabine, Lamont held out his hand. 'I believe we should make our way over to my father. Shall we?'

Usually, Sabine would hesitate, but tonight she took it without a second thought. He walked her in the direction of his parents but changed their course right before they reached the circle of people, instead, leading her to a path just outside. She hadn't noticed how warm it was inside the house until she took a deep breath of the cool night air.

'I hope you are not offended by my rescue,' Lamont said stiffly, letting go of her hand as soon as they were out of sight.

Sabine rubbed her fingers together as she checked behind them. Not Damien nor any of the other guards had followed them out.

They were alone for the first time since their disastrous ride.

'It's quite all right,' she said. 'I'm actually grateful.'

'I trusted you would appreciate the gesture. I remembered your fatigue when you first arrived,' he recounted, a small smile curling on his lips.

'Yes… I thought it was my lack of practice with such festivities.' Sabine cleared her throat nervously. 'Perhaps it is my personality. Maybe I should be grateful I didn't grow up with the expectation of attending these kinds of events. I shouldn't have taken that frustration out on you. I apologise.'

'There's no need, I understand,' he said.

'Pauline mentioned that you are the "crown jewel of suitors". I must admit I don't quite know what she means. I know your family used to be part of the aristocracy.'

'Ah, yes, before the commoners decided we were all better off dead. They were never fond of the lucky ones,' he joked dryly.

Sabine forced a small laugh. 'And how are you lucky?'

'I'm surprised you don't know,' he said. 'My father owns half of the coffee and cocoa plantations in your country – well, the ones owned by the French, thanks to your father. We're working on expanding soon.'

'Oh,' Sabine said, her eyes wide.

'You truly didn't know?'

'My father has been usually busy lately. He probably assumed you would inform me of your family's endeavours,' Sabine forced out as she tried to process Lamont's words. She knew her father was selling Côte d'Ivoire land to foreigners, but she didn't know it was for French plantations, which meant he was in deeper with the government than she thought. 'H–Have you and your father visited often?'

'Occasionally, but personally I quite enjoy civilisation. Not to say your home isn't beautiful but I can't quite see myself spending much time there,' Lamont said. 'Considering how adamant your father was about you being here, I assume you two are of the same mind.'

Sabine bit the inside of her cheek to hide her shock as she realised exactly why her father was enamoured with the idea of her marrying Lamont. 'Yes,' she lied. 'We're quite alike.'

'Even if not, I doubt your father would give any less than the best in the world,' Lamont commented. 'He cares for you deeply.'

'Yes,' she said awkwardly before starting down the path towards the stables. Lamont followed her. She tucked a stray strand of hair behind her ear.

'You're wearing my ring.'

Sabine looked down at her hand to see the emerald ring sitting comfortably on her finger. 'Today is a special occasion,' she told him, not meeting his gaze. She had forgotten she was wearing it, instead constantly aware of her ruby bracelet pressing into her skin under the sleeve of her dress.

'Right,' he said. 'You play the fiancée with great skill.' The dejection in Lamont's voice caused Sabine to look at him. He kept his eyes straight ahead, but she could see the disappointment.

For the first time it dawned on her that Lamont might have been excited about marrying her, that he may have viewed it as more than a power grab or gaining a bed mate. Maybe, he wanted a genuine relationship with her. Yet, considering his family's business, she couldn't imagine why. Sabine looked down at the path, an uncomfortable lump forming in her throat. 'It is my duty,' she responded.

'I know.' He touched her arm softly, signalling her to stop. 'I feel I must apologise for my presumptions. I admit I assumed you would be happy to marry me. I didn't think about what you may have lost in the process. That was cruel of me.'

'As my fiancé, you have that right.'

Lamont laughed sadly. 'And look what it has gotten me,' he replied. He reached out and took her hand. She stiffened as he brought it closer to his lips. She felt his sigh caress her skin as he let go. 'I'm starting to care for you, Sabine, even if you don't feel the same.'

Sabine shifted on her feet, unconsciously stepping away from him. The shadows shifted, and from the corner of her eyes, she could make out Damien blending into the wall of the estate. She looked down at her feet to avoid staring.

'I'll tell the guests you are tired,' Lamont said. 'Perhaps I should fetch Sandra.'

'I can make my own way,' she said gently. 'Good night, Lamont.'

'Good night, Sabine.' He reached out to her again but seemed to think better of it, walking back to the party.

She waited for him to move out of sight before retiring for the night. When she entered her bedroom, a pair of arms wrapped around her. She gasped before digging her elbow into the person's stomach. She heard an 'oomph' but the arms tightened, and she heard a familiar chuckle.

'Your self-defence could use some work, but not bad,' Damien said, kissing behind her ear. She scoffed before turning around in his arms.

'Don't scare me like that,' she admonished. 'I thought you were downstairs.'

'I saw you and Lamont parting in the garden,' he told her. 'Are you okay?'

Sabine tried to smile, but it didn't feel quite right.

'Perhaps we should begin sword fighting again,' she said instead. 'My endurance is dreadful now.'

'If you need to rest—'

'No.' She turned and looped her arms around his neck. 'Stay with me.'

Damien smiled before taking her hand, sliding her ring from her finger. 'Don't worry about this,' he said. 'I'll take care of you.'

They kissed, and for a moment, she could relax and just give in. She let herself be taken apart, pleasure racing against her skin.

She lost herself in every kiss and embrace, letting Damien enjoy every part of her and doing the same in return.

After he left for the night, she could no longer ignore the feeling that settled in the pit of her stomach. She stared at the windowsill, where Damien had put her ring. Studying the gem, she bit her lip as she realised what her marriage entailed.

She was trapped.

Chapter Fourteen

Paris

June 1896

The next few weeks, Sabine got better at pretending – or 'playing the fiancée', as Lamont called it. It became easier to smile and joke in public, to sit next to him and gaze at him fondly when he spoke. She could see the approval in Genevieve's eyes and the jealousy in everyone else's.

Sabine didn't mind the task as of late, mostly because it kept her distracted from the truth: her growing conflict of her feelings regarding her father, even as it pushed the reality of her wedding to the centre of her attention. While Lamont was presumptuous with a tendency to underestimate her, he was undeniably amiable and he enjoyed being in her company. Very rarely did he meet someone that tried to defy him or even could. His brothers were much older, and he had traditional parents. She was his only confidant in his immediate vicinity. Knowing this, it was easy to understand him.

And yet she couldn't ignore the very present reality that, in any other context, she would be his direct property versus only his presumed property disguised as his partner. It may not have been so terrible if she didn't know what it was like to be treated like an equal.

The more time she spent with Lamont, the more she wished she was with Damien. He was the only person that made her feel safe and reminded her of herself. When it was all too much, when she got tired of smiling and pretending that she wasn't intelligent, he was there. She liked how he teased her, how he refused to back down when challenged. He didn't shrink; he didn't waver.

She didn't know how to feel about losing him because the world told her she had to.

'You must have quite an active mind.'

'Excuse me?' Sabine asked as she came back to the present. She and Lamont were watching the horse races, which was much more relaxing than trying to ride together.

'Your eyes are always so focused, but it feels like you're never quite here,' he commented, looking away from the track to her. His eyes softened as they landed on her. 'They're beautiful, by the way. As are you.'

'You must be tired,' Sabine teased. 'You're usually more creative with your compliments.'

'You seem to respond best to truth, so I decided to oblige you as much as possible.' Lamont yawned and she chuckled, taking his hand. Even as she did it, it felt like she was stepping outside her body, watching another woman talk with fondness. She was scaring herself with how easy it was to fall into the act.

'No more late nights for you,' she told him.

'I promise. At least until the wedding,' he smirked. She shook her head with a good-natured smile, hoping it hid her discomfort as she slid her hand away.

The announcer informed the crowd the race was about to start, and Sabine looked back at the track. She watched the horses run around in circles. She cheered when she spotted the horse she had bet on earlier making its way to the front. A few minutes later, it managed to make it to second place. She clapped delicately, turning to remind Lamont that they needed to collect their winnings before they left. He was staring at her curiously, his eyes roaming her face lazily.

'Did you have another suitor at home that you hoped to marry?' he asked suddenly as the crowd settled.

The sudden question caught Sabine off guard, and she couldn't stop the image of her first love from popping into her mind, sitting beneath an iroko tree, smiling under the light of a setting sun as the rays warmed his dark brown skin. If she closed her eyes, she could almost feel him tracing *je t'aime* clumsily against the back of her hand. She cleared her throat before looking away.

'And if I did?' she asked defensively. 'Would I be less desirable to you?'

'Of course not,' Lamont said, and she could hear the frown in his voice. 'I'm just… trying to understand your reluctance. I've never met a woman so angry to marry into a rich family.'

'Because being an upstanding citizen is so wonderful,' she said sarcastically, and Lamont laughed unexpectedly. Sabine had never heard him sound so carefree. 'Yes,' she told him reluctantly after his laughter had died down. 'I did have someone I loved dearly. We were best friends for years.'

'You must miss him.'

She looked down, fiddling with the coin purse in her lap. 'I try not to,' she whispered.

'Do you feel you betrayed him?'

'Sometimes.' she said. *More than once*. The ghost of Damien's lips travelling up her shoulder… she squeezed her eyes shut.

'The more comfortable I get, the harder it is to remember that it wasn't supposed to be this way,' she revealed. She didn't quite understand why she was being so honest other than it was the first time someone had asked. The memory was so big, it was difficultto stuff back in the deep corner of her heart that she buried it in.

'I wish I knew how you felt. Truly. At least I would better understand you.'

Sabine's throat went dry. Hadn't she said those same words to Damien, confused how her father could be so consumed by her mother? And now, here she was on the other side, wondering how he managed to live without her. Loving someone you could not keep was nothing more than a ghost one was forced to remember every moment of the day. Who could withstand such torture?

She bit her lip before turning in her seat to face him. 'Heartache's no fun for anyone. Most of the time, you just wonder if it's worth it.' She could just see him nod before hearing him shift on his side towards her.

'I hope you're not offended by this but… I can't help but wish that one day you feel an inkling of how you felt about him for me,' Lamont confessed.

She could hear the awkwardness in his voice, as though he weren't used to being so vulnerable. It was interesting how the simplest words could be so hard to say. She was about to say something about how they had time when he stroked the side of her face. She pulled back, not prepared for him to touch her. He must have taken the reaction for shyness because he laughed softly before guiding her face to his lips.

The kiss felt very matter-of-fact for her, even as he pressed his lips harder against hers. She squeezed her eyes shut as she kissed him back, the moment feeling obligatory and cold. Luckily, he loosened his hold seconds later. She forced a shy smile to her face when he leaned towards her again, turning her face away.

'You're going to miss the race, Lamont,' she whispered, looking ahead, but it was a long time before she felt the eyes on her face disappear. Instead, he took her hand, and she forced herself to hold onto his.

–

Although he snuck into Sabine's room almost every night, one of Damien's favourite ways to see her was their weekly fencing lessons, a development that came after her terrible outing with Lamont. It was nice to interact with her in public, even if it was only as teacher and student. Seeing her in the sunlight was a luxury that he would not pass up.

So, why was he so nervous as he stepped into the garden?

Maybe it was the troubled look she had for the last few weeks when she thought he wasn't looking. Like now, as she sat on a bench under a tree with golden and burgundy leaves with a pinched expression. It was as if something were haunting her, keeping him out of reach. He wasn't used to this distance between them, nor did he know how to talk to her about it. He supposed he could be straightforward, but he also knew that she could be a good liar when she wanted to be.

So, a roundabout approach would have to do.

'A beautiful day,' he commented.

Sabine jumped, replacing her worry with a small smile.

'They're all beautiful.' She looked over the garden. 'Despite my initial qualms, France is nice.'

'I'm surprised your father didn't bring you sooner, especially since your mother was French.' He sat beside her on the bench, Sabine's hands twisting her lap.

'Mother preferred to be home, which I cannot blame her for after the boat ride.' Sabine shuddered. 'Not the best experience, I'm afraid.'

'Then I shall remain thankful I never chose to join the navy.'

Sabine laughed a little. 'You are much more suited for land.' She was quiet, her hands gripping the bench. 'It crossed my mind after my mother passed that we could have visited for one reason or another, but that seemed too sentimental for my father. It is a "gift only afforded to the feminine".' She rolled her eyes. 'My father is not the emotional type.'

'I know.' Damien's first meeting with Kwame Kouassi replayed in his mind. 'I'm surprised he showed you so much affection.'

She shrugged. 'He always wanted me to have two things: stability and power. It's something he worked for all his life.'

'So, why not look for something more familiar?'

Sabine grimaced before sighing deeply. 'He was never fond of the idea of me being with a local man,' she explained. 'He had to do a lot of things for us to get the power we have, some of which included hurting our own people. He didn't want me to bear the consequences.'

That seemed understandable. However, what caused more questions was the way Sabine now wrapped her arms around herself as if to shield herself from danger. There had to be more to the story. Still, he held back the question, 'What happened?' and instead said, 'That explains the fencing.'

'The fencing, the guards and his insistence of looking for suitors within our newly formed business partners… and I think he was scared.' Her brows pinched together. 'He knows from experience how far someone can go when they fall in love, and he didn't want anyone ruining his plans.'

'He made you a soldier.'

'Yes.' Sabine frowned. 'In a way, he did.' He hummed in contemplation.

'You know what's the best moment of being a soldier?' he asked suddenly.

Sabine raised her brow, meeting his gaze as she shook her head.

'It's that moment when you let go of all your opinions, when you finally bow your head to what's happening. You'll hate yourself for it later but, in that moment, it's a relief to be able to stop thinking. Suddenly, you're not someone no one wanted or deathly afraid of losing the only friends you have to someone just like you on the other side. You're just… ready.'

'Then why is it so hard to live with?' she whispered.

As Damien looked her in the eye, they were one and the same. Under all the gleam of privilege and pride lingered the feeling of being lost. Once again, he felt their connection, unwavering and undeniable, just like when they had first met.

'If I knew I would tell you.'

A tear slipped from Sabine's eye, and she quickly wiped it away. 'Despite everything he's done in my mother's name, my father spent years teaching me love has consequences. It's a fantasy that can never be fulfilled. Perhaps, it was not enough.'

'Why do you say that?'

'Because here I am with you.' She bit her lip before placing her hand tentatively over his. 'I know our time is limited but if I had a choice… you are all I want.' She gripped his hand tightly. 'Please, tell me you understand.'

He paused at the fear in her eyes and pulled free of her grip to wrap his arm around her, pulling her to his side. 'I don't need to understand,' he said. 'You don't need to worry about me. I'll always be okay. Even when all this is over, I'll find my way to you.'

Sabine buried her face in his chest but did not answer. He couldn't say for sure, but he had a feeling she didn't believe him. So, he held on as tight as he could, hoping she wasn't slipping away, that she had enough faith in them to know he would keep his word.

As he made his way down the hall, he knew she would need it. The general waited for him, looking livid as he gestured for Damien to follow him to his study. He instinctively looked out the window and paused when he saw that it looked out to the garden, specifically to the bench him and Sabine were sitting on earlier. He swallowed nervously as he met the general's gaze.

Love had made him reckless.

Chapter Fifteen

Washington, D.C.

August 2013

The sound of the marketplace filled his ears as he wandered through the streets looking for his mother. She had been gone for two days, an absence that was odd for her. She was supposed to come back with food, but night came and went. He went to her employer's house the day before, sneaking through the back when he heard the mistress of the house shouting about his mother being missing. He snatched a piece of fruit from the kitchen before silently slipping out. He continued to wait until his stomach was too empty to bear, hoping that maybe someone in the market would know where she went.

Answers came with pitiful or scathing looks, but the answers were all the same: no one knew where his mother went.

Hours from that moment, he would wander the streets. A baker closing shop would have some sympathy for him and give him some bread. Upon trying to take him home, he would tell her his mother was gone. While the baker was kind, she knew she wouldn't have enough money to care for him. She would do what she thought was best and tell a passing group of soldiers about her predicament. Among them would be General Roulet, someone who took one look at him and noticed that despite being tired, poor and clearly orphaned, the boy wasn't defeated.

–

Jones's eyes blinked open to a dark room. His gaze roamed the ceiling for a moment as he realised he was awake and felt surprisingly rested. He reached over to his bedside table to his charging phone. Squinting at the screen, he read that it was only 2:37 a.m. He groaned, putting his face in his pillow.

This is what happens when you go to bed early after staying up for an all-night session.

He usually would've stayed in New York, but the studio session had been so difficult and the artist so indecisive that the last thing Jones wanted to do was be anywhere where Jair could call him to come back in at the last minute. So, he drank a cup of pure black coffee with two extra shots of espresso and headed out on the four-hour drive. He managed to stay awake long enough to eat and watch a film to unwind before crashing.

Unfortunately, that left him wide awake at the worst time. He rubbed his forehead in frustration as his stomach grumbled. There was no way he was getting back to sleep starving. He threw off his covers with force to look for a hoodie, happy he wore sweats as pyjamas. The idea of cooking was thrown out quickly at the thought of having to wash dishes after. So, he went to one of the few places nearby open late.

Twenty minutes later, Jones hummed happily as he sipped McDonald's Sprite in the parking lot. The radio filled the inside of his car and he bopped his head along to the music as he looked around. There weren't any shady characters he could see, so he eased up a little, letting himself turn the music a little louder before biting into his burger. He swore at that moment a burger and fries had never tasted better.

Just when he started to relax, singing along to the song playing, he heard a thump. Adrenaline flooded his system, and he turned his music off, praying that it wouldn't be trouble. He heard someone cursing quietly but he couldn't quite see them, so he got out the car. God was generous because instead of someone looking for a bone to pick, it was the familiar brown eyes of Dani, who was rubbing her arm.

'Dani.'

'Jones… um, sorry,' she said quickly. 'I accidentally ran into your mirror.' He looked behind him and sure enough, his driver side mirror was bent inward.

'Hey,' he said bemused. 'You good?'

'Yeah, it was nothing. Just stings a little.' She grimaced.

'Do you—?'

'No.' She rotated her arm. Beyond a small wince, she seemed fine. 'Not good as new but probably won't bruise.'

'That's good,' he said, not sure how else to respond. The silence stretched between them, the awkwardness giving him a chance to catch his bearings enough to remember his manners.

'We should probably ask "how are you?"' he suggested.

'That's a good point,' she agreed. 'How are you?'

'I'm good and you?'

'Hungry and exhausted from Rachmaninoff,' she said, making him laugh a little. 'This may sound a little out of the blue, all things considered, but… if you're going to be hanging out for a bit, do you mind if I get my food and eat with you?'

Jones blinked in surprise but didn't hesitate to say, 'Nah, go ahead.'

'Okay! Okay… um, I'll be right back.'

Jones watched Dani jog to the door, her hands clutched tightly around her keys, pepper spray keychain swinging with each step. *Smart*, he thought. Although it would be smarter if he didn't leave her alone… He grabbed his keys and locked his door before following her. Dani looked up as he waited by the door, tapping on his phone like he was busy. He didn't look directly at her, but he swore he spotted a smile from the corner of his eye.

When Dani received her food, he stood and waited by the door. She gave him a small, polite 'thank you' when he opened the door, leading her to his car. He opened the passenger's side and got his food off the seat while she sat on his trunk, facing the restaurant, a line starting to form in the drive-thru. He was certain it was filled with students going just as crazy as Dani or those who finished second shift and were hungry, like him.

'What did you get?' she asked as he joined her. She reached into her bag, grabbing a handful of fries.

'A quarter pounder.' He took a bite, but the euphoria he found earlier was long gone. It was just cheap, greasy food again. Still, it quieted his stomach, so he wasn't too bothered. 'You?'

'Just fries,' she said. 'It's the best thing they got.'

'Fair,' he said, reaching for the last of his own.

They ate quietly for a while, looking at the line of cars going by. The silence was surprisingly comfortable and Jones was able to disappear into his mind, reflecting on his dream. It was rare that Damien thought about his childhood, his life becoming consumed by the military so early in life. In fact, even reliving Damien's life, his childhood memories only came after he met Sabine and his desire to have more to share with her. It was laced with so much hope that he could replace those memories with a family of his own, one he would never abandon. It was a blessing Damien didn't know how it would end. That seemed to be a burden unique to him and Dani.

The sound of slurping interrupted his thoughts. He looked over at Dani, who was staring at the half-moon above them with a straw in her mouth. She didn't seem to even realise her drink was finished as she sucked on air, the obnoxious sound getting louder.

'Okay, okay.' He reached over to the cup to take it, but Dani started to dodge his hand as she realised what he was doing. 'The drink is gone. Please, put it out of its misery.'

'I don't hear the ice complaining,' she commented as she let the straw slip from between her lips. She set it down and he picked it up, shaking it.

'That's the complaining,' he said.

She snatched it back from him, placing it as far from him as she could. They fell back into a lull before Jones broke the silence.

'So, why are you practising so late?' he asked her.

'You're asking me this now? At... 3:12?' He shrugged, waiting for the answer. She crossed her arms and looked at him pointedly.

'You first. You don't seem like a night owl to me.'

'I'm afraid you don't have a choice as a musician. Artists rule the night,' he said. 'My friend is a producer in New York. There's a song he's working on and he asked me to play bass with the singer's band. I've worked with her before but this time we were there *all* night. We didn't leave the studio until ten a.m.'

Dani winced. 'Damn. You couldn't just do the bassline and leave?'

'The singer insisted on the entire band being there and getting it right live,' he said, exhausted by the mere reminder of the session. 'I have never seen someone so obsessively work on a song for ten hours straight.'

'Wait, you didn't start until midnight?'

'The band started at nine, but the artist didn't show up until midnight. They had a concert earlier.'

'They had a concert and then ran over to the studio,' Dani said in disbelief. 'How? I'm tired after sitting and playing Beethoven for two hours, much less having to jump around a stage.' Jones threw his hands up helplessly.

'Either they ran on Red Bull and faith, or they had something extra to get them through. I was tempted to dip out every break, but I knew it would cause hell for my friend.' He laughed a little at the image of Jair pounding at his door for leaving him with the insufferable pop star.

'Do the artist often have "something extra"?' Dani asked.

'Eh, I'd say it's fifty-fifty. Usually, it's nothing more than weed but some get a lot more *creative*.'

'How vague of you.'

'It keeps me in the biz.' He winked, making her giggle. 'You'll learn one day.'

'I doubt I'll be working in a studio a lot. Maybe for soundtracks or live recordings, but I think I'll stay strictly in the performance realm for now.'

'And you think they're any more chill?'

He and Dani exchanged knowing looks both smirking. Jones didn't spend a lot of time with the performance majors when he was at Howard, but he did know enough people to know where there were packed schedules, there were more than a few drugs to be found.

'NowNow, back to you. What's got you craving fries this early?'

'Between Brahms' Double Concerto and Price's Symphony No. 1 in E Minor? Nothing,' she replied. He chuckled at the response as she looked up at the moon. 'My fingers feel like they're swollen. My back is killing me most days and I'm reaching my breaking point with my solo. Younger me who thought grad school would be easier because I could just concentrate only on music was foolish.'

'A solo, huh?'

'It's nothing.' Dani waved her hand as if to brush off his awe. 'Like hell it is,' he said. 'Some people would kill for that.'

'Unfortunately,' she sighed. 'Meanwhile, I've been distracted, so now there's less praise and more whispers of my talent "finally" fading.' She looked away from the moon, shadows falling on her face as she picked at her nails. 'I feel… I feel like I'm being consumed by them, you know? I keep having to remind myself that I'm not one of *them* when I wake up. And their emotions feel so overwhelming. I mean, I dreamed of them before, but to live it is too much. Where's the room for me?'

'It'll come back,' Jones said. 'When the memories are done. It's a headache until then but it gets better. After.'

'So, you just lived your life completely fine?' she said sceptically.

'Oh, absolutely not.' She raised her brow, silently asking for more. 'I got the memories in my second semester at Howard.

I failed all my finals, could barely get out of bed the first half of the summer and then spent the rest of the time begging my professors to let me retake the tests I missed. Not the adventure I would choose.'

She laughed before quickly sobering up, looking down at her hands. 'They're saying that Dr Carver made a mistake when he assigned the solo to me,' she told him, her voice almost a whisper. 'They say I'm too distracted, that I wasn't *supposed* to have a solo like that anyway. I'm not *obsessed* enough. I don't have extra training... I practise a lot but not as much as others—'

'You're gifted and they're not,' Jones interrupted. Dani's jaw dropped before she burst into laughter. Jones's brows raised. 'What?'

'I'm sorry,' Dani said between peals of laughter. 'It was just blunt; I didn't expect it. No one's that straightforward other than my friend Riley and, well, she's my friend so...'

'I'm usually not,' Jones admitted. 'But I've seen you play. And I've been there, so I know. Don't take it personally. There's always a genius, always the one with connections, always the one who made it on their own, and at the end of it, none of it matters. I'm not saying you shouldn't try but sometimes, the only real difference is luck.'

She looked at him warily, as if she were right on the cusp of believing him but not quite. He gave her a reassuring smile but didn't push it. If Dani was already this far into her career, he had no doubt she could handle the performance. A little midnight doubt came with the territory.

Still, he felt his heart warm when she held out her fry box to him. She nodded at his questioning gaze, and he grabbed a couple of fries, luckily still a little warm.

He munched on them as she asked, 'So, how lucky do you think you are?'

'Pretty damn lucky,' he answered, not having to think twice about it.

'Even the studio session?'

He groaned. 'Sometimes, you have to pay for it.'

'Even with…'

The unspoken words lingered in the air and their eyes met. He could see so much of Sabine in them, the worry and the care. But like him, the stakes weren't hypothetical this time. Yet, his breath still caught as he looked at her, wondering not for the first time what would have happened if they didn't remember.

As the more sensible of the two, Dani looked away first, sliding off the trunk.

'I should go and try to salvage some kind of sleep before practice,' she said. 'Want me to walk you to your car?' he offered.

'Nah, it's just over there.' She pointed at a car a few parking spaces away, the space between them empty so he could see her climb in. Yet, she didn't step away. Instead, she looked at him, curious and worried as she tended to be around him. 'What caused you to remember?'

The question made him shift uncomfortably under her gaze. There was an easy side to that story, one perfect for the conversation. But there was more to that summer than just some bad headache and he wasn't ready to tell her that; he already felt like he was lying.

So, he shrugged. 'That's a question for another day.'

Something in her expression shuttered close and she nodded slowly. 'Or another life. Good night, Jones.'

The words felt final but in a much different way than the day they met at the cafe. That was fear but this was logic. The right thing to do.

He got down from his hood and went back into his own car, checking on Dani from the corner of his eye. She was gone within minutes, and only then did he feel comfortable enough to drive home, the adrenaline of seeing her wearing off even as the tenderness stayed.

A week later, Jones was deep in slumber, no dreams visiting him. It was a rare break for him, one that he would appreciate when he woke up. Except today, that would be interrupted by his phone suddenly ringing. He squinted before looking at the clock on his bedside table. 4:25 a.m. *I swear if Jair is calling about a studio session I'm blocking him*, he thought as he scrambled for his ringing phone.

'Hello,' he answered, his voice deep and groggy.

'Hey.' He paused at the sound of a woman's voice. He checked the caller ID and his heartbeat picked up, waking him up. 'Jones? You there?'

'Yeah,' he answered, clearing his throat. 'Hey, Dani. I didn't expect you to call.'

'I'm unpredictable,' she said. 'You should know that by now.'

'Should I now?'

Silence. In person, one of them would have laughed but they both sounded too tired to hit their usual social cues. He blinked a couple of times, almost falling back asleep, when he heard her sigh.

'I can't sleep,' she admitted. 'You said artists rule the night so… do you mind staying up with me?'

Jones didn't have to look at his calendar to know that his day was packed tomorrow. He had a doctor's appointment, needed to email ten different people, co-ordinate with Ross about a project he was working on, and clean his apartment. It was one of those mundane adult errand days that needed him to be well-rested.

And yet, he sat up, getting comfy against his headboard and said, 'I've got all night.'

Chapter Sixteen

Paris

August 1896

'Where's Damien?'

Captain Cadieux closed his eyes and breathed out slowly, reining in his frustration.

'I don't know no more than what he said in his last letter,' he said.

'But you wrote back,' Sabine insisted.

'Exactly what you said to the letter and there has been no response since. More than likely, he is busy with his duties.'

'Captain—'

'Mademoiselle Kouassi, I have no new information.'

'It's—' She caught herself before she could correct the guard. *It's mademoiselle, not princess.* She was a long way away from those days. 'Just… I'm worried. He kept me much more informed than most.' She narrowed her eyes at the soldier, and he sneered at her before catching himself. He knew better than to push his boss's guest.

'Mademoiselle, I assure you, you're well protected here. We can double the guard if you're truly concerned.'

'Look… Damien is my friend. I just want to make sure he is okay,' she said. Cadieux's eyes turned pitying, and she bit the inside of her cheek to hide her irritation. She was no lovelorn girl. Something was wrong and no one was telling her what.

'He's okay,' Cadieux said kindly. 'He's simply on another assignment. You have nothing to worry about, Mademoiselle.'

She gritted her teeth at his words. He had said that last time as well. She doubted he even knew Damien's condition, but she couldn't press further or she would seem unreasonably invested.

'Very well,' she relented, turning on her heel.

She walked off and held back from rolling her eyes. These kinds of conversations were unfortunately common in the household now.

It had been a rough two months without Damien. The letter she had received when he first left, delivered by Cadieux, was a surprise. The words were hurried, saying that Roulet had called him back to the caserns to help with a situation on the outskirts of the city. At first, she had worried, insisting on any and all pamphlets from the city, searching for news about possible conflict. While she spotted many articles about unrest, talking about a growing division because of the Dreyfus case that still lingered over the city years later, there were none speaking of a crucial situation just outside Paris.

After that, suspicion set in. Why would Damien lie about going back to help Roulet? She asked as much in a letter she had Cadieux send him, and then in the next few. The only correspondence she received was letters from her father on how he was thriving back home.

Meanwhile, her activities began to, one way or another, centre on her staying in the house. Because of her concern over possible unrest, General Roulet insisted on her avoiding going out as much as possible and had Cadieux accompany her whenever she wasn't with Lamont or shopping with Madame Roulet. It was technically the same arrangement as before she became engaged, but Cadieux had always followed the orders to the letter, truly never leaving her side. It was suffocating.

The only relief she had was Madame Roulet, who would let her stroll around town while they shopped or waited for her dress appointment. That too, would soon end due to her trousseau being well-stocked and wedding dress almost done. Now, her time mainly consisted of the tinier wedding details and, of course, visits.

'Don't stomp through the halls, dear.' At the sound of her future mother-in-law's voice, she did roll her eyes. But she made sure to smooth out her expression as she entered the drawing room where Genevieve was sewing a baby blanket for Laurent's brother, who was expecting a son in a few months.

'I apologise, Madame Laurent,' she said. 'I was in a hurry.'

'Rushing is no excuse to lack grace. This is a proper household.'

Sabine took a deep breath and hid her balled fists behind her back, her nails digging into her palms. She would not lose her temper over a snide comment. Her father had taught her better.

'Are you not going to join me? Your needlework could use some improvement.'

Sabine dutifully took her seat on a loveseat across from the armchair Genevieve sat in. She picked up the needlework she had abandoned when she went searching for Cadieux. The two women sat in silence as Sabine struggled to follow the sunflower pattern.

'How is your son, Henri?' Sabine asked politely, trying to break the silence. 'Lamont told me he is expecting a baby in the new year.'

'Yes, in the spring. We are very excited for the arrival.'

'It should be an exciting visit for the family,' Sabine mentioned.

Genevieve paused, giving Sabine a surly look. 'Whatever do you mean?'

'I… when Henri's wife gives birth. Surely, you will visit and help,' Sabine explained.

'Why would I do that? She has a midwife.'

Sabine winced as she remembered what Madame Roulet had told her about childbirth customs in France month ago. Her face burned in embarrassment at the misstep. 'Oh, um, my apologies. In my culture, mothers and aunts handle the care of new mothers. We even move in for a while.'

'Understandable considering your conditions,' Genevieve said dismissively.

Sabine felt her embarrassment evaporate, quickly being replaced by the low simmer of anger. She set her needlework down in her lap. 'Excuse me?'

Genevieve sighed deeply before setting down her needlework. 'Instead of focusing on your rural custom, perhaps you should study with Madame Roulet if you ever want your knowledge of our culture to be more advanced than your needlework.'

Sabine swallowed the indignation she felt. How dare this woman speak to her so callously. Her wealth depended on Sabine's father and to act as if it were opposite was absurd. She couldn't say that, of course, but she could draw the line.

'Whether you like it or not, your grandchild will be half Ivorian.'

'No,' Genevieve said, without skipping a beat. It took Sabine aback.

'No?'

'No,' Genevieve repeated. 'Whether you like it or not, your child will be French. *That* is where your value lies and to pretend otherwise would be foolish.'

The words felt like a gut-punch. Sabine was left speechless, trying to find the right words to put together, something that would mask the hurt. Nothing she could say would be respectful and she refused to agree. Genevieve looked her over before sighing, focusing on her needlework again.

'Please do away with the sentimentality, my dear,' she said. 'We're all getting what we want. You will have your status, and we will have access to your lands. There's no need to pretend much more than that. Simply do your duty and leave the rest to the civilised.'

Sabine rushed out the room, her body shaking from the effort it took to not lash out. She rubbed her throat, trying to relieve the fury practically choking her. She was no fool. She knew the opinions, had seen the looks and whispers. But to have it said to her face how thoroughly inconsequential she and her country were viewed was different. She left everything behind to be a stepping stone, her value rooted in a dead mother.

Slamming her bedroom door closed, she sat down on the edge of her bed. She forced herself to stay still, despite everything inside of her begging to destroy everything around her. She tried to take deep breaths as she gripped her bedspread, her giant engagement ring winking in the sunlight, as if it were mocking her.

What was she doing here?

She straightened up when there was a knock on her door. She opened it and saw Lamont.

'What are you doing here?' she asked.

'Can I come in?'

She pursed her lips but stepped aside. 'The general will be displeased to find you up here. Whatever you've come to say, you must be quick.'

'I just wanted to apologise for my mother's words. That was horrible of her,' he said.

The apology took Sabine off guard, and she stared at him suspiciously.

'Thank you,' she said. 'Although, I highly doubt this will be our last time at odds. Quite frankly, she's incredibly rude.'

'I know. It's maddening,' he huffed out. He took her hand and sat down on her bed, urging her to do the same. 'When I found out what she said, I couldn't believe it. I told her, "Mother, just let her be!" Of course, you need time to adjust. Lord knows you grew up in a jungle,' Lamont huffed out.

Sabine swallowed the lump in her throat. She should have expected it. She had been since he told her about his family business. Yet, the fact that *that* was his defence of her was appalling.

'You both come from two different worlds,' he continued. 'Neither of you can control that. It's a process. You'll settle soon and she'll adjust. We'll all get along. Just give it time.' He took her in his arms, hugging her tightly like a child. She was stiff in his arms, unable to speak. Her fury at Genevieve quickly faded into the background replaced by a hallow feeling in her chest, as Lamont's words sunk in.

She, who had been insulted and belittled unprovoked, was a problem. And he was supposed to be her solution, her key to civilisation at last.

'You should go,' she said. 'Someone could come looking for you and we don't want to start rumours so close to the wedding.'

'Of course.' He stroked her face before kissing her cheek. 'Don't despair. It'll all work in time.'

She nodded and he finally left her alone. She listened to his footsteps disappearing down the hall before she covered her mouth with a pillow and screamed. She hated this stuffy country. She hated her crass fiancé. She hated all the rules, being proper and friendly but never close to anyone. She hated how trapped she felt, how it was all her father's fault.

Or mine, she thought between screams.

After all, her father wasn't here to bear her decisions; only she was forced to do that. A bitter laugh built up in her throat. All that fear and anger towards a man who was across the ocean. She laid on her bed until she was sure the Laurents were gone. Only then did she dare to go downstairs. She was starving, not having eaten all afternoon. She was on her way to the kitchen when Madame Roulet came across her.

'Oh, Sabine, dear!' Sabine resisted the urge to turn away as the woman gathered her in her arms. 'It's good to see you on your feet. Genevieve said that you came down with a sudden sickness.'

Sabine forced a smile, not wanting to risk a real dinner for an evening in bed with broth. 'Luckily, it was merely a scare. I feel fine.'

'Wonderful. Would you like to have an early dinner in the garden? The general will not be back tonight, and I have been craving a good game of croquet.'

'Um… sure,' Sabine agreed.

'Fantastic,' Madame Roulet exclaimed, looping her arm in Sabine's.

Hours later, Sabine was full and sipping a glass of wine as she watched Madame Roulet whoop in joy as she scored another point. For the first time in weeks, she laughed, belly ache and all.

'Good job, Madame,' Sabine said as she set up her next shot.

'Well, *Madame Laurent*, you can afford to be generous.' Madame Roulet wiggled her brow suggestively before taking a drink of wine. Sabine ignored the comment; she knew Madame Roulet was excited about her getting married and she didn't want to ruin the fun.

She looked around at the garden. A month from now she may not see it again, at least not for a long time. She hated it here and yet this was the closest thing she had to a home, Madame Roulet the only person she could almost call a friend. Everything and everyone she once had was gone and everything she gained would be lost too.

'Why the long face, my dear?'

Sabine opened her mouth to say she was worried about the wedding but, instead, she asked, 'Was he different?'

Madame Roulet's shot was crooked, taken aback by the unexpected question. The hostess didn't pay any attention to the skewed ball as she turned her gaze to Sabine.

'Who, dear?'

'Your husband,' she clarified. 'The general seems so straightforward, as if he's always been this way so, I can't help but wonder if it was ever otherwise.'

'Of course,' Madame Roulet said, putting her mallet down and joining Sabine at the table. 'People are always going to change. Why?'

'I—' She was tongue-tied as she tried to find a way to explain her confusion without damning herself. Madame Roulet watched her struggle before joining her at the table, pouring herself a glass of wine.

'You know,' she said, 'I always found it so fascinating that you never speak in your mother tongue, even a slip here and here. I speak a little English and Spanish, but I always found the simplest question hard to answer outside of French. Do you mind… demonstrating?' Madame Roulet gestured for her to speak. Sabine felt tears welling up but cleared her throat as she sat up. She looked around, making sure they were alone, before speaking.

'*I'm terrified,*' Sabine said in Fante. '*I have to live my life with a man that hates what I am, even if he ignores it. The love of my life is gone. My father has given me away to this country that belonged to a mother I wasn't allowed to remember. I am trapped and I don't know how I will survive it.*'

Madame Roulet nodded slowly with a glazed look. It was bittersweet, saying the words out loud but it being a secret all the same. Madame Roulet took her hand, squeezing it tightly.

'That's a lovely language,' she said. 'And to answer your question earlier, people only grow into who they really are. My husband is above board and respectable, so much so that I couldn't believe he wanted to marry me; I was quite rambunctious, as I'm sure you realise.' Madame Roulet's smile fell, and her gaze grew distant.

'When we realised I couldn't bear children, he should have left me. At the least, have found a mistress because important men must have a legacy. Instead, he simply told me that he dealt with enough children with the military.' She giggled fondly at the memory. 'It should have bothered me or surprised me, but it didn't. By the time our marriage was tested, I knew who he was. He had shown loyalty and patience a thousand times over…' Madame Roulet took her hand. 'I truly hope you and Lamont find love. Despite what everyone says, it makes it much easier to fight for something when it matters.'

Sabine swallowed around the lump in her throat. She already knew who Lamont was; had noticed it when they first met. She already knew she couldn't love or fight for him. The only one she could fight for was long gone.

'You know, you look like you could really stretch your legs,' Madame Roulet said. 'I suggest a quick walk before dinner. It does wonders for your health. Why, I always feel refreshed after walking through the Luxembourg Gardens.'

Sabine knew she should go on with the charade, say that she simply couldn't before giving in to Madame Roulet's insistence. But she was tired of pretending, so she merely said, 'Thank you.'

Madame Roulet gave her a pitying smile, squeezing her hand before letting go. 'Go on, then. You want to get back before dark,' she urged. Sabine got up immediately and got her coat, slipping out the house before a maid or Cadieux could stop her.

The first few steps outside were calm. Then, she realised she was granted freedom, if only momentarily. She picked her skirt up and rushed away. Her heart beat more and more frantically the further she got from the house. Her mind clashed with the pure instinct to run and the knowledge that it was only a temporary fix. Yet, she couldn't go back, not yet.

Navigating the maze of streets was easy. There were shops upon shops that were familiar, but she didn't want to see anyone that would recognise her, instead heading towards the Seine River. A cool wind caressed her face as she walked along the banks. It was a nice autumn day, golden leaves scattered along the shore, the sky a bright blue. She tilted her head back, eyes slowly closing.

What she would give to stay in that moment... 'Princess!'

Sabine's eyes shot open, and she looked over her shoulder, freezing as she saw Damien strolling her way. He seemed so different, and it took a moment to realise he wasn't wearing his uniform. Instead, he wore a brown day suit and boots. For a moment, she wondered if she were simply imagining him.

'Should I wonder why Cadieux is nowhere to be found?' Damien asked, only a few feet away.

The simple question brought Sabine back to her reality, and she scowled before walking away from him.

'Sabine, wait.' She ignored him as she headed across the bridge. She didn't know what she did to anger God to give her such a bad day but she wasn't going to take it. She heard Damien's footsteps and wasn't surprised when he pulled her to a stop. She pounded her fist against his chest.

'Where the hell have you been?' she snapped. 'I've been waiting to hear from you for weeks and all of a sudden you show up now? What is wrong with you?'

'I'm sorry—'

She pushed him, and Damien grabbed her arms, pulling her into his chest, her face a hair's breadth away from his. Yet, he wasn't angry. If anything, he looked remorseful as he tightened his grip on her arms. She struggled against him.

'Get off of me, you coward!'

'Roulet kicked me out.'

She immediately stopped fighting and stared at him in shock. '*What?*'

'He saw me comforting you in the garden last time I visited. He forced me to go back to the caserns and stay there. There was no way for me to contact you,' he explained.

'B–But you left me a letter. I wrote back to you several times. You didn't answer!'

'Roulet made me write it. I answered your letters, I swear, but I see they never made it.'

It took the wind out of her anger, forcing her to swallow the bitterness of the situation. There was a chance that he could be lying to her, but the disappearance felt out of character for him. If he truly thought it was over, he would look her right in the eye and tell her so. He protected her feelings, but he didn't lie to her.

She felt a small flutter of hope as she looked him in the eye. 'So…'

'I didn't abandon you. Not on purpose. I wanted to come back. I just didn't know how,' he explained.

It felt like a curtain being lifted. Weeks of being distraught at the thought of him no longer being in her life, leaving her, only to find out it wasn't him running away. He'd kept his word. She was right about him.

135

She took a shuddering breath as she leaned on his chest. He wrapped his arms around her and she closed her eyes tightly, barely holding back her tears of relief. She twisted her hands into his jacket, hoping he wouldn't let her go anytime soon. He kissed the top of her head and her shoulders relaxed.

It was good to be home.

'What are you doing out here by yourself? I heard Cadieux was trailing your every move,' he murmured against her hair.

'Madame Roulet suggested I take a walk.' Sabine fiddled with one of his brass buttons. 'Truth be told, she's the only thing keeping me sane these days.'

'Lamont?'

'And his mother,' she said. 'It's like being frozen slowly. I try to imagine living with them and it's just… it'll be impossible.'

She felt Damien sigh, but he didn't say anything. She was glad he didn't. She wouldn't be able to handle him telling her she could survive when all she desired was a chance to live for herself. She nuzzled her cheek against his chest before daring to open her eyes.

The first thing she noticed was how dark the sky had gotten. Madame Roulet had said the general would be gone all night but she didn't want to worry her. She sighed before stepping away from Damien's embrace.

'I have to head back,' she said. She stroked his face, wanting to linger in the moment as much as possible.

He frowned but kissed her palm. 'I'll find a way to write to you.'

'I'll be waiting.'

She stepped back before the urge to kiss him was too strong. It was already dangerous enough that she held him for so long. She adjusted her cape and walked back towards the house, supressing the tears that sprung up with every step. It took her a while to notice the footsteps behind her, and she looked over her shoulder to see Damien lingering a few feet back. She stopped with a raise of her brow.

'What are you doing?'

'It'll be dark soon enough,' he said. 'A young lady shouldn't be out here by herself, and I've heard I make good company.'

'And who told you this?'

'A princess I met a long time ago,' he said. 'A foreigner, but quite charming.'

The words made her pause as affection bloomed. It could have been the way the light caught Damien's hazel eyes or the velvety tone or how the fading sunlight danced over his brown skin – anything equally superficial. It would have been much easier to toy and flirt with that feeling than succumb to the fondness that constantly weighed on her heart. Already it was like being welcomed by a warm flame. How was she to resist it after being cold for so long?

'Let's go see the Jardin des Plantes,' she suggested. 'They're not far and, if I remember correctly, you're as fond of them as I am.'

'That sounds lovely,' he said, gesturing in front of them. 'Lead the way.'

–

Damien shouldn't have been there.

He should have followed her home silently, let her go at the door. He should have ignored how easily they fell back into step with one another. He should have remembered the punishments that awaited him if General Roulet were to find out that he defied his orders again.

Instead, he felt elation walking through the gardens by her side, the sudden switch making his head spin. Yet, he felt torn. Seeing her, finally being able to explain what happened, had put an extra spring in his step initially, but all he could focus on was the lack of vibrancy in her eyes, how hard she clenched her hands together. Whatever pressure she had been previously hiding now hung over her like a cloud. He knew there was nothing he could have done while Roulet had been keeping tabs on him – and still would be until the wedding – but he still felt a pang of guilt.

He should have tried harder to come back.

'The flowers may be gone are still gorgeous,' Sabine commented, looking around with wonder. 'I have never seen anything like this. We never had seasons like this back home. Only wet and dry.'

'I remember,' he said. 'I told you, it sounded much nicer than snow.'

'You were correct…' She trailed off, smiling tentatively. 'You seemed to like my stories.'

'Your home always sounded amazing.' He remembered her animated explanations of the lush, far-off lands. 'I could only wish to have grown up in a place like that.'

Sabine giggled as she faced him, the lost expression from earlier long gone. She looked both vulnerable and fierce all at once as she sat on the edge of a fountain. Damien checked their immediate surroundings. People were exiting the park, but some lingered nearby. Figuring it would look more suspicious if he continued to stand, he took a seat next to her, looking straight ahead.

'I never stood a chance. Not from the first moment we spoke,' she admitted.

Damien didn't dare face her. He wasn't sure he could handle the look he'd seen on her face, or the sweet promises falling from her lips. He almost wanted to ask her to stop, but he still craved the reassurance that he had mattered to her. 'I've never been able to truly hide from you, even when I wanted to. Sometimes, when you would stay the night, we would breathe in sync. Did you know that?'

'I… never noticed,' he said, dumbstruck by her words. He watched the last few people trickle out the garden, guards wandering at the fringes but not paying them attention.

'I wish I never did. Then, I could be the lady I was meant to be… I shouldn't be here, putting you at risk. I need to return—'

Damien cupped her face and brought it to his own. Sabine didn't fight, immediately melting at his touch. It felt like someone had lit a match under his skin, her touch feverish every time her hand brushed him. He pulled her into his arms, the movement muscle memory. How many times had he done this as sunlight warmed her skin? He bit her lip, hungry to recreate that moment with her, his mind turned dizzy with their mutual desire.

And destructive, he reminded himself. She was still engaged, tied to an influential family. Yet, Lamont was no soldier, no fighter like them. The idea that he would ever be stupid enough to try and stop them almost made Damien scoff.

Let him try to take you away, he thought arrogantly as Sabine moaned, clinging to his shoulders.

'Come with me,' he whispered when they separated, both breathing heavily. He was ready for her to be reasonable, to remind him that she couldn't.

'Okay.'

—

'We shouldn't have done that.'

Damien shook his head where it rested on Sabine's chest. 'I think it was your best idea yet.'

He shimmied down to kiss her stomach, and she was very aware of the blanket that separated his lips from her bare skin.

They had escaped to an inn a few streets over. Sabine drew eyes, but Damien kept a proper distance, not stepping inside until the street was empty. The owner narrowed her eyes at them but said nothing at the gold coins Damien tossed on the counter. The bed barely fit the two of them, but it didn't prove to be much of a problem as their bodies became entangled.

Her skin still tingled in the aftermath, hypersensitive with every move he made, and she had to stop herself from sinking her nails into his back to pull him over her again, instead settling for tracing random shapes across the planes of his back as he continued to kiss her. She bit the inside of her cheek before running her fingers through his curls.

'It's a great idea until we have to scramble for our clothes,' she murmured as she stared at the ceiling.

Damien propped himself on his elbows, framing her face. 'Your guardians are not down the hall from us.' He leaned down to kiss the curve of her neck. 'We're fine.'

'What about when I have to go home?' He groaned, tucking his face into her neck. She wrapped an arm around his waist, kissing his shoulder, and breathing in the woodsy scent that naturally clung to him. 'I'm still engaged, and you're still being monitored by Roulet… I don't know how we're going to keep this up.'

He pulled away so she could see his face. 'Then, we figure out a way to get out.'

Sabine raised her brows. 'What do you mean?'

'Let's run away.'

Her eyes grew wide. The words had been an inkling in the back of her mind; an idea easily dismissed. Yet, when Damien disappeared, it became a fantasy. Now… now, she had to choose. If she said no, this would have to be the last time she saw him. Roulet knew there was something between them. Maintaining the affair after she was married would be difficult, especially since she would be leaving the city soon after. They would have to give up everything…

'How do we do that?'

He flipped them over, so she was laying atop him, her hair falling around their faces. Damien's fingers trailed up her exposed back, his hooded gaze making her throat run dry.

'I may not be in the navy, but I have friends there. I can call in a favour or two. I have money saved. It's not a lot but—'

'My trousseau,' Sabine said. 'Between that and Lamont's ring, we'll have more than enough money to disappear.'

'Now, we just have to pick a place and a route,' Damien said.

'My father comes in October,' she told him, remembering the letter he sent before departing from Côte d'Ivoire. 'We have to leave before he arrives, or we won't have a chance.'

'I'll find a way out before then,' he vowed.

'I never have anything to do on Wednesday or Saturday. I'll convince Madame Roulet that I need another walk,' she smirked.

'Okay.' He looked over at the clearly expensive dress that lay abandoned on the floor. 'And maybe come in something more… subtle.' She giggled before nodding eagerly. Her laughter faded as she realised the implication of what was happening.

'We're really doing this,' she whispered.

Damien's eyes grew serious, and he leaned up to kiss her. It was a gentle touch, sealing the promise. They weren't going back; they couldn't. And Sabine couldn't think of all the promises she made to her father. She was here now, and she needed to be happy.

'Yes,' he said between kisses. 'We're doing this.'

Chapter Seventeen

Paris

September 1896

Madame Roulet was right when she said that having something to fight for changed everything.

Now that Sabine knew she was going to run away, she was able to endure the last of the wedding preparations, spending time with Lamont, and could even ignore Genevieve much more effectively. Every night she would sort through her trousseau and pick out the most valuable pieces, wrapping jewellery and expensive but light linens in the kita cloth she brought, knowing she could strap it across her chest and hide it under her coat. The days seemed to slow down the closer she got to Wednesdays, the nights over too soon after being in Damien's arms. While she struggled to hide her excitement, her sudden 'glow' being explained away with her upcoming nuptials.

It was finally happening. She was going to have a chance to breathe, to be in love.

To live.

—

'I can't believe you had Francois by his last franc,' Damien said as they walked towards the city centre. 'How did you manage to learn cards?'

'Madame Roulet has many ways to entertain herself,' she said, fanning herself with her hat. 'Plus, after a few rounds of watching, anyone can pick up on how to play.'

'Your domination was incredible to watch, my love. I think you broke him,' Damien complimented as he kissed the back of her hand.

Sabine laughed, throwing her head back. 'My God, I gave his money back! He shouldn't gamble if he isn't prepared to lose,' she reasoned.

'But lady luck was shining down on you and cards are the ultimate temptress. Who was he to resist?' He grabbed her by the waist suddenly and Sabine let herself be pulled in, smiling against his lips as he kissed her. Damien pulled away a bit, eyes lustful. 'I, for one, cannot imagine.'

'Not even a little?' she teased, stealing a quick kiss.

Damien looked her up and down, forlorn. He dipped down to kiss her neck and up to her ear. 'Not again,' he whispered.

She wrapped her arms around him and sighed happily, glad she didn't have to worry about drawing eyes.

They had met by the river again and Damien greeted her with a wide grin. After weeks of planning, he had figured out their escape. They would go to Tunisia, where they could blend in with the newly educated French citizens starting a new life. He had a friend on the ship that would sneak them on board and papers that would be good enough to establish new identities when they arrived. The ship would leave the day after next, and Sabine hadn't hesitated to say yes.

To celebrate, he took her to a pool hall on a side of town where rumours wouldn't get back to Roulet. They drank and gambled the night away. She wasn't nervous; she only brought a few coins, with all her other valuables tucked away under her bed.

She felt like she would start floating at any moment with how giddy she felt. The only thing that kept her on the ground was Damien's arms around her, shielding her from the cold evening breeze. What she wouldn't give to call this man her husband. She opened her mouth to tease him about marriage when Damien's head snapped to look over his shoulder.

'What?' she asked, caressing his face with the back of her hand, coaxing him to meet her gaze. 'What is it?'

His eyes stayed narrowed on the scene at the end of the street, two protestors screaming at the officer, who raised his weapon towards them. Damien turned her away just as the sky above them rumbled. Sabine was about to dismiss it, since it had been windy and grey all day. Then, she felt a droplet hit her hair. She automatically moved her hands over her head, ducking down. Damien led them out of the middle of the street. The rain picked up quickly, turning into a downpour by the time they found a dark doorway to duck into.

'Well, that won't let up soon,' she commented, looking at the pouring rain. She heard Damien chuckling and turned to him. 'What?'

He tried to control his laughter as he pointed at her hair. She touched it before gasping in horror. The lovely high bun she had created earlier was a ruined, lumpy mess. She groaned as she let her hair down; she refused to look like a lunatic in the street. Just as she set about braiding it, Damien shifted closer to her. 'You better not tease me,' she warned.

'Why don't you let your hair down more?'

Sabine slowed her braiding, self-consciously looking at the ends. 'It's... a bit unruly. The curls don't fall quite right, so I'd rather pin it up.'

'Just how much do you have to hide?'

Biting her lip, she let go of her hair to wrap her arms around herself, the question stripping her bare. When she thought of all the things she had kept tucked away – her looks, her mind, her mannerisms, her culture and her past – she wondered what was left for her to show.

'Everything,' she admitted, clearing her throat awkwardly. 'I'm sure you can understand.'

Damien shrugged and tucked a stray stand into place. 'I don't think there's enough to me to hide something,' he said.

Sabine looked at him in disbelief. 'Standing in front of me is a man so loyal he's willing to give up everything for that which he considers worthy. Surely, there's more to a man like that.' She tapped the tip of his nose. 'You just haven't gotten to know him yet.'

He caught her wrist and kissed her finger. Sabine's face flushed at the sudden intimate gesture.

Damien stared with half-lidded eyes. 'The papers for when we leave… we share a last name.' He swallowed nervously but kept his eyes on her. 'Is that okay?'

Sparks skittered across her skin, joy making her heart feel as though it was about to beat out of her chest. She decided in that moment that those were the most romantic words she had ever heard.

'Yes,' she said breathlessly.

She wasn't sure who stepped forward first but suddenly they were wrapped up in each other, her braid unwinding as she cupped his face. She ran her fingers down his chest, pulling on his jacket and walking backwards until she hit the wall. Damien didn't relent for a moment as his lips pushed and pulled against hers.

She tilted her head to deepen the kiss, gasping against his lips as she felt him lift her from the ground. She clung to his shoulders, kissing his neck, her teeth settling into his skin as she heard him loosen his belt.

The rain beat heavily over their heads, but they could barely hear it over their own intimate sounds. Sabine struggled to catch her breath as he moved within her, slow and steady with an occasional snap of his hips that made her gasp. She was practically shaking out of her skin and every touch from him felt like he was the only thing keeping her in one piece, as if she would fall apart the moment he let go. She clung to him, her nails digging into her palm even through the fabric of his shirt.

Every whisper of his name was a plea to keep him for just one more moment, just one more day. Every breath that caressed her skin was a miracle, the way his unrelenting warmth shielded her from the chilling water was bliss.

There was no price she wouldn't pay for more moments like this.

Though she was sure Madame and General Roulet had retired for the night, Sabine had her excuse ready as she entered the house. Surely, waiting out the rain would be reasonable enough. However, the words died on her lips as she stepped into the living room.

The fireplace roared, a very dapper guest seated in front of it, calmly reading. Her skin suddenly felt cold, and her hands began to shake. She clenched them into fists to hide her fear and approached them.

'Father,' she greeted.

Kwame Kouassi looked up from his book and smiled at her, but she saw an edge to it that made her heart race. He was furious.

'I see you got caught in the rain,' he noted calmly. He clicked his tongue as he set the book aside. 'Although you seemed to have dressed for it.'

Her face flushed as she remembered she was wearing a peasant dress, skipping her usual stop at the inn to return sooner. 'What are you doing here?' she asked as he stood. 'Your letters didn't mention a visit.'

'I thought I would surprise you,' he said, kissing her cheek. 'It seems I've stumbled upon a few surprises of my own. Did you miss me, *mon trésor*?'

'Yes,' Sabine forced out. 'I'm merely… shocked. I can't believe you're here. H–How was your trip?'

'Perfect. Blue skies and good winds until this afternoon, but luckily, we avoided the worst of it. Don't worry, Sabine. We can play host and guest after our business.'

'Our business?'

'Of course. As we speak, Cadieux is fetching an important guest. Or rather a familiar confidant, wouldn't you say?'

'Father—' Sabine jumped as a door opened suddenly.

'Ah, here he is.' Sabine shrunk back from the sharpness in his cruel smile.

'Father, please...' she said under her breath, but he ignored her, clasping his hands together loudly as Damien stepped inside the room. She flinched at the sharp sound but didn't dare look away from the scene unfolding before her. Though Damien was soaked by the rain like her, he walked with confidence, standing tall in front of her father despite the tension in the room. Even Cadieux, who lingered in the corner, looked wary.

'Mr Kouassi.' Damien bowed his head slightly. 'Welcome back to Paris. You look well.'

'Seems you were caught in the same storm as my daughter,' her father replied.

Sabine bit the inside of her cheek, her heart threatening to burst out of her chest. Her mind raced for ways to distract her father but quickly descended into panic.

Don't react, she recited. *Don't show anything. Don't react to anything.* Her father looked between the two of them before chuckling, the sound sending a chill down her spine.

'It appears we have an issue,' he began. 'A little bird told me that there has been some interference in your pending marriage, Sabine. Personally, I found this hard to believe until I took a stroll around town. Some vendors in the market just can't stop gossiping about a young lady and the soldier sneaking all around town.' He made sure to hold her gaze. 'I think we need to remedy the problem.'

'There is no problem,' Damien said. 'Only a rumour.'

'Oh, you underestimate the power of words, soldier,' her father shot back, turning his attention to Damien. 'You see, a

147

whisper is like an ember. One misplaced word overheard by the wrong ear can cause a fire. With every exchange of the story, the details become more sensational until all that remains is an inferno no one can control. But what would a man of so little consequence understand of that?'

'Father, that is uncalled for,' Sabine interjected, but he simply held a hand up to silence her.

'Did you ever think about what will happen to her in all this?' Kwame continued. 'You string her along for sport, for entertainment and folly, ruining her every step of the way. The humiliation alone will force her out the country.'

'Father—'

'Do you think *you* will come out of this unscathed? That you could keep your rank when you would cause such a scandal among one of parliament's favourite families?' Kwame sneered at the man. 'Being demoted may hurt your pride, but the fall from grace my daughter will incur will be one that destroys her.'

Damien's eyes burned bright with defiance but Sabine noticed the wariness in them too, the words unfortunately having a ring of truth. She did her best to seem confident as she stepped in front of her father. She knew he loved her, would never hurt her directly, but she also wasn't a fool. She was well aware of his ability to punish her, even now.

'Father,' she called, bringing the room's attention to her. 'Don't blame Damien for this. I made a promise, and I can keep it. You were right to raise awareness of the mistake. You can trust me to fix it.' She ignored Damien's look of disbelief, instead focusing on how her father seemed to mull over her words.

'I believe you,' he said. Sabine almost let out a breath of relief but she saw his eyes move over her shoulder. 'But I'd like to guarantee that. Cadieux.' He motioned for the man to step forward.

'Yes, sir?' Cadieux asked, a note of nervousness to his voice.

'You are in charge of chaperoning my daughter when she leaves for town, correct?'

'Y—Yes, sir.'

'And you were unaware of these trips?'

'I was only informed by Madame Roulet that Sabine wanted to take a walk,' Cadieux admitted. 'She seemed to need the privacy.'

Kwame sighed and placed his hand on the guard's shoulder, voice heavy. 'You have a good heart, Cadieux. Unfortunately, like I tell my daughter, choices have consequences.'

Sabine noticed the knife only a moment before it was too late. '*No!*'

Her yell was barely audible over Cadieux's scream as Kwame's knife was plunged into his side. He fell instantly, gasping in pain as he struggled to put pressure against his wound.

Tears fell down Sabine's face, blurring her vision as she tried to run to his side, but her father intercepted her, forcing her to look on helplessly.

'This will end now,' he growled. Sabine tried to fight him off, but he grabbed her shoulders, his grip digging into her skin. 'You will not throw away everything we have sacrificed. I will *not* allow it.' He faced Damien again, who was crouched by Cadieux's side. 'Roulet considers you a son, soldier. For that, I will spare you tonight. The next time something like this happens, it's you who will bear the consequences. Take him and get out!'

Damien tensed, baring his teeth, his hands forming fists. Sabine shook her head furiously at him. *Please, don't do this.* She couldn't afford him tempting her father's rage and Cadieux needed help. Reluctantly, Damien relaxed, helping Cadieux up.

'Oh, and Damien, do return my dagger,' Kwame yelled as the men rushed out the back.

Only when the door slammed behind them did Kwame let go of her. For a moment, she wished he hadn't. Her legs felt so weak, she could barely stand. She stumbled back a couple of steps at the sight of Cadieux's blood on the floor, soaking into the carpet. It was a small miracle she had somehow managed to stay on her feet as her father reclaimed his seat.

'He will live,' he said, picking up the book once again.

Sabine watched how casually he moved on, how he always did. She thought back to how he would destroy her world in a mere moment only to pretend everything was normal. Maybe it was, and maybe Sabine, for all her fighting spirit, directed her energy at the wrong people. She never spoke out against her father's punishments. When a decision was made, it was done, but now…

'You almost put his blood on my hands,' she said numbly in Fante, the switch unconscious. 'Just like Daouda.'

It was a name that she hadn't spoken in years, memories rarely let out of a young boy from her childhood. For so long, they were inseparable best friends. Then they shared their first kiss, and everything changed. She started thinking of marriage and a family with him, a thought she had mistakenly mentioned to her father. Her father vehemently disapproved, but she was stubborn, adamant about being with him. It resulted in a dagger buried in Daouda's chest.

Her father shrugged, his eyes still on the book. 'It was necessary.'

Something snapped in Sabine, and she stomped over to him, snatching the book from his hand and throwing it into the fire.

'Who do you—'

'He was a boy! He was good!' Kwame frowned in disapproval, but she continued. 'He didn't do anything wrong by falling in love with me, but you *killed* him for it!'

'And the fact that his life wasn't enough of a warning makes me question the faith I had in your intelligence,' her father snapped, making Sabine flinch. 'He was poor and ordinary. A blip that no one will remember in time. You think you're suffering now? Your life would have been ten times harder with him.'

'He cared for me,' she growled, the aching pit in her stomach a reminder of what her father had taken from her long ago.

'He would have destroyed you,' her father shouted, shooting to his feet. 'He would have given you a life of labour for a "love" that would have faded over time. I saved you from that! And I will keep saving you from ruining yourself, whether you like it or not.'

'I never needed this!'

Her mind whirled and she felt like she could barely catch her breath. She couldn't understand. Had she not been a dutiful daughter? Had she not done everything right? How could he treat her this way when he claimed to love her?

Tears of frustration escaped, wetting her cheeks, and when she spoke, her voice was a whisper. 'Why do you torture me like this? Why do you insist on this life for me? Why do you hate me for being like her? Love and family were enough for mother. Why do you deny me the same?'

Kwame's eyes practically flashed as he towered over her.

'It's not that simple,' he fumed. 'Yes, your mother giving up everything gave me the best years of my life, but I'd be a fool if I did not acknowledge that had I been a man of means, she would not have died!'

Sabine froze at the words. She had only a few memories of her mother's last moments. Her father refused to let her see her mother's deteriorating state. She only knew that one moment her mother was there and then, suddenly, she was gone.

'She had a curable disease. Something that only required medicine we could not afford, and it was made no better by the stress of her working,' he revealed. 'She should have never had to lift a finger, much less die in a room with nothing but darkness and merciless heat. Had I been the man your grandfather wanted me to be, you wouldn't have lost her. And for you to be so careless—'

Kwame raised his hand, and Sabine recoiled. His shoulders tensed for a moment before they slumped. She blinked in surprise as she watched her father finally drop his guard, and his hand, his face filled with worry.

'Ama, I don't hate you,' he replied. 'I love you more than anything in this world. And that means making the decisions you hate now so you can *live*.' He grabbed her by the shoulders and she swallowed nervously at the renewed rage in his eyes. 'That means I will not let you make this mistake.'

The silence between them was tense, and Sabine could already feel her fear giving away to resentment. She wanted to believe him, but she wasn't sure her heart could take such a truth.

'Go to your room,' he instructed, letting her go. 'I'll take care of the mess and be gone by morning.'

She didn't speak as she hurried up the stairs, stopping only to look down at him over the railing. He was holding his face in his hands.

They were both defeated by tonight.

The next morning, Sabine didn't bother getting dressed before going downstairs for breakfast. The sun was barely up but she knew the chef, Hugo, would be in the kitchen preparing as a few maids readied the dining room. She prodded at the dark circles beneath her eyes. She had tossed and turned for hours, but her mind wouldn't quiet. It argued with her father. It agreed with him. The only thing she was sure about was that, in mere hours, she had gone from feeling indestructible to falling apart completely.

Now, she was numb and in need of coffee.

She had only stepped outside her room when Sandra spotted her.

'Madame,' she said with a wary look. Sabine prayed she wouldn't ask about last night. Maybe God decided to grant her mercy because Sandra said, 'You have company. He's waiting for you in the garden.'

–

Damien sat on a small, wooden bench tucked away deep in the garden, shoulders slouched and eyes aching. Between patching

Cadieux up, sneaking him into the caserns, and wondering what would happen all night, he was exhausted.

After leaving the guard in the hands of the doctor, he had spent all night packing, waiting for Roulet to walk in and discharge him. He had enough money to start over somewhere else. Not to mention he knew where to find other work if he had to. He would've been on his way to talk to Roulet himself right now were it not for Sabine.

They still had unfinished business. And judging from the dark circles under her eyes, she seemed to feel the same.

'We should talk,' he suggested softly. Taking a deep breath, she sat on the bench beside him.

He waited for her to say something, anything. He had thought she would be pacing back and forth in a rage or talking so fast he could only understand that she was worried. Instead, she sat completely still, like a statue. Her eyes were haunted just as they had been weeks ago. It made him uneasy, and he decided to break the silence.

'Aren't you going to look at me?' She shook her head stubbornly. 'Sabine, talk to me. Please.'

'I can't,' she said, her voice a shaky whisper. 'Please… don't make me say it.' Arms wrapped around herself, she looked small and lost. Damien frowned, guilt washing over him. He stroked her cheek gently.

'I have the papers. We can leave right now.'

Sabine closed her eyes and bit her lip as she turned away from him. He wrapped his arm around her. 'The protests are getting worse. I wouldn't be surprised if they boiled over soon. I don't want to see what happens to you when it comes. We can have a life away from this place and go where no one will find us.'

While not as prepared as his first plan, he knew the ports well and more than enough soldiers willing to help them out. Even if they had to wait weeks, there were plenty of places to hide in the city. All they had to do was decide where to go. Even if he never saw France again, he wouldn't mind.

He'd give up the world for her.

'Someone will get hurt if I do that and I refuse to have anyone else's blood on my hands,' she told him resolutely. Damien nearly flinched but told himself Sabine was frightened. Last night was fresh on their minds. Still, his heart twisted in his chest when she said, 'We should have never met.'

'No.' He grabbed her shoulders and turned her towards him. He held her face gently, tilting it up so she could meet his eyes. 'I don't regret this. We needed to meet. I needed to know what a life with love – *real* love – felt like, and you gave that to me.'

Tears fell from her hazel eyes with every blink, and he could feel her tight grip on his jacket; she didn't want to let go. He placed his forehead against hers. 'Be with me, Sabine. Please. Let's be free.'

'Free,' she repeated. 'My first love said the same thing. He knew my father would never approve, and he wasn't as lucky as Cadieux.'

'You were young then. I know this city like the back of my hand. We can get away,' he insisted. 'Give us a chance.'

'People will get hurt.'

'No one else is involved. It'll just be you and me. Isn't that all that matters?' Sabine stared at his chest, her brows furrowed.

Believe me, he wanted to beg, the words were already on his lips. He had a feeling that last night wasn't the first time since her first love that Sabine had been exposed to a scene like that, but he knew he could keep her safe. All she had to do was say yes.

When she looked into his eyes, he already knew her answer.

'After seeing what happened, how could you ask that of me?'

His hands dropped from her face, not expecting the crushing feeling that followed. It was like the ground had disappeared from under him as he held her gaze, the unwavering look telling him the hard truth.

There was no more fight left in Sabine. She had seen enough. She couldn't push anymore. She couldn't believe that he would be all right should she take the chance. And despite his words all those months ago, she was no soldier; she was merely a girl who had seen enough death in her life.

With nothing left to say, he placed Kwame's dagger next to her and left, mind hazy as the hope bled from his future.

In his dazed state, he somehow ended up in General Roulet's office at the caserns. He didn't hesitate to knock. He heard a muffled, 'Come in,' and opened the door. Roulet looked up from his paperwork, brows furrowing in concern.

'Captain,' he said. 'Is there something wrong?'

Damien tried to form words, but nothing came out. Nothing made sense to him anymore. He sat down on a couch by the window, his gaze falling to the floor. Silence filled the room, only briefly interrupted by Roulet moving from behind his desk to sit in the chair in front of him. Damien tried to gather his words as he finally accepted the truth.

His time with Sabine was over.

'Allow me to go to the wedding. I'll go wherever you assign, no questions asked… I need to see the ending for myself.' He forced himself to look at Roulet and for once was comforted by the concern he found in the general's gaze. 'I was a fool, wasn't I?'

Roulet sighed, patting his shoulder. 'No more than the rest of us,' he said.

Roulet left his hand on Damien's shoulder as he stared at the floor. He was grateful for the gesture, not strong enough to move just yet. He may have only received half of Roulet's love growing up but, at that moment, it was enough.

Chapter Eighteen

Paris

October 1896

From her bedroom window, Sabine could see the preparations for her wedding underway in the garden. Lamont wanted to go all out for the celebration. It wasn't surprising; she was used to her future husband's lavish taste by now. Today, it was simply magnified, especially thanks to her father's suggestion that the wedding venue be changed to the Laurents' estate to truly 'make a statement'.

Arrangements were quickly adjusted and expanded. More flowers, more food, and more guests. The French may supposedly be private about their weddings, but she would not be surprised if the entire city knew all the details of the affair.

She was sure many would be envious of the layered bright white gown she wore. It had a high collar, and sleeves buttoned at her wrist. Jewels randomly adorned the full, lace-covered skirt. The only adornment left off were ruffles – a small victory on her part. She picked at the skirt, barely looking at herself in the mirror. She was more than happy to close her eyes as Madame Roulet pinned the veil in her hair, letting the fabric fall over her face carefully.

She couldn't help but think about how her hair was down for once, the curls falling down her back past her shoulders. It looked just like it had in the rain… she turned away from her reflection.

'Beautiful,' Madame Rolet said, and Sandra agreed with happy tears in her eyes. Sabine didn't bother mustering a matching smile. She was doing her duty, but she wouldn't walk into it with a smile. It was the only thing her father couldn't force her to do. Her lack of enthusiasm permeated into the atmosphere and Madame Roulet shifted awkwardly. 'Sandra, could you see if they are ready to start?'

The maid nodded, quickly disappearing out the door. Only when the door closed did Madame Roulet return her attention to Sabine. She went to the vanity in the corner of the room – Sabine's future room – and grabbed a handkerchief out of her bag. She lifted the veil and dabbed gently under Sabine's eyes. Sabine blinked in surprise before touching her face.

She hadn't realised she was crying.

She was about to scrub her face but Madame Roulet stopped her hands, squeezing them tightly while giving her a pitying look. It was something she had done since the day Damien left. No doubt the general had informed her of what had happened, which was embarrassing in one way and devastating in another. Yet, Madame Roulet said nothing, taking over as much of the wedding preparations as possible. It was the only thing she could do and Sabine tried her best to appreciate it.

'We have to put on the gloves now,' Madame Roulet reminded gently. Sabine nodded solemnly, letting go. She slipped on the white silk gloves that were waiting on a table nearby. Her outfit was complete just as there was a knock on the door.

'Madame, they're ready,' Sandra said through the door.

Madame Roulet motioned to the door, eyes more despondent than she thought possible for the lively woman. 'Shall we?'

There was only one answer.

–

The wedding was beautiful, a perfect and traditional French affair. Sabine looked beautiful in her snow-white dress and diamond encrusted jewellery, courtesy of Madame Laurent. Lamont looked equally handsome, wearing a formal black suit and white shirt. She contemplated the unintentional black-and-white theme of her wedding. All she could see was the contrast. Light and dark. Foreign and domestic. Before and after, one becoming the other after all papers were signed and the chaste kiss the ceremony called for.

They quickly transitioned to the *le vin d'honneur*, a dazzling reception in the ballroom. Tables were laden with wine and gifts despite it being so early in the day. People milled around in their finest as they drank glasses of champagne. Every person she passed congratulated her on a marvellous event, stating how beautiful she looked in her dress. She barely had enough time to thank them before she was being pulled along to meet someone new. It was dizzying and the wine did nothing to help the sickness in her stomach.

'Excuse me, Madame Laurent,' a familiar voice spoke from behind her. Sabine whipped around quickly, freezing when she spotted her father with a proud look on his face.

'Oh,' she said. 'Father.'

Her cold reception took him aback, but he quickly adjusted his expression to that of a joyous father. She could probably blame the alcohol for her lack of fear as he approached. Or maybe it was the finality that erased any intimidation she would have felt otherwise. Her father took the glass from her hand as he kissed her temple.

'Should I be concerned with how much you're drinking?' he continued quietly under his breath.

'It's a party,' she said through her teeth. 'One you have arranged perfectly.'

'Sabine, smile,' he warned. 'It's your wedding day.'

She scoffed. 'I've secured your business ventures. Now, all I have to do is force a baby out and I'll have used up all my importance for everyone in this room. Enjoy the dinner.' She started to step away when her father pulled her back.

'You don't talk like that to me, Sabine,' he snapped under his breath.

She stared daggers at him, truly offended at the insinuation that she was still his to control. 'Madame Laurent,' she corrected. 'I now have more power than you. And after tonight I will use it to make sure I never have to see you again.'

'Sabine.'

'I will *never* forgive you,' she whispered. Her father's eyes widened and his grip loosened. She ripped her arm from his and stepped back from him. She hoped he could see that her loyalty was gone. She was free to hate him as much as she wanted.

The tense moment was interrupted when Lamont came over.

'Kwame!' He clapped his hand on her father's shoulder and she saw her father's jaw tighten. 'I see you've caught up with my bride. She is the most gorgeous thing in Paris, is she not?' Lamont stumbled over to her to sloppily kiss her cheek. Sabine stiffened from the kiss, nudging him off her.

'Did you need something... dear?' she asked.

'Yes, actually. Kwame, my father asked for you to meet in his study for a cigar,' Lamont said, looking around. 'Ah, Gabriel!'

Her husband disappeared in the crowd and she stared at the ground, the humiliation of being tied to him sobering her.

'You should go,' she told her father. He was silent before kissing her forehead, a lingering touch that made her ball her fists.

'You look beautiful, Ama.' Tears filled her eyes, but she held them back as he walked away. She stood awkwardly in the crowd for a moment before exiting the party.

She found herself wandering the courtyard, the din of the celebration in the background. It was ironic; so many people were here to celebrate and even her husband didn't notice her absence. She looked at her reflection in one of the fountains scattered about and sighed. She barely recognised herself anymore.

She perked up at the sound of footsteps behind her but didn't turn. Instead, she wandered behind a tree, pulling out her father's dagger she now always carried with her, a reminder of her greatest mistake. When she heard the soft footsteps draw near, she moved to press the knife to the person's neck, but they caught her wrist.

'Glad to know you didn't forget your self-defence lessons.'

Any words died in her throat as she saw Damien standing in front of her, gripping her wrist.

It had only been two weeks, the longest of her life. It felt like their lessons and the stolen kisses were memories from years before. She remembered his carefree smiles as they talked in her room, moonlight streaming through the windows. Then, suddenly, she had nothing to remember him by, just her heartbreak to know it was real; her ruby bracelet had gone missing.

Of course, not much had changed in their time apart. He was the same charismatic soldier that could command or blend into any room he wanted. His eyes on the other hand... they belonged to a stranger.

Dropping the knife, she stepped out of the shadows. 'Damien,' she said surprised. 'What are you doing here?'

'I begged Roulet to let me come. I needed to see it for myself,' he answered.

Sabine flushed in shame and embarrassment. 'Right,' she said before stepping back, tugging her wrist out of his loose grip. She cleared her throat awkwardly. 'I... didn't expect to see you again,' she told him. 'I wasn't sure if you had returned to your post.'

'I did,' he said. 'I'm actually a commandant now, much to Roulet's pleasure.'

Sabine nodded, not sure what else to say. She could only reflect on the irony of them being in the exact positions they fought so hard against.

'You look beautiful,' Damien said stiffly.

Warmth gathered in Sabine's chest. It must have been hard for him to say. 'Thank you,' she answered. 'I have to admit I prefer this uniform. It suits you.'

Damien smirked before touching the bright red sash that hung across his chest, and Sabine laughed quietly. His expression sobered at the sound. 'Are you happy?'

Her smile left, and she looked at the ground. 'I am… satisfied,' she answered, her smile becoming strained. 'I made the correct choice.'

'Your mouth says as much.' He stepped closer to her, and she wondered if he would touch her, her nerves tingling in anticipation. At the last moment, he stepped around her. 'But your eyes do not,' he whispered.

Sabine's face fell as memories of the last few weeks flooded her mind, how bleak they were. She clenched her hands into fists and composed herself.

'Well, either way, it's no longer your concern,' she replied.

His jaw clenched at her statement, but his face stayed impassive. 'A martyr through and through,' he said passively.

She looked down so he couldn't see the regret that consumed her. Perhaps, it would be better to retire for the night. She opened her eyes and froze when she saw smoke rising from the estate.

'Damien,' she whispered, pointing behind him.

He turned, his gaze following the smoke above her, and pushed her back towards the party. 'Get out,' he commanded. 'I'll go in and evacuate the crowd.'

'Damien, no!'

'I won't go in,' he said. 'Don't worry and don't look back.'

She nodded, and he took off without another word. Sabine started towards the nearest gate but turned back, watching the flames rise and trickle down the hall. She suddenly remembered a key detail to tell Damien. Her father was inside in Roulet's study.

Panic surged through her as she watched the smoke rise higher. There were soldiers everywhere. She could grab one and maybe they would be able to get him out. It would be better for her to escape and wait... or maybe they would let him die.

I'm sorry, Damien.

She raced through the courtyard, up the stairs and through burning hallways to the study. He was the only family she had left. Despite all the rage and all the pain, she couldn't take a chance on her father's life.

–

By the time Damien reached the main estate, the guests had noticed the fire and were panicking. He didn't pay attention as he led more bewildered guests away from the fire, barking orders at the guards. Frantic, people rushed towards the exits, and he could only hope that Sabine had already left.

'You!' Damien spun around to see Kwame pushing his way through the crowd towards him.

'Where's Sabine?' Kwame shouted.

'She's here, probably in the back of the crowd. She was outside when the fire started,' Damien reassured him, trying not to look worried.

A guard with soot on his face raced towards the group. 'I checked the ballroom. Everyone has been escorted out.'

'Sabine!'

Damien's head snapped to Kwame's direction, expecting to see his ex-flame running towards her father. Instead, Kwame was staring at the house in horror. Damien followed his gaze and saw a glimpse of Sabine through the flames. His eyes widened in shock, trying to work out which room she was in. Why would she go to Roulet's study?

'I'm going inside for Sabine. If I don't make it back in an hour's time, head to General Roulet's home. Captain Cadieux will be in charge from there on out,' he ordered the guard.

Damien charged towards the house, the guards yelling for him to come back. He ignored them, the only thing on his mind, the woman he needed to save.

–

The light was blinding around Sabine. It consumed the room in a way one could call beautiful from afar. Inside, however, there was nothing but terror and relief. Relief that her father wasn't there. Terror knowing she wouldn't escape the fire.

She coughed through the smoke as flames climbed the walls. Flames licked at her ankles as she wove through the burning room, not enough air in her lungs to scream. The door wasn't consumed yet, but it was blocked on the other side by fallen decor. She tried to move the burning furniture out of the way, ignoring the hiss of skin.

She pushed at it desperately, resorting to kicking when it refused to budge. She wheezed as her chest burned, falling to the ground. Her body trembled from the overwhelming heat and lack of oxygen.

She slumped further until she lay on the ground and closed her eyes. It was ironic that the last few years of her life had been spent surrounded by people, only for her to be left alone in her dying moments. She blinked slowly when she heard something bang against the door.

'Sabine!' A familiar voice made its way through the roar of flames. She tried to sit up, but her head was swimming. The door rattled with force but didn't open. The banging and the screams became more desperate. 'Sabine! I'm coming, Sabine!'

She closed her eyes as the cries grew more and more desperate. It was a useless endeavour on her rescuer's end. He wouldn't have time to make it out of the flames now either, and she mourned at the thought.

He, the love of her life, didn't deserve to die this way.

'Damien…' she whispered.

Her fingers brushed the door. For a moment, her body felt suspended in time, a curtain of silence falling over her as images flickered between the flames. She saw glimpses of her father, the cold courtship between her and Lamont and the many nights she had spent silently crying. Yet, what she clung to most were her memories with Damien, stretching out like endless summer afternoons. It should have been a blip in her life and yet… if she had to do this all over again, living and failing just for a few more perfect, ill-timed moments, would she?

Yes, she answered silently.

She had no time to think whether or not she was foolish. She was too busy drowning in smoke.

–

'Sabine!' Damien shouted desperately against the door. He could just make out the sound of her coughing, which was the only thing that kept him beating against the door futilely.

It was the only thing he could do.

There was no way out, which he had realised on entering the house. The more sweat poured out of him, the more he realised he wouldn't survive. He could barely feel his hands anymore as the skin blistered under the relentless flames. It got harder and harder to move his arms. All he had left was the desperate need to break down the door so Sabine wouldn't die alone.

But he was unable to break it down.

Eventually, all he could do was slump against it, his energy dissipating as his vision swam. His mind screamed for him to keep fighting as the flames edged closer to his body, but he couldn't. Yet, something inside him raged futilely. He refused to believe this was the end, but the truth was unavoidable and all he could do was watch the fire consume him.

'Sabine…' he croaked desperately, smoke coating his throat as he took one last breath.

Chapter Nineteen

Washington, D.C.

August 2013

Dani jolted out of her sleep coughing, smoke searing her lungs. She caught her breath as she realised that, rather than a burning villa, she was in her bed. Hands shaking and heart thundering in her chest, her skin felt too tight. The sudden rush of memories spun in her head; she closed her eyes, taking several deep breaths.

It's not real, she told herself. *It's not real.*

Yet, she couldn't help but get out of bed to get some water to run over her hands. The cold stung her but it was much better than the feeling of her skin burning. Then she went to the kitchen and chugged ice-cold water until her stomach felt like it would burst, wishing she hadn't talked her friends out of renting the house that had a pool. She would've jumped right in.

Returning to her room, she grabbed her phone from the nightstand. It was two a.m. but Jones would answer. At this point, it was routine, waking up in the middle of the night, calling him, talking for an hour and then going back to sleep. He was probably expecting her call. Yet, she couldn't make herself press the call button. She didn't know what she would do if she heard his voice that held all the memories.

She closed her eyes as sobs wracked her chest. It was all true. The endings she avoided thinking about, the worst of her 'dreams', they really happened. She was going to die soon and Jones would, too. She pressed her face into her pillow to muffle the sound of her crying.

It was the beginning of the end.

–

Dani should have cancelled her counselling session. She wasn't fond of lying, but she was also not fond of being labelled crazy, as she knew she would be if she told the truth. She huffed and crossed her arms. She had forgotten her stress ball in her room, so she had nothing to distract herself from the current storm raging in her mind. She dug her nails into her palms, the stinging distracting her briefly from the helplessness, Sabine's death still fresh on her mind.

'How are we feeling today?'

'Fine,' Dani answered quickly, staring at the ceiling as if it would give her the answers she needed.

'Did your concert go well?'

'It went spectacularly,' Dani said sarcastically.

Ironically, the concert *did* go spectacularly well. Dr Carver had eagerly approached her afterwards, ready to give her another solo for the next performance as well as offering to help her with her resumé for the New York Philharmonic. She was officially a favourite student.

'And the dreams?'

'The same.'

'You seem tense today,' Dr Castillo observed. 'Things are tense,' Dani snipped.

'Like what?'

'I really don't feel like talking today,' she grumbled, crossing her arms childishly.

'Dani, could you look at me?'

She tilted her head to the side, just enough to make eye contact with the counsellor. Dr Castillo put her notepad on the table next to her and leaned forward, piquing her curiosity. The counsellor only did that when she was concerned. 'That was the third time I asked you that set of questions, and you answered it the exact same way every time. Did you notice that?'

'…No,' she answered truthfully.

Dr Castillo nodded slowly before sitting back again, her bracelet clinging as she intertwined her fingers.

'You've said in multiple sessions that you do not come here of your own volition. It's what your parents want out of concern for your mental state, but from what I can tell, you seem fine, Dani. Yes, you have very vivid, repetitive dreams. Yet, they don't affect your social life, your grades or your general outlook on life. However, your life is more than your dreams. So, if you want to discuss something, this is also a great space for that.'

Dani pressed her arms closer to her chest, holding herself tighter. She immediately remembered her conversation in the garden with Madame Roulet, telling her feelings in Fante and just being able to let it all out. Unfortunately, Dani was limited to English and the words were too heavy to hold.

'I'm developing a bad habit,' she said. 'I'm… I have feelings for someone I shouldn't.'

'And why shouldn't you have feelings for this person?' Dr Castillo asked.

'Because my life will end. As I know it,' Dani added quickly. She couldn't forget the space wasn't completely safe. She scratched her knee nervously as Dr Castillo stared at her sceptically.

'Is this person dangerous?'

'No. He—' *Died in a fire trying to save me.* She frowned, looking down at her lap. 'He would never put me in harm's way.'

'Does he have habits you're concerned about?'

'No.'

'Is he in a relationship?'

'No.'

'So, what makes you so sure that your life will "end as you know it"?'

'Because it's happened before. I've fallen in love with people, and it didn't work out and there were consequences for it.' The answer begged for further explanation, but Dani was already toeing the line and she didn't know how much more she could say without lying or creeping too close to the truth.

'And yet, all these... consequences led you here,' Dr Castillo pointed out. 'You have friends, hobbies and are actively pursuing your dream to be a musician—'

'Exactly! I love the life that I have right here, right now and don't want it to change,' Dani said, panic coating her voice. 'I feel like one day I'll wake up and have everything I want and then it'll be over. How am I supposed to reconcile with that?'

'I thought sleep and death were cousins.' Dani scowled at the therapist throwing her words back at her. The therapist held her hands up in surrender before leaning forward. 'What makes you so sure this one person will change everything?'

'He already has,' Dani admitted. 'I'm different around him. I'm changing and the more I change, the more I want to see him. I talk to him every day and it's not enough. I miss him in a way I've never missed anyone. Sometimes, it hurts to stay away from him.'

'Well, while there can be a concern around the intensity of your feelings, I think you just answered your own question,' Dr Castillo said. 'You've just admitted that he makes you feel different than all the ones before, right?'

'Yeah.'

'So, he's not the same as the other guys before him,' she continued.

'No. There are some distinct differences,' Dani said reluctantly.

'So, what's to say that things can't be different this time around? That you won't make the same mistakes. That the "ending" you see coming won't be for the better? More than likely, you're not the same person you were when you pursued those other relationships. So, instead of comparing him to the past, focus on the present. Maybe he is just as bad as the ones before or maybe he's exactly what you need. The real question is: are you willing to find out?'

Dani shifted uncomfortably on the couch. Logically, her therapist was right. Even now, she couldn't be sure since she only fully remembered one lifetime. From what she remembered, none of her other lifetimes had previous memories but there was no denying the pattern. So, now what? She looked at the clock that hung on the wall.

'Times up, doc,' Dani said. She grabbed her things and walked out, just as confused as she was before. Or perhaps there was no easy way to look at it. She had to choose between this love or life. And if she had to choose, the answer should be life, right?

Before she could process her own doubts, she felt a familiar twinge forming around her temple. She stumbled a couple of steps before she could catch herself. She gritted her teeth as she forced her vision to focus, realisation dawning on her.

She was already starting to remember another lifetime.

Tomorrow, she thought as she headed straight for her car. *I'll start figuring out everything tomorrow.*

–

'Bro, look at this. Someone did this for their history project last year.' Ross tapped Jones's shoulder, holding out his phone for him to see the video playing. Jones squinted at the screen before taking the phone.

A jolt went through him as he spotted Dani sitting in a living room, wearing a floor-length dress holding her cello. There was another Black girl, dark-skinned with straight hair formed into a fancy updo, sitting next to her in a Regency-era dress. Dani started playing Mozart as the girl calmly sipped tea for a few seconds. Then, another girl, also Black and dressed up, walked up behind the two and Dani transitioned to another song as the third girl started to dance behind the pair.

He smiled as he recognised the melody to a song he helped Jair with, reading the caption, 'When Black people enter the history chat.' He chuckled as he handed his friend the phone back. He remembered Dani mentioning that she was helping her friend with a video the last time they talked.

'Dope,' he said. 'I see Carver's protégé is as good as he says she is.'

'What?' Ross tapped the screen to replay the video. 'Oh, is that the girl he introduced to us? What's her name? Dina... Diane...'

'Dani,' Jones filled in, his smile becoming softer, but he schooled his expression as Ross looked up. He snapped and pointed at Jones.

'That's it! I'm surprised you remembered it.'

'What makes you say that?'

'Nigga, you barely remember my name half the time.'

He chuckled. 'She's fine. You're not.'

'And yet, here you are inviting me to a museum and not her,' Ross said as they walked through the doors of the Brooklyn Museum. Jones shrugged, trying to think about a smart comeback before he let himself mull over the fact it had been over a week since Dani had last called him. He wondered if she was still practising for her concert. Even then, it was still odd not to hear from her at all... 'Also, you know we can only be here for an hour before I have to go get ready.'

'I know the drill,' Jones reassured him.

The New York Philharmonic was performing that night, and they were forty minutes away from the theatre. Despite it being five hours before the concert started, Ross treated performances the same as he treated going to the airport: if he wasn't obscenely early, he was late. Luckily, the crowd was small that day and wouldn't take up too much time for Jones to visit the exhibit he wanted.

'Why did you want to see this again?' Ross asked.

'I'm researching something.'

'Researching what?'

'Something for a song,' Jones lied, his eyes scanning over the exhibition poster inside the museum.

There was a dramatic shot of an ancient harp-like instrument with the words 'Griots: Holders of Human Life and Legends' in bold typeface. Walking in, a hush fell over him. The room was dim with the majority of the light coming from spotlights that highlighted various African statues around the room. There were a few people gathered around the exhibit, murmuring among themselves.

'So, is this something for Jair?' Ross asked as he looked around the room. 'Gonna switch from bass to... a kora?' Ross read off a nearby display that held said instrument, a guitar of sorts that had a thin, notched bridge with many strings with a round base. 'Supposedly, it sounds like a Spanish guitar mixed with a harp.'

'Maybe I'll pick one up someday,' Jones said dryly as he walked around, looking at the statues, squinting at them closely to find the right one.

When he convinced Ross to take a detour to this exhibit, he had made it sound like a casual but confident request to see something cool that had caught his eye. He said they might as well see it together since Ross was in town and they, as musicians, should learn more about West African music.

While that was true enough, what he didn't tell Ross was that there was something in him that begged to go, simply from an exhibit advertisement with a picture of a terracotta figurine depicting an archer. It was almost the same feeling he had when he found a relic from his past lives, a bone-deep knowledge that he had held the object, knew of its origin and importance. There wasn't the same level of familiarity but something about it made it hard for Jones to ignore.

For a moment, he wondered if it was all in his head until he stepped in front of a glass case that held the figurine he saw online, accompanied by others like it. They were all soldiers, some standing tall, others on horseback. A tingling feeling sat on top of his skin, and he read the plaque, hoping for some clarity.

Inland Niger Delta artist. Djenné, Mopti Region, Mali.
Archer, soldier, and equestrian figures. 13th to 15th
century. Ceramic.

He grimaced at the spare information before looking through the glass. On the other side was a painting that had bright and bold colours, dominating the wall. It depicted a man in patterned and regal robes on the back of a decorated horse against a yellow background. It was so big and the colours were so vivid, Jones was surprised he missed it at all. It demanded Jones's attention. He approached it and noticed that there was a small stand in front of the artwork, holding a pair of black over-ear headphones with a button under it labelled: 'Press to Play'.

He put the headphones on and pushed the button. The sound of a xylophone-like instrument played for a few seconds before transitioning to a woman singing. He looked around for more information but didn't see a plaque. Instead, the lights shifted around the painting, words appearing on the wall below the frame.

'Listen carefully, for by my mouth, I shall tell you the story of Sundiata Kieta, son of the Buffalo, son of the Lion…'

Jones's eyes followed the words, reading along with the epic of the first king of Mali. After a couple of minutes, he could no longer resist the urge to close his eyes, giving fully over to the relaxing tone of the griot's soothing voice.

As soon as he did, his head went quiet, the griot's voice fading away. Slowly, the black behind his eyelids was replaced with the vision of a blue sky dotted with the occasional wispy cloud. Trees with skinny trunks and thick, vibrant green canopies blocked out parts of the sky, the ends of their branches dotted with spindly yellow flowers. *Babul trees*, his mind supplied, despite never having seen them before.

A moment later, he realised he was on the ground, surrounded by shrub grass, but no part of him felt the urge to get up. Whatever responsibilities the world burdened him with didn't exist and he could truly bask in it. The afternoon was perfect and unending, the breeze provided background music to the scene. That and the occasional sigh he heard from the person lying next to him because he was not alone.

In this life, he never would be.

Jones's eyes snapped open when he felt a hand land on his shoulder, jumping as though he were being jolted out of a dream. The headphones slipped off his ears and he caught them right before they hit the floor.

'Hey, you okay?' Ross asked, his eyes shining with concern. Jones blinked for a moment before remembering where he was.

'Yeah,' he said. 'Yeah, I'm… I was listening to the story and spaced out.' He held the headphones up to his ear and realised the audio ended. He slipped them back onto the stand, reading the words on the floor.

Just as blood is crucial to human survival, the griot is crucial to the survival of West African history and culture.

'What was the story?' Ross asked.

Jones searched his mind for the answer, but he remembered nothing beyond the first minute. One moment he had closed his eyes and the next, Ross was in front of him.

'It was about a king,' he said, still dazed.

'Hey, man, if you're having a bad day…'

'No,' Jones said quickly, even as he felt the telltale signs of a migraine forming. 'I'm fine.'

Ross's brows furrowed and, for once, he wished his friend didn't know so much about his health. 'You're sure?'

'I'm good.' He peaked at his phone, noticing the time. 'And we gotta go. It's been over an hour.'

The next day Jones sat on the floor of his apartment, fiddling with a Rubik's Cube as he finished his daily Sudoku on his phone. He leaned his head against his bed as he tossed the device aside.

He was still battling the migraine from the day before; even walking around his apartment was difficult. In that way, he was lucky he had nowhere to be and there was food prepped in his fridge. It was the small things that made his days easier. Despite his pounding head and wobbly steps, he made sure to complete his daily routine. After the puzzles, he ran through the scales on his piano before switching to guitar. If he felt well enough, he would practise a song or try composing.

Today was not one of those days. Today, all he wanted to do was lay down and let all his memories be as troublesome as they wanted. He contemplated his situation as he ran his fingers over the strings of his acoustic guitar, the soft sound resonating through the room.

He would like to believe he was a laid-back person. 'Live and let God' was his favourite motto growing up. He didn't hold grudges or stay down too long; he'd seen the consequences of that through enough lifetimes.

Now, however, he was getting worried. It felt like his grip on reality was loosening. More and more, he struggled to remember what needed to be done tomorrow or the next day, while his past lives were clearer than ever. Some days, he didn't know who he was waking up as. Just a few days ago, he was throwing punches as soon as he woke up, readying for a match that didn't exist. The day before, his head filled with details about a wedding dress and linens.

A shiver went through him, the chill of fear filling him. What would happen at the end of it all? Who would he be? What would he become? Would he lose himself to a different personality? At this point, what was he even fighting for?

Us.

He rubbed his forehead as his headache intensified. His first instinct was to make yet another doctor's appointment but that wouldn't help. He knew the symptoms and the timeline. If he were to keep up his habits, stay with his memory exercises and was just plain lucky, he would have at least another decade to live. The problem then became that, according to his past lives, he *wasn't* lucky. Two months ago, he wouldn't have been bothered by this but now there was a renewed sense of dread every time he thought about his early demise.

Suddenly, a long-forgotten melody crept into his mind. He frowned even as he pulled his guitar into his lap, unable to resist the urge. As soon as his fingers touched the strings, the music fell out of him, as if he had played the song yesterday instead of seven years ago after his diagnosis.

The piece was a swan song, an ode to a man lost long ago. Originally, he had written it for a summer music programme audition. In his essay, he had described it as a reminder to never give up, to go out fighting. The answer was cliché, but everyone loved it and the piece.

However, as he played the song now, he didn't think of fighting. Instead, what came to mind was the moment when he looked someone in the eye, and they gave him permission to give up.

The relief that came with it.

As if trying to physically push that thought out of his mind, he played harder and louder.

Yet, the memory remained.

Chapter Twenty

Sarah focused on breathing in and out. Despite the smoke in their air that made it feel like someone was trying to choke her, she breathed. She filled her lungs and relaxed, thankful there was another breath to take. She did so until another wave of pain shot through her side, knocking the air out of her. Gritting her teeth, she curled into herself.

Nineteen and her life was already over.

'Keep pressing,' the man, David Wright, barked.

Sarah huffed and pressed harder against her side. She gasped, shuddering as the pain radiated through her chest, but kept the wound covered half-heartedly. Slowly, she blinked as she watched him board up the window.

As if there weren't Zeppelins outside and people panicking every which way. As if they weren't in the middle of a war.

'A pointless one at that,' she mumbled. She felt herself drifting in and out of consciousness, David's thundering foot-steps bringing her back.

'I keep telling you to press on your wound,' he barked, putting his hand over hers and pressing roughly. She cried out. 'Get over it,' he said, looking around the room. 'I'll see if I can find a cloth.'

'It won't help,' she mumbled.

Ignoring her, he looked and continued his search. The previous residents had been away from home, long gone by the time she and David had scrambled inside after the raids. The cupboards and closet doors were open with suitcases nowhere in sight. She could even make out spots on the wall where pictures were missing. She rolled her eyes.

Who was taking pictures at the end of the world?

'You know, I always wanted to go to Paris, but I must say it's probably just like here. Half destroyed with smoke everywhere. If I close my eyes, I could be on a holiday,' she mused.

'Not funny.'

'I'm not even sure it still exists. Maybe all of Europe has finally burned down. Perhaps, all this will finally end…' She trailed off shivering, but it was difficult to tell if it was the cool, night air or the blood leaking through her fingers.

They had never stood a chance.

It had been the end of a typical day for her, heading home with a large bag of laundry. The sky was already dark, and she was readying herself for a full night of washing. She was walking as quickly as she could, arms crossed, shoulders stiff and eyes on the cobblestones so as to not attract any attention from any men leering nearby. She heard some murmuring but ignored it; some people still treated Black people like a carnival attraction. It was only when everyone stopped, the crowd's mumbling growing louder as they pointed towards the sky, that she realised something was out of the ordinary.

She looked up and froze as she spotted the cause for all the commotion. High above, lit up by a searchlight, was a German Zeppelin. It reminded her of a whale, massive, grey and silent as it slipped in and out of the clouds. She had heard of them from the papers but seeing one so close made her dumbstruck.

At least, until the bombs dropped.

The crowd erupted into chaos. People scattered every which way as the ground shook. The screams made her move, dropping the laundry bag as she tried to duck into an alleyway, when another load of bombs dropped. The blast sent her to her knees as the ground rumbled below her. Rocks and glass rained down and she cried out as a shard cut into her, burying itself into her side. She tried to stand but the pain was overwhelming. People started to step on her as they scrambled to get away. She was certain she was going to die in the middle of the street.

Then, a stranger pulled her up.

'Are you okay?' the man asked, propping her against the wall. She started to slide down, her knees weak. 'Hey! Talk to me! What's your name?'

'S–Sarah,' she answered, her throat dry.

'I'm David,' he told her. 'I'm going to help get you out.'

And she, who was usually wary of new people, took his hand.

'Focus on me,' David yelled, and Sarah's eyes shot open and she returned to the present as he roughly wrapped her abdomen. Under the grime and dirt, his expression was grim, maybe even concerned. That wasn't a good sign. 'Keep looking at me.'

'To think the English conquered the world just for this…' she said, futilely trying to push his hands away. He brushed them off as he tied a knot tight enough for her to wonder if that was how corsets felt.

'Just hang on,' David said. 'It'll be over soon.'

'We don't know that.'

'We'll figure it out.'

'No, we won't,' she argued tiredly.

'Shut up. We are *not* dying. I won't let us.'

That Sarah could believe.

David's determination was something she had never seen before. Between sewing her up across from a burning church and dragging her through the city for shelter, leading her out when the shelter started to flood, he had shown her a level of survival she could barely understand. The grit baffled her. Even as the bombs continued to shake the walls around them, he just kept moving on. At first, she respected it, trudging alongside him.

Now, hours later with her hastily sewn wound reopening from the constant moving, her head was pounding, the pain growing and she was tired of pretending to act hopeful. She'd had enough.

'You should stop helping me,' she said. 'Get to a real shelter.'

'We will. I just need to fix you first,' David insisted.

'Is that what you are? A fixer?' she asked, groaning as she shifted, agitating her wound. 'Why did you even help me?'

He looked at her incredulously, as if the answer were the most obvious thing in the world. 'You need it. Why not?'

'Ah,' she said. 'So, you're a hero.'

His eyes widened before he looked away, clearly uncomfortable with her description. She wondered if he did that a lot. He was comfortable showing his frustration in front of her, but from what she could see, every other emotion was off-limits. Meanwhile, she had only grown bolder as her despair did too.

She turned her gaze to the ceiling. 'It won't matter.'

'We'll find another shelter. We just need—'

'No,' Sarah cut off. 'It won't matter if you save me. Eventually, this horrible night will be forgotten, and everyone will move on like it never happened, as humans always do.'

'Don't say that,' he commanded, his voice dipping to a dangerous timbre.

She looked at him curiously. Was he patriotic? He didn't seem like the type, but she doubted she would have enough time to find out. 'It's true,' she said. 'Nothing is going to change.'

'After all of *this*,' he waved towards the window, 'it has to. Humans survive and adapt.'

She sighed, her lids feeling heavy as she continued to half-heartedly press her hand to her wound. 'Well, I don't want to anymore.'

'Fucking ungrateful,' he murmured. 'There are thousands of people out on the battlefields, trying to protect you! And—'

'And what?' she snapped, the anger she had suppressed all her life roaring up like a raging fire. 'They go back home with chests puffed out, "saving the world" like they always have. Then they go back to hating the same people they hated before while we scrape by, hoping that our children's children's children will finally be treated with decency. Finally, not a lamb for the slaughter? Well, you know what? It's tiring. It's exhausting existing just to prove a point or change something that doesn't want to be changed. Dying here, dying there – what does it matter? I'm sick of surviving a never-ending battle with the whole world *hating me*.'

David's face fell and a part of her felt a sick vindication that he knew she was right. After all, wasn't the world falling apart for that very reason? Yet, as quickly as the satisfaction came, it swiftly left. A looming dread replaced it as she watched David search for the right words. She frowned, wondering if she hit too much of a nerve. She may not have any hope of surviving, but she didn't want him to give up with her.

'Can't think of anything to say?' she asked, sarcasm laced in her tone but not in her eyes. *Fight with me*, she asked silently. *Keep going.*

David stared at her before taking a deep breath through his nose. Before he could open his mouth to argue, the familiar sound of explosions filled the air. He jumped, covering her body with his own as the ground shook again. Sarah looked at him, could tell from his wide eyes that he was thinking the same thing.

The bombs were getting closer.

–

David put a finger to his lips before creeping towards the back of the house. He looked out the window, trying to spot something moving in the night sky. It was hard since there was no moon to provide light. Still, he strained his eyes until he saw something slowly traveling across the sky, too small to be a cloud. He heard shouting down the street and ducked away from the window. He shuffled back to the dining room where he left Sarah. He wondered if he would come back to a corpse or not. Logically, this would be the best time to die. All she had to do was loosen the knot and drift off.

He felt a moment of panic, slowing his steps, hoping that she wouldn't leave him alone in this. War was hard enough already. He didn't want to think about having to hide in a house with the body of a girl he had tried to save. He peered at her, her back facing him. Luckily, he saw her body move with each pained breath she took.

David hurried, crouching by her side. 'It looks like the Zeppelin is a few streets over,' he said, nervousness slipping into his tone. 'The best we can do is try to shield ourselves—'

Another explosion shook the house and they both recoiled. Sarah wrapped her arms tightly around herself as David moved the wooden kitchen table, so it covered them. He heard her laugh weakly, when a shiver ran through her.

'I'm cold,' she said, surprised.

His eyes widened and he looked down at the bandage he had rewrapped around her abdomen earlier that night. It was soaked through with blood, meaning that the crude stitches he had sewn hadn't lasted. He pressed his hand to her wound and she didn't flinch. His breathing started to quicken as he looked around the bare kitchen. He couldn't see anything that would stop the bleeding.

So, it is the end.

'… You need to go.'

'What?' he asked. His eyes met hers, the electricity of all the things never said burning between them.

'If you're going to leave, then you need to go now.'

He knew she was right and that the window was only getting smaller. But leaving her alone, on the floor of a stranger's house… he couldn't make himself move to the door.

'I told you, we're in this together. I'm not leaving you by yourself,' he said, his determination winning out against his instinct to survive. Still, her eyes dimmed, glazing over as he made his choice. 'Then, lay next to me,' she said softly.

'Hold my hand until I go,' she pleaded, her voice quivering with all the tears it was too late to shed.

He shook his head, tearing his gaze from her, but she gripped the arm of his shirt. 'Stop—'

'David,' she cut off. 'I—I can't. I'm too tired.'

The silence after the explosion filled the space between them and he gritted his teeth before slipping from beneath the table and her grasp. He frantically opened the cabinets, looking for a sewing kit or cloth – anything that would help. When the kitchen came up empty, he ransacked the bedroom and bathroom but those were also bare. He covered his mouth, holding back a scream. The shouting outside continued, the words 'take cover' echoing as they travelled down the street.

His shoulders slumped in defeat. Time had run out. There was nothing left to do other than wait and pray. And he already knew where that would lead.

Heart heavy and tired, he went back to the table. He had only been gone a few minutes, but Sarah already looked smaller, curled up with tears falling out of her eyes. He took a shuddering breath, joining her on the ground, laying on his side. With his size, it was a bit awkward, but he managed and she shuffled closer until her knees touched his. He looked at her then and he could see the fear he felt in her eyes. She held out her hand. He took it, eyes lingering on their interlocked fingers.

'My little brother volunteered for the navy,' he confessed suddenly. 'He wanted to make me proud, get out and save the world. Every day, I prayed for hours that he would survive, that he would come back. He died in the first battle he went into. I know it's part of war but… part of me couldn't help but feel like this is God's answer. The reaper coming to harvest.'

He could still remember the way the wood dug into his knees every morning he prayed and when he'd collapsed from the news. One of his favourite people in the world, the person with a smile that he swore lit up the world, was gone and no war victory would bring him back. It had been his biggest heartache until that moment. Now, it took a back seat to lying next to a girl with a wounded heart like his that he wanted more than anything to save, knowing he failed her.

'I lost my brother, too,' she told him. 'Years ago. He moved to America, promised to pay for a ticket for me as soon as he could. One day, he was in the wrong place at the wrong time… I loved him more than anyone in this world. Even war was easier to swallow than losing him.'

'And now…' The last part of David's sentence was drowned out by the sound of another bomb exploding, practically on top of the house. His grip tightened around her hand, and Sarah nodded in understanding, another tear falling.

Now, he thought, *this would be the only legacy we have.*

Words left unsaid. Arguments never to be had. A connection forged in the darkest of days. The rare chance to not be alone in the end.

She pressed her forehead against his. 'Close your eyes,' she whispered. He did, holding on tight as a loud whistle pierced the air.

The light that followed was blinding until the building crumbled around them.

Chapter Twenty-One

September 2013

'We really appreciate your help, Stephen.'

'It's no problem, Ms Diane,' Jones replied.

The librarian smiled brightly, and, for a moment, it took him back to Atlanta. She reminded him of some of his aunties, her silk press dotted with grey though there were no wrinkles to be found and her smile was as warm as her mahogany skin. Though he hadn't talked to her much – the Tenley-Friendship Library being fairly new – there was already a level of comfort between them. Every time he visited, she would tell him about a new book, and he would tell her about a new album, going back and forth at the reference desk. Of course, when she asked him to host a music class over the autumn break, he immediately agreed.

'Well, it's not every day we have a world-class musician visiting. Oh, the kids are going to love you,' she gushed, making him feel a bit bashful. He was never good with praise. 'I have to get back to the front desk, but I will send you the details later this week, okay?'

'Okay.'

'Wonderful.' She patted his shoulder before walking off, throwing over her shoulder, 'And make sure you get a book before you leave!'

'No promises,' he teased, even as he headed to the stacks.

Jones explored the shelves with cursory glances and a slow gait. Occasionally, he would pick something up, but nothing caught his attention. It seemed to be a running theme for a while. He looked at his phone, checking his call log. He scrolled until he found Dani's last call, sighing and leaning on the shelf in defeat.

Dani hadn't contacted him in over a month. At first, he didn't panic. She was a grad student; of course, there was going to be a point where she fell off the face of the Earth. But the days stretched to two weeks, and he just called to check on her. He even sent a video, a remake of her friend's video, with a text saying, 'Copycats or a remix?' but there was silence. For a moment, he feared the worst – accidents happened everyday – but a quick Facebook search revealed she was fine. So, after the relief wore off, he was forced to realise the truth: she didn't want to talk to him.

He wished he could wonder why but it wasn't hard to guess. By now, she probably remembered the end of Sabine and Damien, possibly even David and Sarah's, stories. What did people say? Once is an accident, twice is a coincidence, three times would make it a pattern... And who the hell would want this kind of pattern?

He pushed off the shelf and continued to walk around the library. It was smart; it might hurt less when the inevitable happened. Still, it felt like his heart was turning to stone at the thought that it might be all over.

The universe, however, seemed to have another idea.

The moment he rounded the corner, time seemed to halt. He spotted Dani at a nearby table. He watched her pore over a pile of books. Her braids were piled on top of her head, pulled out of the way, showing off her cheekbones and full lips. She almost looked at peace were it not for her furrowed brows. He almost wondered if he should give her a few minutes to study, but she huffed, looking around. It didn't take her long to spot him. Her mouth formed an 'o' and Jones felt it would be too awkward not to walk over.

'Hey,' he said. His voice seemed to break her shock and she looked down quickly.

'Hi,' she said. 'I have to go.'

'What?' She didn't look as she grabbed her books, hastily getting up from the table. She didn't notice that she had left her coat on the back of her chair and he grabbed it. 'Dani, wait.'

She didn't turn to look at him, instead picking up her pace as she weaved between stacks and towards the exit. He jogged lightly to catch up to her. He expected her to stop at the front to checkout her books but she beelined for the doors. *What is she doing?* He hurried to catch up to her as the alarm went off.

'Dani, what are you doing?'

'I have to get away from you,' she said, still not looking at him.

'Why?'

'I can't be near you. We can't be close. It's a trigger,' she continued, walking towards the street.

'What are you talking about?' he asked, seeing a truck speeding down the street.

He dropped the jacket and ran as she stepped out. His heart jumped out his throat as he narrowly pulled her to safety, making her drop her books. He gripped her arms tightly, pinning her to his chest. They were both breathing heavily, hearts racing as the truck drove by, not slowing down for a second.

'Dani, stop! You could have gotten yourself killed,' he snapped, unable to hide his fear. If he had been even a few seconds late... he looked at her, seeing her eyes start to gleam.

'Then, I guess it'd be over. Like it's s–supposed to.' Her words gave into sobs. She gripped his shirt tightly, crying into his chest. The cries were ugly and desperate, the ones reserved for losing someone you couldn't imagine living without. He swallowed the lump that suddenly formed in his throat and held her close, wishing this wasn't their first hug. He could feel her leaning onto him more, her legs probably about to give out. He held her up, refusing to let her fall.

'It's okay.' It was probably the worst thing he could have said but it was all he had, all he could force himself to believe. 'It's going to be okay.'

–

Dani could barely look up from her lap as she waited for Jones to sort things out with the librarian. One of them had followed, after seeing her crying her eyes out. Jones had led her to a stone bench just outside the building, promising to be right back. She had thought about leaving but couldn't gather the strength to get up, much like Sarah. She placed her head in her hands at the thought.

She had researched for weeks but she couldn't find an answer. There was no rhyme or reason to why she was reincarnating, why she was only remembering now when she couldn't before, why she kept falling in love with the same person and why – oh, *why* – did it always end with both of them dying.

She tried listening to Dr Castillo, but everything pointed to their lives repeating. The only way she could think of solving it was by avoiding Jones. And now she almost killed herself trying to do so. She would laugh at the irony if she wasn't so exhausted. She heard footsteps approaching and she moved her hands to her lap. Jones sat down next to her, placing the books she was researching and her coat between them.

'Ms Diana told me to tell you that she likes the variety in your taste of books, just not your checkout method,' he said.

She huffed out a tired laugh, but it was half-hearted and fell flat.

'I'll remember that next time,' she told him. Her eyes softened as they landed on him. 'You have the same eyes.'

He raised his brows. 'As who?'

All of them, she wanted to say. He didn't look like any of their past lives but the look of care and longing in his eyes was one she had lived with for over a century. A prize possession she could only ever cherish temporarily.

'I'm trying to figure out what's happening to us,' she said instead. 'I keep looking but nothing's coming up. All I know is that the closer we get, the more likely it'll be that you'll die, or I'll die, and I can't figure out how to fix it.'

Her voice got wobbly at the end, and she bit the inside of her cheek to hold back her tears. She had been breaking down almost every other day. Every time she reached a dead end, she almost felt like she was dying all over again. It was too painful to bear, too hard to admit, when her friends or professors asked why she looked so tired or sad.

How did she tell them she was going to pass away because the universe or God decided she couldn't have life and love at the same time?

'The dreams started when I was a kid, maybe five-ish,' Jones said, suddenly. Dani scrunched her brows before she recalled their conversation in the McDonald's parking lot. 'Like I said, the memories triggered during freshman year. My first love broke up with me, and I had never felt heartache like it. I guess that pain made it all come back. At first, I thought the headaches I was getting for weeks afterwards were just me missing her, but one day, the veil lifted. I remembered everything all at once, all those memories crashing together, and I had no idea what belonged where.' He grimaced, staring off in the distance. 'Some days, I felt like I couldn't even get out of bed. I had to make one of my senior class projects about memory just so I would have an excuse to spend days mapping out the lifetimes, hoping that sorting it would make it make sense.'

'What's the first story you fully remembered?' she asked.

'Damien and Sabine and then the rest. I think it goes in order before getting chaotic.'

'What do you mean chaotic?'

'Sometimes it jumps to the first life, sometimes the fourth,' he clarified. 'It hasn't jumped to the future yet, so I think we're in the clear there.'

'How many lives do we have?' she asked warily.

'It's… hard to tell,' he admitted. 'From what I've calculated, we're in life five or six now.'

'And all the endings…' Dani looked at him expectantly and he felt the weight of every lifetime, every disappointment coming back; he shrugged helplessly. The feeling of defeat made her shoulders slump. 'We should stop seeing each other.'

'Considering I almost made you run into the street, I think that's fair,' he said, remorse colouring his tone and she immediately wanted to take it away.

'I ran because—'

'You were scared,' he filled in but she shook her head.

'Because I knew I would run to you,' she confessed. 'I would ruin all my plans because I missed you. I missed talking to you, laughing with you. My only foolproof plan and I wanted to throw it out the window the moment I saw you. *That* scared me.'

The implication hung in the air between them but neither seemed to know what to say. Yet, her skin was vibrating in anticipation as she realised that a barrier had just broken. It seemed the further she ran from him, the more they were drawn together. She should be devasted.

She was almost embarrassed by the amount of relief she felt.

'Try Mali,' he said suddenly. 'I went to see an exhibit on the griots and—'

'Wait. Don't tell me right now.' She watched his face fall at her interruption and licked her lips nervously. There was no turning back when she said, 'Tell me when I call tonight.'

Watching the smile stretch across his face was like watching the sun break through the clouds and for a moment, she foolishly thought it might be worth their impending doom.

Chapter Twenty-Two

'Focus! Focus!'

Demir's coach repeated the words so often, they echoed in his head even after his fists finished meeting the wall. His knuckles cried out in pain, but he was used to the burn. It greeted him like an old friend.

'Watch the hook!'

Demir shifted his footing so he could throw a left hook. His speed was good, but his power was superb – in his own opinion. Still, there was room for improvement, especially if he was going to enter bigger, better paying fights.

'Aye, watch it!'

He gritted his teeth as his hand hit the wall harder than he intended. Pain crackled up to his wrist, and he stepped back, cradling his hand.

'Fuck,' he groaned as he unravelled the tape. He cursed again, feeling the bruises beneath his dark skin beginning to form; he tried to bend his pinkie finger.

'Gonna blow your fucking hand out doing shit like that. I keep telling you, D, *focus*,' his coach, Jack, yelled as he walked over.

Out of instinct, Demir looked around to see if there were any peering eyes. The other boxers, scattered around the room, were minding their own business. They were used to the sight, he supposed, of the two of them. Demir, tall and Black with dark brown hair and eyes to match and Jack, a few inches shorter than him, white, blonde, Irish and loud as shit. The fact that they were both twenty-four made it even stranger, with Demir often getting mistaken for thirty while Jack's easy-going smile made him pass for barely twenty.

They were undeniably an odd pair. Most saw the arrangement as Jack, a budding boxer until he blew his knee, using Demir to fulfil his own dreams. Maybe there was some truth to that, but it didn't take away from the fact that he was a great coach most of the time.

Pain shot through his hand as Jack looked it over with a frown.

'Fuck, that's ugly.' He took a pack of cigarettes from his back pocket and pulled one out. 'You're lucky I got a new doc that costs less. Jimmy would've charged me out my ass for this shit.'

'I don't need a doctor,' Demir told him easily. 'Just need to snap it back. Worry about your blood pressure.'

'You *are* my blood pressure. And you doing reckless shit before our fight this weekend will fuck both of us.'

Demir shook his head at his coach, rewrapping his hand. He didn't need some street doctor telling him to pour some weird ass oil over it. 'You don't have to worry about this weekend. I'm fine now. I'll be fine by then.'

'You're damn right, because she's here already.'

'Who?' Jack stepped around him and headed for the stairs, a crescendo of catcalls beginning to rise as their guest descended the stairs.

So, he had heard right when the coach said 'she'. By his side was what Demir classified as the American Beauty: slim figure, curled hair and big, wide eyes. Her dark blue dress clung loyally to her curves; while sheer stockings kept her technically appropriate, she had a smile that was anything but shy. If it wasn't for her mocha-coloured skin and full lips, he was sure she would've been on every motion picture poster.

She walked arm in arm with Jack, talking animatedly while waving at the other boxers. Her wave may have been inviting but Jack's stare was not, so the other boxers stayed in their corners, even as their eyes lingered. Not that Demir could claim any differently; he couldn't look away either.

'The fuck is you doing, D?' Jack asked once the pair got close. 'Why are your wraps back on? Take them off so she can look at your hand.'

'I'm fine, miss,' Demir said politely as he stood. The woman raised her brow before taking the clutch purse from under her arm and tapping it on his knuckles. Demir hissed, snatching her bag.

She whistled. 'Impressive reflexes, but clearly, your hand is hurt, so if you don't mind...'

She held out her hand, and Demir gave the purse to her with a scowl. Tucking it under her arm again, she gestured towards his hand. He sighed and placed it in her palm. Undoing the wrappings with deft fingers, she gently turned his hand to assess the damage. Demir grimaced as she smiled at his crooked finger.

'Fascinating,' she commented. 'I've never seen this before.'

'A dislocated finger?' he questioned, looking at her sceptically. What kind of dainty dame did Jack bring in here?

'Hardly,' she said. 'I meant your knuckles. I've heard of this method of training but have never seen it in real life. You see, what you're doing is slowly fracturing the bones so they can heal and become denser. A knockout from you must really be something. As for the finger...'

Demir couldn't help the cry he let out as she pulled on the digit to snap it back in place.

'There.' Bright eyed, she ran her fingers over his hand. 'All done. Also, you can get the same effect hitting the bag. It'll hurt a lot less.'

She stepped back to Jack's side, arm sliding around his waist. A small stab of jealousy hit Demir as she rested her head on his shoulder, her demeanour calm. He couldn't remember if a woman had ever been so at ease in his arms.

'This will be fun,' she commented before grinning. 'My name is Selene.'

'Selene...' he said slowly. The name rang a bell, and he looked at Jack suspiciously. 'As in your girlfriend?'

Demir had heard about her plenty of times, usually over drinks. Jack tended to go back and forth between complaining about how she drove him crazy and lamenting over how much he loved her, driving Demir crazy, too. He never said anything on the subject as he had no opinion either way. His first and foremost rule was to stay out of business he wasn't a part of. However, he would have never imagined the girl that drove Jack so crazy was Black.

'More or less,' Jack smirked. Selene gasped, pinching his side. He winced before chuckling.

'It's nice to finally meet you, Demir,' she said. 'You better not forget my name since I'm the only one in here who likes fixing broken things.'

His jaw clenched. Now he understood. Her mouth was just as wild as Jack's.

'You'll get plenty of chances, Sel,' Jack reassured her, planting a quick kiss on her forehead before unwrapping himself from her embrace. 'Okay, playtime's over. Arms up, D. Ten more reps.'

A few hours later, Demir picked up his bag, ready to rest his sore body and glad he didn't have to train tomorrow. He was the last boxer in the gym – all the sane ones having left a couple of hours ago, ones that probably had something better to do or someone to go home to.

He shut off the lights in the locker room and walked over to the stairs. Selene was waiting nearby. Petty as it was, Demir hoped she smelled like sweat and it ruined her evening. She straightened as soon as she saw him.

'I hope I didn't offend you earlier.' He must have looked at her confused, because she continued. 'The broken thing. You seemed quite angry when I said it, but I'm a doctor, you see.

Well, training to become one. When I said broken, I meant something more technical.'

Demir looked her up and down. She was quite beautiful, he would never deny that, but Jack's personality was enough for him. He didn't need any more complications. He wanted to box, get paid, and go home. As long as he could do that, he was more than fine with forgetting her.

'I feel no ways about you.'

She seemed taken aback by his bluntness, but just as she opened her mouth to reply, he cut the lights and walked up the stairs. Selene huffed before following him outside where Jack was waiting for them both by his raggedy car.

'What took so long?'

'Lay off. You tortured me enough,' Demir said tiredly. Selene brushed past him, sashaying to the car and getting in without a word. Jack looked at her for a moment before turning to Demir. 'Need a ride?'

'My two feet look more reliable.'

'Saturday at eight,' Jack told him, climbing in after her. 'Don't be late or I'll come find you. You'll regret not taking the ride!'

'I doubt it,' Demir yelled over the roar of Jack's engine. He shook his head as the car lugged down the street, turning in the opposite direction. He tilted his head back to the sky, scanning it for stars, counting five before little prickles of pain ran up his arms.

He reached into his pocket for his cigarettes and matches, ready to light one when he studied the bandages Selene had wrapped tightly over his knuckles. It was much better work than he or Jack had ever done. Maybe Jack was onto something with this girl... he shook his head before pocketing the pack. This wasn't the time to think about that.

A few streets over, sirens wailed in the night, and Demir decided to jog the rest of the way home.

'Good job, babe,' Jack said as soon as they got back to his apartment, placing a kiss on her cheek as they sat down on the couch.

She turned on the radio, a lively jazz song playing. 'You mean I got the job,' she asked with a smirk.

Leaning over, he captured her lips. Selene sighed into the touch. This was her favourite time of the day, when it was almost over and there was nothing else to do but relax. They continued kissing for a few moments before Jack tiredly collapsed beside her. She giggled before wrapping her arm around him as he buried his face into her shoulder.

'You always had it,' he mumbled against her neck. 'Says the one that didn't want me going to the gym.'

''Cause I didn't need the dogs in there slobbering over you,' he said, pulling back enough so she could look him in the eye.

She raised her brow. 'And what makes you think D won't?'

Jack laughed, standing. 'I'd be shocked to death if he did. I've never seen him look at *any* girl with anything close to happiness. I've never seen him with a dame, not once.'

'You sure he just doesn't bring them around? He's handsome,' she yelled out as Jack headed to the kitchen.

'Hey, don't get any ideas, and no,' he said, making Selene giggle. He was always so easy to rile up.

'How do you know this guy again?' she asked, trying to recall how they'd met but nothing came to mind. Of course, she had heard about Jack's friend over the years, but it was always in passing. Selene had stopped going to Jack's fights after his first match; she couldn't handle the brutality. So, she'd never met 'D'.

One day, there had been a boxer Jack was excited to fight, then that same boxer was a friend at the gym, and then that friend wanted Jack as a coach, pulling him out of the dark place he had been trapped in after his knee injury.

For a while, she thought it was another woman, but Jack never changed the way her friends' boyfriends had when they cheated. There were no extra hang outs, hiding or sudden errands. He came home like he always did, and D was mentioned more and more.

Glad I can put that to bed, she thought, remembering the brooding boxer from earlier. If his glare from earlier was a sign, she wouldn't have to worry about him trying to get on her good side.

'I told you. He's the guy that broke my record,' Jack reminded her. Selene's eyes widened. 'The guy that knocked your jaw loose?'

'Same dude,' he said, sitting back down. 'Going 10-0 and he knocks me out within three rounds.' Jack sighed. 'Anyway, I ran into him at the gym a few weeks after I got back from deployment.'

Selene scowled at the mention of returning from war. It was the worst eleven months of her life, wondering if he was going to survive. He got shipped back early with a purple heart and a knee injury that ended Jack's boxing career before it started. Jack hated that he had to give up boxing but loved the sport too much to quit it completely.

'Turns out he didn't have a coach and was never called for deployment,' he continued. 'He'd go to fights and practise the moves he saw from memory. Demir's power is insane.'

'Wow.' She nudged Jack's shoulder. 'If he's so smart, why the hell does he need you?'

'Because while he brings the power, I bring the technique,' he smirked. 'As you know, I am a master of technique.'

'Oh, do I?' Selene said, holding back her laughter as Jack leaned over her. Just before he could kiss her again, a pressing question popped into her head. 'You sure you don't mind me being in your world?'

'I want you by my side, no matter where I am,' he reassured her. 'Do you mind being there? You didn't like it last time.'

'I hated it because *you* were getting hurt,' she told him, gripping the front of his shirt. 'As long as you're fine, I don't care about anyone else.' She pressed her lips to his. He rubbed the back of her neck, massaging it as he laid her down across the couch.

Any more thoughts of Jack's boxer and his glower left her mind gleefully.

Chapter Twenty-Three

Detroit

March 1946

Most people thought boxing was about the punch when really, it was all about the footwork. Where did the speed come from? Footwork. The power? Footwork. The balance? All footwork, and, though Selene would never admit it, Demir's was some of the best she had ever seen.

Even when his opponent, Zac 'Ironfist' Gibbs, threw a left-hook-upper-cut combo that sent him staggering back, he kept his rhythm. The roars from the crowd didn't seem to faze him as he pushed himself off the ropes, blocking the next punch. Zac swung left, and Demir veered right, tossing out a quick cross punch. The other boxer grunted and tried to hug him, but Demir pushed him off, punching the fighter twice in the ribs before throwing another hook.

The challenger fell to one knee, and Demir was sent to his corner as the referee jumped between them, checking on the competitor. Zac forced himself to stand, but Selene could tell by his limp arms and staggering feet, the guy was already done. He let out a yell as he threw a Hail Mary punch. Demir ducked and swung the final blow. His opponent went down, eyes closed, face bruised and mouth bleeding.

She winced while the modest crowd erupted, drowning out the referee's countdown. Demir only relaxed when the referee lifted his gloved hand in victory.

Selene clapped half-heartedly as Demir went to the back room before standing and grabbing the duffle bag at her feet. Wearing a pair of Jack's overalls from his job as a mechanic, with a white work shirt, hair tucked under a tan hat, she didn't stand out like she usually did, though most did a double take when they realised she was a girl. That's also how Demir's opponent reacted when she approached where he sat on the sidelines.

'Damn, I'm seeing things,' Zac slurred around his busted lip, a guy dabbing at it.

'Not really,' Selene said as she took off her hat and sat down. Someone gripped her arm, and she put her hand in her pocket, wrapping it around the hilt of her pocketknife.

'What are you doing?' the coach hollered.

'I'm about to patch your guy up,' she said. 'Or do you want to pay this dummy who's only putting Band-Aids on him?' Selene heard a scoff and mumble behind her but kept her eyes on the coach. The man's scowl deepened, but, after a moment, he let her arm go.

'Move, Ralph.'

Selene let out a breath of relief, releasing the knife in her pocket as the coach and Ralph argued back and forth. She turned her attention to the boxer, carefully placing her hands on his face.

'All right, let's have a look.'

Twenty minutes later she was tucking a few bills into the bottom of her bag as she headed into the locker room. Jack stood over Demir counting money while the boxer subtly cradled his side.

'That was one hell of a fight,' Jack complimented, sitting next to Demir. 'Keep it up and we'll move up to the big money in no time.'

'I'll say,' Selene said, grabbing their attention. Demir's jaw tightened as she stepped in front of him, looking her over with a grimace. When his eyes landed back on her face, she was pursing her lips. 'What,' she asked. 'You thought I would risk my good clothes down here?' She smirked, turning to her boyfriend. 'Although I could get a smaller size. Think one of your tinier work friends could lend me a pair, Jack?'

'Hey, don't be getting ideas about going down to my job,' he told her as she placed her bag on the ground, rifling through it. 'I'll find you a pair. And you're late.'

'Had to finish something. Always so bossy,' she murmured, pulling out bandages and tape alongside bags of ice she had gotten from the shitty bar next door. Demir was still glaring at her when she looked up. She shoved the ice on his face, and he hissed.

'Watch it,' he grunted, snatching the bag from her hand. 'Haven't you heard of bedside manners? Shit.'

'You can take it,' she snipped, grabbing his wrist to lift the ice from his face and gently prodding around his eye. 'Nothing but a bruise, although he got you good here.'

She tapped the left side of his face, just under the cut on his cheek that stretched to the bridge of his nose. Searching her bag, she pulled out a bottle of rubbing alcohol she had snagged from home and dabbed the wound. When it was clean, she carefully covered it with a bandage, Demir so still, he was barely breathing.

'Not too bad,' she reported, checking his ribs. 'Your right rib is bruised some but nothing serious. You'll be fine. Make sure to move around tomorrow or you'll regret it the next time you practise. And take this.' She took out an unlabelled bottle filled with brown liquor from her bag she had gotten earlier that night. 'As needed.'

'How the hell did you get Sam to give you some whisky?' Jack asked incredulously.

Selene smirked at his reaction. Sam tended to be stingy with his best stuff.

'Three bucks and I promised I'd take a shot with him,' she said. 'He thought I was a lightweight, like one of his other girlies.'

'You need to stop hanging around creepy men.' Jack took out a cigarette, jealousy colouring his tone. It sent a thrill under Selene's skin.

'You hang around creepy men, and I'm hanging around you,' she replied before standing. She kissed his cheek. 'It's inevitable, Jack.' He followed her, wrapping an arm around her waist.

'You just like trouble,' he murmured. She laughed as he leaned in. Before they could kiss, Demir cleared his throat. Jack rolled his eyes but stopped.

'The champ is ready to chug this and pass out,' he announced. 'Let's get the fuck out of here.'

Selene frowned at him. 'You really know how to kill a party,' she sighed before gathering her things.

'Relax, sweetheart. Demir here is all about business. Here's the money for tonight for you.' He handed Demir some bills before holding out a few to Selene. She narrowed her eyes at it. 'And you.' She ignored the eager look in Jack's eyes and waved her hand towards Demir.

'Give it to the champ,' Selene said lightly. 'I patched up our opponent before coming in here. D did a number on him, and I got a pretty penny for it, so…' She winked at Demir, trying to add some playfulness to the moment. 'Keep winning.'

'Come on. You're gonna need it for something,' Jack insisted. 'Like a new dress or makeup or whatever shit women get.'

Selene gritted her teeth. She hated it when he got like this, always trying to give her stuff under the excuse of her 'needing' it. She wasn't a charity case. 'I told you I got my money already.'

'Ain't no way those dudes are giving you this much. Don't be so stub—'

Demir snatched the money from Jack's hand. 'Hey!'

'She didn't throw a punch and got to play doctor. I say we're even,' he said tiredly.

Jack opened his mouth, and Demir gave him a steely look, squaring his shoulders. Even bruised up, he could knock Jack clean out if he had to. Everyone in the room knew that.

Jack's face reddened. 'Let's go already,' he gritted out, ego bruised as he stomped outside.

Selene stayed behind while Demir slowly counted the money he'd earned, ignoring her completely. She couldn't think of anything to say. After another moment of quiet, she slipped out and caught up to Jack.

'Don't ever do that,' he demanded when she slid into the car.

'Then, stop pushing money on me,' she shot back. 'You know I hate when you do that.'

'You go on and on about people treating you fairly. I give you money for your work and you have an issue. You're always doing this. Always looking for all these other people to treat you right but got an issue when *I* do it...'

Selene tuned him out but made sure to respond every now and then. She knew it was better to let Jack vent. He would calm down later, and they could *actually* talk then; they were similar that way.

In the meantime, she contemplated how grateful she was that Demir had decided to be selfish.

—

'She's more stubborn than a mule and twice the headache,' Jack declared. 'Pass me the wrench, will you?'

Demir handed it over, looking around the garage for a moment. He heard the other grease-covered workers shouting, their backs bent and faces dog-tired, and Demir was glad he didn't have to do work like this. He would gladly take a fight over fixing engines in a hot garage any day. Honestly, it was surprising Jack still worked here.

'Sometimes, you can't beat an honest living,' he'd told him once.

Demir wouldn't know much about that, and he highly doubted he wanted to.

'You wanted Selene around,' Demir reminded him lazily. 'Should've known it would be too much to work with her.'

'You don't get it, D.' Jack wiped off his fingers, eyes suddenly dazed. 'She's not one of those ditzy chicks. She's not just going to school to find a husband, you know. She wants to do something, which is crazy as hell to me but—' He shrugged. 'I'm crazy, too.'

'I don't get you two,' Demir confessed. 'You argue like cats and dogs, and she flirts with every guy walking around when she's with you. Seems like she's here for more than just a favour.'

'Hey, calm down with all that all right?' Jack lifted his wrench, and Demir held up his hands in surrender. 'Look, I know it doesn't look like we're going steady but she's different, D.'

'Of course, she is,' Demir said. 'She looks more like me than you.'

Jack shook his head. 'Not just that. We make sense together even if the whole world doesn't know it yet.' He looked at Demir with renewed confidence. 'That's why when we get enough money, we're all going to New York. I heard it's wild out there and that's just what we all need. We can go and have more than this shit. Me and Selene... we're soulmates, you know. She sees the ugly in me. I see the crazy in her and we just make sense together. No one gets me like her. You ever feel that, D?'

Demir thought back about the brief moments when there was a body next to his, but that's all he could recall. Bodies, bright red lips, and disappointed eyes when he wouldn't give more. Everything was always so fleeting... his mind shot back to Selene leaning her head on Jack's shoulder, her smirk softening into a smile. 'No,' he answered. 'Nor do I care to.'

'I know.' Jack smirked. 'You are an island, my friend, and not even the prettiest dame is allowed on shore.'

Maybe not. But he liked the image of himself on a lush island, somewhere no one could find him. Yet, he couldn't shake the image of a sailboat miles away, always floating in sight, a moment away from drifting closer.

Chapter Twenty-Four

Detroit

April 1946

Demir never knew why he woke up before sunrise. He just knew that no matter how little sleep he got during the night, he was always awake just as the sky turned red, signalling the start of a new day. It was also the only time he felt comfortable smoking.

He had grown up with his aunt, a woman with a warm heart but high standards. She always hated the smell of cigarettes, forcing his uncle to smoke outside. Demir had picked up the habit when he was fourteen but didn't have much time for it between work, running around with his friends, and the fights he would get into. So, he took to doing it in the morning, when the world was still asleep, just for something to do, and carried it to adulthood.

His apartment was nothing nice. It was a small, one room studio that held the kitchen, his bed, and there was a toilet down the hall, but it was good enough. He didn't need much, just a space to call his own. The one good thing about it was the fire escape. It was the only place he could just breathe and take in the day.

It was his favourite tradition.

–

Demir was cooking eggs on the stove when someone banged on his door. He never had company in the morning. Cautious, he stepped out of the kitchen and grabbed his bat on the way.

'Who is it?'

'D, it's Jack.'

Demir rolled his eyes and unlocked the bolt. 'It's open,' he yelled over his shoulder.

'I need a favour,' Jack said as he came in, eyes landing on the bat as he stepped into the kitchen. 'Put the damn bat away! You're not gonna hurt anybody.'

'I might hurt you for disturbing my peace for a favour I probably won't like.'

'That's why I need you to put the bat down 'cause I know you won't.' Demir narrowed his eyes at him. 'What are you getting at?'

'I swear I wouldn't ask if I didn't have to. I know you and Selene aren't close, but I need you to do this for me.'

This was truly an understatement. It had only been a couple of weeks but Selene and Demir had already had a routine of bickering before ignoring each other before going back at it. It was almost like her and Jack's relationship but without the affection and twice the animosity.

Demir stared at Jack for a solid minute, unnerving the fidgeting man. 'Double my money next fight.'

'What? You don't even know the favour yet! I don't have that kind of cash lying around.'

'Then promote so you can get it,' he replied. 'That girl is a pain in my ass, so if I have to deal with her, I want it to be worth it.'

'Fine, okay. Fuck, I don't have time to argue with you,' Jack said quickly. 'I'm already late. I need you to pick her up at two. She's taking classes at Wayne State University. Ask anyone on campus, and they'll tell you where it is.'

'Wait, you've picked up Selene from Wayne State without any problem?'

'In the beginning they gave us hell, but now no one bats an eye. They think she works for me,' Jack told him as he dug around his pocket. He dropped his keys and a piece of paper on the kitchen counter. 'She's yours for the day. Call that number when you've picked her up. I gotta go. Thanks!'

Jack was out the door before Demir could say anything else.

He shook his head. 'Damn it,' he muttered, ignoring the keys in favour of his breakfast. Scarfing down his eggs with a scowl, Demir pushed the empty plate aside. It was tempting to go back outside for another smoke, but he decided against it. He had things to do today, especially now that his afternoon would be full. He tapped his fingers on the table while staring at Jack's keys.

Old man Eddie was always trying to pass him some work, something he could do until he picked up Selene, and the pay was decent. The man hardly cared when Demir showed up; he was just ecstatic he had an extra set of hands for his bar. With that thought, Demir got ready to leave.

He would never admit the small thrill he felt sitting in the driver's seat of Jack's car, watching the world around him moving faster than it normally did. That was a piece of happiness he would keep for himself.

–

There was only one feeling Selene had when she saw Demir waiting for her outside of her school, leaning on the hood of Jack's car: horror.

She rushed down the school stairs over to him. 'What are you doing here?' she hissed. 'Where the hell is Jack?'

'He asked me to pick you up today. He's got something to do.'

'Do what?' she demanded. What was so important that he wouldn't tell her this morning before he left?

'I don't know. Didn't care to say,' Demir replied, dismissing her as he stood. Her hands balled into fists at the attitude. She couldn't stand this man. 'You gonna get in the car?'

She looked over her shoulder as more students walked their way and she could already imagine the rumours that would start if they saw her with Demir. She could take the taunts of going 'back to black', but she didn't need them connecting the dots to her side hustle. Placing her hand on his arm, she pushed him towards the driver's side. 'You first.'

Demir looked at her hands on his arm, barely budging. She groaned. 'Hurry up, will you?'

He grabbed her wrists and tossed them aside, unhurriedly getting in the car while she stared at him offended. Regaining her composure, she ducked inside, hiding her face from her gawking classmates and slumping down in her seat until they were far from the campus, barely holding back a grumble.

Class was going to be hell tomorrow. 'Where does Jack usually drop you off?'

'Oh, he didn't bother telling you my *whole* schedule?' she snipped. Brows furrowed, he pulled over and parked.

A nervous jolt went through Selene. 'What are you doing?'

'I'm not riding around in circles all afternoon because you have an attitude. I can find other things to do so…' He reached across her and opened the door, leaning back in his seat as Selene gawked at him.

'You can't be serious,' she said. 'We barely got off the campus!'

'Not my problem. You got two feet. Do what you used to do before Jack came along.'

She glared, staring him down but he didn't budge. He didn't have much patience for her on a regular day, much less when they were two feet apart. Granted, she didn't have much for him either but, thanks to Jack, they were stuck together for the rest of the day.

Reluctantly, she closed the door.

'Jack usually takes me to his place,' she answered. 'That or the garage. Lately, he's been taking me to the gym.'

'And your house?'

'Not an option,' she said, being careful not to be too snippy with him. He still might kick her out.

'I'll take you to the gym,' he decided, turning the car back on.

Neither of them spoke the rest of the ride, nor did they utter a word as they entered the gym. Demir set his practice bag in his usual corner and got to work. Crossing her arms, she sat on the stool in the corner of the room and looked around, noticing an office in the corner.

'I'll be right back.' Demir nodded as she walked to the office. She knocked on the open door and the manager looked up from his desk as she put on her sweetest smile, cocking her hip out just enough. As expected, his eyes trailed down her curves.

Like clockwork, she thought, clearing her throat to bring his attention back to her face. 'Do you have a phone?' she asked with a playful smirk.

'Y—Yeah back here,' he stuttered, pointing to the table behind him.

'Thanks, sugar.' Walking past him, she made sure to keep the smile as she dialled the garage. She did her best to ignore the stare as the phone rang. Finally, someone answered, 'Hello?'

'Is this Jack?' Selene asked sweetly. 'Yeah, who's this?'

'Your wife, sweetheart,' she said, an edge appearing in her voice, and she felt the manager's eyes finally leave her.

'Oh, Sel! Hey, I'm super busy, but I'll be there in a couple of hours — wait, where are you?' he asked quickly.

'The gym,' she said. 'But Jack—'

'Cool. Just do some homework or something til I get there. Love you.'

The line went dead, and Selene gripped the receiver, the urge to scream on the tip of her tongue.

Don't lose it, she told herself.

'I love you, too,' she said to no one, hanging up the receiver. The manager was staring down at his ledger. Selene rolled her eyes and left. She returned to her seat, pulling out a textbook from her bag.

'You okay?' Demir asked suddenly.

Selene swallowed before looking at him. 'Fine,' she answered nonchalantly as she opened the book.

'Where's Jack?'

'He said he'll be here in a few hours.'

'That's it?'

'Yep,' she said through gritted teeth. Pulling out a pencil and notebook, she started studying. A moment later, Demir went back to practising.

Eventually, she felt herself start to relax, the rhythmic sound of fists hitting the punching bag steadying her. It felt like they were in their own separate worlds as she focused on anatomy, getting lost in her notes. She didn't look up again until she heard someone rushing down the stairs.

Jack was practically gasping as he approached them, the barest hint of a limp showing as his knee became agitated. Usually, this would stop Selene cold, but today she didn't care. Before either man could even greet the other, she slammed her book closed and stood.

'Where were you?' she demanded.

Jack barely looked at her. 'Don't worry, Sel,' he dismissed before stepping around her. 'Nice form, D. Just be careful when you switch your feet. You looked off-centre.'

'What's off-centre is your head,' she snapped, blocking his path and crossing her arms. Jack stared at her in shock before looking around. Luckily, most of the boxers had gone home or this would have been a spectacle. Not that she really cared. When wasn't she putting on a show?

'I don't do well with being ignored, Jack,' she said. 'Where were you today? You always tell me if you're not picking me up.'

'I was taking care of some business,' he told her. 'Why are you upset? I got you a ride!'

'I don't want *him* coming up to my school!' She pointed to Demir sharply. 'He looks like a street rat. I can tell my classmates that you pick me up as a favour for your boss but how do I explain *him*?'

'Why are you explaining anything? Everyone knows about us.' Jack ran his fingers through his hair in frustration. 'Just let them think whatever.'

'I can't,' Selene yelled. 'If I arrive with you, it looks like I have a job. I arrive with him and suddenly everyone's wondering what the hell I'm up to. If they find out what I'm doing, they'll kick me out.'

'No, they won't. They have no reason to!'

'I'm practising medicine without a license, something the professors don't approve of. If they find out I'm "helping" you, I'm screwed!'

'Well, maybe if you stopped making a fucking scene and just shut up, you wouldn't draw so much damn attention,' Jack barked. 'Fuck being a doctor. Your ass should try Broadway with all these goddamn dramatics.'

'*I'm* dramatic?' Selene sneered. 'When they kick me out for this, I don't even want to imagine the shit show you'd put on "on my behalf"!'

'You need to fucking calm down,' Jack said in a low voice. 'I don't need you doing this every time he gives you a ride or we *will* get caught.'

Selene glared, catching Demir's gaze. A similar look of confusion lingered in his eyes. 'The hell do you mean every time?'

Jack sighed, pinching the bridge of his nose.

'Well, I wasn't sure until you left for class,' Jack said. 'But I got a gig at another garage. It's for a few days a week on the other side of the city. It pays better than Moe's but their schedule's different, which means I can't pick you up. I've worked it out with a co-worker that I can catch a ride with him but D's gonna have to pick you up from now on.'

'What?' Demir asked the same time Selene said, 'No.'

'I second that. I'm not dealing with her childish ass every day.'

Selene scowled at him. 'This "child" is getting a degree while you're fighting lowlifes in a basement,' she snapped.

'Okay, enough!' Jack declared. 'Look, this isn't easy but with this garage, I get better connections. Better connections equal better fights and better pay, all right? I'm just asking you both to *work with me!*' Jack gestured between them. The pair looked at each other sceptically. 'D, we'll split it seventy-thirty from now on if you do this.'

There was an instant shift in Demir's face, and her jaw dropped. And to think they had been on the same page for once. Why had she thought he could be useful?

'Fine,' he agreed reluctantly.

'Not fine. The answer is still no,' Selene said. 'I mean it, Jack. I'd rather walk—'

He suddenly grabbed her arm, pulling her into his chest. 'Stop being a brat and take the favour,' he ordered through his teeth.

She tensed and, for a moment, wished she could reach the blade in her bag. A second later, Jack's eyes cleared, and he loosened his grip. She snatched her arm back and turned away from him, rubbing her forearm as she sat, not looking at anyone.

'Okay, D,' Jack said. 'Let's go through the combos one more time.'

Selene pulled her book back onto her lap, but she could no longer concentrate. Her arm throbbed, and she jumped at the sound of every hit. Each strike brought memories she wished she could forget.

When practice was over, she practically jumped from her seat, not waiting for Jack before heading to the car. She stared straight ahead as Jack got in. They said nothing as they drove home. Jack tried to pull her into conversation with some inane comment, but Selene didn't budge. She was still concentrating on keeping her hands still. Jack didn't say anything of consequence until they parked in front of the apartment.

'I know you and D don't get along,' he started. 'But I promise it's all for the best. I need you to trust me on this.'

It was ironic how she had to hold back the urge to slap him. Trust him? After what he did? He touched her arm, and she flinched.

'I'm sorry for grabbing you like that,' he said finally. 'You know I hate that.'

'I know.'

'My daddy—'

'I'm not like him. You know I'm not,' Jack jumped in.

'But a lot of men can be, you know that,' she said, voice wobbling as she finally looked at him. His face fell, and she knew they were both thinking of their fathers. 'You went to war, too. You could be like that…'

'Okay, okay. Hands off from now on. I got it,' he told her. 'I'm sorry, Sel.'

Despite the anger coursing through her – or maybe because it – Selene's eyes welled with tears, and she pulled back so she could wipe them away. She refused to fall apart. She refused to show any weakness, as if he could apologise his way into her good graces.

'You better prove it,' she said. He nodded with remorseful eyes. He took her hand as gently as possible and kissed the back of it.

'I'll do whatever it takes. You mean everything to me,' he vowed. Guilt practically radiated off him and she let herself relax into his touch. Jack pulled her into his arms, whispering 'Sorry' over and over until she believed him.

Chapter Twenty-Five

Detroit

May 1946

'Good fight, tonight,' a passer-by told Demir as the boxer relaxed in a booth.

The club Jack had taken him to was loud and energetic, a stark contrast to his current exhaustion. Still, he accepted the shot placed in front of him and threw it back easily. Glancing around the booth, he saw Jack talking to the owner on the other side of it, both on the literal edge of their seats. A girl leaned her head on the owner's arm, winking at Demir when she caught his eye. He gave her a small nod before looking out over the crowd.

A singer crooned enthusiastically on a small stage as a band boomed behind her. People danced and twisted around each other while servers weaved through them. It took a minute, but he eventually spotted Selene on the side, dancing in the middle of the floor with a group of girls. He wasn't sure if they were her friends or people she met here; she had a knack for connecting with strangers. He seemed to be the only exception.

'And my guy, D, here.' Jack slapped Demir's shoulder, and he held back a hiss, cutting his eyes at Jack. 'He's gonna be the next Jack Johnson. Tell me one other guy that has moves like him! Just one!'

'Calm down, Jack. He's a good fighter, I'll give you that,' the owner, Mackie, admitted. 'But a sponsorship? You're asking me for money I don't have.'

'Whoa, whoa,' Jack raised his hands. 'Not at all. Hell, with all the attention D's getting, people will be filling up your club just to see him. After every fight there will be an after party here. It's a win–win.'

'The crowd doesn't give a damn about an amateur,' Mackie reasoned. 'Look, he becomes pro, I'll consider it, but right now, it's a no.' He slid out of the booth. 'Drinks on me tonight, boys. Nora, keep the fighter company, will you?' The owner winked at the girl, and she grinned.

Jack watched Mackie leave and cursed under his breath. 'This is bullshit,' he declared. 'I'm getting us a bottle. He wants to ignore us, he can enjoy paying my tab.' Jack stomped to the bar and Demir leaned his head back, closing his eyes.

When were they going to leave?

His eyes snapped open when he felt a hand on his arm, closely followed by the scent of cigar smoke and sweet perfume.

'Don't mind them,' Nora told him, much closer than before. 'Let them have their business while we celebrate your night.'

He chuckled. 'Didn't take you for the type that likes bruises,' he teased lazily.

Nora gently touched his cheek. 'Adds to the charm,' she flirted before leaning in and kissing his neck.

Demir hummed at the touch, enjoying how soft she felt against his skin. He turned his head, and her lips met his, resting his hand on her hip as Nora let him take control, slowly moving his hand down. He didn't realise how short her dress was until his hand met bare skin, giving him the opportunity to grip her thigh. Not that she seemed to mind by the way she wrapped her arm around his neck.

There was a loud knock on the table, and someone obnoxiously cleared their throat. Demir pulled away abruptly.

'What?' he grumbled.

Selene stood at the edge of the table and gave him a cheeky wave. 'Hate to break up the party,' she said. 'But Jack is outside with the car.'

'We're fine here, sugar,' Nora answered for Demir.

Selene looked at her in surprise. 'Oh, so you'll give him a ride?'

Nora smirked. 'One he'll never forget.' She winked and Selene's eyes widened in shock. As much as she used her sex appeal, he was surprised she was taken aback by the innuendo.

'Doubt it,' she said steadily, returning her attention to Demir. 'Stay or leave. I don't care. I'm just letting you know we'll be gone in a few minutes.'

As Selene walked up the stairs, Demir contemplated his options. He could walk or wait to catch an early morning train. However, he was farther from home than usual and the thought of being in bed in the next hour was too tempting. He sighed. 'I should go.'

Nora's mouth formed a pout, and he kissed it quickly, moving to leave. She caught his collar and reeled him back in. She gave him an intense but too-short kiss, pulling away slowly, her lipstick smudged and tantalising.

'I'll be here tomorrow,' she said. 'Come pick me up.'

He smirked before pressing a goodbye kiss to her cheek. 'I'll see you soon,' he told her and slid out the booth. He exited the club to see Selene leaning against the car as Jack ranted. She looked as tired as he felt.

'And he was this close— D! There you are,' Jack said when he spotted the boxer. 'What took you so long?'

'Nora,' Selene answered matter-of-factly as she dug into her purse and pulled out a handkerchief, holding it out to him. 'You should wipe off the lipstick.'

'Wait, he was busy with a girl, and you interrupted him?' Jack asked Selene incredulously.

'We were leaving,' she defended.

'Fuck that. You see me caught up with a girl, leave me,' Jack chuckled, but it quickly died when he saw Selene's scowl. 'By a girl, I meant you, Sel. You know that.' She pushed off the car and walked to the other side, climbing in the passenger seat. 'Sel, come on. Sel!'

'It's late,' she told him before slamming the door shut.

Jack growled in frustration but followed her as Demir slid into the back seat, leaning his head against the window. His eyes started to close, and the last thing he saw before dozing off was Jack reaching out for Selene's hand.

She kept them in her lap.

–

Demir was weeks into picking up Selene and the routine was mundane at this point. He worked out while she studied. He fought; she patched him up. She went home with Jack. He met up with Nora. There were no complaints, no more fights, and overall, very little conversation, which both sides were content with. Now the only tension left was the only person that tied them together: Jack.

Every day, Jack worked at a garage till dark, calling everyone he could to set up matches, coaching and negotiating before and after every match for a place where Demir could regularly fight. It was good work but gruelling for everyone.

Especially as Jack's temper got worse.

'You have to make it stronger,' he yelled for the umpteenth time.

Selene watched Demir snarl before loosening his gloves with his teeth, throwing them on the ground and spinning to Jack. 'What are you talking about? I know what I'm fucking doing,' the boxer yelled. 'There's no making it stronger! I make it "stronger", I leave myself open.'

'You make it stronger, we get one less round and extra cash,' Jack snapped back. 'Look, everyone knows you're a fighter and a damn good one! You get in there with the best of the best around here, but it's not enough. You heard what Mackie said. We need to get you to go pro now!'

'Well, I can't go pro anytime soon, not until the Golden Glove tournament in March,' Demir told him.

'Yeah, if we can scrape by until then,' Jack said.

Selene grimaced as she remembered her and Jack pulling money together for the gas bill that morning. It had been tight, but Selene had reached into her emergency fund to cover the last few dollars. She had claimed that it was from some money he had given her a while back. She doubted Jack would ever tell Demir that. She wondered about the boxer's bills as he narrowed his eyes at Jack.

'What, you're saying we can't afford to keep doing this?'

'I'm saying that extra cash can really help right now.' Jack stuffed his hands in his pockets and Selene looked at him in suspicion. He only did that when he was about to give bad news. 'Look, I went back and talked to Mackie. He agreed to give us some cash in exchange for fighting at his club.'

'What?'

'It would only be between fights, like an exhibition,' Jack argued but Demir raised his hand, silently telling him to stop.

'Jack, I know money's tight, but I'm not getting my face bashed in by some random brawler for a few extra bucks!'

'So, a few more fights aren't worth twice the cash?' Jack snapped. 'We're just supposed to slum it down here? Maybe you're not smart enough to see how fucking stupid that is, but I am!'

'The fuck did you say?' Demir straightened, inches from his coach and a full head taller. If that wasn't menacing enough, his arms bulged with tension as though he were moments away from knocking Jack's head off.

'Hey, guys,' Selene called out. 'Stop!' The men continued to stare each other down, even when she tried to squeeze in between them, Demir only taking a step back when she pushed at his chest as hard as she could.

'Both of you need to calm down *now*,' she snapped. 'We're getting nowhere like this.'

Demir rolled his eyes at her and stalked off to the other side of the room. 'Where are you going?' Jack demanded.

'Piss off, Jack,' he said over his shoulder. 'Fuck you, you son of a bitch!'

'Jack, stop before you don't have a fighter,' Selene hissed as the boxer left the building.

'Maybe we should get a new one,' he grumbled, walking over to the nearest punching bag and swinging his fist as hard as he could.

Selene placed a hand on his shoulder. 'You don't mean that,' she said calmly.

He punched the bag again, watching it swing as he sighed. 'I'm just tired of this shit.' 'I know,' she whispered.

'I have to fight for every little decision to happen. All this work, night and day, and not one person is listening. Nothing's ever enough.'

'Sounds a lot like Demir.'

'The hell do you mean? He's just acting scared.'

'You want him to give more than he should and that's not fair,' she said gently. 'He's not scared either. And even if he were, that would be reasonable. It's risky taking on that many fights in a row. And let's say this works out. What if Mackie asks for more fights? If he gives in to a ton of fights now, he'll be too worn down by the tournament.'

Jack was silent, and she waited for him to admit that she was right. She would tell him to be patient, maybe convince him to go watch the boxing match he had been talking about all week. Or they could call it an early night. She wanted to make him dinner and kiss on their couch, tucked away from everyone for a while. Instead, he said, 'How could you say that?'

'What?' Selene asked, genuinely confused.

'You're defending the guy who just left us high and dry? And now you want to blame me?'

'Blame you?' she repeated.

'What? You're a fucking parrot now?'

'Don't go there,' she warned him. 'Don't play at who can be meaner, Jack, because you won't like the result.'

'Can't believe this,' he scoffed. 'You would rather stick up for him than be on my side!'

'I'm saying there's more than one side to this.'

'How?'

'How – have you not been paying attention?' Selene gestured to the space around them. 'I'm here with him every day. I watched him train. I patch him up after every fight, no matter how good or bad. I see what he goes through,' she explained, shaking her head at him. 'Jack, you're a great coach. You know how to make a great show, but you are asking him purposefully to break his body for you.'

'For *us*,' Jack emphasised. 'What? You don't think I do the same thing? I bust my ass at that garage every fucking day. You think I wanna be covered in grease and sweat all day for fucking pennies? You think I wouldn't trade it all to be in the ring, make this shit easier for us? You're wrong! But I ain't got it and we all know it! Or do you not give a shit anymore?'

'You know I care about you—'

'More than you care for him?' Jack said, voice cold.

Her eyes widened, and she barely stopped herself from slapping him. Did he really think she needed to cheat on him to defend someone? How cheap did he think she was?

'I barely talk to Demir,' she spat. 'The hell are you getting at?'

'Why are you taking his side?' he pressed. 'Why are you acting like this isn't our last fucking shot to get out of here, to have something better? We don't even have half the cash we need for rent, much less your textbooks!'

Selene felt like ripping her hair out. Of course, she knew they were low on money, but they'd always been low on money. She knew it was the proximity that was killing him. They were all so close to succeeding, but was it worth *this*? Their arguments used to be fun. She used to not be intimidated by him. Now, she hated how nervous she was around him, how she always chose her words carefully so he didn't go on a rampage. And even then, it felt inevitable.

'I'm not taking his side,' Selene repeated. 'I know what we need to do, and I get it! I'm scared too! But you have to realise we've *all* made sacrifices for this!'

'Yeah, some more than others.' Jack looked her up and down with disdain before storming out the back door.

Selene rubbed soothing circles into her temples. Knowing Jack, this was only round one, and she already felt defeated. She opened her eyes, remembering if she was going to get home, she needed to go after him.

She looked towards the stairs only to meet Demir's eyes. From the look on his face, it was clear he had heard everything. Selene quickly diverted her gaze to the floor, where she saw his boxing gloves. He must have come back for them. She grabbed them from where they lay abandoned on the ground and met him on the stairs. He took them from her gingerly.

'I'll talk to him,' she promised.

'You don't—'

She looked at him defiantly, a look she would have pulled on Jack months ago when they were on better terms.

Demir's eyes fell to his feet. 'Okay.'

Selene nodded before steeling herself. As she climbed the steps, a trickle of confidence returned. She reminded herself that no one benefitted when she shut her mouth, especially her. Jack may not be himself right now, but he was still *her* boyfriend. If he wanted her to stay and help, he needed to treat her right.

Jack stood outside, smoking as he waited by the car.

'Finally,' he said, throwing his cigarette on the ground, snubbing it out with his shoe.

'Let's go. We're gonna be late for the match, unless you want to give up on that too.' He opened the door for her, and she threw her bag in the back before facing him, hands on her hips.

He looked at her dumbfounded. 'What now?' he asked.

Round two.

–

The tension was always thick whenever Demir picked up Selene in Jack's car, their usual silence weighed down by unresolved issues. After Jack's fight with Selene, he was mechanical when he trained Demir. Any conversation between the two was sharp and to the point. So, it comforted him to see Selene back to her normal, stubborn self instead of shrinking under Jack's attitude as she had been.

Still, it didn't change much between them and Demir didn't know how to feel about that. Their old truce was now unbalanced since she'd stuck up for him. He had tried his best in the week since to figure out how to repay her, but she never wanted anything from him. There was nothing to give or provide other than silence, so he did that. Still, it nagged at him relentlessly that he couldn't find a way to thank her.

Demir did his best to put it out of his mind as he and Selene entered the gym, starting their usual routine. Selene began to pull out her books while Demir went to the locker room to get ready. Halfway through wrapping his hands, he heard a commotion outside the door, a female voice filtering through. He sighed.

Another argument, he thought before pausing.

Jack shouldn't be here this early.

He stood from the bench and opened the door.

Instead of seeing Selene and Jack arguing, he saw a boxer he'd gone against a while back, Zac, crowding her against the wall. The terror in her eyes was obvious as she tried to push him away, textbook clutched to her chest. Still, the guy leaned in further, pinning her wrist to the wall.

'Hey,' Demir called out as he stomped over. The boxer looked up, loosening his grip. 'Get the fuck off her.'

'Oh, this your girl?' Zac asked. 'My bad. She asked me to come over to help her study. She wanted some hands-on training.' He smirked, and Demir opened his mouth to threaten him only for a textbook to hit him across the face. Both men turned to Selene, who stood there furiously gripping her anatomy book.

'Crazy bitch,' Zac spat, grabbing her by the throat.

Demir ripped him away, throwing him to the ground and grabbing his shirt. His fists rained down on the boxer's face. He ignored the blood and breaking bones until two other people dragged him off. Four others crowded around and, as the noise rose, the gym manager came rushing out of his office.

Demir shrugged off the strangers' holds and walked over to Selene, who was looking at the scene in shock, a hand cradling her neck. Carefully, he reached out and touched the back of her hand. She recoiled and looked up, relaxing when she saw it was him. He tilted her head so he could take a closer look. He didn't see any bruises; hopefully, he pulled Zac off before he could do any real damage.

'You okay?' he asked her quietly.

Selene shook her head. Demir nodded, taking her hand. She squeezed it before shifting to hide herself from the crowd behind him. He stepped closer, and she closed her eyes. The world faded away as he watched her try to catch her breath. He didn't look in the mirror to the commotion happening behind him as he intertwined their fingers. All he could focus on was the fact that she was okay. And for the briefest moment, it was the most important fact in his life.

'Get out!'

Demir turned to see the gym manager's livid eyes on them. 'And stay out! You're banned from here.'

'What?' Selene stepped from Demir's shadow and stomped over to the manager. 'This is ridiculous. He attacks me in your gym, and we're getting kicked out? Are you out of your mind?!'

'It's fine,' Demir said. Selene stared at him in confusion. 'Just get your stuff.' He gathered his things from the locker room and took her hand when he came back out. He led them outside, only dropping her hand when they reached the car.

'You shouldn't have done that,' she said as he opened the trunk, placing their bags inside before slamming it closed. 'We weren't in the wrong.'

'There's no winning battles like that,' he replied. 'Why waste the time?'

Selene opened her mouth before something over his shoulder caught her eye. 'Fuck.'

He followed her gaze to see Jack rushing down the street. 'Well, there goes my freedom.'

Demir wanted to ask what she meant, but she stepped around him to meet Jack halfway. 'Jack, what are you doing here?'

'I left early. I wanted to talk to you,' he said, rubbing his neck nervously before his eyes flickered to Demir. 'What are you guys doing outside?'

'Everything's fine,' she said. 'It—'

'I knocked Zac out,' Demir stepped in. 'The guy got cocky. He said something, and I gave him a quick reminder of who the champ is. Manager's not too happy about it, though.'

Jack stayed silent, which was unnerving; he always had something to say. Now, he looked torn between laughing and ripping his hair out. He seemed to go back and forth, and nearly a minute passed before he spoke. 'Well… I'm glad your head's back in the fight,' he replied before pinching the bridge of his nose. 'I'll, uh, I'll talk to the manager. See if he's willing to let us back in.'

'Or we could go to the gym by Mackie's club,' Demir said. Everyone froze, even Demir. Why the hell would he say that? His eyes flickered to Selene's, seeing the apprehension in them, and continued. 'I think you got a point. What's a couple more fights? It'll get us to New York quicker, so…'

Jack's face broke out with a smile.

'That's what I'm fucking talking about, D!' He embraced him, thumping him on the back heavily. He was beaming when he stepped back. 'I'll call Mackie tomorrow and set up a fight.'

'I only have one condition,' Demir cut in. 'Make sure the fights are worth it. Have to remind everyone who's the best.'

'Hey, couldn't agree more. We need to make you look good – so good Nora's gonna have to fight broads off you,' he teased, punching him lightly in the arm.

Selene furrowed her brows in disbelief but said nothing.

Demir shrugged off the punch. 'It's nothing,' he said, climbing into the car. 'Let's get the fuck outta here.'

Chapter Twenty-Six

Washington, D.C.

September 2013

Dani and Jones were friends.

That was a reality that was easy to swallow as she sent him memes and videos throughout the weeks following their run-in at the library. They talked about the random shows they caught on TV. Sometimes, she just called him to say a quick 'hi' or with a random story. It was an escape – which made it not romantic.

Jones had read enough books to know that escapism is not a good way to start a relationship and, considering that she had stopped talking about their shared past, he was pretty sure she was on a similar wavelength. After all, he understood that they couldn't avoid each other – the universe had other plans – so therefore, they had to settle for friendship.

At least, that's what he chose to believe despite the satisfaction that he felt every time she laughed at one of his bad jokes or any time she mentioned something cool she discovered through her research unrelated to them. If he were lucky, she would play a bit of cello, showing him a glimpse of what she was practising. He had only seen her play a few times, but he hoped one day she would invite him to a concert to fully experience her skill.

Today was not one of those days but he still listened attentively to her explain the solo she had been practising for weeks.

'So, what's the plan now?' Jones asked.

'Panic while running in a circle, SpongeBob style,' she said. 'This is *the* cello solo of a lifetime. There's no way I can actually learn to play Prokofiev's Sinfonia Concertante, Op. 125 in four months. To call the piece a solo is somewhat a disservice. It's basically me featuring everyone else. Professional cellists can barely pull it off and they literally have nothing else to do. The only favour Dr Carver is granting me is that we're only playing the *allegro giusto*.'

'You can do it,' Jones said without missing a beat.

'How do you know?' Dani asked. 'You've never seen me play.'

'Funny you say that considering your fifteen minutes of fame a while back,' he mentioned with a smirk.

'Oh, God no.' He could practically see her covering her face in embarrassment.

While intended only for her friend's class, the video spread like wildfire across the internet. The video was fun at first, inspiring quite a few re-creations but after a while they wore out the song and the videos became less funny. While he did get a lovely royalty cheque from the song's brief boost in popularity, he and Dani were more than happy when everyone moved on.

'It was a good rendition,' Jones said.

'I guess you would know,' she said and he could picture her smirking. She was probably remembering his reluctant admission that he was the producer of the song on one of their earlier phone calls. Another thing that bonded them together, even if it was just on the internet. Jones chuckled but said nothing else, the line becoming silent as they both fell into their own worlds. It was almost scary how easy it was to spend time doing nothing with her, letting the day go by...

Not that you have many left.

The thought was chilling and unfortunately common. He had come to terms with dying a while ago, deciding that all he could do was live his life doing what he wanted. He had his music, his friends, and time to have his own little adventures if he wanted. He finally had the freedom that he longed for in all his other lives and it was enough. Then, Dani showed up and it felt like every time he talked to her, something was different. He felt himself lingering on the thought that maybe, maybe, this life would be different.

'You'll do a good job,' Jones said suddenly, remembering to focus on the conversation and not a mere possibility.

'What?'

'The solo,' Jones clarified. 'Carver doesn't challenge you for the hell of it. He already knows you can do it. So, just trust him.'

'You would know,' she said quietly. After a pause, 'This is getting too dangerous.'

'How?' Jones asked, his voice becoming alert. He hoped she wouldn't suggest that they didn't see each other again.

'You're like a sedative,' she told him. 'You calm everything down. It's so unfair and is gonna make me go to sleep.'

He felt a flutter in his chest, one that had been lingering there for months as he thought back to Dani's curious eyes when they first met. If he were braver, he would tell her that she left him a little off balance, making him wonder about things he had given up on a long time ago. That he loved how she didn't just accept what was happening with them, that she was fighting and made him want to, too.

He had been a goner from the moment they met.

'That will come in handy for our bass lesson tomorrow,' he said instead. 'I doubt you're a "go with the flow" type of learner.'

'I'm that type of learner's worse nightmare,' she teased.

'Perfectionist.'

'Hippie,' she shot back before giggling.

There were noises in the background suddenly and Dani was saying something away from the speaker. 'I gotta go,' Dani said. 'Going to a concert with my friends tonight.'

'Same time, next season?' he said, referencing a quote from *The Fresh Prince of Bel-Air*, one of her guilty pleasure shows.

'Same time, next week,' she said, alluding to one of his favourites, *In Treatment*.

'Have fun.' Too soon, Dani's voice was gone.

Jones stared at his phone screen, already longing for the next time he would talk to her. He turned on his back, staring at the ceiling as music filled his head. That too had also been happening lately. As the days passed, he craved to create again, notes haunting him after every conversation, begging to bring to life all the things he couldn't say yet.

He got up from the floor and went to his room to grab an electric guitar he had been gravitating towards for the last few days. He wanted a sound that couldn't help but fill up the room, brighten even the darkest corners of his mind. He played until the sun disappeared below the horizon, doing everything he could to breathe so much life into the piece that it created a small bit of alchemy. If not to get them to live, then at least to help remember.

–

Jones's apartment reminded Dani of an old neo soul music video, with the muted green walls and the wicker chair in the corner that stood out from all the other brown or jewel-toned furniture. It was cosy and a bit overcrowded with the vinyl records piled up around the piano, TV and on the bookshelves. A couple of abstract pieces hung on the living room wall that made Dani think of stormy seas.

While they had talked on the phone every day, whether texting or calling, it took a while for her to find time to visit as her next concert loomed closer. Fortunately, Dr Carver had to leave early that day, resulting in a half day of practice. There was a part of her that knew it would be much more productive to book a practice room, but the thought was quickly pushed aside when she saw the random meme Jones sent the night before. After all, she would be no good if she overworked herself and novelty was necessary for creativity.

Maybe the excuses were flimsy, but she couldn't find it in herself to care.

She touched the leaf of one of the plants on the windowsill and figured this was what hipsters strived for but could never quite capture. They wanted to look effortlessly cool, but it always felt too clean to Dani, a tad too organised. Jones's place felt… authentic. Lived in.

'What do you think?' Jones asked.

'You have very good taste,' Dani said. 'Although, I do expect Maxwell to come out of your guest room asking if he got any mail today.'

'I'll let you know if he stops by,' he said, handing her a glass of water. 'How was the concert?'

'Good but tiring. My friends wanted to go to a hookah bar after and since I've been a bit grouchy lately, I gave in. The fun almost makes up for the exhaustion,' she said. She took a sip, the drink refreshing after hours of practice. She contemplated the drink as she sat down on the floor in front of his coffee table.

'You know, one good thing about our connection is that you can't kill me without karma taking you with me,' she said.

He huffed out a small laugh, sitting down in front of the couch. 'I figured it would at least get dark outside before the intrusive thoughts came out.'

'I'm just saying,' she said. 'But let's switch topics. What's your favourite colour?'

She expected him to answer the question after a quick but knowing laugh. Instead, his brows raised in concern, and he asked, 'Are you okay?' She closed her eyes at the question, sighing.

Her first instinct was to tell Jones how much she was struggling, maybe even ask for his help, but she liked the middle ground they'd struck. They didn't ignore their past lives, nor did they go out of their way to bring them up. They walked the conversational middle ground, and she would be damned if she broke it first.

Yet, looking at his expression, the worry in his eyes that he did his best to hide behind an upbeat smile, it felt cruel to leave him out completely.

'Jones…' He put his hands up in defence.

'I'm not talking about it. I'm just asking if you're okay,' he said. 'But you know, you can talk to me about it even if you haven't found anything.'

'I know.' Her nails clinked against the glass as she searched for the right words, feeling more tongue-tied than usual. 'It's easier in a way and harder in another. I'm looking into Mali. There's a thread there, I know there is. I just need to figure out what it is.'

They stared at each other, and she could practically hear what he was thinking, that she could ask him for help, just as she knew her eyes were asking him to be patient. Being friends was enough for now. It had to be. Yet…

'I just feel like… once we cross that line, it'll be all I ever think about with us. That I'll spend all our time together looking for a way out and if I'm wrong…'

She didn't dare look at him as she spoke, the words barely coming out above a whisper under the weight of all that she didn't say. Why did it matter if all they did was work on a solution unless she wanted something more? She cleared her throat to fill the silence. 'Besides, the memories are already occupying 90 per cent of my brain. It's better if I don't let them take up any more.'

Her tone was joking but her words were truthful. She thought it would work like the regular memories, first being prominent but fading as new ones came in. Instead, it felt like it was more like a box set of films that she could rewind and play in complete clarity, Demir and Selene sliding cleanly next to Sabine, Damien, Sarah and David often leaving Dani with a migraine. Her mind felt like it was expanding to accommodate the new information. All the lives – and the feelings they were drenched in – weighed on her like a hangover.

'You should make memory palaces,' he said. She raised her eyebrows as she stared at her faint reflection in the water. 'It's a technique that helps people remember events in their life by creating a place in their mind specifically for that memory or set of memories. Makes them easier to carry. And instead of trying to remember everything, you just remember the thing that made it special.'

'A memory palace,' she murmured before meeting his gaze. Her heart squeezed at the understanding look in his eyes with a smile that matched Selene's perfectly. She wondered if he saw parts of their past in her too. Who were they without it? Or did it even matter? The thoughts came faster and faster, but she forced herself out of the spiral, focusing on the warmth in his gaze.

They could have been a million people, but they weren't. And while there were remnants, Jones wasn't like anyone else they had been before, and it made him that much more tempting.

'So, if I want to remember today, I'll just have to remember how you taught me bass,' she said casually.

'I haven't done that,' he said.

The word *yet* hung between them, just waiting for a little push.

'I haven't seen you play since that day in class.' She nodded to the bass in the other corner of Jones's living room, partially hidden by a curtain. 'Care to correct that?'

Jones chuckled before standing up. He grabbed his bass and started tuning the strings as he returned to her side.

'Deal,' Jones agreed. He picked up an amp that was tucked away in the corner and plugged the bass in. 'But you have to sit closer if you actually want me to teach you something.'

'Just the basics,' she said, scooting until she was right next to him, their knees within inches of touching. 'But play something for me, just so I know what I could be doing.'

'Sure,' he drawled, tuning the instrument until the sound was just right. He launched into a breezy, romantic song. He strummed effortlessly, breathing the song into existence. His fingers were an extension of that action, and she could only imagine the hours it took for him to make it look so easy. She felt a tug in her chest as she rested her arm against the couch, staring at him in awe.

She had heard plenty of skilled musicians; she was surrounded by them every day. But a part of her had gotten used to people playing for the accolades or to be number one, even she had to give into that mentality to be where she was. So, to see Jones play for the joy of it, no more, no less… he was mesmerising. He always had been.

'Okay.' He removed the guitar from his neck and held it out to her. 'Your turn.'

'Yeah, because I definitely want to follow *that*,' she commented as she eased the bass strap over her head. The weight of the instrument was heavier than she expected, and she had to straighten her back to counterbalance it. It was strange having to support the instrument with her shoulder instead of her arms and legs like with her cello. She thumbed the frets curiously, not used to those either.

'We're going to leave it unplugged until you get the hang of it,' he said. 'You ever played a bass before?'

'Just a little bit of acoustic guitar,' she replied.

'Well, the concept is basically the same,' he said. He walked her through the different notes that the frets marked, some tips for strumming and plucking. She listened attentively as she would in any other music class. She picked up on his instructions pretty quickly and soon he was scooting back to let her run through a basic scale.

'Pretty good,' he said. 'Although, you don't have to pluck so literally. It's more like a slide.'

'Like…' She slid the side of her thumb against the string the way she would play an acoustic guitar, but she grimaced at the wobbly sound.

'More like…' He leaned over and slid her thumb up from the second string, so her thumb rested against the first. 'Imagine it like your fingers doing the moonwalk.'

She snorted. 'Really?'

'Give it a try,' he pushed. She shrugged before doing so. Surely enough, the note was smooth, just like his had been. 'Good. Now, alternate your middle and index finger… Good… Now do that for each string.' She did, and he clapped.

'I think it's hardly worth a standing ovation,' she said as she rested her fingers against the body.

'No, but it is a good first step, one you picked up in…' He looked over to his kitchen clock. 'Roughly five minutes. Pretty impressive if you ask me.'

'I just think you're easily impressed,' she said, mentally basking in the praise. 'Now, what's next?'

'Now,' he plugged the bass into the amp, 'we get serious.'

He walked her through various beats and the sound of each note, repeating it until she had the E and A notes somewhat memorised. Then, he got another bass to play a simple bassline for her to copy. She felt self-conscious about being able to hear herself over him – he didn't plug the second one in – and started to fumble. Jones was patient, restarting with the same patience as before, slowing down until she got it. Still, she could hear her notes, and it sounded so… bad.

'Can we stop?' She had held back the question for as long as she could, but she was moments away from ripping the cord from the bass and the last thing she wanted was to damage anything.

'Sure.' Jones immediately put down his guitar and set it aside just as she did hers. 'If you're tired, we can wrap this up.'

She sighed, picking at the loose thread on her jeans. Truthfully, she could probably go another hour or two if she wanted, but she just couldn't take it. She had been studying music for over ten years, had won all the right contests, played with state-level bands. It had been a very long time since she sounded so mediocre.

'I sound so rough,' she said.

'You literally just started learning two hours ago,' he pointed out.

'I know, I know,' she said. 'And I know I'm not going to sound perfect or anywhere near like you, but I sound like I'm in an elementary school band, learning a nursery rhyme.'

'Still good in my book.'

'How are you so positive?' she asked, annoyance slipping into her tone.

'Why are you so negative,' he countered. 'You just started. You have to give yourself some time.'

'The thing we don't have,' she snapped, bitterness coating her words.

'Exactly,' he said without missing a beat. He pulled his guitar back on his lap, strumming a much quicker bassline than they'd practised with. 'Why waste it being disappointed that you're not perfect?'

She gritted her teeth, a wave of frustration running through her, and she couldn't tell if it was aimed at his laidback attitude or herself. She rubbed her temples, which brought minimal relief, as she heard muted notes filling the air. She strained her ears trying to recognise the song but couldn't quite figure it out.

The question came reluctantly from her, but she knew it would bother her more if she didn't ask. 'What are you playing?'

'Listen,' he said. He sat up and played full out. She tried to make sense of the beat but couldn't quite place it. It was naggingly familiar though, something she was sure her dad would recognise.

'I can't figure it out,' she said.

'Yes, you can.'

'Jones.'

'Listen,' he urged. 'Close your eyes and listen.'

At first, she narrowed them defiantly, his instructions bringing out a stubborn streak in her. He returned her gaze, his mouth pulling down in frustration but his eyes gentle. They were always gentle, and it drove her crazy. Did he ever get angry? Maybe he was more like Sabine and Demir, with their feelings under lock and key, while she was Selene and Damien, hers much closer to the surface. Not that it mattered as she tried and ever so clearly failed to keep up her walls. She closed her eyes all the way, crossing her arms but listening as he started playing again.

The sound was definitely older, easily Seventies or Eighties. She unconsciously started bobbing along, finally finding the rhythm. Just as she got comfortable, he stopped. She scrunched her eyebrows, about to tell him she hadn't figured it out yet, when he played a very distinctive set of notes. The memory of her dad dancing in the front seat to the song on the drive to school came to her like lightning and she could suddenly hear the whole song.

'"Never Too Much",' she said, opening her eyes. 'Luther Vandross.'

Jones stopped playing, staring at her with wide eyes that did not answer her question. For a moment, she was sure she got it wrong, but his smile instantly washed away her worry. He lifted his hands from the guitar and slow clapped. She shook her head at the dramatics but was preening on the inside. Now, she felt like she was back on track.

'You only picked up bass the last two years of undergrad,' she said, remembering the titbit from one of their phone conversations.

'Yes,' he confirmed.

'How in the world are you so good?'

'Oh, that's easy,' he said. 'Fucking up. A lot.'

Her jaw dropped at the answer, and something close to a pained but understanding laugh spilled out of her. She related completely but was not used to someone saying it so bluntly. She found herself facing the ceiling minutes later when she calmed down, the laughter making her lie down. She felt a tap on her foot and looked over at Jones, whose gaze had become fond and tender. Something definitely *not* friend-like, like they'd silently agreed. Still, she met it head on, finding that she didn't really mind that.

236

'I get that you have to drill like crazy to do what you do,' he said, 'but this is supposed to be for fun. Don't stress about making it perfect. You have time to get better.'

She bit the inside of her cheek to avoid asking the question, 'Do we?' She pushed it far away in her mind, knowing that the only ones with that answer were the powers that be.

'It's a bad habit,' she said instead. '*Being* perfect, not trying.' She winked at him, and it was his turn to laugh, dispelling the knot forming in her chest.

'In the meantime, I'll show you how to play "Return of the Mack",' he said. 'Come on.'

'I don't know. Isn't this how all the coolest bassists play?' She pulled the bass into her lap and went through her very basic plucking. 'Oh! Could you teach me how to play "I Want It That Way"?'

'Absolutely not. You'll have to learn that on your own.'

Just as she had in the museum and for a hundred years before that in probably a hundred different scenarios, she laughed and let her worries slide away, allowing him to become her sole focus.

Chapter Twenty-Seven

Detroit

May 1946

'The deal is done so, tonight, we celebrate, champ,' Jack announced as he entered Demir's apartment. The boxer took Jack's excitement in stride as he closed the door and the curtains over dirty windows before pulling out a bottle of brown liquor. 'Bourbon straight from Kentucky,'

Jack said. 'A little gift from Mackie. He says we're good to start fighting next Tuesday, and I already got us a spot at the gym nearby. The best part: I found a garage that is closer so no more traipsing across town. It's all finally working out!'

Jack cracked open the bottle and took a long swig, making a face as he swallowed before holding out the bottle. Demir took it and followed suit, his own face contorting at the burn; it was stronger than he'd expected. 'Cheers to us,' he forced out. He gave the bottle back to Jack and went to sit on his bed.

'Thanks to you,' Jack said, taking another drink. He stared at Demir's ceiling for a long moment before speaking again 'Sel says I should apologise for the shit I said the other day.'

'It's fine.' Demir shrugged. 'It was just a bad day.'

'Still, I owe you.' He held out the bottle, an unspoken olive branch. Demir accepted it and after a beat, asked, 'You and Sel doing okay?'

'Yeah,' he answered. 'She's been more sensitive than usual though. I think school's starting to get to her.'

Demir's mind flashed back to the gym, Selene pinned against the wall, the fury on her face after hitting the guy, and how she had hidden behind him, eyes closed. He forced himself to shrug. 'Life's tough,' he said. 'She'll be okay.'

'Oh yeah,' Jack agreed, chuckling. 'But I wouldn't be surprised if she burned the whole place down at this point.' He took another drink. 'You catch the baseball game the other day?'

They talked sports and other useless shit for the rest of the night, the noisiest Demir's apartment had been in a while. There was a small part of him that wished he didn't enjoy it as much as he did.

—

'Shit,' Demir hissed as Selene pressed an alcohol-soaked cloth to a cut on his brow.

'He got you good,' Selene commented as she disinfected the cut. 'On the bright side, there only seems to be a few bruises, so a little rest will be all you need.' She taped the bandage to his brow and stepped back. 'Mackie looked happy. I'm sure Jack is making some kind of deal with him now for more money. Seems New York's gonna work out after all.' He watched her nervously tap her nails on her knee.

'Do you want it to?'

Selene blinked in surprise at the question before staring at the floor. 'Umm… I guess. I mean, the sooner we don't have to do this, the better. I finish school in December. So, once I'm a doctor, and you're fighting in the pros, it'll be worth it, right?'

'What kind of doctor do you want to be?' he asked her instead of answering.

'A surgeon,' she replied, laughing bitterly. 'I already fix broken things so why not get paid for it? Don't worry, this time I'm not talking about you.' She paused before leaning towards him, lowering her voice. 'Thank you for… everything.'

'Don't mention it.'

'Always so humble.' She shook her head even as a small smile made an appearance. 'But I'm serious—'

'Did you tell Jack?' Demir asked suddenly. The question had been burning in his mind for days. He had been watching her act the same around Jack while his friend was none-the-wiser. He was sure she had her reasons for keeping the incident to herself, but he couldn't imagine what they would be. Weren't they in love? Then again, what did he know about that?

Selene's smile dropped and her eyes flickered to the door. 'No,' she replied in a low voice. 'And he doesn't need to know.'

'Then, don't mention it,' Demir replied. 'Ever.'

Selene furrowed her brows at him, smoothing her expression when the door opened. She subtly slid back so she was out of Demir's personal space as Jack and Mackie came in.

'And here is the star of the night,' Jack announced, holding out his hand in Demir's direction. He tried to muster up a smile for the club owner, but it fell somewhere closer to a grimace.

Mackie didn't seem to really care. He simply nodded and put his hands in his pocket. 'Hell of a fight you put on tonight.'

'Thank you,' Demir replied, trying not to stare at Selene as she went to stand by Jack, his arms wrapping around her as he kissed her temple.

'I should be thanking you. I've never seen the crowd so riled up,' Mackie chuckled. He reached into his pocket and pulled out an envelope, holding it out to Jack. 'But I hope this will be sufficient.'

He opened it, and instantly his eyes widened. 'This is… very generous of you.'

'Now, don't get too excited. It's merely an investment. I want him fighting every other week, especially on the last Friday of the month. You know, to keep things exciting,' Mackie informed them. 'I assume this will be more than enough.'

'Y–Yeah,' Jack cleared his throat awkwardly. 'This, um, this looks good.'

'Wonderful.' Mackie tipped his hat. 'See you all next week, then. Especially you.' Mackie took Selene's hand and kissed the back of it with a wink.

She giggled before winking back. 'Looking forward to it,' she replied, right on the cusp of flirty despite leaning her head on Jack's shoulder.

Demir didn't understand how Jack could stand it. Hell, *his* blood boiled at the interaction, and he wasn't even supposed to care. He looked down at his feet. What the hell was going on with him?

'Lemme see,' Selene said once Mackie left, taking the envelope. She squealed at the contents before hugging Jack.

'Gonna show the man who got his face busted for whatever's in there?' Demir drawled. Jack laughed before holding the envelope to him. He took it and stopped short at the contents. He had never seen so many bills in one place, much less for him.

'How much is this?'

'Two hundred and fifty dollars,' Jack answered excitedly. He took the envelope from Demir and divided the money, the envelope still thick when Jack handed it back. 'We're in, D.'

–

When Selene really thought about it, being in the library was the only place she had a chance to be alone. Everywhere else in her life, she was surrounded by people. Her two siblings and mum when she went home, Jack when she went to his place, other students in class, and Demir everywhere in between. Some days she could feel herself getting lost in the commotion of it all; her life felt like it rarely ever stopped.

Within all the havoc, the library was her sanctuary. It was the only place where she felt fully in control, where she wasn't being dragged along to the next place. It was also the only place she was forced to be quiet, even if her thoughts weren't. They bounced back and forth between biology, boxing and how much Jack had changed in the last few months. The brooding man from before was long gone, and he was finally back to normal.

But he's not, she thought frustratingly. She huffed loudly, earning a few looks, as she put down her pencil.

She had known Jack since they were children. Even trying to remember her life before him, there were only a handful of memories. She had grown up knowing the five blocks between their neighbourhoods like the back of her hand. Before he found boxing, she was his fighter. She had fought kids on the playground to leave them alone, for them to be together, and even to get into Wayne State – who only *just* had their first Black, female graduate a couple of years ago – for her own sense of independence. Jack didn't always get it, but he was always in the fight with her.

Now... Selene wasn't sure what she was fighting for or who it was with.

Their new life was nice, but she couldn't shake the feeling that something had changed within him. She shook her head, refocusing on her textbook. With an exam in a couple of days, she couldn't think about that. She still had a dream to fight for, if nothing else.

She studied for another hour before heading outside to wait for Demir. A shiny new car pulled up in front of the steps and her eyebrows raised when she saw the boxer step out, a slow smile spread across her face. She may have been wary of their new money, but she couldn't deny that it came with perks.

'I got a good deal from a guy I know,' he explained as they headed into the city. Selene ran her fingers over the dash. 'I'm guessing it's not one of Jack's guys then.' 'I know more people than Jack. Have to.'

Selene smirked knowingly before leaning back in her seat. 'So where to? Now that we're not borrowing a car, we could go anywhere.'

'Says the one not fighting every week,' Demir pointed out.

Selene laughed but held up her hands in concession. Lounging in her seat, she tapped on the window idly.

'Where do you wanna go?' he asked after a while.

She chewed her bottom lip for a moment before her eyes lit up. 'Do you have a radio?' 'There's a radio in here.' He pointed to the dash.

'No, I mean, one where I can listen while stretching my arms or dancing,' she insisted. 'Unless you want me to dance on top of your car.'

Demir smirked at the suggestion. 'As much as I'd enjoy that, I know a spot,' he said, making a left turn.

—

'You'll never know how many dreams I've dreamed about you...' 'It's Been a Long, Long Time' crooned through the radio in Demir's living room. He had moved it from the kitchen counter to a spot near the window so he and Selene could listen as they sat on the fire escape. He peeled an orange while Selene smoked.

She thought it was ironic that people found the activity relaxing when it did nothing but agitate her. 'I hate smoking. It tastes disgusting.'

'And yet here you are,' he drawled, eating an orange slice.

'If I didn't, I'd lose my mind.' Selene stared at the cigarette in disdain before taking another drag. She sighed, blowing out smoke. 'Between school and Jack...' She shook her head, bringing the cigarette back to her lips.

Demir's hand shot out, taking it from her. Instead of being offended, she only looked at him curiously as he put it out. He handed her an orange slice. She stared at him, lips pursed before taking it from him and popping it in her mouth.

'For someone who supposedly has a soulmate, you sure lie to Jack a lot.'

'That's how you keep a soulmate,' she said around the orange. She swallowed, looking through the grates. It was all so tiring when she thought about it. 'Lying's just easier sometimes.'

'Than telling the truth?'

'Than not always being the girl he wants,' she clarified. 'I know Jack accepts who I am, but sometimes it's easier to shield him from things he'll never understand than to argue with him about why the world is the way it is. We argue enough.' She ran her fingers through her hair. 'It'll be better later. We just have to make it through now.'

'So, the flirting at the club…'

'Not my favourite activity, but a good way to start conversations with the right people. At least, most of the time.'

Demir stared at the fruit in his hands. She laughed softly before tapping his knee, bringing his attention back to her.

'You don't get it.'

'No,' Demir admitted.

She shrugged. 'I guess someone like you doesn't have to.'

'Like me?'

'Someone who doesn't need anyone,' she explained. Demir's face stayed blank, so she sat up, turning her full attention to him. 'You don't bring any friends to fights. I only ever hear about you hanging out with Jack. Well, Jack and Nora. Has Nora even been over here?'

'We meet at her apartment.'

Selene smirked and shook her head. 'You let no one in your world.'

'I prefer it that way,' he said. 'You're here. Doesn't that count for something?'

Selene faltered as she sat back, turning away from him. 'I mean, I don't know.' She shrugged awkwardly.

It shouldn't have mattered, really. They had been alone together for months in many different places. Yet, this was the first time it felt *personal*. Selene hadn't asked to come to his apartment, and he could have suggested using the radio in the gym or taken her to a diner.

Instead, here they were in a space that must be special to him, at least special enough to keep to himself. Suddenly, it didn't feel like two people thrown together for better or worse.

It felt like… more.

'Why didn't you tell Jack?' she asked quietly. Demir sighed and she felt a pang of guilt. She knew that he didn't want her to bring it up. It would be better for her to forget about it, but she couldn't help it. She needed to know why this man who used to hate her – maybe still did – would keep her secret.

Protection always came with a price.

'I couldn't tell what scared you more: being attacked or Jack finding out.'

'But… you don't like me,' she pointed out.

'I'm not cruel for sport.' He turned towards the city, his hand almost crushing the orange but stopping just before he did. Selene scoffed.

'Plenty of men are.' She wrapped her arms around herself tightly.

'Well, not me,' Demir told her, popping another orange slice in his mouth. 'My social skills ain't that bad.'

Selene opened her mouth and thought better of it. Beyond arguing, Demir had never harmed her. He drew hard lines but was never malicious. Maybe that's why it was so easy for her to defend him to Jack. He plucked another orange slice, and Selene's hand shot out to steal it.

'Hey!'

'You won't miss it,' she dismissed. 'And if I do?'

'It went to a good cause.' She winked, and there was a small thrill that went through her as she saw his eyes linger. It was good to know that she could get his attention, no matter how short-lived the moment was.

'You're trouble,' he murmured.

'At least I'm fun.'

'*I hope you do believe me, I've given you my heart…*' Nat King Cole sang, and a sense of calm fell over her.

'I like it here.'

Demir chuckled. 'It's a shit apartment,' he said.

Selene scooted closer until their shoulders touched. 'I like it *here*,' she emphasised.

Demir paused and a small smile formed on Selene's lips as she looked at the building across the alley. Beneath them, people walked by and sirens sounded somewhere in the city. It was far from peaceful, but something about it soothed her.

She was so caught up taking it all in that she almost missed it when he said, 'Me too.'

Chapter Twenty-Eight

Detroit

June 1946

The streets of Detroit were busy under the gloomy sky that had hidden the sun for hours. The bustling crowd of people was on their way home, to the store, or their second job, with cars in the street honking as they raced from one point to another. There was so much activity, you could get lost in it as people hurried away from the slim possibility of rain. It was Demir's favourite kind of day.

Well, except for one thing.

'Why are we here again? The last thing I wanna do is walk around.' Demir held back a sigh as Selene whined.

'Because I can't sit in the house and listen to the radio all day. I need to move around to stay healthy. Shouldn't you know that, doc?'

Selene rolled her eyes. 'Of course, I know that. I just prefer to ignore it.'

'God forbid I take your big head out your books.' Demir picked up his pace little by little until Selene was lagging behind.

She scowled at him, speeding up. 'Those books are why I can patch you up, so watch it,' she snipped. 'And my head is not big!'

Demir looked her up and down with a sceptical expression. 'Hmmm…'

Selene hit his arm and an easy smile formed on his face. 'Don't even try it!' She reached out to push him and he grabbed her hand. She snatched her hand away and huffed, making him laugh.

It had been a month since Demir had started fighting at Mackie's club and not much had changed for him. He still spent the week with Selene and weekends with Nora. His days were filled with odd jobs, practice and fighting, sometimes drinking with Jack afterwards. There was only one new thing.

He *enjoyed* getting under Selene's skin now.

The banter between them was refreshing although her constant questions made him think more than he wanted to. To distract her from how few he answered he teased her about everything he could think of. No matter how obvious he made it, Selene always got offended before nagging him about something mundane and safe. He talked to her more than anyone he'd ever talked to in his life.

'Oh, let's go in there,' she suggested, pointing to a corner store across the street. She started to cross, but he grabbed her arm.

'Nope.' He steered her back onto the sidewalk. 'We're just walking.'

'Just *walking*?'

'Just walking,' he repeated. She groaned before stuffing her hands in her coat pocket. 'This is my warm-up before the gym, so no distractions. Just walking.'

'Okay, fine,' she conceded, crossing her arms. 'It's just a shame that on a day like this we can't do something interesting.'

'Walking doesn't have to be interesting.'

'But it should be. I mean, why do something if it's not?'

'To get to one place or the other. Or are you too used to sitting pretty in Jack's car?' 'I'm used to doing *something*, which I guess isn't your forte.'

'My what?'

'Your specialty,' she clarified. 'If you have no one around you, no one's there to force you to do anything outside the ordinary.'

'If that's the case, shouldn't you feel at home?' He motioned to the people around them. 'You're in a crowd with no one to stop you. You can make your own entertainment.'

'Oh, please, you should know better than anyone else that this isn't a crowd,' she said. 'These are strangers. If anything, it's the best way to not feel alone, even if you are.' She stopped suddenly, and Demir turned back to see what had happened. She was staring across the street; he followed her gaze to a couple kissing goodbye in an apartment doorway, not caring who saw.

'Until you see something like that.' Demir raised his brow at her reaction. 'But you have that.'

'Not exactly.' She turned to Demir; her face was wistful. 'Have you ever seen something simple and common, but its everything you wanted? And you knew you couldn't have it?'

Demir's first instinct was to say 'No,' but the word got stuck in his throat. His mind raced as he tried to figure out why that was the wrong answer while the hope died in her eyes at his silence.

'Maybe not,' she said. 'I guess you already have most of what you want, right? You're lucky.' She started walking again. 'Come on, let's finish this distracting but not distracting walk. It's just so much *fun*,' she drawled. 'You know, there has to be one interesting thing about this, I'm sure of it…'

Demir ignored the tightness in his chest as he joined her. 'There is,' he said, interrupting her rambling.

'And that would be…?'

'Well, for one, it's definitely a good way to find out what's going on in the neighbourhood.' She gasped before smirking. The look put Demir at ease; she was back to normal.

'So, you're nosy,' she accused.

'I'm aware,' he corrected.

'Oh no, D, you may be good at fooling others, but not me,' she said smugly.

'Doubt that,' he replied. Selene slowed, but he kept walking figuring she would catch up. He almost faltered when he heard her say, 'You shouldn't.'

—

The punch only clipped his chin, but it was enough to send Demir staggering back against the ropes. Selene winced as, left eye swollen shut, he struggled to dodge his opponent's blows, the hits reverberating through his body until the bell rang. He was panting by the time he sat in his corner.

Johnny 'Havoc' Lawson was, unfortunately, living up to his name. 'D, you gotta listen to me out there,' Jack screamed over the crowd.

Who they were cheering for, Selene couldn't tell. She focused on pouring water down Demir's throat only for him to spit it out seconds later, staining the floor with blood. Grabbing his face, she took a better look. His eye was almost completely swollen shut. He wouldn't last much longer.

'He's favouring his right,' Jack continued. 'Aim for the ribs. Make him use his left side. The swings are gonna be slower. Stop fucking around and get in there!'

Demir nodded weakly, and Selene waved a hand in front of his face. 'How many?'

Demir tried to focus on her hand, but his gaze was sluggish. 'Four,' he guessed. She put two fingers down.

'How many?'

'Three.'

'Two,' she sighed, turning to Jack. 'We might have to tap out.'

'He can make it.'

'He's punch-drunk and can't see straight,' she insisted.

'We're too close to give in now,' Jack stressed.

'If something happens to him—'

'Nothing's going to happen to him, we're good. Come on, Sel,' Jack snapped. Selene scowled and turned towards the boxer.

'Hey.' She tapped his knee to bring Demir's attention back to her, frowning at the effort it took for Demir to meet her gaze. She frowned but forced herself to focus on the outcome she knew Jack wanted. 'You have about two more rounds in you before you fall out. Do you think you can knock him out before that?'

Breathing harshly, Demir looked around, not answering. Uncertainty settled in his eyes, and it unnerved her; she had never seen him look like that.

'Demir...' Before she could suggest quitting, he gave her a jerky nod.

'Yeah,' he answered. 'Let's get this over with.'

She ignored the twist in her gut at his answer. 'Okay,' she relented. 'Just listen to Jack's instructions and bring him down quick. Otherwise, I'm throwing in the towel. Got it?'

'Yeah, yeah,' he said dismissively.

She grabbed his face, forcing him to make eye contact. 'Demir,' she said, her eyes boring into him. 'Can you do this?' His jaw tightened at her touch; her expression defiant. He wasn't going to give up and she knew nothing she could say would make him.

'You know I can,' he answered. Selene bit her lip nervously but nodded, stepping out of the ring.

Legs stiff, Demir made his way back to the middle. The bell rang and he swung out. The hit landed but Johnny was quick to follow. They traded blows with Demir taking more than he was giving.

The crowd sounded like a roaring monster, the fight in front of her a raging bull. Selene wanted to look away, didn't want to watch as he got sloppier with each second. At one point, she couldn't help but yell, 'Demir, duck!'

Luckily, his body moved at her command, weaving under Johnny's fist to punch him in the jaw. The fighter dropped his hands and that was Demir's cue. He threw two quick jabs to the boxer's right side and an uppercut before the fighter hugged him.

The referee pulled them apart, forcing them to take their stances again. At his signal, Demir's fist shot out and hit the man's nose, dropping Lawson to the floor. The crowd cheered wildly as the referee counted. Selene rarely prayed, but all she could do was thank God when the referee's countdown finished.

A half hour later, Demir winced as Selene bandaged his ribs so tightly she worried that he might have difficulty breathing, but she wasn't taking any chances. The cuts and swelling on his face were bad enough.

'That was close,' Jack muttered from where he paced in the middle of the room.

'There's no way you can fight that guy again any time soon. Though he might be good for an end of the year rematch… I need to talk to Mackie and see who he's thinking of next. We need to get you ready.' Jack sped out the door, and Selene groaned.

'Always thinking of the next thing while everyone else is trying to get through tonight,' she grumbled, grabbing the notebook by her thigh and quickly scribbling across the page.

'What are you writing?'

'Notes on your condition,' she told him. 'I'm making a medical history for you so I can keep track of any damage.'

'Sounds like a lot.'

'Nothing compared to what I'll do when I'm a doctor.' She finished her sentence and closed the notebook. Eyeing the knot over his left eye, she dug into her bag for her switchblade. She sterilised it with rubbing alcohol before touching the knife to the bulge. 'Hold still.'

'Shit,' Demir hissed as she cut into him.

'I suggest you don't see Nora tonight,' she told him, her gaze as steady as her hand. 'It's gonna hurt like a bitch to breathe, much less do anything else.' She held a rag to his face, pressing down to soak up the pooling blood. He gripped her knee tightly, breathing through the pain. She rubbed circles into his wrist with her free hand to try and soothe him, but there was little she could do. The only way to fix him was to cause more pain.

'The answer to your question is yes,' he said suddenly.

'I ask you a lot of questions.' Selene checked the wound, throwing the towel down and grabbing more bandages. 'This wouldn't be so confusing if you answered more of them.'

'The question you asked when we were walking,' he told her. She paused before looking at him. He met her eyes bravely, even though he had to fight past his busted lip to speak. 'Pick any time in my life, and there was always something that I wanted... something everyone else had but me.'

Selene gaped at him before forcing herself to focus on patching his cut, though she was suddenly more aware of the hand on her knee and every struggling breath he took. Once finished, she clasped her fingers together.

'Tonight,' she said softly. 'What did you want tonight?'

'To give up,' he revealed quietly.

Selene nodded slowly before taking his hand, leaning her forehead gently against his as she closed her eyes. It was the safest way to comfort him. She didn't care if it was inappropriate; she needed to be reassured that yes, he was still there. That he would be okay.

'Make me a stupid promise.' 'What?'

'Don't scare me like that again,' she pleaded.

Demir laughed a little but stopped short, his breathing becoming laboured for a moment. 'Okay,' he promised. 'I'll try.'

'Good.' Selene pulled back and helped him stand. 'Let's get you to Jack's because there is no way you are spending the night by yourself.'

A couple of hours later, after the niceties and ride home, Selene was throwing a blanket over Demir, who had practically passed out once his head hit the couch. She set a glass of water on the table in front of him before putting the back of her hand to his forehead, not feeling a fever. She checked his pulse next. It was slow and steady, comforting. She pulled away before she could wake him.

That was too close.

Walking into the room she shared with Jack, her hatred of fighting returned, renewed. All the fears she once had for Jack came rushing back. Walking on the edge of death like that… she couldn't understand the appeal or the drive it took. Jack was lucky enough to get away with only a bad knee, but she doubted Demir would be so fortunate.

Jack had been fierce, but Demir was brutal. The calibre of fighters that he would entice would be dangerous, and Selene couldn't just watch him get hurt. As reluctantly as their relationship had formed, Demir was her friend now, and he needed her help.

So, she made sure to wipe the worry from her face as she stepped inside the bedroom, closing the door behind her.

Jack paced the room, grumbling under his breath as he looked through the newspaper. 'What'cha looking for?' Selene asked casually.

'Seeing if there are any fights happening tomorrow,' he explained. 'How's D?'

'He's gonna be sore in the morning but okay. He'll have to skip a couple of practices though.' Jack cursed under his breath before sitting on the bed.

'Mackie wants to bring Johnny back soon,' he said, tapping his foot nervously. 'He's not telling me who we're fighting next, but if it's anything like tonight, we may be out in a couple of months. I gotta double D's workouts.'

'Hmm.' Her mind churned with ideas as she changed for bed, feeling Jack's eyes lingering on her as she did so.

'What are you thinking about?' Jack asked, his voice suddenly raspy.

She looked over her bare shoulder at him. 'Don't worry about that.' She quickly changed into her nightgown and climbed into bed. 'And don't worry about Mackie. We'll figure something out.'

'Sel, I don't know—'

'Shhh…' She grabbed his shirt and pulled him closer. 'No more fighting tonight.'

–

The last place Selene expected to be the next day was back at Mackie's club. It had a different atmosphere during the day. Warm and lazy, it begged you to take it easy before the chaos of the night rushed in. It wasn't a bad place to play hooky but unfortunately, that wasn't her plan as she sipped her sidecar.

'My, my,' Nora said as she walked up to the bar. 'I must say this was the last thing I ever expected.'

The feeling was mutual for Selene. She couldn't explain why but the girl stayed under her skin. Maybe it was Nora's brazen demeanour, the cockiness that she carried around, but Selene pushed that aside. She was going to need that for her plan to work.

'Life is better with surprises,' Selene said dryly. She motioned to the seat next to her.

Nora sat delicately, her caramel legs revealing themselves through her deep green dress's high slit. 'And what surprise do you have for me?' She waved the bartender down, smirking as she ordered. 'A martini, please.'

She waited for the bartender to walk away before speaking. 'I need your help fixing Mackie's line-up.'

Nora's smirk fell, and she was silent as the bartender placed her drink on the counter before returning to his tasks. 'I see you've gone mad,' Nora took a long sip from her glass before standing up. 'No, thank you. See you around.' Selene's arm shot out, blocking her path.

'The fighters Mackie is picking are too tough. At this rate, Demir's gonna get knocked out of the game too soon.'

'Knocked out?' Nora snorted before looking her up and down. She lifted her chin, daring the dancer to continue with the insinuation. Nora pursed her lips, backing down. 'I can't tell Mackie how to run his club.'

'But you can convince him to book the new hotshot fighter you heard about. One that's a little easier than what Demir is used to,' Selene urged. 'It's smart, and you know it. Not to mention it keeps him around longer.'

'D's gonna hate it when he finds out. He doesn't want to be babysat.'

Selene rolled her eyes. 'D needs to focus on practice, especially after last night.'

'Watch it,' Nora warned, an edge to her smile.

Selene's gut twisted uncomfortably. So, Nora really did like him. She pushed down a sudden flare of annoyance and focused on the task at hand.

'Look, men don't know what they want. They just act like they do,' Selene reasoned. 'We on the other hand, see a lot more than they ever will.' Nora hummed in contemplation, taking a sultry sip. Selene held back a scowl. Not everything had to be a show.

'You know, we'd have to go and find them,' Nora pointed out.

'I love a chance to get dressed up.' She smirked, channelling the dancer's confidence. 'I'll pass along the names. All you have to do is get them to Mackie.' Nora looked at her up and down and Selene dared to venture she was impressed.

'You really wanna do this?'

Selene shrugged. 'We're already here.' She took another sip of her drink, staring into the amber liquid. 'Why not go all the way?'

'All the way, huh,' Nora murmured, running her fingers around the rim of her martini. She waved, catching the bartender's attention. 'Two champagne cocktails, please!' A minute later, he returned with the drinks. She held one of the glasses out to Selene.

'We'll have to talk about my cut but,' Nora's trademark sultry smirk returned, 'let's do it.'

They clinked glasses, and Selene downed the cocktail quickly, hoping she hadn't made a terrible mistake.

Chapter Twenty-Nine

Washington, D.C.

October 2013

'I'm telling you; I'll be there tomorrow. Really, I'm good now.'

'Fine, but if you pull out at the last minute like last time, I'm beating you with your own guitar,' Ross threatened. 'I almost had to call Oliver to fill in.'

'Oliver's a cool dude.'

Ross scoffed. 'Nigga wants to pretend he's Jimi Hendrix but takes an hour to get a decent take. Be there tomorrow.'

Jones chuckled at his easily frustrated friend. 'Relax, man. I'll be there.'

Hanging up, he went back to the task at hand, flipping through albums in Som Records, decorative vinyl records covering the walls and encouraging him to explore the small shop further. It was no larger than a basement, the room split by a row of pillars. Shelves stood on either side of the far walls; random baskets of vinyl albums tucked into corners. Despite the size, Jones often spent hours in the store for one reason: finding music for his dad.

Though he didn't regularly talk to his parents, he kept in touch with them in his own way. His dad, a former musician, had a vinyl record player that he'd kept from the Eighties. Growing up, Jones had watched him take it apart more than once to fix it. Sometimes, he would help while his dad recounted stories of discovering hip-hop or the concerts he had been to.

During high school, his dad had screened in the back porch of their Atlanta home and moved his record player outside to play every Sunday – his version of church. After Jones had moved out, he created a way to add to the tradition. Every month, he would send his dad different vinyl records, adding to the memories.

Jones was flipping through the R&B section, picking out a few safe bets: Marvin Gaye, Curtis Mayfield and other greats his father had lost over the years. He was looking for something more contemporary when someone stopped in front of him on the other side of the aisle.

'Hmm… I give this album a six out of ten.'

He looked up and saw Dani leaning over the records, staring at his selection. At the top of the stack lay *House of Balloons* by The Weeknd.

'Hello to you, too. But I can't give this less than an eight. It's a classic in the making,' Jones defended.

'True, but how can someone be that sad for so many tracks? Not to mention toxic,' she said, scrunching her nose up.

'Toxic *but* talented.' Jones moved the album to the side so he would remember to buy it. 'Plus, he knows how to stand out, especially nowadays.'

'Fair enough.'

Jones smirked as he spotted an album and grabbed it. 'Speaking of someone who always sings sad songs…' He held up *The Best of Sade* vinyl.

Dani's jaw dropped before she grabbed it from him. 'First of all, not all her songs are sad,' she said. 'Second, her voice is sultry, not whiny.'

'The Weeknd isn't… super whiny.' While talented, Jones wasn't always in the mood for the singer's falsetto tone.

'Say The Weeknd is a better singer than Sade and I will riot,' Dani warned.

Jones looked at her perturbed. 'Never,' he said, taking the album out of her hand and putting that one aside, too.

Jones tilted his head curiously as Dani continued to browse the store, wondering how deep in the memories she was. He would guess their third life, but it was impossible to know if her mind was still going in order like his or—

Don't spiral, he reminded himself.

He almost hated how a question about her memories or research was always on the tip of his tongue. He knew she was doing her best to find a solution and he didn't want to put pressure on her search. On top of that, he couldn't decide whether to feel resigned to the fact that she might not find anything or to start giving in to the flicker of hope that flared up every time she said nothing, thinking maybe she was inching towards something. So, no matter how much he itched to ask, he left it alone.

He blinked, bringing his attention back to the moment as she held up another vinyl. 'Now, *this* is a classic.' She tapped on the cover of *Rapture* by Anita Baker.

'Ay,' he said, reaching out to take a closer look at it. 'This is it. Altos are underappreciated.'

'Oh, absolutely. Alto voices are rich like dark chocolate. But people can't appreciate that either.'

' 'Cause it's bitter as shit,' Jones commented as an idea popped into his head.

Dani opened her mouth to say something but panicked as he pulled the vinyl out of its packaging. She looked over her shoulder, moving so that she was blocking him from the view of the cashier, Carter.

Cute, he thought as she leaned towards him. 'What are you doing?' she whispered.

'Relax, the guy knows me,' he reassured, nodding towards Carter. He removed the paper sleeve and placed it on top of the album cover. 'Now, guess the song.'

Dani watched him nervously as his hand hovered over a set of grooves and he hummed the melody of 'Sweet Love'. Her eyes widened and she turned her ear towards him, listening carefully.

Bobbing her head a couple of times, he expected her to say the title but instead she hummed along, harmonising as they covered the chorus.

He moved his hand and 'played' another song. It took her a few seconds before she switched over. He did that a couple more times. Each time, Dani kept up with him, even dancing a little to 'Same Ole Love'. It was Jones's turn to be impressed.

'It seems like we finally have something in common,' he said, sliding the album back into the sleeve.

Dani chuckled. 'One or two things,' she commented straightening up. Her eyes lit up as she held up Aaliyah's *I Care 4 U* album. 'I love this one.'

'Yeah, Aaliyah was super talented. Had all the potential in the world.' Dani nodded, smile fading as she stared at the album.

'The phenomenon of losing the young and talented.' She slouched, their hands almost touching, and he couldn't help but be hyper aware of the small distance between them. 'How do you live with it?'

'I didn't have to before now,' he said. She looked at him pointedly and he sighed, looking around. 'I guess... I came to terms with it. I can't control life doing what it does.'

'Even if it's tragic?'

He smirked. 'The tragic stories are the best.' Dani cracked a small smile.

'Can't beat potential.' She slipped the Aaliyah out from his pile before walking to the checkout counter. 'I'll text you later.' She didn't look back as she paid for her records and headed for the exit.

'Hey,' he called softly. She turned, looking at him expectantly.

He was about to invite her back to keep the game going. Yet, the words got stuck in his throat. The craving to be near her and the need to protect her from what was coming battled inside him as he looked for something to say. The longer he stared, the more flustered he became. He looked around for a hint, the jazz section catching his eye as he forced himself to smile. 'We'll always have Charlie Parker, right?'

Dani's expectant look transformed into fondness, and she held the Aaliyah album to her chest.

'Charlie is so last century,' she said with a playful eyeroll, nodding just to the side of him. 'Let's have Brandy instead.'

With that, she left, longing piercing his heart, his eyes staying on her until she was out of view. Only then did he look to where she had pointed and chuckled. He picked up the album and headed to the checkout.

'You two are the cutest music nerds I've ever seen,' Carter commented dryly as he rung him up.

'Yeah, maybe.'

He looked at the Brandy album in his hand. The songstress's sultry expression dominated the cover, the title, *Full Moon*, tucked into the corner. He made a mental note to keep the album for himself.

Chapter Thirty

Detroit

June 1946

'Knock, knock.'

Demir looked up from where he sat lounging on Jack's couch to see Nora standing in the doorway. Dressed to the nines, she wore a floor-length, satin pink gown with a matching coat and a pair of chandelier earrings that gleamed in the low light. 'There you are.' She stepped inside and knelt by his side.

'You look nice.'

'I thought I'd recreate the surprise you could've gotten if you'd come to the club the other night,' she said, stroking his face. 'That was one hell of a fight.'

'Shoulda seen the other guy.' He sat up slowly, making room for her on the couch.

'I did.' Nora giggled. 'He needed a few more stitches than you.' Her hand hovered over his ribs as though unsure.

'I wouldn't do that.' The couple turned to see Selene enter the room. 'He's still healing. You could aggravate something if you're not careful.'

'And you're what? His doctor?'

Selene smirked. 'Actually, I am. Nice to see you again, Nora.'

'It's always a pleasure to see Jack's girl,' Nora said. Selene pursed her lips in displeasure. 'Well, don't worry. I'll make sure that your prized fighter is in the best of shape.'

'Sure.' Selene cut her eyes towards Demir before walking out of the room.

Nora scoffed. 'She likes to hover.' She sat on the couch next to Demir, mindful to leave some space.

'She's just cautious. She's seen some shit.'

'Well as long as she's not getting too close…' Nora laid her head on his shoulder, her voice practically a purr. 'I missed you yesterday.'

'I've missed you, too,' Demir responded almost automatically. 'Wish I got a chance to see you in this dress earlier.'

'Well, you have time now,' she whispered, scooting closer.

Demir put his arm on the back of the couch. 'I'm still healing up.'

'We don't have to do what we usually do.' Nora shrugged. 'We can just… talk. I'm really interesting, even with my clothes on.'

'And yet clothes off is so tempting,' Demir teased, leaning towards her. He stopped short as pain shot through his back, groaning as he leaned back.

Nora giggled, moving closer until she was hovering over him. 'I think that's out of the question.' She stroked his face, quickly kissing his lips. He moaned quietly against the touch, leaning into her. 'But we can stay like this for a little while.'

'And talk,' he reminded her, her eyes lighting up as she grinned.

'And talk,' she repeated before leaning down, so her lips met his again.

–

'So, you and Nora are together now,' Selene said on their next walk.

They were circling the block so they could both stretch their legs. Demir was looking a bit better after a couple of weeks of rest, but his movements were still careful. The exercise was good for him and the perfect time to ask the question that had been burning in her mind all weekend.

Demir shrugged. 'No more than before.'

'Wait, you're not?' Selene raised a brow. 'That's surprising.'

'We don't take things seriously,' he said.

She snorted. 'Okay, that's not surprising for either of you.' Demir shook his head in amused exasperation before flicking her nose. Glaring, she tried to slap his arm, but he dodged.

She scowled. Sometimes, she hated that he was so agile. 'Don't be a snob,' he told her.

'You're the one saying she's for play, not me,' she snapped.

'What's with you?' he asked with furrowed brows. 'I thought you and Nora were friends. You're always talking at the club.'

Selene sneered but said nothing. No matter how it appeared, all she and Nora had to discuss was business, and she wanted to keep it that way. Between dipping into her emergency fund to secure the new fighters and juggling everyone's expectations, she didn't have the energy to hide her disdain. She highly doubted the dancer cared for her opinion; clearly, she did not like Selene either.

Meanwhile, Selene was trying to keep everything together and clearly none of the men in her life appreciated it. As per usual, she was the one bearing all the criticism. She and Nora both had the same slick mouth, but *she* was the one getting scolded? Give her a break.

'Did you know that Nora's travelled to Europe? She regularly writes to her friends in Paris,' Demir continued. 'She also works at several clubs, making enough money to live downtown. Mackie's is just her favourite.'

'So what?'

'Maybe you should talk to her instead of judging her. After all, she's living her life by her own rules. Isn't she doing what you wanna do?'

'For the love of…' She rubbed her temples to fight against the burgeoning headache.

'I saw your hustle back at the old gym, how you would patch up the opponents first after fights for extra money. You don't do that now.'

'What can I say, boxers can be dangerous,' she replied coolly, her anger turning sombre. They were both silent. Some days, she could still feel his fingers digging into her neck. 'He was one of my first clients, you know.'

Demir tilted his head curiously.

'The guy who cornered me at the gym. He tried to flirt with me when I patched him up, but he was so out of it, I thought nothing of it. And then...'

'I'm sorry,' he said softly, regret filling his voice.

I bet, she thought with a scowl. She didn't need his pity.

'I can dislike Nora all I want,' Selene continued. 'She won't care. So, leave it alone.' She looked at Demir long and hard before continuing to walk. He didn't try to catch up, opting to trail behind until they found their way back to the car.

–

Everyone in Jack's apartment gathered around the radio, eager to hear the Sugar Ray Robinson fight. While Demir usually preferred to listen to fights by himself, he couldn't deny that he was having a good time as people leaned closer to the radio in anticipation. He also found himself enjoying the way Nora held his hand, her body trembling in excitement.

'*Rubio throws a hook and misses. Robinson counters. Rubio goes down!*'

Jack's friends cheered loudly, some arguing about bets made earlier in the night as their conversations drowned out the radio.

'Shut up!' Jack turned up the volume.

'*That's it! Rubio is down for the count. Robinson wins!*'

The cheers returned and Demir joined in as Nora jumped up, hugging people randomly before coming back. She planted a kiss on his lips that was more of a smile than anything, but he returned it all the same.

He smirked. 'Having fun?'

'Tons,' she replied and pecked him on the lips again. 'Now, time to get my money from Stella. Stella, don't think I forgot!' Nora shuffled off to the kitchen, following one of her friends.

Demir relaxed, settling against the couch. News about the WWII aftermath started to come through, but someone switched to a music station. A couple of guys moved the chairs and dining table from the middle of the room, creating an impromptu dance floor. A few of the girls pulled their dates to the floor and started jiving, their legs moving lightning quick. Chatter rose around him, some people playing cards in the corner as they smoked while others seemed caught in a debate of one philosophy or the other.

Surprised Selene isn't over there.

Just as the thought crossed his mind, she appeared from another room. She sat on Jack's lap, whispering in his ear, making him laugh as he wrapped his arm around her waist. Demir quickly turned away, not wanting to feel what he always felt when he saw the couple. He didn't have to linger on his own thoughts for long though, as Nora came stumbling back into the room with a glass of wine. She took a long gulp and fell on the couch, glazed eyes staring at him.

'I wish…' she started before falling silent.

He turned towards her and tugged at a curl that had escaped from its bun. 'Wish what?'

She blinked a couple times, her eyes clearing up as she straightened. 'I wish you would dance with me,' she said quickly, plastering a forced smile on her face. 'Dance with me, D.'

'Oh no,' he protested as she grabbed his hands. 'I'm better here.'

'Oh, come on. You're all healed up and no one's gonna care if you're not good. Everyone's drunk anyway. Just one little dance for me.'

'I'm fine, Nora,' he told her, pulling his hands out of her grip.

'Of course, you are,' she said, lips pursed as she sat back down. 'What does that mean?'

She scoffed. 'Of course, you're fine with us doing nothing,' she elaborated. 'It's what we always do. Oh, except sex. You always have time and energy for that.'

'Yeah, well, so do you,' he shot back. 'I don't get it. You never had a problem before. What's wrong now?'

'What's wrong is that we've been at this for six months,' she snapped. 'It's not just a casual thing for me anymore. You know I care about you. We talk. We're getting to know each other. You're telling me you don't want more than this?' Nora stared at him baffled. 'When are you gonna take me on a real date, D? When is it gonna be more than just the club or parties or random nights spent together? When are you gonna be in this for real?'

'I never asked for any of that. I haven't changed, so why are you expecting something different?' he defended. 'Look, Mackie asked you to keep me company for one night. No one forced you into this.'

'Wow.' She shook her head, blinking back tears. 'You're awful. Just like the rest of them.'

'Sure,' he said passively as he got up. 'Where are you going?'

He ignored her and grabbed his jacket from the back of the couch, shrugging it on. He headed up to the roof.

The distant skyline twinkled, feeling impossible to reach as Demir leaned on the edge, brooding in the dark by himself. He wished he could be the same. This was the reason he avoided people; the expectations that came with them were unbearable. He patted his pocket, sighing when he realised it was empty. 'Fuck.'

'Looking for these?' He turned to find Selene holding up his pack of cigarettes. It must have fallen out when he left. The door swung closed behind her as she stepped onto the roof, holding out the pack to him. He snatched it from her, too agitated to be gentle. She didn't seem to mind as she joined him. He quickly lit one of the cigarettes and took a long drag before exhaling.

'Nora asked me to check on you, which I didn't expect. The crying was a surprise, too.'

Guilt welled up inside him, and Demir frowned, continuing to smoke and determined to ignore the feeling. Selene took the cigarette from his fingers and inhaled. His stomach curled like the puff of smoke she let out. It reminded him of when they would hang out on his fire escape, something they hadn't done since their spat earlier in the week. He wondered if it was normal to miss someone after only a few days.

'What's going on with you two?'

'Nothing,' he said quickly. 'And that's why she's annoyed. Now, she's suddenly asking me about dates and shit. We didn't need all that before tonight. Now, we get in front of people, and she wants to be a girlfriend.'

Brows furrowed, she put his cigarette out. 'Demir, do you care about her?'

'Of course I do,' he answered. 'But I don't want anything serious.'

'With her or with anyone?'

He looked over to the city again and tried to imagine a world where he wasn't always fighting or living one day at a time. The picture was fuzzy in his mind. 'I don't know,' he admitted.

Selene shifted awkwardly beside him. 'You know, I hate to be the bearer of bad news,' she said after a moment. 'But you did kind of lie to her.'

'How did I do that?' he snapped.

'Calm down, big guy,' Selene said with a small smile. 'What I mean is, from the outside looking in, it looks like you guys are together. A guy like you doesn't give people attention. So, when you do, it feels like a big deal. You make people feel… special when you talk to them.' She looked at him with an intensity he wasn't used to seeing from her. 'It's… addictive, talking to you. You make people want to figure you out.' She shrugged, her nonchalance feeling strained. 'We just can't help it.'

'We?' he asked quietly.

Selene's eyes widened as if just realising what she said. However, instead of looking away like he expected, her gaze dropped to his lips before returning to his eyes. A jolt ran through Demir as all the tension between them came into perspective. For a moment, his mind dared to go into territory he had been denying himself for months. He felt a thrill go up his spine as she swayed towards him, tempting him to move closer.

Just a taste…

Selene took a deep breath before stepping back, breaking the spell over them and he turned so she couldn't see his disappointment. His eyes stayed on the sky as she started to walk away.

'If you like her, don't ruin it just because you can.' Demir looked over his shoulder. Between her cautious steps and hesitant gaze, she seemed just as conflicted as he felt. 'You should try to be happy as much as you can while you can.'

And then, she left without another word.

Demir tapped his fingers on the roof's edge before following her back to the party. It was surreal stepping inside, the chaotic energy jarring after the quiet of the rooftop. He looked around and saw Nora, teary-eyed and talking to her friends. Her gaze roamed the room, widening when she saw him. Putting down her drink, she went to him. 'D, listen—'

'I'm sorry,' he cut in. 'I didn't mean to upset you. I was just surprised.'

'I mean, you're right,' she admitted uncomfortably. 'We're just having fun and…'

'Maybe,' he sighed. 'But I shouldn't have done that. I do care about you, Nora. So, let's just keep talking about it. Okay?' A small but wary smile spread across her face.

'O–Okay.'

He grabbed her hand and pulled her into an embrace. They stayed like that until the song switched to something much slower.

'We can dance to this,' he offered. 'It's more my speed.'

Nora looked at him in disbelief before laughing. 'Yeah, we can do that.'

Eagerly, she pulled him to the middle of the room, his hands settling on her lower back, her arms around his neck. Demir followed her steps, the two of them swaying side-to-side. It was slow and sweet, Nora looking at him with wide, earnest eyes. 'I am sorry,' she repeated. 'You know that, right?'

Demir tried not to shift uncomfortably beneath her gaze. Instead, he pulled her close, resting his cheek against hers. 'I know,' he whispered in her ear. 'Me too.'

Nora let out a sigh of relief and laid her head on his shoulder.

Nearby, Selene swayed to the music, peering over Jack's shoulder. Gaze filled with uncertainty, she caught his eye. Demir tried to look away – like he always did – but stopped as her eyes stayed transfixed on him.

They stared, each waiting for the other to break, but instead, their gazes softened. Only then did he notice the yearning in her eyes and the short distance between them. How easy would it be to cross the room and take her into his arms? How easy would it be to kiss her like he had wanted to on the roof? In his mind, he was already taking the first steps and reaching out. She was meeting him halfway; his arm was wrapping around her waist just as her hand reached to caress his cheek…

Jack whispered something in Selene's ear, and she looked away, burying her face into her lover's neck.

Demir closed his eyes for a moment, remembering where he was, who was in his arms, and what it would really mean to cross that line.

Chapter Thirty-One

Demir struck the punching bag, darting around as he worked on his speed. He'd been lagging in his last few fights and was tired of getting hit when it could be avoided. Stepping back from the bag, he practised several different combinations.

From the corner of his eye, he could see Selene talking on the gym's phone. He couldn't hear her, but hand on her hip, she kept gesturing the same way she always did when she argued with Jack. Clearly, they weren't having a good day. Shaking his head, he focused on the punching bag. With another fight around the corner, this wasn't the time to be distracted.

The sun sank lower as he practised, arm aching, throat parched. Sweat dropped off him as he went to get his water bottle. Selene was sitting next to his bag, but he said nothing while taking off his gloves.

Much like their first month together, they didn't really speak anymore. He wished he could go back to when their silence was to avoid agitation. Now, it was chock-full of questions he couldn't bring himself to ask.

Digging into his bag, he found the bottle and took a long gulp before wiping his mouth.

He ignored the way Selene's eyes lingered on him.

'Jack can't make it today. He's checking out some new fighter Mackie told him about, an Italian he's been doing business with.

He's trying to get in good with the coaches to see if they rig fights.'

'Jack the Spy,' Demir replied dryly. 'Go figure.'

'Yep. He also said he found a sparring guy that should be here tomorrow to help.'

Demir nodded as he started to pack his things. She slid off the seat, following suit. 'You can, um, drop me off at Jack's.'

He opened his mouth to agree when Selene's stomach growled. Her eyes widened as she covered her face in embarrassment. 'I skipped lunch,' she explained, refusing to look at him.

Chuckling, he closed his bag. 'Then, we'll go get something to eat before I drop you off.' 'Demir... we don't have to—'

'Jack would kill me if he knew I let you starve,' Demir reasoned. 'Besides I'm hungry too, and this makes things easier.'

'Right. Guess easy won't be so bad,' she said reluctantly.

'Good.' He nodded towards her stuff. 'Get your books and let's go.'

—

They found a diner around the corner from Jack's place. The food was good and the coffee decent, so they didn't have much to complain about. Or at least, Demir didn't; Selene always found something to fuss over. As to why it no longer bothered him anymore, he chalked it up as part of her charm.

'You shouldn't eat so fast,' she chastised.

'You just like telling people what to do,' he told her around a bite of food, wiping his mouth with a napkin before continuing. 'You must have a bunch of brothers and sisters.'

'Just two,' she said, picking at what was left on her plate. 'Two sisters. Dad works all the time, and my mum used to wash clothes. Now, she stays home to watch my sisters since I'm not there and I send money home.'

'She knows what you do?'

'Hell no. She thinks I'm getting it from Jack to "stay pretty."'
Selene rolled her eyes before taking another bite.

'So, she likes Jack.'

'She adores him.' Selene sighed. 'Meanwhile, my dad can't stand him. He would drag me out of school if he knew that I was staying at his place.' Demir grimaced before continuing to eat and Selene let out a short laugh. 'Dramatic, I know, but it is what it is. No use in trying to change it now.'

'So… you and Jack have always been tied at the hip?'

'More or less,' she said, taking a sip of coffee. 'He was just… there. I can't remember a time he wasn't. I miss those days sometimes. Now…' She shook her head. 'I shouldn't be telling you all this.'

For a moment, the air became thick with the same tension they had at the party. Demir pushed past it; it was a momentary lapse in judgement. It shouldn't have so much sway over them. They just had to get over the awkwardness.

'You might as well finish the story,' he said, trying his best to sound like a supportive friend.

Selene stared at her plate with a frown. 'There's just been space between us lately,' she murmured.

'You're worried about him going out on his own.'

'Please, Jack can hold his own. I'm not worried about that.'

Demir held back a laugh, trying to be understanding of her frustration, but it was kind of cute watching her stuff her face like a brat.

Selene chewed quickly, swallowing and placing her fork on the table. 'We used to check out fighters together all the time,' she said suddenly. 'It was our date night. We would get dressed up, watch fights, and would celebrate at a nearby club. Now, he just wants to go out whenever, and I don't like it.'

She tapped her spoon on the edge of her coffee cup until Demir covered her hand. He made sure not to linger as he took the spoon and hoped she didn't notice his nervous swallow. 'You're going to hate me for asking this and I mean no disrespect by it,' Demir warned her. He placed his elbows on the table, leaning forward and lowering his voice. 'Do you think he's seeing another woman?'

'What? No! He better not!'

The certainty in her voice stabbed him in the chest as he sat back.

Selene's eyes widened at her outburst, and she sighed, rubbing her temples. 'I mean, he's not that type of guy. He's very loyal.'

'Then, you have nothing to worry about. He'll come back around soon. He adores you.' The words were forced but true. He saw no point in trying to manipulate Selene's view of Jack. She was too smart for it, and he was still trying to be a good friend.

'Speaking of time, the night's still young, and I'd rather not be in the apartment by myself. Let's do something else,' she suggested.

'Like what?' She bit her lip, looking around. Demir breathed slowly as he felt the urge to reach out and press his thumb against her bottom lip, releasing it from her teeth. He almost closed his eyes to compose himself. Overnight, what used to be a simple gesture had become torture to him and telling her probably wouldn't help. She'd either avoid him or worse – do it even more. Her eyes lit up and she leaned forward with an innocent smile, her voice sweet.

'Mind if I drive?'

His answer was automatic. 'Yes.'

Eyes narrowed, she scoffed. Something about how quickly the switch happened made him laugh. This girl was the worst... but he liked it.

He let out a loud sigh before holding out his keys. 'Where are we going?'

–

'Ta–da!' Selene turned the engine off before holding her arms out as much as she could inside the car.

Demir's grip on his seat loosened finally as he warily looked out the window. 'We're by the river,' he said before looking at her. 'Are you about to kill me?'

Immediately, her smile disappeared as she sucked her teeth.

'Boy, stop it. Come on.' She stepped outside and took a deep breath, soaking in the sight in front of her. A full moon shone in the night sky, revealing the outline of Belle Isle in the distance. Moonlight made the water shimmer and dance. 'Beautiful, huh?'

Demir followed, joining Selene as she lay across the hood of the car, the leftover heat from the engine providing enough warmth to make her comfortable. 'Sure,' he drawled, still on edge.

'Will you relax?' She patted the space next to her. 'No one knows about this place.' 'That's what everyone says until it's too late.'

'Well, if some crazy white man wanted to murder me in the middle of the night, he's already had plenty of chances,' she told him. 'My daddy found this place years ago. When I was little, we used to come here every full moon to "get rid of our anger".'

'Clearly didn't help that much.'

But instead of getting irritated, Selene merely laughed. 'Oh, if you think I'm bad now, you should have seen me back then. I raised hell with my mum every chance I got.'

'Why?'

She shrugged. 'She wanted me to be mature, look out for my siblings and help her with the cleaning. I wanted to be a kid. We've never been the type to get along.' Her mind flashed through the arguments she had with her mum as a child. It was disheartening how few good memories she had with her. Even then, most everything was riddled with disagreements… or fear. Her head suddenly felt light, and she reminded herself to breathe. 'I think my daddy saw his anger in me and wanted to stop it in its track before it was too late.'

'What would you guys do out here?'

'Just throw rocks in the water. It was kind of silly looking back but it's some of the best memories I have of him. Wanna try?' She didn't wait for his answer, instead sliding off the hood to grab one of the rocks under her feet. Smooth and flat, it warmed the palm of her hand.

Picturing her nightmare of a biology professor, she flung it as far as she could. The distance was satisfying, the stone disappearing with a *plunk* beneath the surface. She picked up another rock, focusing on one frustration or another, and threw it.

After a few more, Demir joined her. She didn't ask him what he was picturing; her dad had warned her not to.

'That's another man's burden,' he'd said. 'You don't need to be a part of that.'

The memory made her pause, and she grunted, flinging the stone as far as she could. That one didn't feel as great as the others.

'Your father may be onto something,' Demir said.

She tried to force a smile, but it was lacklustre. She tossed another rock so lightly it barely made it into the water.

'You okay?'

Selene opened her mouth to lie, to say something clever but something stopped her. The thought of lying about it, like she always had, exhausted her. For once, she was tired of hiding.

'…I don't know what happened to my father,' she confessed. 'My sisters and I had heard about the war and all the other shit that's always happening, but he was a good dad. He was strict but he never hurt us. Not until he got fired from his job and started drinking more… it was like a switch. One day, he loved us and the next we were the reason his life was shit. You and Jack are lucky. You can punch your way through life while I'm stuck. If not with him, then another man.'

Demir said nothing, making her nervous. He didn't want to be out here and now she was telling her life story. She knew better than that.

It was only when he took her hand that her mind stopped churning.

'Punching only gets you halfway there,' Demir told her. 'Walking away, well, that will take you anywhere you wanna go.'

Selene looked up at him, his skin blue in the pale light of the moon. It made her think of the river in front of them as the light danced across his striking features, and she wished she had asked more about him. Over and over, she realised she didn't know much. Even worse, she found the desire to know more growing stronger every day. And the thought of him one day not being in her life… 'What do I do if someone wants to walk away from me?'

'Jack won't do that. He's just figuring it all out. Give it some time.'

She faced the water, watching the moon's shimmering reflection. She didn't want him to see her disappointment at his answer, one she wasn't even sure about herself. She pulled her hand out of his.

'Is that what you needed with Nora?' Selene asked. 'She seems happier when we go to the club. Or at least hates me less.'

'Why does she hate you in the first place?'

'She probably thinks I'm pretentious, just like I think she's a whore. Not that either of us were wrong,' she said with a shrug.

'Sel, come on.'

She put her hands up as if surrendering. 'I promise, I am not talking bad about her. I'm just saying we've had our views of each other from the beginning. We're not supposed to get along. We understand each other better now and that's enough. But you haven't answered my question.'

'Which is?'

'Are you and Nora better now?'

Demir was quiet as he thought about her question. From where Selene stood, the answer was obvious. Nora had been smiling more, and Jack was always mentioning Demir going on dates. She swallowed the bitterness that seemed to appear every time she saw the two together.

They're good together.

Demir was her friend. She needed to be happy that he'd found someone that suited him. And yet…

'Yeah,' he finally said. 'We are. We're still taking it slow but I'm not ruling it out like before.'

Selene bit her lip, holding back a frown. Slowly, she nodded. 'Thanks for talking to me that night. I needed it.'

'It's the least I could do. You've looked out for me since the beginning,' she said.

'Wouldn't be too sure about that,' he replied. 'Once upon a time, we hated each other, remember?'

Selene huffed, laughing. 'How could I forget?' she said. A sudden wistful smile crossed her face. 'That's kind of the ironic thing about our relationship. The first time you helped me, you were actually being an asshole.'

Demir tilted his head in confusion before motioning for her to continue.

'I can't thank you enough for taking the money Jack wanted to give me after that first fight. Do you remember?'

Demir nodded.

'It was the first time someone was on my side for that kind of thing. Maybe you won't get it as a man because, no matter what, you can own *something*. Jack will never see a problem with it, because he's always taken care of me, but I always feel like I have to prove I own everything I've got, which is why I don't want Jack's handouts. He's already given me too much. I'm not even his wife.'

Demir's eyes flickered to her hand, her fingers bare, but they both knew jewellery only amounted to so much.

'You might as well be,' he pointed out. 'Everyone knows you're his girl, no matter what you do or who you talk to. You might as well have a ring on your finger.'

'I'm *not* his wife,' she snapped, her skin hot from the implication. 'Don't matter what anyone has to say about it, that's the truth. Got that?'

Demir blinked several times, probably shocked by the intensity of her words. She fidgeted under his lingering gaze but didn't take back what she had said.

Selene could see herself spending the rest of her life with him, but being a wife was different. It came with responsibilities she didn't want. It also meant being tied to someone for better or worse, and she had seen how quickly people could change. Hell, she changed all the time. Just the thought of Jack becoming a stranger to her in the worst kind of way made the hairs on her neck stand on their ends.

'Loud and clear,' he answered. 'Are you ready to go?'

Selene opened her mouth before closing it, uncertain. She stood instead and walked towards the passenger side.

Demir didn't comment on the change as he went around. 'You heard about Mackie booking Parker this weekend?' he asked once they were in the car.

Selene paused, looking at him in surprise. 'I… no. He got Charlie Parker?'

'Nora said they go way back,' he said. 'Apparently, the place is going to be packed.'

'I–I mean of course it is!' Voice budding with excitement, she squealed. 'It's Charlie Parker! I love his record with Dizzy. I can't believe Mack made that happen! I have to find a new dress!'

'Of course, that's the first thing you think off,' he said dryly.

'Of course it is,' she repeated and stuck her tongue out at him. 'I'm seeing someone important.'

'And why would he want to see a brat like you?'

'Don't call me a brat.' Scowling, Selene smacked his arm. 'I'm way smarter than you'll ever be.'

'Oh, I know,' he said, the corner of his lips lifting into a smile. 'But you're still a brat.'

'Nobody asked you,' she grumbled, anticipation bubbling up inside her as they drove home.

She wiggled in her seat, humming one of her favourite Charlie Parker songs. At some point, Demir put a hand on her leg to stop her from moving, but she just grabbed it, singing into it like it was a mic. The song was off key, and, for a moment, he stiffened awkwardly while driving with one hand, but eventually her bad singing made them both laugh the rest of the way home. It was the most fun Selene had had in a long time, and she was glad it was with him.

The sudden thought made her laughter stop short as they parked behind Jack's apartment building.

When did that happen?

The change in energy was immediate, and Demir's smile disappeared. He looked at her curiously, but she shook her head, getting out and waiting for him to exit the car so they could take the back way in.

'And here we are,' he announced once they had reached Jack's door.

Selene dug into her purse for her keys. 'Thanks for walking me,' she said politely. She stopped before unlocking it, facing him.

'Maybe next time…' She licked her lips nervously before clearing her throat. 'We shouldn't talk about Jack or Nora.'

'Seems like we'll run out of things to talk about.' 'There's other things.'

He raised an eyebrow before stepping closer. She tensed but didn't move away, despite having the room.

'Like what?' His voice was quiet, and she stared at him, a sudden sense of longing punching her in the gut.

Tongue-tied, she tried to force a smile. 'Jazz,' she whispered and turned to unlock the door, slipping inside.

She leaned against the door, heart racing a mile a minute. She felt her cheeks heat up and patted them in an attempt to calm herself. This needed to stop. It was bad enough she had wanted to dance with him at the party weeks ago, but now this?

'Baby, is that you?'

Selene jumped, turning to look in the living room. Groggy, Jack lay on the couch. He must have fallen asleep there.

'Hey,' she said breathlessly. 'I thought you were at the fight.'

'It ended early. Guy was a dud,' he grumbled as he sat up. 'Called the gym but no one answered. Figured you left so I came home.'

'Oh, I grabbed some dinner,' she explained, taking off her shoes. She went over to him and held her hands out. 'Come on. Let's get you to bed.'

Slowly, Jack blinked and took her hands. She almost laughed at the sleep lines on his face. He had definitely been dreaming. Wrapping his arm around her shoulder, they walked to the bedroom. He flopped down on the mattress, and she giggled as she pulled off his shoes.

'Who did you go with,' he asked sleepily. She froze.

'Huh?'

'Dinner,' he clarified. 'Who did you go with?'

'Oh, just Demir. We got sandwiches.'

'M-hm,' Jack mumbled and drifted back to sleep.

Selene felt a pang of guilt as she watched him. She had no real reason to lie to him. Yet, it didn't stop her from standing over the sink, scrubbing off the mud from her shoes.

Chapter Thirty-Two

Detroit

September 1946

Demir felt like he was standing on an edge, seconds from falling, and he loved it. The adrenaline from his fight still coursing through his veins, he entered Mackie's club, Jack's arm around his shoulders and Nora on his arm. The crowd parted for them, whistling and cheering as the band played an exciting tune cued for their entrance. Demir didn't smile, his body was buzzing.

With a record of 23-0, Demir was officially eligible to fight in the Golden Gloves.

'Now, that's what I call a welcome,' Jack yelled into his ear as a blur of people congratulated him, and he thanked as many as he could as they made their way to a booth.

The trio sat, and, instantly, people crowded around them, a couple of photographers hounding them for pictures. Demir scowled and held his hand out, blocking his face from view. He started to lean forward to grab the camera when Nora pulled his arm down.

'Let's just take one,' she said, her eyes bright from the excitement in the room. 'It'll be our first picture together.'

They snapped what felt like a million photos, the lights temporarily blinding him. At some point, Jack put his hand on Demir's shoulder, smiling; he was the only one who wasn't.

'See, that wasn't so bad,' Nora said as the photographers stepped away.

Demir shrugged as a server filled everyone's glass with champagne, placing the chilled bottle in a bucket in the centre of the table. He doubted she would have the same sentiment when she saw the pictures.

'Hey, Sel!' Jack hopped out of the booth, meeting Selene on the dance floor. She shone under the club lights, a sparkling silver dress hugging her figure nicely. She kissed Jack's cheek, embracing him tightly, glowing every step to the table.

'Evening, everyone,' she greeted when Jack escorted her to the table.

'My, my, Selene.' Nora's eyes lit up as she looked over Selene's outfit. 'That dress is marvellous! Where did you get such a stunning outfit?'

'My aunt is a seamstress for a boutique downtown. They had some extra fabric and, when I told her I was seeing Charlie Parker tonight, she wanted me to look nice.'

'Well, you succeeded. If only you were here when the cameras were,' Nora smirked, but it was more playful than usual. Even Selene cracked a smile, stepping out of Jack's arms to do a spin. His eyes widened before he headed towards the dance floor, but she caught him before he could step away.

'Where are you going?'

'I'm going to get the photographers,' Jack said, cupping her face. 'So, people fifty years from now can still be jealous of your beauty.' He placed a quick peck on her lips, and she laughed as he raced into the crowd.

'Come sit down.' Nora reached over Demir's lap and patted the seat next to him. 'We missed you at the fight earlier.'

'I had a test at school,' Selene said, her eyes focusing on Demir. 'Congratulations!'

'We're going to New York,' he told her.

'Once we make it through the tournament, and we still have a few more fights before that,' she said. He knew she was trying not to get her hopes up, but she could barely contain her smile as she grabbed his chin gently, turning it side to side. 'Looks like you didn't get beat up too bad.' She lightly touched the bruise on the side of his face, ghosting over where his lip split, and his skin tingled. Demir grabbed her hand and, reluctantly, moved it away.

'Because I'm good,' he replied. 'And I didn't want Jack trying to patch me up and fuck something up.'

Selene laughed and leaned back. 'I wish I could've been there for the knockout.'

'It was spectacular,' Nora jumped in. Selene and Demir looked at the dancer. She still wore a smile, but there was an edge to it. 'One of his best fights yet. Wouldn't you agree, honey?'

Demir looked at her in confusion. 'I guess,' he answered, trying to figure out where the pet name came from.

'Seems like one of those lucky nights,' Selene replied coolly.

'I'll say.' Nora snuggled into his side. He and Selene made eye contact, him puzzled by the sudden affection while she moved a couple inches away. Their eyes lingered a second too long and she grabbed one of the glasses of champagne, finishing it seconds later. The trio sat awkwardly until Jack came back with a photographer in tow.

'Ready,' he asked the group as he slid into the booth. Nora rested her chin on Demir's shoulder while Selene adjusted her hair. Jack rested his arm on the back of the booth. Demir made sure to look straight ahead, his face as stoic as usual.

Click. Click.

The night continued in full swing. Demir couldn't call himself much of a fan of jazz, although he preferred it to the classical music his aunt had seemed obsessed with throughout his childhood – but watching Charlie Parker blew all his preconceived notions of the genre out the water. He could see why Selene vibrated with excitement as they watched his band; it was thrilling.

'I can't believe this,' Selene kept saying over and over as Charlie's fingers glided over his saxophone. Demir was inclined to agree as he could barely keep his eyes off the musicians as the sound of horns blared. Suddenly, the song slowed. There was a quiet, almost romantic tone that calmed the crowd before the horns screeched and took off lightning quick.

The transition caused Selene to jump in her seat and grab his hand. Demir glanced down at their hands and then back at her, but she seemed mesmerised by the band, head moving with the music, her lips stretched into a wide smile. She had never looked happier.

He squeezed her hand lightly.

Selene seemed to snap out of her reverie, but she didn't look at him. She also didn't pull her hand away until the song ended. Only then did the pair separate to clap, Selene standing as much as she could in the booth.

Charlie stood up and made his way to the microphone. 'Thank you, thank you. Now, according to my friend, Mackie, tonight is a special night, and I know only one way to celebrate. So, grab a partner and come along.' He turned to his band. 'Are we ready?'

The band agreed as the crowd started to clap. Charlie lifted his saxophone to his lips and the song jumped straight into a high-speed melody.

'We *have* to dance.' Selene urged Jack out of the booth and pulled him quickly to the dance floor.

Nora laughed at the couple before standing as well. 'Now, don't you leave me on this dance floor by myself.' She placed her hand on her hip and looked at him expectantly.

Smirking, he followed, taking Nora into his arms when they reached the dance floor. He made sure to stay near the edge, so they didn't get in the way of the real dancers. While he didn't consider himself the best, he could keep up with the rhythm, which was good enough for him.

They danced, occasionally stopping when someone brought him a shot for winning the fight or when one of Nora's friends would come to say hi.

Eventually, the songs became slower, and he could just sway for a little while Nora stared into his eyes, and he felt a certain fondness for the girl in his arms. Nora was beautiful, smarter than she let on, and unflinchingly honest. Everything about her was desirable. It would be easy to make a life with her. And maybe, just maybe, he could want it…

A glimpse of silver caught his eye, and he turned his head. Jack was spinning Selene in circles, her dress catching the light before she was pulled into Jack's chest, beaming. Demir's heart skipped a beat at her smile.

He didn't even realise he was slowing down to watch her until he heard Nora say, 'How many times are you gonna do that?'

Demir tore his eyes from Selene to look down at Nora. 'Do what?'

Her hands slid from his shoulder to his chest, palms resting over his rapidly beating heart.

'Look over my shoulder to watch her… look at her the way I want you to look at me.' Nora swallowed, her eyes shiny. 'If I didn't know better, I would say she's the reason you dance with me. Why you're with me at all.'

They stopped, and the crowd moved around them without care. Demir felt a wave of guilt as he peered into her glazed eyes. 'What's the other reason then?'

She looked down at their feet before resting her head on his chest. 'You're almost a good guy. Too nice to break my heart but too cruel to let me go.' She stepped away from him, her expression sombre. 'Thanks for the dance. I won't be needing another.'

'Wait…' He reached out to her, but she avoided his touch, weaving between the dancers until he lost sight of her.

'D!' He felt someone's hand on his shoulder and looked to see Jack grinning.

'Mackie's about to introduce us to Charlie! You gotta—' His grin fell. 'What happened?'

She saw how I feel about your girl.

Demir clenched his fist as the thought swiftly came across his mind. Before he could make up a lie, Selene waved at them excitedly, beckoning them over as she stood beside Charlie Parker with a wide grin. Ignoring Jack's questioning look, Demir went to her side.

'There you guys are!' She hugged Demir and then Jack. 'Just in time.'

'I'll say,' Jack told her as he took the spot on the other side of the jazz musician. 'Nice to meet you, Mr Parker.'

'Same to you.' Charlie nodded his head towards Demir. 'Nice fight tonight, champ.'

He nodded but stayed silent as the group posed for the picture.

Suddenly, Selene gasped. 'Wait, we forgot Nora,' she said. 'Let me find her real quick.' Demir grabbed her by the waist, stopping her.

'Don't worry about it,' he said quickly, urging her back to her spot.

She looked at him baffled as the first flash went off. The photographer yelled for her to look forward and she did with an easy smile, though a small pinch of concern furrowed her brow.

Hopefully, the camera wouldn't pick it up.

It took three more pictures before he remembered to move his hand from her waist.

–

'It's just perfect.' Selene stared at the newspaper before hugging it close to her chest. 'Aren't you afraid of ruining it?' Demir teased from Jack's couch.

'I bought extra copies,' she said, waving away the worry. Chuckling, he closed his eyes.

Two days had passed since the night at Mackie's club. For the most part, he had healed up, but Selene could tell he was still sore. As such, she insisted he rested a bit longer. Despite the short time frame, Demir had already become restless. She had done her best to distract him with conversation, sharing stories about her childhood or with card games. The times he didn't want to talk or play games, she would re-read the Charlie Parker article.

It always made her giddy when she saw the picture. She had stood right next to him! Well, next to Demir, who was next to him, but it was good enough.

'I still can't believe it. Actual proof that me and Charlie Parker were in the same room. He liked my dress. Ugh, I wish they got a picture of him kissing my hand,' she gushed. 'I'll never throw this paper out.'

'Jack might,' Demir murmured.

Selene's jaw dropped and she chucked the newspaper at him. 'That's not even funny!'

It didn't stop Demir from chuckling as he gathered up the pages. He stared at the picture before frowning.

'What's with the face?'

'They didn't put your name.' He handed it back to her. Her eyes roamed over the page for a moment before spotting the caption.

> *Charlie Parker (right) with amateur boxer, Demir 'Doomsday' Elliot (left), his coach (far right), and beauty (far left) at the Blue Rabbit Club.*

'Oh,' she said and shrugged. 'That's all right. I didn't expect them to. Besides, I look fantastic.'

'You don't mind no one knowing your name?'

'Nope. Besides, Charlie Parker does.' She winked.

Demir shook his head but said nothing as he stared at the ceiling. 'I guess. It'll be a nice surprise in a few years when the papers have to start calling you Dr Robinson,' he surmised.

Selene paused, once again finding herself stunned by his words. So many times, people had dismissed her when she said she would be a doctor. The few times they would acknowledge it, they always attached Jack's name to it. She should be used to it but there was a unique sting every time she was called the 'future Dr Sullivan', like she wasn't even allowed to have her own dreams.

It was nice about having someone who didn't question her ability to make something happen by herself. She could fall in love with a man like that.

'What?' he asked, and realising she was staring, she looked away, changing the subject quickly.

'Nothing. So, what do you want to do? Make it count. It'll be the last time you will get the privilege of my presence for a week.'

'So, you and Jack are going on a trip soon,' Demir noted dryly.

The holiday had been months in the making with Selene and Jack bouncing around ideas of where to go and how long they could be away. She hadn't thought much of it – just another plan that could fall through at any moment – until Jack showed her a map a few days ago with a route already marked out. He'd had stars in his eyes when he told her about the lake and all the things they were going to do. Selene was glad he'd been distracted; the panic on her face would've been too obvious.

Jack rarely went big but when he did, he pulled out all the stops. And there were only a few 'surprises' left in their relationship.

'Yep,' she said, forcing a light tone to her voice. 'We finally found some time to be alone.' They sat in awkward silence before she cleared her throat. 'So, um, what to do. What to do…'

'What can I do that doesn't involve you chasing me down?'

Her shoulders relaxed as she eased back into the conversation.

'I don't "chase you down".' She rolled her eyes before looking around. 'We could play cards, listen to the radio. I guess I could get you a few magazines, if you can read 'em.' She winced before looking at him apologetically. 'Not that I'm assuming you can't. I just— I mean, I know everyone's not the best. Not that it means you're dumb. Jack struggles with it sometimes. I'm not comparing you to Jack—'

'I can read,' he replied, so calm it bordered on bored. 'I don't like magazines though.'

'Oh,' she said awkwardly. 'So... what do you read? Those crazy crime novels?'

Demir fiddled with his hands as he reluctantly told her, 'I read poetry.'

Selene's eyes widened and she giggled, covering her mouth with her hands. 'Wait, wait, don't tell me you're one of those secret poets that go to the clubs to start revolutions,' she teased.

He huffed out a laugh. 'Hardly,' he said, making eye contact with her. 'I don't have a lot of patience with books, so I read poetry because it's shorter and gets to the point. A lot of them are stupid as shit, but others help things make sense,' he explained. 'Like, Langston Hughes... "I've known rivers ancient as the world and older than the flow of human blood in human veins. / My soul has grown deep like the rivers." Or Shakespeare, "When in the chronicle of wasted time / I see descriptions of the fairest wights / And beauty making beautiful old rhyme." Or "I love thee to the depth and breadth and height / My soul can reach, when feeling out of sight..."'

Selene stared at him in awe, her eyes never wavering.

'Elizabeth Barrett Browning,' she said. 'I've read that poem before. It's beautiful.'

His gaze suddenly became distant. 'It was one of the first poems I ever read.'

'Why do you sound so sad about it?'

Demir sighed, clasping his fingers together and staring at the ceiling. 'Because,' he said. 'It's also the reason I started fighting.'

Her brows furrowed in confusion as she put the paper aside. 'I... don't understand.' Demir took a deep breath, and she could tell it would be a long story.

He told her about how his parents had left him in the care of his aunt and uncle when he was young. How his aunt used to work as a maid for a family, the Keene's. Sometimes, she would take him with her to help. One day, his aunt was dusting and accidentally knocked over some books. Mrs Keene started screaming, insulting his aunt how she couldn't even read the books.

So, Demir, determined to prove to her that he and his aunt were smart, grabbed the fanciest one and took it home, knowing Mrs Keene wouldn't notice because it was just for decoration. It happened to be a volume of poetry by Browning. His neighbour taught him how to read using that book. He studied for weeks, memorising as many poems as he could. When he was ready, he went into the living room in front of Mrs Keene and recited every poem he learned.

'The minute I was done, she slapped me across the face, screaming about how I stole from her,' Demir said. 'She fired my aunt. On our way out, Mrs Keene's son said something stupid. I don't even remember what it was, but it made me mad enough to punch him in the face. He didn't even try to hit me back. He just ran inside, yelling for his mama.'

Demir clenched his hands into fists, anger radiating off him. Selene leaned over and placed her hand on his. He looked down and let out a long sigh, his shoulders drooping in defeat.

'I had never seen my aunt look so terrified,' he confessed quietly before clearing his throat. 'As soon as we got home, she beat me. I talked back, trying to tell her I did it for her. She didn't care. She wished that I had just taken the slap, and I couldn't accept that. I ran away that night.'

Selene bit her lip, her heart aching as she imagined brave, little Demir getting punished for trying to protect someone he loved. 'Did you ever go back?'

'I see her a couple times a year,' he told her. 'But I never lived there again, no matter how bad it got. I never asked for her help either.'

'Do you ever regret it?'

'No,' he answered. 'I love my aunt, but I couldn't be small for her.'

'I know the feeling,' she whispered. 'Being forced to be small… until you feel like you can't exist at all.'

They locked eyes for a moment. In his eyes she could see the same pain she'd felt when she lived with her parents, the unique feeling of betrayal when the person you loved and protected unleashed their pain on you.

So, she stood up and went to her bedroom. Crouching, she searched under her bed – where most of her books resided – until she found what she needed, returning to the living room and holding out a book of poems by W.H. Auden.

'At least, you got a good hobby from it.' She handed him the book as she sat down on the other end of the couch, folding her legs under her. 'Mind reading to me?'

'You might not like how I say it,' he warned.

'Maybe I will.' She propped her arm on the back of the couch, resting a cheek on the back of her hand. 'Don't rule me out just yet.'

She stared at him expectantly until his eyes became resigned. Clumsily, he flipped through a few pages before settling on a poem. He cleared his throat, purposely not looking at her. She smiled at his shyness while waiting patiently.

'This one is called, "Lullaby".'

Chapter Thirty-Three

Detroit

October 1946

Demir splashed water on his face as he tried to catch his breath. Practice was kicking his ass today. After his last few victories, he thought he would be bouncing around the ring in excitement; instead, he felt the same way he had the first time he started fighting: in way over his head. He groaned in frustration and exhaustion, gripping the sink.

Why am I here?

It was a question he rarely asked himself anymore. He'd finally reached a point when he had enough money to rent an apartment and buy food. He'd buried the question deeper once he started garnering respect as a boxer. While he didn't care about the fame, the security was something he couldn't part with, not when he didn't have to worry about his next meal, and it allowed him to postpone seeing his aunt until Christmas.

Now, the question lingered in the hollow look of his eyes. Every ring looked the same and he could barely keep up. He could no longer remember which fight was for cash and which one went to his record. It didn't matter; they all hurt the same. His hands shook, but he clenched them into fists, staring into the mirror. He needed to get back to practice.

Just a few more minutes, he thought, hands already itching to be free from the gloves.

'Fucking exhausted,' Jack declared. He stumbled inside his apartment, reeking of gin, and Demir followed, Selene guiding him as he limped along.

The match was rougher than usual. While he could have knocked his opponent out in the first three minutes, Mackie hated paying for fights fewer than three rounds. Unfortunately for him, the challenger was more adaptable than he expected, and the fight had lasted all twelve rounds before going to a decision.

It was only mildly satisfying that he'd won.

Demir headed to the couch, Selene holding him steady as she helped him ease down onto the cushions. He groaned, leaning his head against the wall behind.

'I'll get you some water,' she muttered, heading to the kitchen where Jack was going through the cabinets.

'Did we run out of booze?' he slurred.

Demir heard Selene sigh tiredly, the sound of cabinets closing following. 'You don't need any more,' she told him. 'You've had enough for everyone tonight. Go sleep it off.'

'Fuck, I was going to put the bottle in your suitcase,' he said.

'You will not have my clothes smelling like liquor,' she sneered as the two stepped into the doorway. 'And we might not be able to leave tomorrow. You'll be hungover.'

'Oh, no.' Jack waved his finger clumsily before cornering her against the wall. 'I'm not missing a single day of this trip. It's a celebration.'

'It's not,' she said, pushing him aside to head to the bedroom. Jack looked at her in surprise before following. 'Not yet.'

'Keep your voice down,' she hissed, the pair disappearing.

Slowly, Demir closed his eyes, too exhausted to do anything else. It wasn't until he heard a soft thud on the table in front of him that he realised he'd dozed off. His eyes snapped open, body tense and fists up. He relaxed when he saw it was only

Selene setting a cup of water down on the table in front of him, the moonlight from the window making her partially visible.

He wanted to thank her, but that was quickly followed by the urge to tell her to sit down so they could talk all night before she left him for a week. It was a dumb idea; it wouldn't change the inevitable.

After the night they saw Charlie Parker, he realised something. Despite all his guilt over Nora, he didn't regret how he felt about Selene. What else could he have done? She was captivating and too smart for her own good. She drew him in from across a room. She made him think of too many things that scared and excited him. He wanted her more than he should and couldn't find a way to stop.

So, when her gaze met his in the moonlight and he saw the tenderness in her eyes, he did what came naturally.

He leaned forward.

Selene froze as his lips met hers, his hand tracing her cheekbone. Part of him was scared to touch her more, to move beyond the softness of the moment. Reason told him that he shouldn't be doing this, that Jack was only a few metres away, but it quickly quieted as Selene relaxed into the kiss. She placed her hand on his arm, leaning more into the embrace. Ever so slightly, her lips parted, allowing him to deepen the kiss as she shifted until she was kneeling on the edge of the couch, leaning over him.

Their lips created a quiet rhythm in the dark, only hinting at the intensity of the moment.

Demir let his hands explore her hair, her spine, the curve of her face, the waist he had desperately wished to wrap his arm around so many times, and Selene seemed just as eager to touch him. Her hand gripped the collar of his shirt, the other stroking his arm as she slid her tongue against his.

He straightened, dragging her onto his lap so they could be chest to chest. It felt good to be wrapped up in each other, melding into the night so easily. She was like a star – or was she like the moon as her name suggested? Something that shone bright while he twinkled away in the back, so far and yet so close.

She placed her hand on his cheek before gently pulling away. They panted against each other's lips, and he leaned in to taste her breath again. She let him steal two more kisses before placing a hand on his chest to stop him, and then she slipped off his lap. He could barely see her as she left, footsteps fading as she disappeared down the hall.

He let his hands fall from where they once held her, touching his lips absentmindedly; they still buzzed from her touch.

He lay down, unable to stop the smile that came to his face. He had seen people high on angel dust with pupils blown and a wicked grin on their face. If someone saw him now, he imagined he'd look the same.

He stared at the ceiling until his eyes were too exhausted to stay open, his mind replaying the moment until it finally surrendered to sleep.

–

A couple days after Selene and Jack left for their trip, Demir found himself at his aunt's apartment for dinner. It was a visit he tried to do every few months, equally out of love and obligation. Perhaps, it was the talk him and Selene had a while back, but the ugly memories weren't constantly marching around his head like they usually did. Instead, he savoured the scent of food wafting from the kitchen, remembering when his aunt would cook dinner. He remembered her fussing over him at the table while his late uncle talked to him about 'man stuff' he wouldn't understand for years to come. He missed those days more than he wanted to admit.

'Come on and sit down. Dinner's almost done,' Demir's aunt instructed as she walked out to the table with a bowl of collard greens without so much as a glance towards him.

He sat at the table tucked in the corner opposite the stove and watched his aunt cook in thick silence. She never listened to the radio, despite Demir scraping together enough money the first year after he moved out to buy them one in an attempt to prove he was fine. Having grown up poor in the south before her family uprooted to D.C. and then moving to Detroit, his aunt got suspicious when too much money went to one object. It was more of his uncle's preference. Demir turned it on every now and then when the quiet was overwhelming during visits but the longing in his aunt's eyes burned guilt into his gut every time.

A few moments later, she placed two plates and two cups of water on the table, handing him a fork and knife. He accepted them and dug in, almost groaning at how good the food was. It was his favourite part of the visit; he'd deal with *any* awkward conversation for a bite of his aunt's greens.

'What did you do today?' Her eyes were piercing.

He swallowed and wiped his mouth before answering. 'Worked at Old Eddie's bar mostly.'

'And yesterday?' she asked pointedly.

He smirked. 'I won,' he said smugly, enjoying the downturn of his aunt's frown. He took a sip of water. He looked at the couch, spotting a newspaper on the arm rest of his uncle's side of the couch 'You still put out the newspaper?'

'Every Sunday,' she said breezily. 'And had I not, I wouldn't have seen your picture with Charlie Parker. You looked nice, except for your busted lip.'

'It was a fun night.'

She scowled. 'I can't believe you're still working for that white boy.'

'With,' he corrected. 'And everyone works for some white boy.'

'You could do more, or at least find something better than getting your face bashed in. Everything this family endured just for you to go fightin'.'

'All they endured so I can make my own choices,' Demir said calmly. 'I told you I'm not arguing about it, Auntie.'

'Then, at least tell me you have someone who makes you happy, someone that makes sure you're not so alone in this world,' she insisted.

His mind immediately flashed to Selene, to rooftops and moonlight and secrets and kisses and how much he missed her and how she was with someone else and how that was nothing new.

The last part hurt the most.

'I have friends,' he said instead, picking up his fork again. 'But you don't have to worry. I've always been fine on my own.'

His aunt huffed out a laugh.

Demir paused. 'What?'

'You are so much like your father and the spitting image of your mother.' She grimaced. 'Me and my sister may have the same blood, but she was always running from some ghost. I never knew what it was. I don't think she knew either. All I know is that it led her to a man who ran away, and it made her do the same. Now, here you are, always runnin' from things you care about.' She placed her hand over his, concern colouring her tone. 'And what you can't run from, you fight your way out of. What are you running from? What are you fighting, Demir?'

He swallowed around the sudden lump in his throat and looked down at his plate. In his aunt's eyes, he could see the response she expected, that he was running from her. But that wasn't true; it wasn't even close. He didn't even know how to articulate what made his heart feel like a machine that kept him moving rather than something meant to connect him to people.

'I'm fighting to stay in this world,' he said instead. 'That's good enough for me right now.'

His aunt's disdain was obvious, but she didn't say anything else. Rather, she simply retracted her hand and told him that the bathroom sink was clogged. He promised to come by and fix it soon. They talked about small things after that, things they'd heard around the neighbourhood. By the time his plate was empty, he didn't remember anything from their conversation. He just placed his dishes in the sink, hugged her goodbye, and left an envelope of money for her on the newspaper that she would never read.

Exiting the building, he gazed up at the orange-stained sky. He walked down the steps, stuffing his hands in his pockets as he began to make his way home, which was only a few blocks away. He was glad he didn't take his car. Evening was the perfect time to enjoy a moment of fresh air.

'Aye, champ!' A man across the street waved his hands.

Demir squinted, recognition washing over him. He was one of Jack's friends. They met at the fight party after his argument with Nora. If he recalled correctly, he went by Haze. Demir nodded, and Haze took that as a cue to make his way over.

'What's up?' he greeted, his thick, black hair flopping into his face as he grinned. 'I haven't seen you since the party. That night was insane, right?'

'Yeah. It was fun.'

'Hell yeah. I kept telling Jack to bring you around more, but he says you're busy.' 'All the time.' Demir shrugged as he started walking again.

Haze followed suit. 'I bet. How's the record?' He shadow-boxed the air in front of him, and Demir couldn't help but crack a smile at the enthusiasm.

'Still undefeated.'

'Damn. Next time there's a fight, let me know. I'm betting my next payday on you.' Haze whistled, making a passer-by turn his way. He winked and the woman flashed her middle finger at him before walking off. 'Hey, you doing anything now? I'd usually bother Jack with all this but you're good company, too. I'm checking out this party downtown at Eddie's. Some people from Jack's will be there.'

Normally, Demir would turn his offer down, but the opportunity to not go home and overthink his aunt's words was too tempting. Plus, Jack's friends weren't that bad. He had quite the knack for finding good company. So, for once, he agreed.

–

'A poetry club,' Demir deadpanned when they arrived.

Haze chuckled as he leaned back in his seat. Chairs and tables were scattered around a dark dance hall. The only lights were candles flickering on the tables, creating silhouettes out of the crowd. A spotlight illuminated the stage where a poet recited his lines passionately.

'Don't knock it yet,' Haze told him, taking a sip of beer. 'Most get lost in the clichés of what they think they should expect. Open your mind, D.'

'I'll keep it closed for now.'

Haze laughed, the soft sound of snaps filling the room as the performer descended the stage. Demir pulled out a cigarette, lighting it with a match. Reluctantly, he settled into his seat to watch the next act. He had to admit that the poets were pretty good. Most knew how to own the stage while others had clever word play that outshone their nerves.

Haze cracked enough jokes in between acts to lighten the mood, and after a while, he found himself feeling comfortable in a room where people exposed their greatest weaknesses in front of a crowd; the mere act confused him. He couldn't imagine being so vulnerable, much less so publicly.

He stubbed out the last bit of his cigarette as another person took the stage, a tall, dark-skinned man with his hat tipped so low his eyes were hidden. His sleeves were rolled up his forearms, and he stood in front of the microphone beneath the spotlight. He cleared his throat before the low timbre of his voice filled the room.

"'*You made me a body 'Of cogs and fixes'.*'"

Demir's throat closed up as the words brought back the memory of that day his aunt beat him, surfacing like it nearly drowned and finally gasping for air. The confusion and betrayal flashed hot across his skin like it only happened yesterday. The images persisted as the poet painted pictures of a screaming engine waiting for anyone to notice its pain.

He couldn't help but remember Selene on the roof all those months ago. His mind ran through all the times he had watched her from across the room without being able to touch her. How the one time he did, it was in darkness and silence.

"'*But I couldn't avoid the quiet*
'*And you had a house to run.*'"

The words rang out as the poet stepped off the stage. Silence reigned for a moment before the crowd started to clap enthusiastically, a couple whistled, cutting through the noise.

'Now, you get it.'

Demir almost jumped, forgetting Haze was there.

Haze wore a knowing smile. 'Not such a cliché after all, huh?'

It took a moment, but Demir forced a smirk to his face. 'Of course it is,' he replied.

Haze laughed easily, waving down one of the servers milling around the room. Only when he turned away did Demir take out another cigarette, lighting it with shaky hands. It took another two acts before they stilled, but the sting stayed with him even when he laid his head on his pillow in the early hours of the morning.

Chapter Thirty-Four

Detroit

October 1946

Whenever people asked Selene if she liked the beach, she was quick to scrunch her nose up. Everyone was always surprised at her reaction, and she understood why. The ocean was this great, magnificent thing but all Selene could feel was how small it made her.

It was easy for her to dominate a room and command attention. She had perfected the skill after years of wishing her father would acknowledge her as more than just a burden. Refusing to be ignored was second nature to her, her greatest weapon. It also caused some of her greatest regrets.

Subtly, she touched her lips, watching the sunlight dance on Lake Michigan on a small beach just outside Chicago. A pair of arms wrapped around her, and she forced herself not to tense.

'It's not the ocean,' Jack said in her ear. 'But I figured it would be a great substitute.'

'Definitely.' She gripped his arm tightly, smiling up at him. 'You did good.' Looking over her shoulder, she kissed his chin. 'Though I'm surprised we're here at all. Everything's been kind of crazy lately.'

'Exactly,' Jack muttered into her neck. 'I needed to see you. I mean, how the hell do we sleep next to each other every night and I still miss you?'

A lick of guilt curled in her stomach as she leaned against him, but she ignored it.

'Because you won't listen to me about the next fighter.' Jack groaned, his arms loosening from around her waist, but she grabbed his hands, making him stay. 'I'm telling you it's not a good match.'

'It's a great match. The guy's a machine. Stop worrying about it.'

Selene turned around to face him. 'He's good in all the places Demir is not. Or so I've heard.'

Jack sighed. 'I know you wanted to go to the fight, but you always complain about never having time to study—'

'Don't use my school as an excuse. You know you've been holding out on me.'

'You don't even like watching them,' Jack protested.

'I liked being with you,' she snapped.

She watched as his jaw moved in a way it did when he didn't know what to say and bit the inside of her cheek, trying to reign her anger in. The metallic taste was already on her tongue, she was sure Jack would taste it the next time they kissed.

She gripped the patio railing, staring him down. 'I miss when we were a team.'

'It's just life right now,' he murmured. 'We only have to do this for a little while longer, you know?'

'I know.' Despite the steely tone, she did understand where he was coming from. Truly, it was her own frustration at the lack of a replacement name to give Nora. It would be too late by the time they got back.

Jack pushed her hair behind her ear and kissed her forehead. 'Just be patient.'

'Nope,' she said defiantly before pouting. 'I hate waiting. Patience is the worst virtue.'

'I like waiting for you,' Jack said. 'When you come around, it means you want to be there. And when you show up, the way you support me, I feel unstoppable. You got a mouth on you.' He gave her a pointed look that made her crack a smile. 'But I love it and you. I almost couldn't ask for more.'

Selene quirked her eyebrow. 'Almost?'

'I could ask you for one more thing…' Jack stepped back a little, getting on one knee.

Selene straightened up, her heart starting to race. The wood dug into her palms, but it felt like the only thing keeping her upright. Jack smiled as he reached into his pocket, but Selene waved her hand frantically, making him stop. He tilted his head in confusion.

'We're… not that simple.'

'Since when was marriage ever simple?'

Selene cleared her throat before it could tighten more, tucking her hands behind her back to stop from fidgeting under his gaze.

'We don't have the life for those kinds of promises,' she explained. 'I'm too ambitious and what kind of marriage lasts hopping from one place to another? Hell, it's not even legal in half the country!'

'It is in New York City.'

Selene raised her brows. 'So, I'm just supposed to stay there my whole life?'

'Right, because you're the world traveller,' he quipped, and Selene glowered at him.

'Be realistic. With marriage, there's kids,' she continued. 'What kind of life can we build for them? There are things you don't understand about me, things that I'm not even sure you want to know and I'm sorry, but I refuse to be the wife that lives a whole separate life from her husband. That's the only way my parents are surviving now. It's a nightmare, but what if they were us *before* everything? You never even talked about a future with me!'

'I didn't have to.'

'Why?' Selene pushed.

'Because of our life now!' He stood up, pinning her in place with the blazing look in his eyes. Selene swallowed nervously but didn't look away. 'Anytime anyone has given us hell, we got

305

through it. We faced it together. We never cared how it looked to everyone else. Why should we care now?'

'Because *this* includes the law,' she whispered. 'You keep acting like it doesn't matter, as if I still don't use the back door to go home unless you're there.'

'Sel, it's because of the law I need to do this. I need to know that you're safe and cared for, that this life doesn't leave you with nothing,' he insisted. 'I'm not saying it's perfect, but if there's a chance…'

'It's still too dangerous,' she hissed. '*Everything* changes after marriage.'

'I have been there every time you have changed,' Jack pointed out, her argument dying on her tongue. No matter what had happened in her life, he had been the one thing she could trust to remained consistent. But was that still true?

'Things can't stay like this forever. And even if they do, I don't care. I refuse to let some greedy, fat politician who wished I died in a fucking war tell me who can be my wife,' Jack declared.

She shook her head. 'You're reckless.'

'But you like that about me. Sometimes, I think you admire it.'

He winked at her, trying to be playful, but she groaned. The mere idea was insane. Still, she felt the same enduring weakness she always had whenever he had a crazy plan. She hated how part of her wanted to try, the curiosity that urged her to give in to the excitement in his eyes that told her that *her* Jack was back.

Yet, for a moment, Demir's face flashed in her mind, and she paused as Jack pressed his forehead against hers. She closed her eyes, feeling the caress of his breath against her lips.

'You're the only thing I've never questioned in my life,' he said softly. 'No matter what. So, if you have to say "no" right now, it won't change anything. I'll be here arguing with you regardless.'

Selene laughed, her voice a breathless whisper.

It felt nice to have something so familiar. She didn't fool herself into thinking Jack would be a perfect husband or that their marriage would be a dream come true. She knew it would be a very harsh reality. She also knew she could trust it and him.

Perhaps Demir was a fantasy. There was an honest, good man in him under the rough exterior he'd created to move through life. She'd seen whenever Demir let his guard down. Even when he didn't, he was still everything she wanted in a man but never had the courage to admit. Yet, that alone made him the scariest thing in her life.

Selene closed the inch of space between her and Jack, her frayed nerves smoothing out under his lips.

'Okay,' she whispered between kisses. She felt Jack's smile grow against her lips, and he lifted her off her feet. She let herself get lost in the excitement, Jack's elation rubbing off on her. Suddenly, the thought of taking on the world didn't seem so bad.

She wanted to keep kissing, but he pulled away, reaching into his pocket to pull out a small box. Selene froze at the sight of it, unable to take her eyes off the black velvet square as he opened it. The ring was fairly simple, a row of three diamonds on a gold band, the centre stone slightly bigger than the other two. Even in the low light, the stones sparkled, hinting at how much money Jack had spent. He slid the ring on her finger. It was heavier than she expected, the weight of change lingering around her as he pulled her into his arms.

'See? That wasn't so hard,' he whispered. Selene didn't respond; she just kissed him again.

The next morning, she woke up crying from a dream that disappeared as she tried to remember it. The band of her engagement ring was smooth against her cheek as she wiped her tears, and she paused as a faint memory of smoke resurfaced, but the dream faded beneath the morning light. She looked at her hand, frowning.

She'd made the right choice and yet…

She didn't dare finish the thought, instead, flipping onto her side to look at Jack, still fast asleep. She scooted closer, wrapping an arm around him, and buried her face in his shoulder.

–

Demir ducked under Benny's arms, weaving out of the way. The punches were slower than they would be in an actual fight, but it forced him to focus on his movement, which would later turn into instinct. It was hard to resist sneaking in a punch. After all, he was a fighter at heart.

Hit or run?

The thought popped into his head suddenly, sounding an awful lot like his aunt, and the question made him pause long enough for Bobby's fist to graze his ribs before he twisted out the way. He quickly put distance between them, his fists coming up defensively.

'Lookin' good 'cept that last one!'

Dropping his stance, Demir looked over his shoulder to see Jack walking over to the ring. He motioned to Benny to take a break and approached the ropes.

'Welcome back,' Demir greeted, touching his glove to the fist Jack held out. 'Had a good trip?'

'Best yet,' he declared with a secretive smile. 'Don't know how another will top it. Well, I can think of one but that won't be for a while.'

Demir didn't pry into what that meant. Jack would tell him sooner or later, whether he wanted to know or not. Instead, he looked over Jack's shoulder. 'Where's Selene?' Demir smirked. 'Let me guess: her hair got wet.'

Jack chuckled and, for some reason, it made Demir narrow his eyes in suspicion. It wasn't like him to roll with quips like that.

'Hardly. She had to stay late at school to catch up on some assignments, but she'll meet us at the apartment later.'

Part of Demir bristled at the casual way Jack assumed he would be going over after practice, but he also couldn't blame him. He had spent more time there in the last few weeks before their holiday than in his own home. It was only natural that he was invited.

'In the meantime,' Jack heaved himself into the ring, leaning on one of the corners, 'let's see what you've been up to while I've been gone.'

Benny met Demir in the centre of the ring, and they began. They threw themselves into practice, going through all the drills from top to bottom. Jack's energy was higher than usual as though he was mere moments from jumping in, excitement pouring from him in a way that Demir hadn't seen in a long time.

'That's it!' Jack clapped. 'That's fucking it, D. Finally got that shit down.'

'I been mastering it.' Demir wiped off the sweat from his face as Benny made his way to the bathroom. 'And with your jumping around, you might as well be in the ring with me.'

'Hey, don't let the knee fool you. I can still throw a couple blows,' Jack defended. 'Jump in, old man. I'll make sure not to knock you out.'

Jack laughed but shrugged off his jacket. 'Don't forget I taught you everything you know, pretty boy.' He threw it on the ground and put his hands in front of his face the way he'd shown Demir hundreds of times.

Demir smirked as he mirrored the stance.

They circled each other, throwing out a couple of playful jabs and talking shit. Jack's speed and accuracy were surprisingly good considering he hadn't fought in years, but there were plenty of openings. Despite that, Demir never took advantage of them, keeping the match friendly; it wasn't about winning. If anything, it brought him back to the beginning of everything.

Though similar in skill, Jack and Demir only met in the ring once. How they ended up working together was a blur of memories and conveniences. Times like this, he was reminded why they had become friends, even if he had betrayed him.

Demir waited for the regret to hit him, but it stayed at bay. He had already decided: he wouldn't interfere with Jack's relationship. There was no reason to make things difficult if the kiss was a one-time thing. He only hoped Selene didn't regret it. He could deal with everything but that.

'You better not be fighting.'

They looked to the side of the ring where Selene was resting against the side of the ring and Demir's heart lifted at the site of her so close after being gone so long. Her smile was soft and welcoming even though her eyes were tired. He took a step towards her, but Jack beat him to the ropes, pressing a kiss to her cheek before smiling at her fondly.

'Nothing wrong with a few blows every now and then,' he teased her.

The moment snuffed out the light in Demir, leaving a dark cloud over him and a sour taste in his mouth. Neither of them seemed to notice as they stared lovingly at each other, and he swallowed the acid-like taste in his mouth as he approached them. Though the way Selene looked at him, gaze full of warmth, helped to soothe the hurt.

'Hi, Demir,' she greeted. 'Have a good workout?'

'Boring as always,' he shrugged. 'How was school? Jack said you had a good time away.' She looked away, stuffing her hands deep in the jacket she had yet to take off.

'It was.' Her voice was smaller than before, and she cleared her throat before looking at him again. Still, she hesitated. 'School was fine, though. Luckily, a classmate of mine took good notes, so it was easy to catch up.'

'You would've caught up quickly anyway,' Demir said easily. 'With how deep your nose is in those books, I'd give it two days before you were back at it.'

The edge of her lips quirked up into the beginnings of a smile before she quickly schooled her expression. 'Flattery gets you nowhere.' Despite the words, fondness coloured her tone, filling her eyes.

'It's not flattery if it's true. You're a genius,' Jack added.

And just like that, Demir was pushed to the outskirts again as Selene's attention shifted.

This time, he did better at ignoring the burn in the back of his throat. Stepping back from the pair, he pretended to go through some combinations again as Benny returned to the ring.

'Ready to go?' Benny asked, and Demir nodded.

Taking his stance, they started. He ignored Jack's shouts from the side, narrowing down his world to his gloves. It was hard to tell how long he sparred with Benny, but by the time he looked up, sweat streaming down in rivulets, Jack and Selene were already long gone as if they were never there.

–

Selene's body felt like it was full of lead as she knocked on Demir's door the next morning. She fiddled with her ring, starting to slip it off her finger before she stopped, deciding against it. No more hiding. She had gotten lucky yesterday that Demir had decided not to come over. Maybe she would have that same luck, and he would notice her ring quickly so she wouldn't have to explain anything. She scoffed. If she were *really* lucky, she would have been smart enough not to kiss him in the first place.

Someone moved behind the door, and a shadow appeared beneath. She swallowed around the knot in her throat as she spoke. 'Demir, it's me. I'm alone.'

There was a brief pause before the door opened. They stared at each other for a moment before Demir pulled her inside. She went willingly, heat entering her veins.

Selene shrugged her coat off and barely removed her gloves when he grabbed her by the waist. He pulled her into his chest, burying his nose in her hair. She couldn't help the way she leaned her head back, relaxing in his arms. His lips ghosted over the curve of her neck, his breath causing goosebumps to rise on her skin. Just as she reached up to touch his face, she stopped.

She could *not* give in this easily.

'Demir.' Her voice, deep with desire, was a whisper. She held onto his arms, her face flushing under the sudden heat in the room. Everywhere his skin met hers felt like fire and it was intoxicating. Merely breathing near him was tempting, the air thick with desire and anticipation. Her words were strangled when she spoke. 'I need to talk to you.'

'Then, talk,' he encouraged. She pulled away, his hands settling against the small of her back. Her breath caught as she looked at him. There was no denying that Demir was handsome with his defined cheekbones and piercing eyes – she had always thought that, but it wasn't what made her melt.

Going a week without talking to him, being free to be as bratty as she wanted to be, felt wrong. She missed pulling him out of his shell for a brief moment, finding out more about him… she missed getting to know him.

She kissed him without another thought.

Her lips moved eagerly over his, and he returned it just as enthusiastically. Her tongue touched the seam of his lips, and he parted them willingly. The kiss turned hungry and heated so quickly, it made her head spin. Lust thrummed in her veins as she took her gloves off and pushed him against the wall, a moan escaping her lips.

Something sizzled along Selene's spine as Demir spun them around, so she was pressed against the wall, grabbing her thigh. She let out a breathy moan as he hitched it over his hip. She wrapped her arms around his neck and sucked on his bottom lip, pulling him closer as his hand crept up her thigh.

She didn't know how to stop. The thought of it being the last – the only – time kept hammering in her head. The moment was everything she had wanted and giving in felt amazing, especially when she soon couldn't have more. Any moment they would have from here on out would be tainted by the absence of what could have been. Couldn't she at least have this?

But can you do this to him?

Selene's thoughts drifted beyond the next few hours, beyond all the impossible scenarios, and focused on the ring slipping down her finger.

Could she betray both the men she loved?

No.

The thought rang out, loud and clear, and she pushed Demir away. The boxer stumbled back in surprise. Panting, she refused to meet his gaze, instead pressing her right hand to her lips.

In love with Demir? Suddenly, all the pieces fell into place. Why she was always aware of him, why she constantly defended him, why she had never liked Nora, and why she rarely lied to him. She had been in love with Jack for so long it never occurred to her it would look different with someone else.

She loved Demir... and she couldn't do this to him.

'I want this... God,' she whispered. Tears gathered in the corners of her eyes as Demir approached her again, his footsteps echoing in the silence. 'Demir, I *really* need to talk to you.'

'We can talk later,' he told her, voice still dripping in lust. 'You don't understand.'

'What...?' The words died on his tongue as desire turned to confusion. She placed her hand on his chest, and he covered it with his own. Demir froze and, just like that, it was all over.

He looked down, lifting her hand so that he could fully look at the diamond ring gleaming in the morning light. He kept staring at her finger as he stepped back, her hand slipping from his grasp.

'Please, say something,' she said, her voice strained.

He didn't. He just kept staring at the ring, even when she moved her hand to her side. She searched for an explanation, but none would save him from the betrayal of her decision.

At the end of the day, there was no excuse. She had made the choice that everyone saw coming except for him.

Suddenly, laughter spilled out of him, hollow and painful. Tentatively, she stepped towards him but was unable to do anything except watch as he broke. He gripped his midsection as if he'd heard the funniest joke, as if his hands were all that kept him together. She bit the inside of her cheek as a stubborn tear escaped.

What had she done?

She flinched when his laughter died out and his eyes met hers. They practically flashed, and anxiety flooded through her. He cupped her face, his eyes holding hers, and she shrunk beneath his gaze as he held her there. His lips were soft as he kissed the tear away. 'We never talked about us. Not one single moment,' he murmured against her cheek, his lips dragging up to her ear. 'Why talk about it now?'

She felt his hands tremble, his breath ghosting her lips, eyes full of sorrow. Despite her attempts to look away, he forced her chin up so she would have to face his pain. Another tear fell; he didn't bother to take that one. 'Get out,' he rasped.

'Demir…' She reached out to touch him as his hands slid from her face. He didn't step away, and they stood, chest to chest, as her hand hovered between them.

Jaw clenched, she forced her hand to return to her side. She tore her gaze from his to grab her coat and gloves before she left, the door slamming shut so loudly behind her, she jumped. She waited to hear something – a crash, a scream – but there was nothing, adding to the finality of his words.

Hands covering her mouth, she stepped back until her back hit the other side of the hallway, sinking to the floor and sobbing into her hands as devastation hit her full force, weighing down her heart.

'I'm sorry,' she murmured. 'I'm so sorry.'

–

Distance would make the heart grow fonder if there was any fondness left to be had. Otherwise, all distance did was leave space to remember everything that had gone wrong.

Demir guessed he should have expected the latter.

'Hey, can you focus?' Jack snapped his fingers in front of Demir's face, which the boxer smacked away. 'Don't be pissed at me. I told you not to practise yesterday. You know better,' he growled in annoyance. 'You better pay attention in the fucking ring.'

'I always do,' he answered nonchalantly.

Jack huffed before leaving the room. *Finally.* Demir stretched in an attempt to keep himself loose as he paced the back room. He was ready for the night to be over.

Stepping into the ring, he felt ready enough. His opponent, Victor 'Fury' Stone, was a heavy hitter but lacked control, so, with a little patience, Demir quickly overtook him with a few well-placed hooks and jabs to the side. The referee started the ten-second count, and Demir knew it was over by the time the referee hit eight. He didn't bother looking at the other boxer, already thinking of how long it would take to get home.

However, the thing about fighting was that every second counted. The tide could turn at any moment.

He was reminded of that when he looked towards the edge of the ring. Not because of Jack watching him with dollar signs in his eyes; he was used to that. It was the look of horror in Selene's eyes. Her mouth was forming his name as he looked over his shoulder to see what was scaring her.

The fist came out of nowhere, and it felt like his jaw was being knocked into his brain.

He stumbled back as the fighter launched his whole body on him, putting his hands up and falling as his head spun until everything went black.

–

'Demir!'

Selene was launching herself into the ring before she could think better of it, the referee finally able to pull Victor off Demir. She crouched next Demir's side, pulling out his mouth guard and using a nearby towel to soak up the blood pouring out his mouth. His pulse was strong beneath her touch, and she scanned his body for any other wounds, but beyond the cuts on his face, there didn't seem to be anything out of the ordinary.

Except he wasn't moving.

'Here.' Jack held out her medical bag. She snatched it from him, practically tearing it open to grab hold of her penlight. Demir groaned, his eyes fluttering open for a moment.

'Demir, can you hear me?' She forced his eyes open, shining the light from one side and then the other. His reactions were delayed, but his eyes eventually found the light, his pupils constricting.

Behind her, the crowd was a cacophony, people running about while Jack looked like he was on the verge of a fistfight with the other coach. Demir blinked, his eyes focusing, and he reached up as if to grab the rope. Selene took his hand, squeezing it.

'Hold on,' she told him. 'Hold on for me.'

He squeezed her hand tightly, not letting his eyes close again.

With Jack's help, she managed to carry him out of the club and to the car. They took Demir back to their apartment, where Jack called up John, the guy who had patched him up before she came along. In the meantime, she stuck to Demir's side, keeping him awake. While she could diagnose him, she didn't have any supplies to treat him beyond a bleeding wound. Usually, she was against hospitals, especially since the closest one that would admit him was miles away. This time, she kept a close eye on the car keys, ready to drive.

John came quickly, entering with a small duffle bag over his shoulder filled with any medicine he might need. He reminded her of a gruff uncle that had seen too much. Just as Selene expected, he didn't say much of anything, just shooing her out of the away and getting to work. She hovered nearby, watching the doctor closely. Demir had told her that he was sloppy, and she was not taking any chances.

'Mind getting us some water,' John asked with a pointed look.

She scowled but went to the kitchen, nonetheless keeping an eye on John as she searched the cabinets for a glass, eyes narrowed in suspicion. Someone tapped her shoulder, and she jumped, quickly spinning to see Jack.

His tone was strangely neutral. 'You all right?'

'No,' she snapped, filling the cup with tap water. 'Don't worry too much. He's gonna be fine.'

'This should have never happened.' Her eyes were blazing as she pointed her finger at him. 'I told you to switch fighters.'

'Demir was on track—'

'I'm sick of you not listening to me,' she hissed. 'And I'm tired of people getting hurt because of it.' She started walking back, but Jack blocked her path, his gaze steely.

'Who else is getting hurt?'

Selene glared, tempted to throw the water in his face. She couldn't believe she'd ever found his jealousy attractive.

Ever since coming back from Demir's apartment, she had felt unsteady. She had tried her best to get back to normal, yet everything felt forced. And in that moment, she was suddenly aware of how much she wasn't the girl she showed Jack. She hadn't known how much she pretended until she realised there would never be a stopping point.

Before she could open her mouth to make a snide remark, there was a groan from the couch. Clutching the glass of water in her hand tightly, she stepped around Jack.

'Demir, can you hear me?' John asked.

'...Yeah,' he croaked.

Selene pressed the glass to his lips, tipping it so he could drink. She only stopped when he started coughing. John took away the cup and helped him up.

'You're okay,' he said, his voice deep and soothing. 'Just make sure you stay hydrated and don't go to bed anytime soon. Your head's gonna hurt, so take these. One pill per meal.' He pulled an unlabelled bottle of pills from his bag, placing them on the table. 'And try not to look in the mirror. You might crack it.'

Demir started to laugh but winced, clutching his head. John patted his shoulder before standing and going over to Jack, who was gazing at her suspiciously as she sat next to Demir. She fought not to scowl.

A little late for that, she thought bitterly. She looked at Demir, noticing he had closed his eyes. 'Hey, hey.' Selene shook him until they opened. 'You need to stay awake.'

Demir sat in a daze until his gaze landed on her. She couldn't help but stroke his face gently, her fondness for him battering against her chest. If Jack asked about it later, she could say she was just concerned. Another not-lie to dump in the distance growing between them.

'You'll be okay in a few days,' she reassured him, not looking at Jack as he escorted John out. 'But for now, you need to stay up. Okay?'

She waited for Jack to return but, after a few minutes, had a feeling he would be gone for a while. Maybe at a bar nearby. She frowned and got up to turn on the radio. Jack could stay out as long as he wanted; she doubted he would be useful right then.

She went back to the couch and placed a pillow on her lap, coaxing Demir to lay on it. 'You need to elevate your head.'

He groaned as he laid back down, her fingers softly stroking his face and hair. Music filled the room, and his gaze focused on the ceiling.

Selene's thoughts drifted back to the fight, images of Demir hitting the floor over and over flooding her mind. She tried to stay quiet but every now and then a shaky sob snuck out. For a moment, she had been sure he was gone... she raised her hand to wipe away the tears, but Demir caught her wrist clumsily. She paused and looked down at him. His eyes didn't move from the ceiling.

'Why are you here?' he asked, his voice monotonous. Another shudder ran through her as he waited for her to answer.

She didn't.

It was only when sunlight filled the room that she finally let him drift off, enough time having passed for him to be out of danger. She let out a shaky breath as she kissed the back of his hand.

'I don't know.'

–

When Demir woke up alone on the couch, he was tempted to stay for the day. He wanted Selene to take care of him a little longer, imagine a different life for a few more moments. But, between the ring on her finger and the notebook Selene left on the table, he knew he had overstayed his welcome.

He shouldn't have opened it, but curiosity of his condition got the best of him. At first, it was just as she said, notes about his injuries and recovery. Then it changed. Rows and rows detailing his fights and opponents filled the pages. Quick notes about who was 'too strong' and who he should fight again littered the margins. Dollar amounts that looked like something out of a gambler's notepad next to Nora's number.

He's trying to get in good with the coaches to see if they rig fights.

To think he believed she cared about him when this whole time, it was all about New York. Granted, didn't he already know her and Jack were the same from the beginning?

He scoffed at his own foolishness. He wanted to be angry, but he was simply exhausted. So, when Selene had run to the store, he slipped out. He took the long way home, wondering how he got here and why the hell he was staying. So often, he ran around with questions in his head, when the answer was quite simple. By the time he entered his apartment, he had clarity that made it easy to pick up the ringing phone.

'D, what the hell is going on?' Jack snapped. 'I came home and Selene was a mess worrying about you. God knows how many times I had to stop her from running around town to look for you or going to the police!'

'Jack,' Demir spoke, his voice deceptively calm. 'I quit.'

Chapter Thirty-Five

Occasionally, Dani needed to run away. She never went far, only looking for a place that forced her mind to be quiet for a while.

Today, she kept it simple and went to the cinema, picking a random action film. She didn't truly care what would be on the screen; sitting in the dark by herself in a room that wasn't her own sounded blissful enough. She picked a seat in the back row, far from a group that had gathered for the showing. As the lights dimmed and the trailers started to play, she let her mind drift to her research.

After weeks, it seemed that her one and only lead had fizzed out. While she had learned the role of a griot, understood the importance of West African oral history, she couldn't quite connect it to her and Jones. There were griots in Côte d'Ivoire but they were inherited roles and Kwame didn't seem to be connected to them. Of course, everything after was long disconnected.

The closest she could get was the role of griots being record-keepers for tribes. Maybe her and Jones were supposed to be that, but then it didn't make sense why they were just now remembering. They would have had to remember earlier for that to make sense. And, with that, there was nothing left to explore.

So, another dead end.

She fought back tears as explosions happened on screen, the defeat settling in. She rubbed her eyes, trying to compose herself.

The more she remembered, the harder it was for her to accept what was happening. Maybe it was watching Alexis celebrate her birthday over the weekend, or Talia and Riley making plans for trips after graduation or Dr Carver helping her with her application to the New York Philharmonic last week, but it hit Dani that Selene would never grow old. That more than likely, she herself wouldn't escape her twenties. She wouldn't have a future to look forward to. All her work, everything she did to build a life and a career... it meant nothing.

The anxiety around that thought had been a low hum in the background for days but it kept creeping closer and closer to the surface. She didn't know what to do or how to escape it. How did someone accept death when they never saw it coming?

Dani grimaced as the sun hit her eyes when walking out of the cinema, feeling even worse than when she went in. *So much for that.* She walked a few blocks to her car, pulling out her phone to check the time. There were multiple notifications waiting for her, social media likes and comments, reminders, emails and texts. She opened the latter, ignoring the one from Dr Carver, and focused on the one about it from Jones sent ten minutes ago.

Still coming for bass lessons?

She chewed on her bottom lip as she stared at the screen. She had promised to meet him at two thirty and it was creeping closer to three. Her first instinct was to ignore him as well, go home and scream into a pillow. Then, she remembered how Dr Castillo would always push her into therapy to seek help among her friends instead of leaning on her instinct to be painfully independent. It was annoyingly good advice, especially since Jones would be the only one to understand her fears. And she would have to break the news eventually.

Heading over now, she typed back before getting in her car.

–

Jones was standing outside when Dani pulled up, bass strapped across his back. Her grip on the steering wheel tightened and she had to force herself to let go. Jones had dealt with everything well so far. At this point, she wouldn't be surprised if she was the one breaking down at the end of the conversation. The least she could do was put on a brave face until then.

'You know, I can meet you in one of the practice rooms,' he said.

'Yeah, but your apartment is too nice and too expensive not to spend more time in,' she said, keeping her tone light and playful. 'Shall we go?'

'We shall.' He gestured for her to go up the steps to the entrance.

She stepped inside his apartment with a sense of familiarity that she suspected she shouldn't have after only a few visits, considering that it took her two months to get used to the house she rented now. But the place was so undeniably cosy, she couldn't help relaxing as she flopped on his ridiculously soft burnt orange couch.

As he went to the kitchen, Dani flipped through the artbook on the coffee table. Under it, there was sheet music and she ran her fingers over the notes, playing the song in her head. He set a glass of water in front of her, as he always did, before going to his room to grab one of his basses. He had a collection of ten so far, all mounted on a wall in his bedroom, and he planned on getting another around Christmas.

'A present to myself,' he had explained when he first showed her.

She closed her eyes for a moment, hoping he would make it to the holiday. She opened them back up as he returned with a blue-grey bass with a police line neck strap.

'A Fender Aerodyne Jazz Bass.' He placed the instrument carefully in her lap, easing the strap over her head when she leaned forward.

'Such a gentleman,' she commented as she ran her fingers over the metal strings, mapping out the notes of the frets. 'If only cello were this easy.'

'You need some help?'

'I got it,' she told him as she tuned the strings, listening carefully to the muted notes. He chuckled as he eased onto the floor in front of her. 'An expert already.'

'It's not exactly a hard transition. It's this,' she sat the bass up so the neck pointed to the ceiling, 'to this.' She turned it sideways, resting the curves against her thighs. 'And then plucking. Plus, these handy dandy frets make finding the notes much easier.'

'So, you're ready to plug it in,' he suggested.

'Absolutely not.' She couldn't help but smile, her first one of the day, at the sound of his laugh. She was thankful she could bask in the sound for a little while longer. She straightened up and walked her fingers along the frets of the bass, focusing on the tiny vibrations the motion caused versus the giddy feeling filling her chest. 'Let me be delusional for a bit longer.'

'Fine, but next week we're plugging it in. No more running for you.'

She nodded but her smile faded, the words making a lump form in her throat. Jones noticed the change immediately, his gaze becoming cautious as he looked her up and down.

'You okay?'

She opened her mouth to say, 'Yes' and continue learning 'Feel Good Inc' by Gorillaz, and ignore the world for a little longer. Instead, she asked, 'You remember all of our lifetimes, right?'

Jones's brows shot to his hairline as he leaned back against the couch. 'As far as I know, yeah.'

She plucked the string a couple of times before removing the bass from around her neck, setting it aside. 'Why do we fail every time?'

Jones bit the inside of his cheek, scratching the back of his neck nervously. 'We had good reasons at the time,' he answered politely.

'All for them to be our downfall,' she said flatly. 'Nothing but bad timing and missed opportunities painted as a love story.'

'It's not that simple,' Jones said, his eyes wounded. The look punched her in the gut, and she wished she could take it all back, fall back into their lesson. Yet, reality was knocking on their door, and she couldn't take it anymore.

'I failed,' she whispered. 'I can't figure it out, which means…'

Dani's words clogged her throat, tears that she had been holding back all afternoon escaped her eyes. Something in Jones's eyes shattered and it was too much to witness. She laid down and stared at the bright, blue sky out the window, the wisps of clouds easing along. She took a stuttering breath.

'Maybe I can wrap my head around the inevitable but, more than anything, I just wish I knew why,' she settled on.

The two were quiet, letting the hum of appliances take over the conversation as the air remained tense. It felt like walking along a cliff edge, each step being monumentally important. Part of her was tempted to say the wrong thing – whatever it was – and end this friendship, go back to her original solution. Unfortunately, it hadn't worked the first time and now that she knew Jones, it wouldn't be the same.

It was almost unfair how easily he filled a gap in her life that wasn't even missing. He walked into her life, changed everything, and now she had to figure out a way to live without him or live with him to an early grave. She took a deep breath, biting the inside of her cheek to hold back the tears that started to spring up again.

She tensed up at the thought just as Jones settled on the floor near her, still not touching her as if he could tell she needed space. Or maybe it would've been too much for him, too.

'What are you thinking?'

Dani forced her hand to relax from the fist it formed, surrendering to the truth as she spoke.

'That I can only imagine how great it would be if we were more than friends,' she said quietly, as if the words would create a cosmic shift if said too loud. 'We would be by now if we didn't remember, just like our other lives. But I can't get over the mortality of us. We barely get to start before everything is over and it's not fair. Why did we have to remember now?'

'I… honestly can't tell you,' he told her. 'This lifetime has had its ups and downs with me, but I haven't been this scared of death in a while.'

Dani was tempted to tell him she didn't know which was worse but kept the thought to herself. She doubted it would help the hopeless conversation. They were truly damned no matter what they did. She scooted a tad bit closer to him to feel a little of the warmth radiating from him to fight the chill settling under her skin.

'You wanna know something?'

'What?'

'Sometimes, I wonder if we truly experience death,' Jones said quietly. 'As awful, as the endings are, as soon as we close our eyes for good, we're in new lives. Better ones than what we had before. And knowing what's coming, in a weird way, it makes it easier for me to enjoy my life right now. The hard part is knowing I keep taking you with me.'

The lump in her throat seemed to grow and she closed her eyes, forcing it down enough to quip, 'It's quite the crappy consolation prize.' Something that sounded between a snort and Jones choking lifted the tension.

'Can't argue with that,' he said finally before falling into silence.

'What if…' Dani's words faded as she tried to figure out what she wanted to ask. What was it all for? What was the lesson? What if he regretted meeting her?

What if this is our last life, our last chance to get it right?

'Are you happy?' he asked suddenly.

'Yeah,' she said without hesitation. She turned her head so he could see her sincerity when she said, 'The happiest I've ever been, according to my other lives.'

'Then I'll say this much.' He drummed his fingers on the floor before speaking, his tone sombre as he met her curious stare. 'As much as we genuinely loved each other before, one thing that happened in every life before this one was that we were always trying to escape the world around us. This time we don't have to. So, if nothing else, we at least beat that part of the story already.'

'Maybe the universe is throwing us a bone,' she sighed. 'One step closer to getting older.'

Though his shoulders slumped in defeat, his smile only looked a little tired. 'If so, then I guess I'll meet you at the retirement home.'

'I'll be the one playing shuffleboard,' she said, causing him to chuckle. The sound made her relax, the restlessness she felt all day finally disappearing though nothing had changed. They could still die tomorrow but they couldn't change that now. She had worried enough for the day.

She leaned over, running her fingers over the guitar, a muted melody playing. She suddenly wanted to tell Jones to get his amp so she could hear herself. It didn't matter if she was bad or not; she just wanted to know.

'Maybe it was as simple as a wish,' she said finally. 'You wanted to see me again. I wanted to save you. All things are possible through God and magic and whatever else is out there beyond what we understand.'

'A wish strong enough to bring us back to life… guess we'll have to wait and see.' He finally sat up and reached over her to pick up his bass. She bit her bottom lip as his arm brushed her knee, her nerves zeroing in on the sensation as he held the instrument out to her.

'Shall we?'

She stared at it for a while, eyeing the frets, the colour of the body, all the little knobs and stringers until her eyes landed on the fingers gripping the neck steadily but not too tight, just enough to let it go. She sat up before taking it gently from his hand, placing it back on her lap.

'We shall,' she said, stretching out her legs so they were pressed against his. She held back a smirk as she heard him clear his throat, shifting his body, but not moving away. 'I'm thinking "Seven Nation Army" this time. You know that one?'

'Yeah, it's practically bass 101,' he said as he showed her how to play the first few notes. And for a few hours, she didn't pretend to be normal or ignore death looming around the corner. She just let the moment be more important and it was more than enough.

Chapter Thirty-Six

Detroit

November 1946

Old Man Eddie's bar was different during the day. It didn't carry the undercurrent of all the impromptu parties it hosted or the drunken secrets it kept. It was bright and open, the most fitting place for Demir to be.

He had been lucky that it was poetry night when he stumbled up into the place the night he quit boxing. He was also lucky that Haze was weirdly loyal to people he had only known for a short time, which the man chalked up to being biracial with a lot of siblings. Either way, Demir was grateful that for once he wasn't running to a fight. He wondered if his aunt would be proud of him or would accuse him of doing the same thing he always did.

Wiping down tables in preparation for opening in a few hours, he heard someone whistle behind him.

'How's it going?' Haze approached, an easy smile stretched across his face.

Demir shrugged. 'It is what it is.' He straightened and gave the man his attention. 'I thought I wouldn't see you till tonight.'

'I figured you would dip out before then.'

'I was going to work a few hours before heading your way. Eddie offered extra money plus tips if I stayed a while,' he explained.

Haze hummed before sitting in a nearby chair. 'Well, I figured I should stop by and check on you. Jack just called me about trying to find you. Sounds like he has cash waiting for you. And before you ask, I didn't say nothing. I'm a messenger, not a snitch.'

'I don't want it,' Demir answered gruffly. 'I'm tired of fighting.'

'I don't blame you. Tough taking hits like that. The old man might call me soft for saying so, but I'm not one for bloody noses. Too pretty, you know?' Haze smirked as Demir rolled his eyes.

'I wouldn't recommend it,' he said, returning to the counter to soak the towel. 'It's like you're a bird trapped in a cage they keep forcing to sing. All the while, you're left wondering how they don't understand that they're war cries.'

'That sounds like poetry to me,' Haze pointed out. Yet again. Demir held back a sigh.

'Come on, D. You know you have something to say,' Haze pressed.

Demir stayed silent even though he agreed. He knew a lot of truths, harsh ones that could make the world feel hopeless. But was that the truth he wanted to tell the world? No.

If he was going to say anything, it would be how running never solved anything, but it was the only thing he knew. How sweet memories were crueller than reality, that hope killed more than men. It tortured and killed dreams, too.

'He's not wrong.'

A chill went down Demir's spine as the sound of heels echoed through the bar. And it was like a trance fell over him as Selene walked over, looking just as sultry and mysterious as she had when they first met. Except this time, he could point out the smallest trace of stiffness in her gait as she approached Haze.

'Hi, honey,' she greeted sweetly.

Haze stood and kissed her on the cheek. 'Looking lovely as ever, Ms Selene,' he complimented.

She smiled, tossing her hair over her shoulder before giggling. Every movement was scripted, right down to the way she squeezed Haze's arm. 'You're not so bad yourself,' she winked, glancing at Demir for a moment before turning her gaze back to Haze. 'Looking for another artist, I see.'

'What can I say?' He held his hands up and shrugged before clasping Demir on the shoulder. 'I'm a patron of the arts. And I'm telling you right now, this one right here is better than any of those washed-up Ivy League brats. Bet he could knock out Shakespeare without using one fist.'

'I wouldn't be surprised.' Her tone was soft, genuine.

Demir ignored it, talking to Haze instead. 'I'm sure some racist piece of shit is rolling in his grave right now,' he said dryly, earning a bout of laughter from Haze.

'Eh, fuck them. They never had taste anyway.'

He snapped the towel at the man. 'Get outta here, Haze. I'm trying to work.'

He raised his hands in surrender, grinning as he made his way to the door. 'All I'm saying is it can't hurt to try.'

Shaking his head, Demir started wiping down the tables again.

'Well, hello to you, too.' Selene sat down in Haze's former seat. 'I've been looking for you.'

'Can't say the same.'

'I'm sure.' She smiled blandly before looking around. 'Nice gig you got.'

'I'm not fighting again.'

'Because of me?'

'Because I'm tired of getting knocked out and cleaning up your bullshit after,' he snapped, staring her down.

She scowled, pushing her hair behind her ears. 'But you still go to the gym. Late at night. Benny told me he ran into you the other day.'

Demir almost sighed. He should've known Benny would tell her that, probably even told her that he had stayed there until dawn. Some days, the only way he could sleep was punching out the hurt. Not that it helped much; five minutes in front of

Selene, and he felt just as raw as that day in his apartment. 'It's an itch. It'll go away.'

Selene stared at him for a moment before opening up her purse, and he narrowed his eyes as she pulled out an envelope, placing it on the table.

He picked it up carefully, looking inside. It was a stack of bills. 'What is this?'

'The money from the last fight that Jack keeps telling everyone he has for you,' she said. 'Figured you didn't want to talk to him either so I'm getting rid of his excuse.'

'Won't he ask about this?' He lifted up the envelope.

Selene laughed, but it sounded bitter. 'Don't worry about that part. I'll handle it.'

He sighed tiredly. 'Selene, why are you here? What do you want?'

'I wanted to make sure we were done.' She looked up, sadness slipping from beneath her flirtatious façade. 'And now we are.' She stood up, her hips swaying invitingly as she walked away, leaving Demir feeling cold.

If this was going to be the last time he talked to her, he refused to talk to the character.

Fists clenched around the money, he got up and caught up to her halfway to the door, stepping in front of her. She stopped short and he grabbed her hand, placing the money into it. She struggled to pull out of his grip, but he held on.

'What are you—'

'Why didn't you believe in me?'

Selene stilled as their eyes met, hers full of remorse. She opened her mouth, but nothing came out.

His grip loosened as his heart dropped to his stomach. 'You should have told me you didn't.'

'Of course, I believed in you,' she said quickly, pulling him back. 'You're an amazing fighter. But Jack was lining up wild cards and, after that fight with Johnny, I couldn't watch you get hurt like that again. I figured if I arranged easier fights between the official ones, it would help. That's all.'

'You should have trusted me to get better.' 'It wasn't you,' she whispered.

A shadow fell over her face, one he had seen too many times when she didn't think anyone was watching. How much longer did she plan on carrying the weight of the world? With her determination, it could be forever. For a moment, all he could do was sympathise for the woman in front of him, someone who spent all her time protecting everyone but herself until it was too late.

And he couldn't save her. All he could do was hope she would do it herself.

'You can't fix his mistakes, Sel,' he told her. 'And we both know you don't want to.'

Selene bit her lip, and he had a feeling that the habit came from keeping in all the things she never said.

'One day, when you do share your words, you'll be great,' she told him, but he knew what she really meant.

I won't be there.

He took back the envelope, running his fingers through her hair as he placed a kiss on her forehead, her hand resting comfortably on his chest, right over his heart.

'I know,' he whispered.

Selene didn't look at him as she slipped out of his arms and Demir didn't watch her go. Instead, he went back to work, arranging the tables and checking inventory. He didn't linger on the thought of what could've been, choosing to look ahead.

–

'I'm telling you this is it,' Haze said as he scribbled Demir's name on the setlist. He'd wanted to put Demir last, but the former boxer convinced Haze to put him in the middle. It was his first performance after all; he didn't think his confidence would last the whole night.

'Let's just get this over with,' he said, feeling the sudden urge to stretch like he did during a fight. He kept flexing his hands, so they didn't become fists; the last thing he was in the mood for was another pep talk from Haze about rivers and letting things flow.

If life was a river, Demir was a rock.

'You know what, let's get a drink to celebrate. You don't look like you can stay on your feet much longer,' Haze teased.

He scowled in his direction, but Haze wasn't looking at him. Instead, his friend's gaze was locked on a beauty at the bar. She wore a lavish, purple dress that was dangerously short under her winter coat, hair pinned in tight curls, her smile wide as she threw her head back in laughter. She was stunning but Demir didn't expect much less from Nora.

He followed Haze, staying in his shadow as she greeted him with a flirtatious smile and a kiss on the cheek. Haze smiled at her, his dimples showing, and Nora's eyes softened.

Oh.

'I got an old friend here, for ya,' Haze said, motioning to Demir. Her eyes widened in surprise as he nodded to her. It wasn't their first time seeing each other since their break-up months ago – they saw each other at Mackie's all the time – but this was the first time they had to say more than a quick hi.

'Good to see you,' she said.

'You, too.' Demir's voice was reserved, making Nora purse her lips in displeasure. He waited for Haze to say something, but someone yelled his name from across the room.

'Ah, fuck,' Haze said. 'I'll be back. Get me an old fashioned, will you?' Before Demir could respond, Haze was walking away.

'I'll do it.' Nora beckoned the bartender over and ordered a round of old fashioneds for the trio.

Demir shifted on his feet, unable to remain still in the awkwardness. Times like this he missed boxing; no one there expected him to socialise. It wasn't until he started hanging out with Haze, who seemed to know someone everywhere he went, that he noticed how bad he was at it.

'Mackie misses you,' Nora said suddenly. 'Jack's new fighter is fine enough, but he lacks your confidence. And record.'

'Oh,' he responded as the bartender dropped off their drinks.

She looked him up and down before giggling. 'What's got you so on edge?'

'I'm, uh, performing. Tonight.' Demir motioned to the stage.

She paused before her cup could meet her lips, eyes lighting up. 'That's amazing!' Suddenly, her smile fell. 'Oh, God. I hope that's not why he invited me tonight.'

Demir was taken aback by the words. 'Wow.'

'No, no.' She shook her hand quickly. 'I'm happy for you, honest. I was just… hoping for a different intention.'

He raised an eyebrow before looking out over the crowd for Haze. He spotted him talking to one of the other poets. However, instead of being focused on the conversation, he kept looking their way while running his hands through his slicked back hair, hands stuffed in his pockets when he wasn't.

'You guys are together,' Demir concluded.

Nora sighed, taking another sip. 'Not really. We've just been hanging out.'

'Like us?'

'Ha,' Nora barked out. 'No. I've learned my lesson.' 'Does he know about us?'

'Yeah. I told him that it wasn't serious but maybe he's testing out the theory.' Nora touched up her hair, a nervous habit she had, and Demir returned his attention to his equally nervous friend.

He was very familiar with jealous men, whether it was the audience in his matches or guys like Jack who glared at anyone who looked at their girl. Nothing about Haze had been resentful or possessive. The moment Demir said he wanted to perform, Haze pulled all the strings he could to get him on stage. They practised together and he pushed Demir beyond his comfort zone. He also knew how annoyingly good Haze was at noticing details, ready with advice on how to fix a problem at any given moment.

Suddenly, a wave of clarity hit him, and the corner of his lip turned up.

'No,' Demir said. 'Haze is a good guy. He doesn't hold onto stuff like that. If anything, he's probably seeing if we're okay. And we are.'

Nora stared at him, tilting her head as if she didn't quite recognise him. Maybe she no longer did, but he was okay with that. He preferred it.

'Always a good guy.'

Demir shrugged. 'Trying to be. But he's better.'

Nora smiled gently as she reached out to take his hand. 'Well, in that case, I can't wait to hear your poem.' She squeezed it just as Haze returned.

'All good?'

'Yes,' she answered. 'Now, let's go find a good seat.'

The wait for his turn was agonising. The trio sat in the middle of the crowd, snapping after each performer. Nora and Haze murmured to each other throughout the night, but it didn't bother Demir; he was too busy trying to calm his nerves. He tried to picture a boxing ring, but he wasn't trying to just survive this. This was a different type of fear and by the time they called his name, he wasn't sure whether or not he would run out the door.

He took a deep breath, holding it as he walked up to the stage. He only released it when he got to the mic, wincing when it picked up the sound. He wasn't sure where to put his hands and could barely look higher than the edge of the stage, the spotlight making everyone else invisible, only intimidating him more. The sudden silence made his throat tighten up, and he couldn't help but close his eyes.

Though his mind calmed a little at the sudden darkness, his thoughts raced as he tried to figure out what the hell he was doing up here.

Tell her the truth.

The words were Haze's but as he eased his eyes open, he could imagine Selene sitting at the edge of the crowd with the same nervous energy she'd had on the rooftop all those nights ago. With that vision, his heart calmed, and he felt he could breathe.

Then, he spoke to her, told her all the dreams he'd had for them, how much he savoured every second beside her. He allowed himself to be mad at her. He gave in to wanting her to come back. The only truth he kept for himself was how much he loved her. By the time he left the stage, the crowd snapping with a couple enthusiastic hoots, he pretended he wasn't disappointed she wasn't there.

He headed to the back door, trying not to look off-put by the compliments he got on his way outside. It was strange being praised for something so personal to him. The snowfall greeted him the moment he stepped out. He took a deep breath, letting the winter air fill his lungs before slowly letting it out, his restlessness leaving with it. Pulling out his cigarettes, he brought one to his mouth and lit it. His sigh created a cloud in the chilly night air just as the back door opened again.

'Mind sparing one of those?'

Demir turned quickly to the familiar voice, his eyes going over her head at first before landing on Selene. He caught himself before his jaw could fully drop. She looked beautiful as always but subdued in a black wrap dress instead of one of her more colourful dresses under her grey winter coat. She leaned against the wall, seemingly relaxed but the awkward shift of her feet told him much more.

'Hi,' she said, sounding just as breathless as he felt.

'Hey.' He opened his mouth to say more, but he couldn't formulate a sentence, still caught up in the surprise of seeing her.

She rubbed her arms before crossing them with an expectant arch of her brow. 'I'm still waiting, you know.'

'Oh.' He quickly searched his pockets for his cigarettes before holding the box out to her. She gingerly took one, reaching into her own pocket for matches. He watched as she lit the end, taking a couple of drags. If someone walked by, they would think they were strangers – and perhaps, they were again. It was an odd realisation. One day, she would be someone he no longer knew.

She might already be, since he had no clue why she was currently mere feet from him instead of in bed with Jack.

'What are you doing here?' he asked.

'I ran into Haze a few days ago,' she said, talking through the smoke that drifted out of her mouth. 'He told me about your show and said to invite Jack along.'

'He didn't want to come?'

'I didn't tell him,' she confessed. 'He's not ready to talk to you like an actual adult. I figured tonight wouldn't be the best time to try.' Demir hummed in appreciation, glad that Selene always had better judgement out of the two.

'You did great,' she added.

'Oh,' he said, his nerves returning, feeling too exposed under her eyes. He fought the urge to look away, instead doubling down as he asked, 'You heard the whole thing?'

'I think I missed the first couple of lines, but it doesn't matter.' She stepped carefully towards him, stuffing her hands in her pockets. 'I think the last part would've been my favourite either way. It was quite insightful.'

Demir swallowed nervously as he recalled the last few lines of his poem.

My throat is still dry with the words I'm hiding
Waiting for when you'll touch the edge of my lip
And say, 'Your tongue is bleeding.'

'The hardest part to write,' he told her.

She looked at the wall as she asked, 'Hard time finding the words?'

He shook his head at her guess, her sombre eyes making him brave enough to be honest. 'I had a hard time being honest with myself. And you, metaphorically.'

She bit her lip and bowed her head, her hair almost brushing his chest. 'I'm sorry.' 'You said that last time,' he reminded her.

She sighed, the puff of air rising to caress his cheeks, her words almost disappearing into the night. 'I have so much to apologise for.'

He knew it was a bad idea, but he still lifted her chin, urging her to return her gaze to him. She did and he was immediately brought back to all their stolen moments, all the things they should have never said to each other but did, stroking her cheek with his thumb, savouring the way her eyes threatened to close.

'Only if you have nothing else to say,' he said. 'What are you doing here?'

She sighed, leaning into his touch, her eyes softening. 'Being fickle and dramatic and probably stupid.' She took his hand and took a deep breath. 'Demir, I think I made a mistake.'

Before he could ask her what she meant, hope budding at the slightest chance that maybe she had changed her mind, a whistle cut through the alleyway. The pair looked towards the trio of drunken men at the end of it heading their way.

'Hey, miss, lady,' one of the men shouted. 'It's chilly out. Mind warming me up?' Selene sneered at them before stepping towards them.

'Look—'

'Forget them.' Demir grabbed her arm, shielding her from their eyes. 'Let's just go back inside. They're drunk out of their minds.'

Selene was still glaring but nodded, heading towards the dance hall. Demir was right behind her when one of the men said, 'Wait, is that Doomsday?'

Demir ignored them, but the loud one stepped in his way right between him and Selene. 'It *is* the champ,' he greeted, eyes blown. 'We've missed you in the ring. Where you been?'

'Retired,' Demir answered, stepping around him.

'Hey, hey, hey.' The man grabbed Demir's jacket, and the ex-boxer twisted his wrist and pushed his arm away. The man let out a chilling laugh as he cradled his wrist. 'Ah, still got the fire. That's good 'cause my pockets been a little thin since you left. Bets ain't coming through like they used to. Can you spare a dollar? I mean you wouldn't mind, right, champ?'

'Get out of the way,' Demir warned, his hands clenching into fists.

'Come on, brother. Just a dollar! Or maybe your dame can spare some time—'

Demir struck him, and the guy fell right to the ground. Unfortunately, his friends didn't take that as a cue to leave. Demir put his hands up, dodging their wild blows. He fell right back into the mind of a fighter, no longer in an alleyway with a couple pissed-off fans. He was in the ring and his opponent was no match for him.

It took nothing more than a couple jabs to knock them out. It was quick and instinctive, the mindset to strike first and worry later slipping on like an old coat. He was barely breathing hard by the time he realised it was over. He stared at the men groaning on the ground, uncomfortable with how easy it was to fall back into his old role.

He should have looked behind him.

A scream pierced the air as pain erupted through his head as he felt something heavy meet his temple. He fell forward, unable to stop the world from spinning even as he met the ground. He tried to open his mouth to yell out in pain, but no sound came out. The edges of his vision blurred as someone came outside. He could vaguely make out someone else yelling. He blinked, and Haze stood over him, Selene bending down to cradle his head. They kept asking questions, but he couldn't answer. He suddenly wanted to sleep.

Close your eyes.

The words were crystal clear in his head along with an image of a woman, tired and resigned, holding a hand over her side, blood seeping through her dress. It left just as quickly as it came but, all the same, he listened.

The chaos surrounding Selene was a distant echo as she cradled her coat to the back of Demir's head, trying to stop the bleeding, watching his eyes drift close. Her mind scrambled trying to remember how to treat head trauma while blood started to drip from his nose, his chest stilling. Her hands shook as she checked his pulse. It was slow, too faint to mean anything good.

'No,' she whispered, before looking around. 'Help! Someone, help me!' She looked back down to see his blood dying the snow red. She tried to turn him over, her heels slipping in the snow as she positioned his chest against the ground, his head to the side. Dread filled her but she did her best to ignore it as she positioned his head over his hands and started applying pressure to his back, a resuscitation method she learned from one of her professors who was a field army nurse. She knew if she could get breath back into his body, he would have a chance.

So, she didn't look at the wound on the back of his head or how the blood seeped more and more into the top of his coat. She just kept pushing, hoping to hear him take a breath over Haze's yelling at the end of the alley or her own sobs. She just needed one breath. Just one...

'Sabine,' Nora called gently from over her shoulder. She shook her head, not stopping until a pair of arms pulled her away.

'Get off of me!'

'Sabine, he's gone,' Nora said, her voice cracking. 'He's gone. You have to stop.'

Sabine shook her head, but there was too much blood, and he wasn't moving. Yet, she still shook Nora off her to grab his wrist. She searched for a pulse. There was none to be found.

She couldn't contain her anguished cry as she collapsed over him, gripping his coat tightly. He was strong, too strong to be gone like this. He didn't deserve this. After everything... how could this happen? She cried futilely onto his shoulder, the snow falling over them. If felt like the cold had seeped into her skin, down to her bones as she felt his body grow colder. She didn't move, couldn't let go of him. *Let the snow bury me*, she thought, *this is all my fault*.

Sirens filled the air, and she looked up for the first time since Demir fell. It felt like everything came into focus as she heard them get closer. Suddenly, she remembered that Jack would be back from the fight by now, wondering where she was. Fear pierced through the numbness, and she looked down; she was covered in Demir's blood. If she got held up by the cops, she wouldn't get home before morning.

'I'm not supposed to be here,' she gasped. She looked around in panic, catching Nora's eyes as she tried to figure out what to do. The dancer quickly shrugged off her jacket.

'Put this on.' She threw the jacket and Selene scrambled to catch it.

'W–What are you doing?'

'That man hit Demir, right?' Selene froze at the question, her brain trying to catch up to what was happening. 'Selene, focus! Did that man do this?' Nora pointed to the drunk from earlier that Haze had pinned against the wall. Selene nodded. 'With what?'

'A brick,' she answered.

'Okay. Demir got hit with a brick by that man and…' Nora closed her eyes for a moment and swallowed. When she opened her eyes, they were piercing. 'Me and Haze will explain everything to the cops. Go. *Now!*'

Nora left no room for discussion as she pushed Selene away from Demir's body. Selene opened her mouth to protest but the sirens were close, only blocks away. She scrambled to her feet, throwing Nora's coat over her ruined dress as she ran the opposite way.

She practically sprinted through the streets towards Jack's apartment, her heartbeat spiking every time she almost slipped on the ice under her feet. She didn't look at anyone nor did she slow down, ignoring the shouts of people when she bumped into them. Her legs were burning by the time she got to the back entrance. She fumbled with her keys, the chill from the night following her as she rushed to Jack's apartment. She didn't dare take a deep breath until she reached the apartment door.

Only when her hands stopped trembling did she open the door as quietly as possible. She stepped inside cautiously, taking her shoes off so as not to make any unnecessary sound. Her steps were silent as she eased towards the bedroom. The door was open, and she could make out the soft sound of Jack's snoring. Relief almost made her collapse, but she forced herself to keep standing. She quietly opened the linen closet and grabbed a towel.

She hoped the closed bathroom door muffled most of the sound of her filling the bathtub, having no energy to explain anything to Jack if he woke up. Her arms were already stiff as she stuffed her ruined dress and Nora's jacket at the very bottom of their laundry basket, knowing Jack wouldn't look there.

She couldn't tell if the water was warm or not as she slipped into it. Everything felt cold and harrowing as if it were snowing inside. Images of Demir filled her brain as she scrubbed the blood from her skin.

Demir performing with all the confidence he carried in and out the ring as he bared his truth.

Him lifting her chin, longing and promise shining in his eyes.

Him falling only moments later.

The blood rushing out of his head.

His limp wrist in her hand as she checked for a pulse.

Tears streamed down her face as she looked at the door, making sure it was locked. Once she was sure, she slid down until her head was fully submerged. Only then did she scream.

Chapter Thirty-Seven

Detroit

December 1946

It was all snow and shouting. And blood; that was never missing.

In the midst of it, Selene felt the weight of weary eyes on her back. She tried to run, but her legs didn't move. Still, she kept trying; something kept pushing her towards the body on the ground. It was a blur, but there was something gruesome about its stillness. She reached out—

She gasped out of her sleep, struggling to catch her breath and trying to ignore the tears that wet her cheeks. Slowly, she sat up, the sweat from her nightmare sitting uncomfortably on top of her skin. Looking over, she saw Jack, still asleep. There was a small wrinkle in his forehead, but she didn't bother to smooth it out. Instead, she slid out of the bed and headed to the kitchen, parched.

She gulped down two glasses, gripping the edge of the kitchen sink, but the unease remained. For the fourth time that week, she reached into her purse and pulled out a rumpled cigarette pack. She grabbed a pack of matches and went over to the living room window, the only view of the brick apartment building next door. Delicately, she slid the cigarette between her lips and lit it, holding the smoke in her lungs as long as she could until she was forced to let it go.

It had been three weeks.

Regardless of all her knowledge of people and the human body, she couldn't wrap her head around it. He had stood right in front of her, stronger than ever. He was moving on, becoming who he was supposed to be. Her visit was supposed to make everything better. She was going to tell him of her plans to leave Jack, whether he wanted her or not. She was going to be brave for once. One hit from an angry gambler shattered that and she became a coward once more.

She managed to go the rest of the night without shedding any tears, pretending the news of Demir's death was new when Nora called the next morning to tell her what happened after she had left the scene. She wished she could say she collapsed in Jack's arms as an act when she told him, but it felt like her heart was being ripped out every time she said it. The man had been stone-faced about the news, only growing colder when he saw how devastated she was.

She sighed and stamped out the cigarette angrily in a nearby ash tray. From the outside looking in, her heartbreak didn't make sense. She could barely understand the magnitude of it all herself, especially as the world kept spinning, pushing her to move on. Selene rested her head against the window, the helplessness and grief exhausting her. Three weeks down; only the rest of her life to go.

–

'Sorry it took so long for me to get over here,' Selene told Mackie as she entered his club.

He kissed her cheek. 'Understandable. You're a busy woman. I hear you're graduating soon,' he said with a proud grin.

She forced herself to smirk, ignoring the hollow feeling in her chest as she realised it was yet another event Demir would miss. 'Only one more week.'

'Well, congrats to you.' He tipped his hat towards her. 'I have to handle a couple of things before we talk business but have a drink while you wait. On the house.'

Selene hummed in vague agreement as he walked off, dragging her feet to the bar and placing her bag on the counter.

The bartender stood in front of her expectantly while wiping down a glass.

'A gin rickey, please. Courtesy of Mackie,' she told him. He nodded, leaving to prepare her drink. She mentally ran through the terms Jack wanted her to talk to Mackie about, but the thought of talking about boxing at all sent a pang in her chest. She checked that no one was looking her way before allowing herself to slump over the bar, holding her head in her hands.

Would the world always feel this heavy?

'Well, well, well. Haven't see you in a while,' a familiar sultry voice greeted her. Selene looked up quickly to see Nora perched on the seat next to her. She wore one of her usual bright and glitzy dresses, but her eyes were dull.

'Hi,' Selene said, voice uncertain. They sat silently while the bartender placed her drink delicately in front of her. She thanked him quickly before taking a sip.

Nora sighed. 'It's awkward, huh?'

'I don't see how it wouldn't be. We're not exactly friends.'

'Not at all. But we are familiar.' She shrugged, unsure of how else to react.

Nora was a strange acquaintance. The only thing tying them together was gone, yet there was a history and understanding she couldn't ignore. For better or worse, Nora was one of the few people left who knew the real her, and it wasn't something Selene was ready to let go of yet.

'You should be happy, you know. Graduating is a good thing.'

'Maybe.' Selene took another sip, concentrating on how the burn of the alcohol coursed through her. Perhaps shots would make the conversation easier. It was getting more and more tempting to lose herself, to escape. Her guilt felt like the endless ocean she hated so much.

'I promise I wanted to make his service,' she told Nora. 'There was a test and I tried—'

Nora patted her arm, the touch soothing her guilt a bit. 'Nobody's blaming you, hun. It's good you're focusing on your life.'

'I left him,' she whispered, the full weight of her guilt covering the three words.

'The first words out of your mouth after he died were "I can't be here." I've never seen you look as scared as you did right then,' Nora told her, running a finger along the rim of her glass. 'Whatever reason you had for leaving must have been good enough.'

Selene bit her lip. She didn't know why she had been terrified of Jack finding out but something in her gut told her to hide. She looked down at the diamond ring on her finger. The sight of it brought a bone-deep dread that had her longing for the caress of smoke on her lips; nowadays, she never seemed to smoke enough. For the moment, she settled for a sip of her drink.

'Jack said the service was beautiful,' she said, trying to get the conversation back on track.

Nora stayed silent, and Selene looked up to see the beauty staring pensively at her before her gaze turned pitying. 'It was, but he wasn't there.'

The revelation felt like a punch to her gut and Selene couldn't help but drop her jaw. 'Wait. No… no, he went. He told me about the service and how Haze called most of the attendees hypocrites for only showing up after Demir was dead.'

'You should talk to your fiancé, because I don't think we're close enough for me to go any further in this. However, I do know he wasn't there, and I stayed until the end.' Nora waved down the bartender. 'Park, make me a sidecar, would you?'

The world was a blur as Selene got out of her seat and stumbled out of the bar, her mind spinning with images of Jack in a black suit as he dropped her off at school. He hadn't even picked her up because he was supposedly at the repass. So, now… neither she nor Jack were there for Demir in the end.

Her stomach twisted dangerously, and she stepped onto the kerb quickly, throwing up the drink and small breakfast she had. She heaved painfully until the noise turned into sobs. She struggled to pull out her handkerchief to calm herself as she realised Demir had been doomed from the moment he met her.

Wiping her mouth, the sour taste of bile was heavy on her tongue, but there was nothing she could do about it. She shivered as she walked home. The tremors felt like they came from deep within her gut, exhaustion urging her to lie in the street and let the world be done with her. Instead, she pushed on.

There was something she needed to make right, even if it was too late.

–

'Sel, this is crazy,' Jack announced as Selene stuffed her things into a suitcase.

'Maybe' she said. 'But it's over. I can't do this anymore, Jack.'

'Do what?' She didn't answer him as she focused on gathering her clothes. She shoved her notebooks amongst the hastily packed clothes and trinkets. She hadn't been diligent, grabbing whatever was hers without regard of whether she truly needed it; she wanted to make sure she didn't have a reason to come back.

'Sel, just stop! You're out of your mind!' He grabbed her bag and tried to pull it away from her.

'*Stop it!*'

Startled by her scream, Jack dropped the bag's handle. The sound of their heavy breathing filled the room as they stared at each other, and he looked at her in disbelief. She didn't know how to feel. Years of her life were being torn into shreds by her decision, a whole lifetime with someone she still loved, over someone that she'd met less than a year ago.

But she could no longer hide behind the dreams Jack had for her. She'd had someone that believed in her, whether or not he was by her side. Demir had made her feel grounded and without him, there were only whispers of the things that made sense in her life.

Still, a part of her wanted to stop, if for nothing else than to not break Jack's heart. He was hurting, too. Yet, even as the thought formed in her mind, she knew she couldn't. He had created this reality just as much as she had, and she couldn't marry him as if she were okay with it. She couldn't keep that big of a lie.

'Take it,' she said. 'I don't care. I can leave the bag, but I have to leave.'

'Sel, enough. This is just your grief talking,' he reasoned, almost desperately. 'It's okay; I get it. I miss him, too! But we can't let his ghost dictate our lives.'

'You miss him,' she asked incredulously. 'You didn't even go to his funeral! You lied to me!'

His eyes widened and she watched him scramble for an excuse. He threw his hands up hopelessly. 'S—So, it can't be hard for me to see him like that?'

Selene narrowed her eyes in disgust. Even now, he was trying to act as though she was ignorant. Knowing this wouldn't be a quick conversation, she dropped her suitcase. 'That's not why you did it,' she seethed. 'And that's rich, considering he was your friend first.'

Jack's expression darkened, and she took a cautious step back. While she would love to trust him, there was no telling how he would react.

'You know what, forget it. You want honesty? Fine. I didn't go. Actually, fuck him! All right? You happy?' Jack's yell pierced her chest, and his own façade was gone. Now that she was looking, it was clear it wasn't just jealousy. A part of Jack *hated* Demir. 'He could do all the things I couldn't and didn't appreciate it for a goddamn second. Hell, he screwed us over! He took New York from us! And don't bullshit me, Sel. I know you two were too close. You're doing all this over a man you once said you hated! Hell, I don't even know if you would mourn me like this!'

Selene winced but straightened her shoulders. 'You know good and well that if you died, I would feel like my heart was ripped out. I loved you for most of my life!' The look of shock on his face made her anger dissipate, and guilt ate at her resolve. Still, she took a deep breath and forced out the words, 'But you're right. I lied about, Demir.'

Jack stilled before turning his gaze to her, eyes guarded. 'What do you mean?'

She crossed her arms, looking at the floor as she spoke. Every word was a struggle to release from her throat. 'It was innocent in the beginning, but we spent more and more time together and things just changed.'

'Sel, stop.'

But she couldn't. Now that the truth started flooding out of her mouth, she wasn't sure she would ever be able to stop.

'He understood me in ways you can't. He listened and I didn't have to hide from him or put on a show. He just let me be myself, which has been damn near impossible with you since we started all of this. I didn't know a relationship didn't have to be a constant struggle until I met him.'

'So, you liked him because it was easy?' he asked incredulously.

She looked up, finally, meeting his gaze. 'No, I loved him because our relationship was honest!' The echo may have been in Selene's head, but the words lingered all the same as Jack's heart broke right in front of her.

He rocked back in shock; his voice was barely a whisper. 'What?'

An apology rushed to the tip of Selene's tongue, but she bit it back, the weight of the truth lifting from her shoulders as she spoke. 'All I do is lie about who I am so we can be together.' She cleared her throat of the tears that were building. 'And I can't take it anymore.'

'What are you saying? You haven't been lying,' Jack exclaimed. 'We're still good. I can forgive you, okay? I–I wasn't paying enough attention. If that's all it takes, I can do that. I can fix this.'

'Jack…'

'Don't do this,' he pleaded, grabbing her arms desperately. 'We're soulmates. It's been you and me from the beginning, always. We've always been all we had. That's all we ever needed. We're supposed to be together. I know you know that.'

Selene stared into his frantic eyes. She placed her head on his chest, giving into his warmth for one last time. Before he could wrap his arms around her, she slipped her engagement ring into the front pocket of his shirt.

'I need more,' she whispered.

His devastation was too painful for her to watch, so she stared at the floor as she grabbed her suitcase. She turned on her heel, placing her keys on the kitchen counter and walked out the door.

One of the things she had once loved so much about Jack was his persistence, so she was only mildly surprised when he followed her.

'You can't just walk out,' he continued as she headed down the stairs. 'We need to talk about this!'

She ignored him, determined to leave, when a sudden jerk stopped her. She looked behind her to see Jack gripping her suitcase. 'Jack, stop.' She pulled harder, her heels digging into the stairs for leverage, her back braced against the stairs' railing.

'No! You can't leave!'

'Let go!' Her scream echoed down the stairs, reminding her that they were five storeys up. 'Enough, Jack!'

Face red and pupils blown, he looked as desperate as he sounded. 'You want me to let you go just like that? After you fucking cheated on me? I was willing to forgive you!'

Selene sneered as she tried to pull her suitcase away from him. 'Right, 'cause you're some kind of hero! I don't need your forgiveness!'

'You really want me to let go?' Jack bellowed. A trickle of fear ran through Selene, remembering when he grabbed her in the gym, bruising her arms. 'Fine!' He pushed the suitcase into her chest with all his strength.

A part of her knew Jack was acting out. She knew he'd meant for her to land on the stairs, maybe tumble down a few while he stomped back to his apartment.

Instead, she went over the railing.

Jack's face turned from rage to shock, and she caught a glimpse of his hand reaching out, but she was already too far away. As the wind pushed against her back, she realised there would be nothing to catch her but the concrete floor. Her ears barely caught the scream she let out, heart hammering against her chest in an attempt to escape her doomed body.

For a split second, her mind conjured up images of the sunset and Demir. He was smoking, his expression peaceful. He looked over at her, holding out a cigarette to her. She reached out to take it.

The darkness was sudden and heavier than anything she had ever known.

Chapter Thirty-Eight

Washington, D.C.

October 2013

Dani shot up from her bed, clutching her bed sheets and breathing heavily. Her body shook uncontrollably as she reached out to turn on the bedside lamp. She knocked several things over in the process as she struggled with the switch. The room flooded with light just as her door swung open, making her jump.

'What's wrong?' Riley stood in the doorway, holding a broom in her hand, bonnet askew. The sight made Dani laugh, even though she was sure her own bonnet had fallen off during the night as well. 'What?' Riley snapped.

'Why do you have a broom?'

'I thought someone broke in!'

'Oh, um, no.' She glanced awkwardly at the mess on the floor 'I just dropped some things while turning on the light.' Sliding out of her bed, she crouched down to pick up her phone along with a couple pens and a bottle of lotion, checking under her bed for anything else. She tried to place them on her bedside table, but her hands didn't want to co-operate, her belongings falling through her shaky grip.

Growling, Riley snatched the items up and slammed them on the bedside table, making Dani jump from the sharp sound in the quiet room. 'Okay, what is wrong with you? You have been weird as fuck for a while. This is more than you just being Cave Dani.'

'I'm fine,' Dani insisted. 'Honest. It was a bad dream. That's all.'

Riley rolled her eyes. 'You always have weird dreams and while I would usually insist on knowing what happened, I'm too tired tonight. I have an exam tomorrow. Call your therapist or something.' She stood and turned off the light. 'Next time, freak out quieter.'

Dani kept her mouth shut as her cranky friend left. Tomorrow, she would tell Riley what was going on. Or maybe she wouldn't because she doubted someone as straightforward as her would believe she was part of a reincarnation love story. That may be more of Talia's speed; she wrote fanfiction whenever she was stressed out.

Grabbing her phone, she pulled the covers over her head, squinting as she turned on the screen. It was 2:03 a.m. Talia could still be up, but she couldn't bring herself to go to her friend's room. She could barely focus beyond remembering she was alive and breathing. Everything was okay.

She threw off her covers, stuffing her feet into a pair of sneakers and grabbing a denim jacket as she headed to the attic. According to the landlords, it was supposed to be off limits, but Riley had jimmy-rigged the lock a long time ago. The door opened easily, and she went to the window, climbing outside and onto the roof. Tiles dug into her legs as she sat and stared at the sky.

There weren't many visible stars but there were enough to be comforting, lifting some of the weight from her memories. Not just Demir and Selene, but everyone's. She reminisced on all the small touches, the conversations, all the lines they'd crossed to have a piece of *something*. So many moments someone could've said yes but refused. So many chances that were never taken, all because of fears that didn't even matter in the end. She brought her knees to her chest, burying her face as sobs wracked her body, remorse and heartache crashing over her.

The remorse of unspoken words was too much to bear. To know that she would have to carry their regrets for the rest of her life felt like too much of a responsibility to survive. There was no winning.

Another crappy consolation prize.

A laugh broke through her sobs as she recalled her bass lesson with Jones. The phrase had become a catchphrase for them, something that made accepting everything that was happening just a tad easier. They said it for the tiniest inconveniences, news headlines or just funny moments they saw. The worst moments of her day had soon become the most bearable, most understandable because it could have been worse, and it wasn't yet.

She felt a familiar swell of longing fill her chest and for the first time, it hit her how ridiculous she was being. If she had learned nothing else from her past lives, she knew it was better to do everything she could to be happy now instead of waiting for it to be perfect. Just like Jones, Dr Castillo, and her friends had been telling her. After all, avoiding her feelings hadn't solved anything and, even if there was a slim chance it did, it didn't change that she was in love with him.

'All right, universe, you win,' she whispered through the tears, a half-moon the only witness as she promised, 'Never again.'

—

Jones sat on a bench at the edge of the Meridian Hill Park, basking in the beauty of a lovely day. Jair, on the other hand, sat on the top of the bench, his feet planted on the seat and his eyes glued to his phone as Jones watched people pass by, walking along the crisscrossing pathways. The clouds above them moved languidly across the sky, and sunlight glinted off the fountain in the middle of the park, shining like a beacon. While he didn't venture outside often, he liked to stop at the park whenever he could.

It felt like the world slowed down just for a while.

'Okay, I'm thinking we can knock out the rest of the soundtrack on Sunday and Monday. Everyone should be available then except for Tim,' Jair said, sighing. 'We really need a new bassist. Dude is never available until the middle of the week or the dead of night.'

'We all know Tim is nocturnal.'

'Doesn't make him any less of a pain,' Jair mumbled, tucking his phone in his pocket. He seemed to contemplate something before speaking again. 'I could see if he can come in on Thursday and record separately but that means we'll have to rearrange the sessions…'

It was easy to tell that's what Jair wanted, even if he had the decency to pretend otherwise. Jones sighed good-naturedly before giving in.

'Let Tim relax. I'll cover bass for him,' he said.

'Thanks, man.' Jair dapped him up. 'Aye, I'll make sure to put a little extra on top of your cheque for it.'

'Damn right.' Jones smirked before wincing at a sudden pressure that filled his chest. For a moment, his entire body ached to the point where he could barely move, head-splitting pain falling over him.

'Hey, you all right, man?' Jair spoke, but his voice seemed far away. Jones gritted his teeth as he tried to breathe. 'Jones, what's wrong? Jones!'

'Huh?' His eyes snapped open, the sudden pain dissipating like a memory. Jair looked at him with wide, panicked eyes. 'What the hell just happened?'

'Nothing, nothing,' Jones said, still trying to catch his breath. 'Just these random headaches. I'm seeing my doctor soon anyway, so I'll ask him about it then.' This was not a lie, necessarily. He *did* have an upcoming doctor's appointment.

His best friend looked at him sceptically for a moment. 'You sure?' 'Yeah.' He leaned back against the bench, relaxing his shoulders.

Jair's brows furrowed but he kept a straight face. Was it messed up to gaslight his friend? Absolutely. But at this point it was almost instinctive. Only his parents knew the full extent of his condition, and he was determined to keep it that way.

'You sure you'll be good for the studio this weekend?' Jair asked. 'I can drag Tim there.'

'Nah, I'm good. I'll be fine. It's just a routine thing,' Jones reassured him.

Besides, I can't afford to miss it.

'All right, man, don't scare me like that,' Jair said, laughing awkwardly.

'Gotta keep you on your toes, man.' He grinned and Jair rolled his eyes but chuckled anyway, checking his phone.

'Listen, I gotta head out, but I'll catch you later. Let me know how it goes at the doctor's.' They dapped again, and his friend jumped off the bench. 'And remind me to send you the info for the Ty Rivers project!'

'I will,' Jones called. Only when Jair was gone did he pull out his phone to set an alarm. He tried to ignore the number of reminders that cluttered his calendar; it was an eyesore.

A sense of dread filled him as he tucked his phone away, and he considered cancelling the appointment. He already knew the outcome. His body was no good, and it wasn't getting better.

Clasping his hands together, he rested his chin on them, his elbows digging into his legs. He didn't know how long he could keep doing this.

You need a plan! He bit the inside of his cheek as his mum's worried voice cut through all the noise in his head. *You keep running around like this, you're going to drop dead.*

'I'm fine,' he muttered, leaning his head against the back of the bench, and tilting his head towards the sky. Closing his eyes, he took a deep breath of the crisp autumn air. The smell of grass and leaves was glorious after the humid summer. Trees rustled with the wind and the birds chirped as they flew off for winter. It was a beautiful symphony. He didn't need to linger on the thought of not being able to enjoy it one day. He was here now, he'd likely still be there tomorrow, and that's all that mattered. There was nothing else to worry about.

357

A camera shutter went off, and someone frantically cursed under their breath. He peeked, and smiled, sitting up as Dani sheepishly made her way over to him.

'I can't remember the last time a camera shutter got someone in trouble outside of a TV show,' he said as she sat next to him.

'I didn't tell you? I, uh, got a new phone.' She looked at the ground, refusing to meet his gaze directly.

He eyed the little nicks along the phone's case and smirked. 'So, you wanted me to be one of the first pictures on your "new" phone?'

'No!' She clamped her mouth shut, and he couldn't help but laugh at the denial. Huffing, she hid her phone under her arm, still not looking at him. 'The phone isn't *that* new,' she explained.

'M–hm.' He leaned back, leisurely resting his arm along the back of the bench. Dani eyed it but didn't move from under it. He figured that was a good enough sign. At least, he hoped so. 'You know you have to show me the pic, right?'

She blanched before scooting away. 'It's not that big of a deal.'

'Hey, if you're going to have a picture of me that can circulate at any moment, I need to at least authorise it.'

She grimaced but reluctantly unlocked her phone, handing it over. 'It's not a bad picture.'

He took it, head tilting curiously as he looked at the photo. She was right. It wasn't bad at all. It wasn't goofy like the pictures his friends had of him or serious like the few pictures his dad could convince him to take. He looked… relaxed. It had been a long time since he'd seen himself like that.

'It's not,' he agreed, handing her back the phone. 'I guess I can allow you to keep it.'

She raised her eyebrows at him and inched closer. 'Allow me?'

He nodded despite her intense gaze. 'Yeah. It'll keep you from missing me so much.' Her eyes widened, and the faintest traces of blush appeared on her cheeks.

'I— It's not—'

'Relax.' He smiled, raising his hands up in surrender. 'I'm done teasing.' Dani scowled and leaned against the bench, her shoulders brushing his arm. He ignored the electricity that skittered across his skin. 'How's... everything?' he asked. 'Anything new?'

A shadow fell over her face. 'Other than watching Demir and Selene lose their lives just as they were getting started? The memories were straightforward this time,' she said, looking down at her lap. 'We're kind of bad at picking each other, huh?'

Jones chewed on the inside of his cheek; this time there was no laughter. Instead, he felt an age-old hollowness fill his chest. So many years spent alone, so many days waiting for her, so little time to savour what they had.

'It's not like I don't understand why.'

She tapped her foot anxiously, head still down. When she spoke, her voice was rough with unshed tears. 'I'm sorry.' She finally looked at him, eyes reddened and lips trembling. 'I don't enjoy hurting you. I never wanted to hurt you. Not then or now. I just... I don't know. I can't...'

'Hey,' he said softly, taking her hand in his. Her fingers were slender, but the tips were rough from years of playing cello. He liked that he could feel her dedication.

'This thing between us has never been simple,' he whispered. 'We can't stop the world from being against us.'

'I just don't understand how we... or rather Demir and Damien could be so brave, when Selene and Sabine couldn't.'

Jones sighed, shrugging weakly. 'I don't know if it was bravery,' he confessed. 'Maybe it was selfishness, too, wanting things I— we couldn't have.'

She didn't say anything, instead moving so they were hip to hip, her head resting on his shoulder. The scent of her hair – cocoa butter, almond and rosemary – filled his nose, and all at once he just wanted to fall into her. He squeezed her hand, hoping he wouldn't have to let go anytime soon.

'I think we're also not good at being fair to each other either.'

He huffed out a small laugh. 'There's... room for improvement,' he agreed.

Dani giggled before sitting up, her face mere inches from his. 'Okay. Let's make up new endings for our lives. We can call it Alternative History.'

'And this is helpful how?'

'Well, the worst has already happened, which means we can only go up from here. I mean, why not? We're here. We're alive and together again,' she pointed out. 'So, Damien's alternative life: go.'

'Okay, umm... Sabine never went back in the house,' he started. 'We escape the estate and go to the countryside, get a plot of land to farm on and rebuild our lives.'

'We move to Monaco,' Dani added, a smile forming on her face. 'We start a whole new life, have a kid or two.'

'Of course,' Jones jumped in. 'Teach them to fight and everything.'

Dani grinned before continuing. 'We get a home with an ocean view and live happily ever after.'

'Pass down the house, which the kids can sell and start their own lives.' 'Look at you, being practical.'

'Says the girl who picks an oceanfront house in one of the most expensive places in the world.'

She giggled, rolling her eyes playfully and pulling their hands into her lap while he resisted lowering his arm to wrap it around her. They weren't quite there yet.

'Next, David and Sarah,' he said. 'David finds a better shelter and Sarah is able to get actual medical attention.'

'They survive the bombs, become close due to their experience, and move out of London. It would take a little time, but I think they would get married. No kids, though,' Dani chimed in.

'It would probably be too much for them.' The words were gloomy, but he doubted Sarah and David would have been sad with that particular outcome of their lives. He knew from experience that being alive and in love made up for a lot.

'Okay, what about Demir and Selene?' Dani asked.

'Easy,' he said. 'Selene actually doesn't show up to see Demir perform.'

'They catch up later on and Selene realises she wants to move on, too,' Dani adds. 'She probably even packs a bag in the middle of the night, but she decides to give Jack one more try.'

'Meanwhile, Demir doesn't go into the alley that night. He starts dating but doesn't quite feel the same connection as he did with Selene.'

Dani smirked. 'I stay on your mind, huh?'

'Eh…' He pinches his fingers close together, earning a laugh. 'Keep going.'

'Okay, okay. So, Selene breaks up with Jack right before their elopement. Leaves a note on the bedside table and disappears in the middle of the night.'

'Damn. Not even a wedding?' Jones asked.

'They did not have the patience to deal with each other's families so I'm going to say no.'

'So, you have no faith in them getting married? Not even a little?'

Dani hummed in contemplation before shaking her head.

'Looking back on it, Selene was already gone,' she said. 'Maybe she wouldn't have left him so soon, but I think she would've eventually. Whether or not she still had feelings for Demir, the one thing he showed her was that she and Jack didn't fit well together. She just wasn't ready for the truth.'

'Wow.' Jones was impressed at the insight. Dani nudged his shoulder, bringing him back to the moment.

'Go on,' she urged. 'Selene leaves…'

'Dizzy Gillespie comes into town,' Jones continued. 'They both go to the concert and see each other there. They talk, maybe have a moment of denial but, ultimately, they decide to try. It works, and they live happily ever after.'

'No kids or marriage?'

Jones shook his head. 'It doesn't suit them.'

'I was thinking the same thing.' They stared at each other, the idyllic endings lingering just out of reach.

What beautiful dreams…

'Let's go on a date.'

Jones froze for a long moment before clearing his throat. 'Doesn't that go against our unspoken agreement?' Heat crept up the back of his neck, his damn hopes rising once again.

'It's a stupid agreement,' she said. 'We're here, together again. We get to try again. Why pass that up? I mean, I don't know how much of this is past me talking or present me being tired of being in limbo but… I don't want to have to get close to losing you to realise – again – all the things I'm missing. So, let's just try.'

'Dani…'

You are going to lose me. You're a lot closer than you think.

As much as he knew he should say the words, they got caught in his throat. Hope brightened her eyes even as she nervously chewed her lip. The temptation was too much. This was the first time almost nothing stood in their way. Every part of him wanted to savour that, to be reckless just for a little longer, but he had been reckless before and what had that gotten him?

Still, the answer was inevitable.

'Yes.' He watched as her face lit up before she tried to contain her glee. 'Yeah?'

He nodded, and Dani smiled. He allowed himself to return it, to cherish the moment before he cleared his throat. 'But I want to help you look for an answer. There might be power in numbers there.'

She rolled her eyes playfully. 'I guess a research assistant wouldn't hurt,' she agreed reluctantly, a smile on the edge of her lips.

His chest clenched at the sight, knowing what he said next would take it away. 'And… I need to tell you something important.'

The words hung heavy between them, and her happiness turned solemn. He took a deep breath, ready to tell her the truth about everything but the words died as she cupped his face. She leaned towards him, stilling for a moment, her eyes questioning. He answered by closing the gap between them.

He had expected their first kiss in this life to feel familiar, having the lingering scent of French roses or the quietness of midnight. Instead, he could only focus on how slowly Dani moved, revelling in each kiss for as long as she could before giving him another. He breathed into her, enjoying the taste of honey and mint on her lips just as much. He felt her tremble when his fingers brushed her cheek, but she sank into him the moment he pulled her closer. She felt like relief, a salve to all the wounds he'd been carrying. They lingered in that moment for a small pocket of infinity before pulling away to catch their breath.

'Tell me later,' she whispered.

For a moment, Jones was lost, and it took a while to remember his unspoken confession. He opened his mouth to protest, but she shook her head, her eyes pleading for more time to linger in the promising feeling of the moment. Time was the most precious thing he had to give, so how could he deny her that?

'You pick the date and I'll bring the snacks,' he said instead. *I'll give you all the time I have left.*

Dani raised her brow. 'But what if we don't need snacks?'

He looked at her indignantly. 'Every date needs snacks,' he insisted.

She laughed again, the beauty of it soothing his longing. After all these years, all their lives, she was finally right in front of him, ready to try again.

Dani's phone, forgotten on her lap, buzzed, and they jumped. She looked at the screen groaning. 'I have to go to practise.'

'Mind if I walk you to your car?' 'You better.'

Dani didn't bother to hide her smile as they stood up. Their shoulders brushed every few steps as they walked side by side. Jones decided to savour the anticipation. As it was, his condition would be hard on them, and he had enough regrets from his other lives. This lifetime, he refused to rush out of fear.

One way or another, he knew they had a future together.

'By the way,' Dani said suddenly. 'You do know that Demir would have definitely been one of those old-school jazz poets, right?'

Jones smirked. 'You said the game was called Alternative History.' She looked at him curiously. 'Is that a clue?'

He smiled as he gave into the urge to put his arm around her shoulder.

'I don't know how much you remember about our next lifetime, but I'll save you some suspense. Look up the book *Because I'm Merely a Song* by a guy name Dominic.'

Her eyes sparked in recognition, and she looked at him in awe. 'Poetry?' 'Poetry.'

Epilogue

Paris

February 2080

Yousef Gabrie wondered if humans were creatures of the night.

Not to say he didn't enjoy the day, but a certain energy emerged under his skin when the sun set. Or maybe it was the fact that it was a little easier to remove the thin VR lenses that always covered his eyes, whether for work or to talk with a friend, and just observe the people around him. He took out his vape, dialling down the strength level for his evening smoke before taking a puff.

He didn't know why he was outside.

His fiancée, Nadia, didn't care if he smoked inside. They had air filters in every room, so the smell never lingered, and their balcony had a better view of the stars. So many choices of comfort and still he donned his coat around midnight, walking down five flights to the building entrance before stopping at one of the convenience stands for a snack and heading to a nearby bench to smoke while trying to understand the restless energy under his skin.

Some nights, he enjoyed it. It felt tangible and real in a world wrestling with the artificial too often. On other nights, like tonight, he couldn't help but tilt his head up to look at the stars for answers. He wanted to ask them:

What do you want?

But the universe was nothing if not silent. He sighed before taking another drag. 'They used to be harder to see.'

Pulling his gaze from the stars, Yousef turned.

The person – she, from the red pinkie ring that indicated her pronouns – was leaning against a nearby lamp post in jeans and a lace hoodie that somehow looked both delicate and street-smart. She smiled at him mischievously as if she knew an inside joke that he wasn't privy to. He tilted his head curiously, and she pointed to the sky.

'The stars,' she clarified. 'A few decades ago, you would have only ten or fifteen on a good night.'

Yousef looked up again at the hundreds of stars above his head. He couldn't imagine seeing such an empty sky in the city. 'Huh,' he said.

'Anything particularly special up there?'

'Only the answers to every question we ever asked,' she shrugged. 'Probably. Seems only right the heavens know everything.'

'Much better than humans, we're a bit reckless,' he smirked. 'But we're all lucky.'

'Would a lucky man look so pensive?'

Yousef huffed out a laugh at the odd question. 'Only if he's the luckiest one of them all,' he answered.

A flashing advertisement showed the time. Already thirty minutes had passed, and he didn't want to leave Nadia by herself for too long. He stood up, straightening his coat. Yet, he hesitated to walk away, noticing that the woman's attention was still on him.

'Hope you and your peculiar questions have a good night,' he said, prolonging the moment.

Her eyebrows quirked, but she simply shrugged. 'Same to you and your interesting answers.'

For a moment, something sharpened in her gaze that made Yousef hyperaware of his body, the space between them, the way her eyes never moved from his and the smile she held back. He stared at her, wondering what he could say, but soon the moment passed. He had to get back home; he'd said all he could. He tipped his head towards her.

She nodded in return, her gaze boring into his back. He ignored how the thrum beneath his skin was soothed by the interaction, instead pretending that it was the walk home that helped. Still, he went straight to the balcony to stare at the stars a little longer, contemplating how lucky he truly was.

–

Ava Keïta had seen the man a few times on her walks around the city. She figured he lived nearby as she'd often caught him buying something from the local convenience stands or smoking while looking lost in the night. He moved in sync with the community around him, clearly woven into the neighbourhood. Honestly, she was surprised he'd never noticed her. She always felt like an outsider when venturing beyond the vintage beauty of downtown Paris, like she was standing still in a moving crowd.

Now, Ava knew he wasn't particularly special. She had roamed many neighbourhoods, and there were always one or two people who stood out to her. Still, something about the way he seemed so comfortable and yet so confused called to her. It was a contradiction she understood. As a fashion designer, she always felt as though she were on the edge of rejection, despite her skills and the praise she often received. She rarely met a person who displayed that feeling so openly.

So, she figured she would do what she always did: try to satisfy the curiosity. Only this time, receiving one answer wasn't enough. Instead, it felt like a fire was being set off in the distance. It did nothing but intrigue her, making her wonder if it was warmth or danger.

'Curiouser and curiouser,' she murmured as she watched the flame disappear into the night.

Author's Note

Hi, reader!

I would like to take a moment to say that while this book is a work of historical fiction, I am not a historian. I am not of Ivorian or French descent and much of my family does not come from Detroit. Research for this book was diligent but chaotic, leaving a lot of room for misinterpretation. Although this story was made with the best of intentions, I do apologize for any inaccuracies presented and hope the heart of the story, as well as the message, prevail.

For those curious about the time periods mentioned in the text, I encourage you to reach out to your local library or historical society for sources that will likely be much more thorough than ones I can provide.

For those who don't like the book because it balks against racism and colonization, the systematic ~~crimes~~ practices carried out because of another country's greed and thirst for power and resulting attitudes from these time periods are well known and, unfortunately, still prevalent. These systems still plague many of our societies in the present day and ignoring them will not change the truth. I also encourage you to reach out to your local library and historical society to understand the depth of this history, so we are one step closer to it being eradicated in the future.

-C.D.

Acknowledgements

This is my Oscar speech, so prepare to cue the orchestra.

Thank you, GOD (literally)! This book was an endeavour 10 years in the making. This not the first or second book I've ever written or tried to get published, but it is the hardest book I've ever written. And there were *plenty* of days I was sure it would never be finished. I'm super proud of myself for completing this project and am ecstatic that it's now out in the world!

That being said, I definitely did not get here by myself.

I want to thank my agent, Lary Rosenblatt of 22MediaWorks. Thank you for fighting so hard to bring this story to life. I am so happy I get to go on this publishing journey with you. Thank you as well to Nicole Frail, my first developmental editor.

I would also like to thank the entire Hera Books team, especially Editor Dan O'Brien. The first green flag was how cool your name was, and the second was how clearly you saw the vision of this story from the moment we started working together.

Big, big, big thank you to all my friends, but especially my best friends Carmen, Jessica, Laura, Lucy and Maureen. You guys have stuck beside me throughout this whole process, reassured me "*Man at The Garden*" style that I deserved the best and that I'm a great writer when I couldn't say that to myself. You've read chapters, gave me hugs through the highs and lows, let me relax on the hard days, and told me to "get my ass back to work" when I needed it. I love you guys!

Extra special shout out to Tamar who, on top of being my best friend, doubled as a developmental editor. You pushed the story even further, helping me with research, and just being an amazing supporter from the very beginning when the story was *extremely* different. This story wouldn't be half as good as it is without you. (Quick piece of advice: Don't write like no one will read it. Write like your friend who will let you go as crazy as you want, will read it.)

Almost last, but definitely not least, I want to thank my amazing family, especially mom, dad, Drew, Julian, and Paige. You all have picked me up when I thought I was down and out. Your faith in me never wavered. You kept the dream alive even when it seemed lightyears away. I love you all and am extremely blessed to have you by my side every day.

(Special shout out to Kobe, my partner-in-crime, who has napped, barked, and let me stress pet him through all of this. I love you, bud.)

Finally, I want to thank the readers. You all are actively making my biggest dream come true and I am forever grateful.